Her Mother's
Secret

Also by Catherine King

Women of Iron
Silk and Steel
Without a Mother's Love
A Mother's Sacrifice
The Orphan Child
The Lost and Found Girl
The Secret Daughter
A Sister's Courage

Digital-exclusive short stories
Stolen passion
The Professor's Daughter

Her Mother's Secret

Catherine King

sphere

SPHERE

A CPI catalogue record for this book
is available from the British Library

ISBN 978-0-7515-5428-1

Typeset in Bembo by Palimpsest Book Production Limited,
Falkirk, Stirlingshire
Printed and bound in Great Britain by Clays Ltd, St Ives plc

Papers used by Sphere are from well-managed forests
and other responsible sources

MIX
Paper from
responsible sources
FSC
www.fsc.org FSC® C104740

Sphere
Little, Brown Book Group
100 Victoria Embankment
London EC4Y 0DY

An Hachette UK Company
www.hachette.co.uk

www.littlebrown.co.uk

Acknowledgements

I had a fascinating time researching early twentieth century health hydros in Yorkshire and Derbyshire. I found that they were thriving during the Edwardian era, despite some of their now questionable practices. I am indebted to the wonderful Mavis Baird of Champneys Forest Mere for her detailed knowledge of the rigorous routines from earlier years, including her reference to Russian cake. I found a recipe in *Mrs Beeton's Book of Household Management*. I am also grateful to Simon Brian of London who, as a young man, was a 'health farm patient' and remembers the Spartan regime well. Many thanks to both of you. The original Forest Mere country house has an interesting history in its own right and is in such a beautiful tranquil setting that it inspired my fictional Mereside Lodge.

As ever, my thanks also go to my agent Judith Murdoch and my editors Manpreet Grewal and Hannah Green at Sphere. Their constant help and support during the creation and production of the finished book makes the writing an enjoyable experience for me.

PART ONE

Chapter 1

Waterley Hall, South Riding, Yorkshire, 1885

'Do I look beautiful, Father?' Ruth stood in the middle of the butler's pantry and twirled around, showing off her fashionable bustle.

Seth Hargreaves leaned back in his chair, a satisfied expression on his face. 'You look more of a lady than Her Ladyship.'

'Yes I do, don't I?' It was dark outside and Ruth examined her image in the glass of the window. 'Her Ladyship is an old frump, though, so that's not difficult. Do you think His Lordship's friends will like me?'

'They won't be able to take their eyes off you.'

Ruth felt a thrill of excitement run down her spine. Lord Laughton was young and handsome and clearly rich enough to buy Waterley Hall, complete with its resident servants and surrounding farms, without worrying about the costs of renovations. His friends in the Riding came from wealthy families who lived in grand houses. Ruth's father had been butler to the old family at Waterley Hall, but that family had simply died out, and he was already a favourite of the new master.

'Won't Her Ladyship mind me being there?' Ruth asked.

'You leave all that to me. She's gone to the shipyards for a few days. It's up to you to assist His Lordship entertain his guests. I shall be serving dinner to keep a watch on you.'

'Oh, Father, I'm so excited! Who else will be there?'

'His Lordship's London friends have already arrived with their lady escorts. One or two have brought their sisters. They will be the unattached ones, Ruth, but make sure you're nice to everybody. They're all young folk like His Lordship.'

'Will they know that I'm your daughter?'

'No, why should they? You'll be presented as Miss Ruth. The guests will think you're a relation. If anybody wants to know, say you're a family friend.'

'Oh! Am I a friend of Lord Laughton?'

'His Lordship has asked for you and I'm honoured that he did. But don't let me down; I have to keep in his favour if I want the house steward position.'

Ruth was indignant. 'I do know how to behave like a lady,' she said.

She had grown up with the previous family in residence – long-established aristocrats with a centuries-old family tree that had dwindled to nothing over the years.

Nonetheless, Ruth had decided at a very early age that she wanted to be one of them, and her father had too.

'Well, His Lordship is still seen as new money so just remember everything you've learned at that ladies' college of yours. You can be a real lady if you play your cards right and this is your chance.'

'Yes, Father.'

The door opened wide and Ivy Hargreaves walked in, her arms full of clean linen. She was much younger than her husband, who had been the butler at Waterley Hall when she had arrived as head parlourmaid over twenty years ago. Ivy was a small energetic woman. She read her bible, prayed every night and walked several miles to the nearest Methodist chapel on Sundays. The previous housekeeper then had been old, arthritic and, frankly, quite dotty. From the day she arrived at Waterley Hall, Ivy had done most of her work, and done it well.

'You look very nice, my dear,' Ivy said, 'but I still don't think this is a sensible idea. Not when Her Ladyship is away.'

'Oh, Mother, don't spoil everything now,' Ruth moaned.

'It's a good opportunity for the girl, Ivy,' her father argued. 'There's no point in spending all that money on a fancy ladies' college if she doesn't mix with real gentry.'

'I'm not disagreeing with that. I just think, with Ruth being only seventeen, Her Ladyship should be present.'

'If I were the daughter of the house I'd be a debutante, Mother,' Ruth protested, 'and attending dinners and balls every night.'

'Seth,' Ivy appealed to her husband, 'His Lordship is known to have an eye for the ladies.'

'I'll be with her all the time. And what if he does flirt with my Ruth? It won't do me any harm at all when it comes to the steward's position.'

'Besides, Mother,' Ruth added, 'If I'm to marry well, it isn't enough for me to look beautiful. I have to know the right people, too.'

'Well, just remember, dear,' her mother replied, 'if you're not happy with anything, then excuse yourself and come down to me. I'll be in my sitting room all evening.'

'You don't have to stay, Ivy. You go back to the cottage and I'll bring Ruth home with me.'

'But if she waits for you she will be very late.'

'She doesn't want to miss any of the fun, do you, Ruth?' her father responded.

'No, I don't. I can talk to the ladies if the gentlemen go off to play cards or billiards. You want me to do that, don't you, Mother?'

Ivy sighed. 'Very well, dear.'

'That's settled then.' Seth Hargreaves stood up. 'Off you go, Ivy, and let me get on with the champagne.'

Ruth's pretty blue eyes lit up. 'Oh, champagne, how lovely. Don't worry about me, Mother,' Ruth said, as the two women walked out into the dimly lit passage outside the butler's pantry. 'Father will look after me.' She turned towards the green baize door that led to the main house and felt her mother's eyes on her as she walked through it and into a different life.

*　*　*

The reception hall of Waterley Hall was large enough for a small dance. It had a mosaic tiled floor and four fluted marble pillars on each side. Opposite the large front door, a wide staircase with gilt balustrades rose grandly to the first floor. Wood-panelled doors led off the hall to the dining room, drawing room, library and morning room.

This will be my world, Ruth thought. Not for her the world below stairs that was her parents' existence. They were respectable and comfortable as butler and housekeeper at Waterley Hall, but they were servants nonetheless. Ruth was determined to have a different life, to be mistress of a great house like Waterley, with servants of her own.

Seth Hargreaves shared his daughter's ambition; he also knew how to please his betters. He was master of his own domain in the servants' hall and ruled it with a proverbial iron rod. Servants who did not comply did not stay. The footmen may gossip in their dormitories about Ruth's elevated status to guest at His Lordship's table, but if one word of it reached her father's ear they would be 'asked to leave'. This autocratic regime had impressed the young lord, and Seth had quickly secured his patronage.

Michael, head footman at the Hall, was on duty outside the drawing-room door and opened it as soon as he saw her. 'Miss Ruth, My Lord,' he said. His face was expressionless but Ruth knew that he was in love with her. She might have considered him, too – he was a fine-looking man – if he wasn't a servant. Perfect for my future butler, she thought.

'Over here.' Lord Laughton was standing in the bay window, staring out at the driveway. He had dark hair and eyes, and features that some described as 'craggy'. But he looked very handsome in full evening dress with a tail coat and white tie. However, when she stood by his side, she realised that he was rather short. The door clicked shut behind her and they were alone. 'Turn around,' he said.

Ruth twirled for him as she had for her father. She noticed that his eyes narrowed and his fingers twitched slightly and she feared he did not like what he saw. 'Father said I looked beautiful,' she said nervously.

'He's right. Come closer.'

She did and he stroked a finger over her cheek and lips. She hadn't expected him to touch her and recoiled instinctively.

'Stay where you are!' he exclaimed.

'I'm sorry, My Lord. You surprised me.'

'And don't call me "My Lord". I'm Laughton to my friends.'

She knew that! Father had told her that! She recovered immediately and replied, 'Of course, Laughton.'

His hand travelled down over her throat to the exposed swell of her breasts. It lingered over their fullness, continued to her tightly corseted waist and returned to her breasts. She held her breath, suppressing the instinct to flee. A clock chimed somewhere, breaking Laughton's reverie. He dropped his hand and turned his attention back to the window. The first carriage was approaching.

The door opened again and Ruth's father announced

the first of the guests who had arrived earlier for a few days' shooting. His face was as expressionless as Michael's. Ruth put on her welcoming smile and prepared to do her best. Over the next hour she smiled a lot, drank champagne and joined in the conversation with suitable comments and questions.

Dinner for twenty people lasted over three hours. Everyone drank wine and voices grew louder. On two separate occasions she caught a glimpse of one of the gentlemen watching her and acknowledged his interest with an incline of her head. When her father removed her dessert plate, he whispered in her ear, 'Now, Ruth.'

She caught the eye of another lady guest, nodded, and they stood up together. 'Shall we leave the gentlemen to their port and stilton, ladies?' She smiled and led the way to the drawing room. Her mouth was beginning to ache with constant smiling.

Michael brought in coffee for the ladies and murmured to her, 'Your father sends his compliments.'

Ruth relaxed with a sigh. Father was pleased. She had performed well and the evening was almost over. Later, one of the ladies played and sang at the piano and some of the gentlemen joined them in the drawing room. His Lordship was not among them but Father came in afterwards and announced cards. Within minutes, the footmen under Michael's supervision had set up the tables and the remaining gentlemen wandered in and took their places. A few of the ladies sat down with them.

'Ruth,' His Lordship called, 'come over here and bring me luck.' Ruth didn't know how she was going to do that but she obeyed. His Lordship was in high spirits. The party broke up about an hour later except for the card table with His Lordship and his friends who were house guests, which carried on.

'Shall I retire as well, Laughton?' Ruth said.

'Certainly not. I'm on a winning streak thanks to you and these gentlemen are chasing their losses.' He raised a hand in the air and called, 'Hargreaves, more brandies, and bring sandwiches.'

The cigar smoke was hurting her eyes but Ruth kept smiling. She was tired and she was bored. Her father sent his footmen off duty and stood to attention in the shadows. The cards fell right for His Lordship. His winnings mounted and eventually the others called a halt. But the gentleman who had caught Ruth's eye at dinner was now so drunk that he could barely stand up and Father was obliged to assist him upstairs. Ruth found herself once again alone with His Lordship in the empty drawing room.

'He's a fool,' His Lordship said, referring to his drunken guest. 'He falls for it every time. I ply him with drink until he can't think straight and then I take all his money off him.' He laughed and held out his arm. 'Come here, Ruth.'

She hesitated. It was very late and she was exhausted. But she felt safe because His Lordship wasn't drunk and Father would be back soon.

'I said come here.' Laughton stepped forward, grasping her hand and pulling her towards him.

Ruth bumped against his chest and his mouth was on

hers before she could protest. He held her firmly and thrust her lips open with his tongue. This wasn't supposed to happen! He was hard up against here, pressing his hips into hers and she wanted to push him away.

But he would stop soon, she reasoned, and then she could voice her disapproval. The worst she had imagined was a brief stolen kiss in a dark corner from a single gentleman who might ask if he could take her for a carriage ride.

His mouth moved to the swell of her breasts, giving her a chance to breath. 'Please stop this, Laughton. Father assured me you wouldn't—'

'I am master here,' he growled and tore at the neckline of her gown with his teeth to expose more of her flesh.

'What are you doing?' Ruth demanded. A frisson of fear shivered down her spine. What if he didn't stop at a kiss? He ignored her question and steered her forcefully back to one of the couches.

She began to panic and push at him with her hands. 'Father will be back any minute,' she cried.

'Then we'd best hurry, hadn't we? I'm not going to hurt you so don't fight with me, Ruth.'

This made her feel easier and she let out her breath.

'That's better,' he said. 'Just relax and do as I say.'

Ruth felt that she hadn't much choice. He was strong and he had pinned her down on the couch. He sat on the edge, facing her, and then buried his face in her exposed breasts, nipping and nibbling at her flesh. She hated it but his weight pressed into her. Her frightened eyes gazed at the chandelier in the ornate plaster ceiling

11

and she pushed ineffectually at his shoulders. One of his hands was fumbling at his clothes between them. To her horror the other reached down and under her skirts following the line of her thigh to the gap in her drawers.

'No, you can't do this! You're not supposed to do this!'

'Shut up,' he said harshly. 'I said relax. You don't want me to hit you, do you?'

'Hit me? Why would you hit me?' she cried. His fingers were between her legs and she was frightened. 'Stop it, Laughton, stop it!'

But he didn't stop. He found what he was searching for and bunched up her skirts, her beautiful new silk skirts, until they exposed her drawers. The silk covered her face but he didn't seem to notice. He was stretched out on top of her with his knee between her legs, prodding and poking at her. She recoiled and pushed her bottom backwards into the couch. Her bustle made this movement useless and her hips remained raised towards him. With a sickening grasp of the situation, she realised what he was about to do whether she wanted it or not and she could not escape from him. Her continuing protests were muffled by her skirts.

It didn't really hurt that much. Or maybe she was too shocked to feel anything. He was heavy but he didn't seem very big inside her. She couldn't see his face but she could hear him grunting and feel him pushing and pushing and pushing. She could smell him, too, or maybe it was her. It was over quickly and he flopped on top of her, groaning and panting. Then he stood up, fastened his trousers and said, 'Not a word to anyone about this, Ruth.' He wandered over to the window.

Ruth closed her legs. Her flesh was damp and sticky where he'd been. She wanted to wash him away and pulled down her skirts to cover her legs.

'Why did you do that to me?' she muttered.

'Didn't you like it?'

'No.'

'Well, it was the first time for you. You'll enjoy it next time.'

Next time? Ruth thought. How can there be a next time when I'm supposed to be wooed by a gentleman suitor? And what about him; he had a wife, for heaven's sake. He was an adulterer! She was sitting on the couch pushing her breasts back into her gown when Father returned.

He took one look at her dishevelled hair and said, 'Ruth, what have you been doing?'

'She fell asleep on the couch, Hargreaves,' Laughton answered from the window. 'Didn't you, Ruth?'

'Yes, My Lord,' she replied, hating herself for lying. What else was she to do? Admit to her father that she had allowed His Lordship to take her virtue? She felt like crying.

Lord Laughton crossed the room from the window to the door. As he passed her father he patted him on the shoulder. 'Good work tonight, Hargreaves. We'll talk about your new position in the morning.'

'Goodnight, sir.' Her father opened the door for His Lordship and closed it after him. 'On your feet, Ruth, and buck up. It's late.'

'Yes, Father.'

'And tidy your hair before I take you home. Your mother will have a fit. What happened to your gown?'

'The stitching tore. I'll take it back to the dressmaker tomorrow.'

'I've got your coat in the servants' hall. The trap's waiting.'

She followed her father back through the green baize door and shivered in the cold passage while he extinguished the last of the candles. She continued to shiver all the way home in the trap.

'You're quiet,' Father commented.

She pulled up the collar of her coat. 'I'm tired.'

'You can sleep in tomorrow. You did very well tonight. His Lordship is pleased.'

Ruth choked back her tears. Father stopped the trap at the front of their cottage and she climbed down. Mother opened the door before she reached it.

'Did you enjoy yourself, dear?' Mother asked.

'Yes, thank you,' she lied. 'I'm going straight to bed.'

'Don't you want some chocolate?'

'No thank you.'

'I'll bring it upstairs for you.'

'*No thank you*,' she cried and ran up the narrow twisty staircase to her bedroom.

She left her silk gown in a crumpled heap on the floor, put a pillow over her head to muffle her sobs and wept until she fell asleep.

Chapter 2

She heard Father rise early the following day. He fed the pony and harnessed the trap while Mother raked the fire and pumped water for the kettle. They left shortly afterwards to breakfast at the Hall. As soon as the water was warm enough she carried it upstairs to wash and put on clean clothes. Then she spread a calico sheet on the bed and wrapped the gown to take back to the dressmaker. It had cost Father a lot of money but the joy she'd felt when it arrived had disappeared and she couldn't imagine ever wearing it again. In fact, she never wanted to see it again.

She was drinking tea when she heard the first guns go off in the distance. The old family used to shoot at their lodge up near Harrogate. But the railway line had cut through the land and ruined cover for the birds.

They had been well compensated and bought up forest in the South Riding instead. The locals were pleased. They were beaters and dog handlers by day and poachers for the pheasant by night.

Father would be supervising luncheon out in the field, Ruth realised. Mother would be busy making sure that Waterley Hall was at its pristine best for His Lordship's guests. But the Hall would be quiet until the shooting party returned at the end of the day. She took down her coat and hat from the peg and set off walking.

She felt soiled and miserable but the brisk fresh air helped her to think and gave her strength. Losing her virtue was a disaster for her only if others knew and His Lordship wouldn't tell anyone. He had a crabby old wife who was easily angered. However, Ruth had to talk to someone about last night or she would go quite mad.

The only person she could trust was her mother. She had argued with Father against Ruth being there last night anyway. Also, Ivy knew more about Lady Laughton's tantrums than Father. Ruth didn't understand why His Lordship had married her until Father explained that it was a 'business arrangement'.

Lady Laughton's first husband and His Lordship had been second cousins; their fathers had owned shipyards on the east coast and steelworks in the South Riding. As partners the cousins possessed the largest industry in Yorkshire and numbered amongst the richest men in a prosperous country. A generation on from the Great Exhibition of 1851, Britannia led the world and Queen

16

Victoria ruled much of it. Steel and shipping basked in this wealth.

But when Lady Laughton was widowed, her husband left his share of the industry to her. His Lordship's father had been the youngest of the cousins and although the widow was much older than he, His Lordship was keen to secure total control – he could not risk her marrying someone else and taking her share with her. As it was, another cousin who had emigrated also had a share, but he was content to be a sleeping partner despite approaches from lawyers to sell.

It was rumoured that the present Lord Laughton's father had bought his title by lining the pockets of politicians in London. He was 'new money' and it showed, Father said. But Ruth was beginning to think that her father was cut from the same ambitious cloth as His Lordship. It was a trait, she guessed, that she shared. She had gone along with his plans for her to mix with the gentry and marry well. However, she had not realised the price she would have to pay.

She stood in the servants' passage waiting for her mother to hurry by. The Hall might be quiet while everyone was out shooting but below stairs was buzzing, not least because guests had brought their own servants with them. Visiting valets and footmen always caused a stir among the maids. She wondered if any of them had lost their virtue last night.

'Ruth, what are you doing here?'

'I want to talk to you, Mother.'

'About last night? Yes, I thought you might have

something to say to me. You looked quite worn out. Have you had breakfast?'

She shook her head.

'Wait in my sitting room. I'll be as quick as I can.'

Ruth felt safe in the housekeeper's sitting room at Waterley Hall. It was her mother's private space and even Father did not often intrude. Ruth had spent many childhood hours occupying herself in there while Mother worked. She made up the fire, took a ladies' journal from the bookshelf and settled in a comfortable chair.

The door opened and Mother came in followed by a kitchen maid with a heavy tray. The maid placed it on the table and said, 'Will there be anything else, ma'am?'

'We'll have a pot of tea and cake in an hour. I want today's cake, mind.'

'Yes, ma'am.'

Ivy lifted the lid off the tureen and a steamy spicy aroma escaped. 'It's the soup that went out to the field for His Lordship.' She sniffed the contents. 'Mmmm, mulligatawny.' She placed her hand upon a bulky white napkin. 'With warm bread from the oven. I'll have indigestion but it'll be worth it.' Then she turned her attention to her daughter. 'Dear me, Ruth, you look awful this morning. Did you drink wine last night?'

'Just a little.'

'Well, you know my feelings on that.'

'Father says I must learn about wine.'

Ivy frowned but only said, 'Come and sit to the table.' She ladled out the soup and drew out a chair. 'Now, what

18

have you to tell me? Did one of the gentlemen guests take an interest in you?'

Ruth had rehearsed what she would say . . . Yes, a gentleman had taken an interest but it wasn't the one she had expected and she . . . she . . . she didn't know what to do . . . *She didn't know what to do.* It was as this last phrase ran through her head that Ruth broke down and cried. She spluttered and sobbed and tried to speak but choked and coughed on the words. Ivy was silent. Ruth couldn't see her mother's expression through her tears but when she had hiccupped to a halt Mother was sitting staring at her with a stony face.

'What happened, Ruth?' she asked.

The hiccups hadn't stopped. 'He – he – I was . . . on the couch . . . and he was on top of me . . . I tried to stop him . . . I did try . . . but I – I . . . couldn't.' She covered her face with the clean white napkin. The tears were flowing again. She couldn't help herself.

'What did he do to you, Ruth?'

She inhaled with a shudder, but her throat was closed.

'Tell me what he did.'

Ruth jumped at her mother's angry tone and every nerve in her body jangled.

'Did he open his trousers and push himself inside you?'

Ruth pulled the napkin down and away from her face. It was exactly what he had done and she nodded.

'Ruth, Ruth, Ruth!' her mother anguished. 'I expect it from my maids but not from my own daughter. Where was your father when this happened?'

'He . . . he . . . he was putting someone to bed.'

19

'We'll have to tell him.'

'Oh, please don't do that, Mother. No one need know if we don't tell anybody.'

'Except the gentleman concerned. He's ruined you, don't you see? Well, he has to take responsibility and marry you because no other gentleman will even look at you now.' Ivy stood up and paced around the room. 'I knew it! I told your father it was a bad idea when Lady Laughton wasn't here to keep her eye on things. Would he have it? Well, we'll see who was right now, won't we?' she fumed.

Ruth sobbed and hiccupped and eventually croaked, 'I'm sorry, Mother.'

'Be quiet! I'm thinking.'

The fire died down and the soup went cold. There was a tap on the door. 'Not now!' Ivy snapped. Ruth needed a cup of tea but she didn't protest. Eventually, her mother had calmed and sat down again.

'We have to tell your father because he'll know what to do. He's a favourite at the moment. Lord Laughton has made him house steward. We were planning to celebrate tonight. *Dear heaven, Ruth, what were you thinking of?*'

'I . . . I t-t-told him to stop and he . . . he wouldn't listen to me.'

Ivy let out a sharp impatient sigh. 'Well, all is not lost. At least he's a gentleman. He'll have to marry you, that's all. It's not how we wanted it but if your father can get His Lordship to persuade the gentleman to do the right thing . . . His Lordship will help us when Father tells him.'

Ruth was startled into sensibility. 'No he won't. I mean, he can't! You don't understand, Mother! It was His Lordship that did it!'

'*What?*' Ivy covered her face with her hands and cried angrily, 'Ruth, what have you done, you stupid, stupid girl?'

She ought to have known better than to expect sympathy from her pious mother and retaliated, 'I didn't do anything! He did it to me. And he seemed to think he was going to carry on doing it! It's not what *I've* done, Mother, it's what you and father have not done. You didn't warn me about that! You didn't tell me that might happen!'

Ivy stood up. 'That's enough, Ruth. I've brought you up properly to value and guard your virtue and this is how you repay me at the first opportunity. The sooner you are married the better, as far as I am concerned.'

'Yes, well,' Ruth muttered, 'as you say, who will marry me now?'

'Who indeed.' Ivy sighed.

The door opened without prior knocking and Father walked in with a picnic basket. He glanced at the table and placed the basket on the floor. His face was ruddy from being outdoors and drinking left-over sloe gin from the shoot. 'His Lordship has ordered a buffet dinner for tonight so I'll be home early to celebrate,' he said. 'Has Mother told you my good news, Ruth?'

'Yes, Father.'

Seth rubbed his hands together. 'His Lordship's had a good day and he's in fine spirits. He has a proposition for me. I'll be home as soon as he's seen me. You two take the trap with this food.' He kicked the basket. 'I'll hitch a ride or walk.'

'Are the guns back already?'

'Only one or two of the lady followers who want first dibs at the hot water.'

Ivy picked up her chatelaine. 'They'll need linen. Stay here, Ruth, and don't breathe a word to anyone.'

'Is something up?' Father queried.

'No.'

'Nothing at all.'

Ruth and her mother had answered at exactly the same time.

Ruth unpacked the basket of cold roast beef, the cook's own mustard pickle, beetroot and a bottle of wine. Dessert pears and the end of the stilton were in the bottom. The cheese smelled too strong to eat. It was last year's because it was too early for this year's to be ready yet. She laid out their tea attractively on the kitchen table and scrubbed some potatoes to bake in the oven. She was hungry now and nibbled at the beef. There was plenty. Lord Laughton fed himself, his guests and his servants well.

Father was subdued when he arrived home and opened the wine straightaway. He drank it instead of tea with his meal. They were nearly finished before he said, 'I thought he was going to offer me a new house, now I'm steward.'

'It's nice here,' Ruth said. 'I like it.'

'It was you he wanted to see me about,' he said.

Ruth exchanged an alarmed glance with her mother who shook her head silently.

'I always knew you'd catch the eye of the gentry and live in a fine house one day,' he went on. 'But I didn't expect it this way.'

'What did he say to you, Seth?'

'He's taken a fancy to our daughter, Ivy, a proper shine to her, he has. He said he'd noticed how lovely she'd grown. Well, I knew he had, otherwise he wouldn't have asked her to the party last night, or paid for the gown.'

'You told me the silk was from you!' Ruth cried.

'Be quiet, Ruth,' her mother responded. 'What do you mean, Seth? He's a married man.'

'Yes, but look at who he's wed to? Who in their right mind would want her for a wife?'

'Isn't one of the marriage vows "for better or for worse"?'

'Oh, don't go all religious on me, Ivy. He's a young blood. He wants a pretty woman on his arm and, well, we want our Ruth to mix with the gentry, don't we?'

'Yes, but not on His Lordship's arm. He has a wife.'

'He likes our Ruth. I mean he really likes her. He said he'd marry her if he could.'

Ruth saw her mother's eyes widen and looked down at the table. 'Why would he say that?' Ivy demanded. 'What else has he told you?'

'He told me I should be very proud of her as she behaved like a perfect lady last night.'

Mother seemed relieved but spoke tartly. 'Well, he would say that, wouldn't he? It's what you want to hear.'

They were talking about her as though she wasn't present and Ruth wanted to tell Father the truth about

23

His Lordship. 'Mother,' Ruth interrupted, 'please can I say something?'

'No!' Ivy answered sharply. 'Leave this to me, my dear. If you've finished your tea you can go up to your bedroom.'

'I think she has to stay, Ivy. I haven't got to the proposition yet. She's still a bit young, you see, and His Lordship's aware of that. I think it was the attraction for him. The Prince of Wales has . . . well, he has his young ladies, you know, and the upper classes take their lead from him.'

'What is this proposition, Seth?'

'It's about our Ruth, Ivy. He's made up his mind and he's determined to have his way. My position, this cottage, your position, all is at risk if he doesn't get what he wants.'

'My position as well?' Ivy queried.

But what does he want? Ruth thought anxiously, remembering that he'd implied there'd be a next time with her. Nonetheless, she couldn't imagine Her Ladyship putting up with that sort of behaviour. She was bound to find out sooner or later. Anyway, it didn't matter to Ruth what His Lordship wanted because she didn't want him. She wanted to meet a young gentleman who was free to marry her.

'You're her mother, aren't you?' Seth explained. 'His Lordship says she has to marry soon.'

'Oh, I see. He wants her out of the way.' Ivy let out her breath audibly. 'That's a relief. I was thinking the same myself earlier on today. Ruth agreed with me, didn't you, dear?'

'Well, yes, but that was because—'

'Be quiet, dear,' her mother interrupted her. 'It's because you want to marry, isn't it?'

Ruth nodded. An early marriage was probably the best option for her now; before anyone found out – or guessed – that she was ruined. Perhaps she was wrong about His Lordship and he had a guilty conscience about his behaviour towards her? If that were the case, he might help her to find a rich husband. Ruth, like her mother, began to relax.

Seth said, 'Her husband has to be a fellow who owes me a favour or two, and will stay loyal to His Lordship.'

'Loyal to His Lordship?' Ivy repeated. Ruth noticed her mother sit up.

'To keep them out of Her Ladyship's sight,' Seth explained.

Her mother and father exchanged a glance that was, apparently, meaningful to them. But not to Ruth who watched her mother's body go rigid in her chair. 'Oh, Seth, no,' Ivy said, 'you can't do that to her. *She's your daughter.*'

'She'll do as I say. So will you. It's His Lordship's orders.'

No one spoke a word for several minutes. Ruth was aware her mother's anger had moved from her to her father. Father usually ignored both of them when it suited him. His word was law in their house. Ruth wanted to ask questions but she knew better than to inflame the situation. The rule for her was 'speak when you're spoken to'.

Father stood up. He was a big man. Tall men were favoured for male servants. Their height gave them stature and authority. 'That's settled, then,' he said. 'I thought Michael, my head footman, would be right for her. I had been training him up to take over from me as butler but he's pliable so he'll agree.'

'He's not daft, though,' Mother argued. 'Michael's already asked your permission to court her and you turned him down. He'll wonder why you've changed your mind.'

'He'll comply when His Lordship pays him off with a dowry. His Lordship hasn't got stacks of hard cash to give away so it'll be a property he has no other use for. Michael won't turn down a chance to live in a country house. He likes the gentrified way of life.'

'Well, he likes the brandy bottle, that's for sure,' Ivy commented.

Ruth grew more and more agitated as she listened to her parents speaking over her head. Michael? They'd chosen *Michael* to be her husband? 'Michael's not a gentleman!' Ruth cried. 'I'm not marrying a footman!'

'Don't you contradict me, my girl!' Her father raised his voice. 'You'll do as I say. He has to be one of His Lordship's servants. You wouldn't survive as a farmer's wife and His Lordship wouldn't do it to one of his own kind.'

'Do what? I thought you said His Lordship liked me and would wed me if he could!'

Her father was losing his temper and he turned on his wife. 'Good God, Ivy,' he shouted, 'you know what His Lordship wants! Tell her, will you?'

Ivy's back was ramrod straight in the chair and her

mouth was set in a thin tight line. 'Oh, yes, Seth. I know right enough and I wish I didn't.'

'Tell me what, Mother?' Ruth asked.

Ivy didn't mince her words. It was a characteristic that helped to make her an effective housekeeper. 'His Lordship wants you in his bed, Ruth,' she said. 'He wants you to be his mistress.'

Chapter 3

Ruth swallowed. 'But I can't,' she protested. 'I'm going to marry a gentleman.' Neither of her parents was showing her any of kind of sympathy. Father was suggesting that she married one man because another one wanted her as his mistress?

'Mother?' she squeaked, but her mother was tight-lipped.

Seth went on, 'She'll be well treated. She'll have fancy gowns and hats, and her own carriage.'

'Don't be ridiculous, Seth! Do you think Her Ladyship will stand for that? As soon as she gets wind of it, she'll have our Ruth scrubbing floors or worse.'

'Well, obviously His Lordship can't have it going on here at the Hall, right under her nose. But that's where the dowry comes in. If Michael marries her, His Lordship will give him Mereside Lodge, the old hunting lodge up country. It's been no use for shooting since the railway took half the woodland. But the lake has fishing; it has been leased as a fully staffed country residence lately. Michael will have a pension and he'll be able to turn his hand to something if he wants.'

'I suppose His Lordship will take up fishing and Her Ladyship will think he's reformed,' Ivy commented sourly. 'Seth, you can't agree to this. She's our daughter, not some jumped-up parlourmaid.'

'You wanted her at that fancy college in the first place!' Seth rubbed his hands over his thinning grey hair. 'His Lordship's made his mind up, Ivy. He won't let her go and he can ruin us all if he wants. He would, too. He's a man without scruples.'

'Well, it takes one to know one,' Ivy retaliated bitterly.

'Oh, get down off your high horse, woman! We'll stay here in comfort. He's doubled my stipend. We're having another room built on and a bigger carriage.'

'Shut up, Seth,' Ivy snapped. 'I don't care about a carriage. I need to think.'

Ruth could not stomach this conversation any longer. She stood up and declared, 'Well, I don't need to think. I'm not doing it.'

'Go to your bedroom this minute, Ruth,' Ivy ordered. 'You've played your part in this too.'

'*It wasn't my fault.*'

'That's enough!' Ivy waved her index finger in the air. 'Upstairs now. I'll be up to talk to you when your father and I have discussed this matter further.'

Ruth shook her head in exasperation. This would be a discussion of arrangements, not an argument against her father's decision. She was glad of an opportunity to escape from the pair of them! Last night she had been on the edge of a new and exciting period in her life.

She couldn't understand why everything had gone so wrong. She had dreamed of a life in a gentleman's country residence just as her father was describing. Except that in her dream she would be married to the gentleman himself and not to his greedy head footman. And why? So that His Lordship could have what he wanted, regardless of her wishes?

It wasn't fair! She wished she hadn't told her mother about His Lordship now and flopped on her bed in despair. She had hoped that she might fall in love with her husband, that he would love her in return. Where was love in all of this? Was this what Mother had meant when she had warned Ruth not to expect too much from marriage? Ruth's heart sank. Mother had told her that kind of romantic love didn't last. For her, the love of God was the only enduring passion.

It occurred to Ruth that her mother might not love her as much as she loved God, possibly because Ruth didn't love God as much as her mother did. Neither did she love Michael or His Lordship! And her father was asking her to be a . . . a sort of a wife to both of them? Actually, he wasn't asking her. Ruth knew her father well. He was telling her and he expected to be obeyed. As she sat in her upholstered chair by the window staring at the darkening sky, she was no longer sure that she loved her father either.

The pony and trap were still by the front gate and when she heard the front door close she guessed her father was going out to stable it. She leaned forward to watch him. But it was her mother, clutching her prayer book, who climbed in and set off in the direction of Waterley Edge and the nearest Methodist chapel. Then Father did something he had never done before. He tapped on her bedroom door and came in with a cup of tea for her.

'Your mother'll come round eventually. She's gone to pray and she wants you to wait up for her,' he said.

'Do I have to do this, Father?' Ruth asked.

'Yes, you do.' His tone was firm.

Ruth lit the lamp, did some sewing and tried to read. The journals about London fashion had lost their appeal. She picked up her bible and put it down again. Waterley Hall had its own church in the grounds that servants were expected to attend. Her Ladyship worshipped regularly but His Lordship didn't. Neither did Ruth's father. Ruth occasionally accompanied her mother to the Methodist chapel. The commandment was the same in church or chapel: thou shalt not commit adultery.

It was dark when Mother returned and Father went out straightaway to stable the pony. However, they talked in the kitchen for a long time before Ivy came upstairs. Ruth was on her feet to open the door when her mother arrived with cups of chocolate. Ruth could see that she had been crying.

'Father says I have to do it,' Ruth said.

'Your father is a wicked man and so is His Lordship. But the damage is done and you must listen to me now. Your father will not change his mind. He's house steward now and pleased that His Lordship has chosen you. He regards it as an honour. If he had any doubts about the . . . the . . . morality of the situation, His Lordship has persuaded him otherwise.'

'What will Father do to me if I refuse?'

Her mother shook her head. 'I do not advise you to disobey your father. He can be quite unprincipled in his reprisals.'

'But I want to marry a gentleman. You want me to marry a gentleman.'

'You lost that choice when you gave yourself to His Lordship.'

Ruth opened her mouth to protest, but Ivy silenced her with a raised hand and a pointed index finger. 'His Lordship is more heartless than your father. He has the power to ruin your reputation across the Riding and he will do so if you do not give him what he demands.'

'It's not exactly giving, is it?'

Ivy look horrified. 'Ruth! Do not even think that what you have to do for him requires payment in return, let alone voice that thought.'

Payment? Goodness, she wasn't thinking of payment! That would make her a . . . a . . . She began to feel sick. That's what mother *had* thought! And that is why she went to pray in chapel. Well, what *is* the difference between a woman kept for pleasure and a prostitute?

'I wasn't thinking of payment,' Ruth said. 'I was trying to say that His Lordship took what he wanted from me without asking. I did not give myself to him willingly.'

'Well, don't ever speak of that encounter to anyone. Do you hear me? From what your father has said, I don't think His Lordship has told him that he took you down.'

Ruth's hopes were raised. 'Then if nobody knows, it won't matter. I can carry on as before.'

Her mother lost her patience and snapped. 'Are you listening to a word I say?'

'I can deny it.' Ruth shrugged.

'You can't do that if you turn out to be with child.'

Ruth's mouth dropped open in shock. 'I can't be. I mean, it was over very quickly and . . .' She pulled a face. 'Well, he isn't very big, you know.' From those whispered conversations after dark in her ladies' college she had expected something more – well, something different anyway.

Mother glared at her. 'I hope with all my heart that you are not with child, but it is not impossible, even the first time.'

Ruth was subdued by this knowledge. 'His Lordship said he would do it again to me, Mother.'

'My dear, there are ways of avoiding becoming with child. I have had enough maids through my servants' hall to know the most effective remedies. I shall take you with me to the linen suppliers in Sheffield next week and find a chemist for you. Don't look so frightened. It's only sponges and douches.'

Ruth didn't like the sound of that at all and moaned, 'I don't want to do this, Mother.'

33

'Nor do I and I have prayed for guidance!' Ivy covered her face with her hands. 'I shall continue to pray every night that you are not with child. For that would make things ten times worse. His Lordship will not want a bastard child; or its mother.'

Ruth realised that her mother was holding back her tears and Ruth felt her own throat close. 'It's not fair,' she whined. 'If I were a man I could run away to sea.'

Ivy inhaled with a shudder. 'For heaven's sake, buck yourself up! We have to make the best of a bad situation. Your father and I agree that you should marry as soon as possible. If Michael agrees to the wedding, the banns will be read at Waterley church on Sunday and we'll have the ceremony in four weeks' time. His Lordship will give your union his blessing.'

'But Michael will say yes, Mother,' she wailed. 'Does it have to be him?'

'Of course it does. He's able to run Mereside Lodge and Michael will have an income from it as well as his pension. Your father will speak to him tomorrow.'

'He's a *footman*, Mother,' Ruth reminded her.

'Your father will make him up to butler until the wedding. It won't be so bad for you. Father says he's admired you for ages. However,' Ivy leaned forward to emphasise her point, 'you'll have to keep him at arm's length: His Lordship won't want to share you.'

Ruth's frown deepened. 'But if Michael is my husband . . .?'

'Don't worry about that now. You'll have your own rooms. The upper classes always have separate bedrooms.'

Ruth's chocolate had gone cold. She didn't want it anyway. It was a rich sweet drink and her stomach felt queasy. Her life was turning upside down and she found it hard to take it all in. 'Do I really have to marry next month?' she muttered.

'Yes. It is the best I can do for you. I don't want it any more than you do. Believe me, I am more sorry than you will ever be. But, to the outside world you will be a respectable married lady whose gentleman husband owns a country residence.'

'Shall we walk?' Michael held out his arm to Ruth.

This was the second Sunday of reading the banns for their marriage and in two weeks the vicar would perform the ceremony. Last Sunday they had made a show of walking out together after church and Michael had droned on about her father coming to his senses at last. She thought he was far too full of himself but Lady Laughton was watching them so she took his arm.

'Her Ladyship is very pleased with me,' he said.

'Why, what have you done for her?'

'This, of course.' He lifted his elbow. 'Marrying you. She came up to me specially to congratulate me. I've done her a big favour.'

'I don't see how.'

'She doesn't like pretty women around His Lordship. She doesn't trust him and that new lady's maid of hers tells her everything. She heard about you at the party the other week when she was away.'

Ruth went rigid. 'What did she hear?'

35

'Only what I told her. I was serving at the banquet,' Michael added, 'and I saw you dressed up in silks for His Lordship.'

'It wasn't for him. He was going to introduce me to his friend.'

'Not that one who was ogling you across the table? He wouldn't have wed you. When it comes to heirs they marry their own kind. I reckon you're well out of that one, Ruthie. He can't hold his drink. Now me, I can finish up all the leftover wine and still serve the coffee without spilling.' Michael put his hand over hers and tucked his elbow closer to his body so Ruth was obliged to move nearer to him. 'Anyway, Her Ladyship will be at the ceremony and I'll get a nice bonus from her afterwards.'

Ruth reflected that everyone was benefiting from her marriage, except her. She had seriously considered running away. But without money or anywhere to go she might die in a ditch. She had learned about the Married Women's Property Act at her ladies' college. It was all very well for those who had means before they married. They could keep it for themselves nowadays. But if you went into a marriage with nothing, you stayed with nothing. She couldn't see a way out of her situation no matter how much she tried.

They strolled on in silence. Waterley Hall estate was vast, with woodland deer parks and rolling Yorkshire countryside punctuated by the blackened winding gear and growing slag heaps of coal mines. You couldn't see the pits from here. Pastures dotted with sheep and ancient forest surrounded the Hall itself.

'Where are we going?' she asked.

'The old charcoal burner's place.'

'That's a long walk into the wood.'

'The shepherd's wagon is there, waiting for repair. They've brought it down from the high pasture before the winter sets in. It'll be nice and cosy inside.'

She stopped. 'Oh, it's too far. My mother's expecting me at the Hall for tea today.'

He pulled on her arm. 'Come on, Ruthie, we're betrothed. We can have a taste of married life.'

'I don't think so.'

She saw a flash of anger in his eyes. 'Two weeks won't make any difference.'

'Yes it will. I can't.' His expression didn't change so she added, 'I won't.'

'Oh, won't you? We'll see about that.' He grasped her hand and strode on ahead, jerking her after him.

'Stop a minute! Listen. I can hear something.' Ruth wasn't prevaricating. His Lordship's wealthier friends and neighbours often rode across the estate, although they didn't hunt on Sundays. She could hear horse's hooves thudding on the ground. Someone was out riding, off the bridle path and crashing through the trees behind them. 'Out of the way!' the rider yelled.

'Good God, it's His Lordship!' Michael exclaimed.

The horse veered on to the track and they stepped aside into the undergrowth. However, His Lordship slowed when he saw them, reined in his sweating horse and swung down from the saddle. He held onto the reins, walked his horse back towards them and said, 'You're a long way from the Hall.'

'We've been to church,' Ruth explained.

His Lordship's face was shiny with perspiration and spotted with blood from a graze. He took off his tall hat and wiped the back of his hand across his forehead, streaking it with dust. He smiled at Ruth and said, 'You're walking in the wrong direction for the Hall.'

'We are just taking the air, sir,' Michael said.

'Go back now,' His Lordship ordered.

Michael did not move. He was stony-faced.

'Now,' His Lordship repeated.

'Very well, sir,' Michael said and turned round. Ruth followed suit.

'Ruth, wait,' His Lordship called.

She had to stop and face him but Michael didn't walk on either. He stayed with her and she was grateful. Ruth kept her eyes on the ground.

'Look at me when I'm talking to you.'

She obeyed.

'Come and see me at the Hall after tea.' He glanced over her head at Michael standing behind her and grinned, 'I have a wedding present for Ruth.'

She couldn't speak. She didn't want any gifts from him. She didn't want anything from him.

'Her Ladyship is talking to your mother about your wedding breakfast,' His Lordship went on. 'I shall be in my study. Five o'clock.'

'Very well, sir.'

He nodded and flicked his hands in a gesture for them to move on in the direction of the church. They did and Ruth heard him remount and spur on his horse.

Michael was gripping her hand so tightly that he was hurting her.

'Let go of me,' she said, trying to snatch her hand away.

'Bastard,' Michael hissed through his teeth. 'Bloody bastard.'

'Michael!' Ruth was shocked by his language, especially on a Sunday.

'Who the hell does he think he is?'

'He's your master, Michael.'

'Well, Her Ladyship is right. He's got a fancy for you, right enough. That's plain to see. But if he thinks he's having his *droit de seigneur* before me he can think again. Nobody's having my wife before I do.' Michael pushed her off the bridle path and into the fern undergrowth. She was so surprised that he was unhooking the waistband of her skirt before she realised his intentions.

'You can't do this here, Michael,' she protested. 'You have to wait until we're married.'

'No I don't. I've wanted you for weeks and I'm having you now. Take off your skirt.'

Ruth had some idea of what to expect and she considered a struggle. But Michael was bigger than His Lordship in every respect. He was taller, more muscular and had strong hands. When he tugged at her skirts he could easily rip them if she resisted, and his fingers on her arm were tight enough to bruise them. She told herself he was practically her husband and therefore he had a right.

His face dripped sweat on to her forehead. All she could see over his shoulder were the dried-up fronds of dying ferns scratching at her hair. His weight pressed her down while he jabbed at her. He seemed to have some difficulty getting inside her until he probed around with his fingers. Then he went on for longer than His Lordship. And all she could think about was that she hadn't put in a sponge and whether or not she would tell her mother.

Chapter 4

Ruth was silent afterwards, all the way back to the church and onwards to the Hall. Michael talked about himself and how he would be well off when they were wed. He'd have Mereside Lodge, anything he could make from it and an account with a bank. Ruth wondered miserably what she would have that she could call her own? Michael didn't seem to notice she was quiet. Her mother did, though, later, when they were having tea in her house-keeper's room in at the Hall.

'Well, have you nothing to say about that, Ruth?'

'About what, Mother?'

'Do pay attention, my dear. Lady Laughton has asked me to take five o'clock tea with her in the drawing room so we can talk about a wedding breakfast for you. It won't be in the drawing room, of course, but here in the servants' hall.' She picked up a plate. 'I shan't have my piece of cake now. You have it.'

'I'm not hungry.' Ruth's fingers were winding round each other nervously. 'Mother, His Lordship wants to see me in his study at five.'

Mother frowned. 'Calm down. You will have to see him when he says so. He'll be nice to you, I'm sure. Your father says he's very keen on you.'

'Well, can you . . .? I mean, if he does it to me can you put the sponge in afterwards?'

Mother looked shocked at first and then very sad, as though she was going to cry. She swallowed and answered, 'I don't know but I suppose it's better than nothing. The douche is for afterwards. Try not to worry about it now. He won't do anything like that here, not with Lady Laughton at home.'

But he did; on the button-backed maroon leather chesterfield behind the locked door of his study. Ruth's eyes roamed over the high shelves of books until he'd finished. He was quite admiring of her; her hair, her eyes, her lips and her breasts, especially her breasts. 'I told you it would be easier the second time,' he said.

He did have a wedding present for her, as well. It was a sapphire set in gold and threaded on a gold chain. He fastened it around her neck, underneath her gown and put the velvet lined box back in his desk drawer. 'Make sure to wear this on your wedding day,' he ordered, and sent her away.

She went home with her parents in the trap that evening. Ruth asked Father to bring the hip bath up to her bedroom and Mother helped carry the hot water.

'I'll stay and help,' her mother said.

Ruth stood fully dressed in her bedroom and shook her head. 'I can take care of myself, Mother. You and Father have done your . . . your best for me, but you are not responsible for me any more now that I have a . . . a patron.' Ruth managed to raise a weak smile. She was aware that her mother was holding back her tears.

Ivy said, 'You must understand that I have to keep Lady Laughton's approval. After your marriage, you will not be able to return here, no matter what.' She raised her eyes to the ceiling. 'Lord help all of us if Her Ladyship finds out the truth.'

Ruth supposed that Michael wouldn't be too pleased, either, when he realised that he'd been duped into this marriage. 'Do what you have to, Mother,' she said. 'I'm learning fast about what I have to do. The ladies' college has prepared me well.' Ruth saw that her mother wasn't quite sure how to take this remark so she added, 'I shall be a perfect lady at all times for His Lordship and . . . cultivate his favour for as long as I can.'

But Ruth was thinking, If I don't I'll end up on the streets, because no one will want me when His Lordship's finished with me, least of all Michael. In this instance the ladies' college might be more useful than mother ever imagined. She remembered a girl who was known to be the daughter of a 'kept women'. In some respects she had seemed wise beyond her years about marriage and money, but her mother had prepared her well to understand the needs of men. Ruth was just beginning.

She fingered the sapphire hidden under her gown and

thought, His Lordship will pay well for me. I'll make sure he does, in jewels and horses and anything else I can sell in the future. It crossed her mind that she was more her father's daughter than her pious mother's.

She said, 'I won't ever come back here, Mother. And I shan't expect you to visit me. You and Father may carry on as before. I know how to make my own way through life now.'

'Dear Lord,' Ivy whispered. 'What have I done to you?'

Ruth shrugged and muttered, 'What's done is done.'

Mother left, fishing in her pocket for a handkerchief and Ruth heard her take the trap over to the Methodist chapel that night.

Ruth refused to go for a walk after church the following Sunday, arguing that she had too much to do before the wedding. She sent sketches and torn-out journal pages to her dressmaker with instructions to arrange delivery to Mereside Lodge of everything except her wedding gown. For that she chose a modest high-necked affair in dusky pink with long tight sleeves and a bustle. The small private church was full. Lady Laughton occupied the front pew alone, with Mother and Father behind her. The remainder of the congregation included Michael's widowed father, his spinster aunt and Hall servants. Ruth was relieved that Lord Laughton had stayed away.

It was a fine autumn day and they lingered amongst the gravestones in the churchyard afterwards. Lady Laughton spoke to the vicar first and then came over to Ruth and Michael and their respective families. She ignored Ruth's father but said something complimentary to her mother. Then she turned to Michael and gave him an envelope.

'Thank you, My Lady,' he said and tucked it away inside his Sunday-best jacket.

Her Ladyship left immediately in her carriage. Michael extracted a leather-covered hip flask from his pocket and took a swig. He offered it to her father who declined and said, 'I have beer and cider set up in the servants' hall.'

Michael shrugged. He was a fine-looking man, tall and straight, but Ruth noticed he had developed a swagger about him recently. 'We won't be there,' Michael said. 'His Lordship has lent a carriage to take us to the railway station.'

Ivy was surprised. 'Are you leaving now?'

'His Lordship gave me tickets for a first-class carriage in the railway train.'

Ruth was as surprised as her mother but maintained her composure. She was becoming quite adept at that these days. 'I shall want my travelling coat, Michael,' she said.

His aunt stepped forward. 'I've put everything in the carriage for you, Ruth.'

They walked towards the waiting carriage. Before Ruth climbed in her mother took her to one side. 'This is goodbye, then,' Ivy said. She leaned forward to make a show of kissing her daughter on the cheek and whispered, 'Encourage him to drink and he won't bother you in the bedroom.' It was the last piece of advice her mother gave her.

Michael didn't need Ruth for encouragement to drink. The picnic basket, prepared by the Hall cook, contained bottled beer and he had brandy in his luggage. It was a long journey by carriage, two railway trains and another carriage at the end. Night was drawing in and Michael's brandy was finished when they arrived at Mereside Lodge.

The house appeared to be a respectable size and set beside water: the fishing lake, Ruth realised. She looked forward to seeing it in daylight. A manservant opened the front door to them and Michael pushed past him and looked around. There was a decanter and glasses sitting on the hall table, intended to warm travellers coming in from wintry weather. Michael poured himself a drink and sat in a chair with his legs stretched across the tiled floor. 'This is the life for me,' he said. His speech was slurred and his eyelids drooping. The manservant stood by and watched as he drank.

Apart from Michael, Ruth liked what she saw. A chandelier of about twenty candles suspended from a high ceiling illuminated the spacious reception hall and grand oak staircase leading to the first and second floors. She heard a movement on the stairs and looked up. His Lordship, dressed in a tweed Norfolk jacket and trousers, stood at the top. He was smoking a cigar.

'Pour the gentleman another drink,' Ruth said to the manservant, indicating Michael.

His Lordship walked slowly down until he reached the last few steps. Michael's attention was diverted by his manservant and the decanter he carried towards him.

When the manservant moved aside, Michael had sight of His Lordship. He was visibly shaken.

'What the blazes is he doing here?' he demanded.

'Don't you know?' Ruth said. She actually felt sorry for him. But she had been used in a similar fashion and had to come to terms with it. He would have to find his own way through.

Michael tipped the brandy to the back of his throat and held out the empty glass.

Ruth nodded at the manservant who stepped forward to refill the glass. 'See him safely to bed,' she said, and turned towards the stairs. She gave His Lordship her widest smile. 'Good evening, Laughton,' she said, 'how lovely to see you.'

'Good evening, Ruth. Come this way.'

Four Months Later

'Where is your husband, Ruth?'

'He doesn't stay in the house when you are here.' And very rarely at other times, she thought. But it suited her so she did not complain. Michael had a carriage and pair with a groom to drive him.

'Where does he go?'

Anywhere he can drink his brandy in solitude, Ruth thought. But she said, 'He's employed a woodman to manage the forest. He spends much of his time with the man's family on the other side of the estate.'

She was sitting in her morning room. Laughton had joined her after a gallop in the icy air and a gargantuan breakfast. Ruth was unable to stomach food at present.

Laughton stood at the bay window that looked out over the lake. 'There's profit in wood,' he commented. 'Michael was a good choice of your father's.' He moved to the fireplace and added a few coals. 'I'm moving abroad, Ruth.'

Ruth's heart stopped. Surely he had not tired of her already? Yet it had not seemed so last night, although he had commented that she was thinner. It was the morning sickness. She wondered how long she could keep it a secret from him and how he would react when he found out. She wondered, also, when he'd be going abroad and how long he'd be away. She fingered the sapphire ring he had given her and then the matching bracelet. She wore them all the time when he was here, even at night; actually, especially at night, when he demanded she wore nothing else. He liked her that way.

He pulled her to her feet and ran his hands up and down the curve of her corseted waist. 'I want to be the envy of my club, Ruth. I want you on my arm at the races to show them how beautiful you are. I can't do that in Yorkshire, let alone the rest of England. I'd be shunned by every society host.'

'Do you mean you want me to go abroad with you?' Her mind was churning with possibilities.

'France,' he said. 'I've got stock over there that I don't want Her Ladyship to know about. I'm liquidising it to buy a stud farm in your name.' His eyes gleamed as he added, 'Racehorses.'

'This is quite a surprise, Laughton.'

'A pleasant one, surely? You'd like to own a string of racehorses, wouldn't you?'

'I should, Laughton. I should.' She hoped the sale would be completed quickly and before her baby began to show. She could disguise it with her gowns, but not so easily between the bed sheets.

She gave a light laugh. 'But oughtn't you to be breeding heirs instead of horses?'

His tone changed and he answered harshly, 'I'll not bed her and why should I? She's too old anyway.' He glanced at her shrewdly. 'What is it, Ruth? Your father assured me that you knew better than to yearn for a bastard. Don't let me down. I won't stand for that.'

'Of course not, dearest. When shall we leave for France?'

'Soon. Very soon. Her Ladyship has found out about this arrangement and there's going to be a hell of scandal. It could cause lost orders, a drop in share prices and God knows what else, so I'm leaving the country.'

'Does Her Ladyship know it's me?' she squeaked.

'That's what I'm trying to tell you,' he replied impatiently. 'Get your maid to start packing. She can come with you if you want, but she'll have to learn French.'

But Ruth's mind wasn't in France yet, it was still in Yorkshire. Everyone would know it was her! She would be blamed as the temptress who had caused the rift in His Lordship's marriage and the name of Hargreaves would be dragged through the gutter. His Lordship was running and so should she. But her parents would remain at Waterley Hall. They had nowhere else to go. Their home, their livelihood, their future depended on the patronage of the incumbents. She had to hold herself rigid so that her trembling did not show. 'What will happen to my mother and father when you leave Waterley Hall?' she asked.

He wasn't interested. 'Not now, Ruth,' he said. 'I've more important things to think about. We'll break the journey in London until I've completed my negotiations with the French. I'm staying at my club and I've reserved a suite for you at The Admiral.'

'It's all arranged, then?'

'I'll be in the library writing letters until luncheon. I suggest you do the same.'

He fondled her face and kissed her. She had come to the conclusion that his affection for her was genuine although he did not say he loved her, not ever. He treated her well, as long as she behaved as he wished. But he was intolerant of argument if she transgressed so she was obliged to obey him. However, she feared for her safety when he found out about the baby, as he would – eventually.

She had no way of knowing whose baby it was. She believed she had conceived very early in her marriage, perhaps before the ceremony. Michael drank less between Laughton's visits and when he was sober he insisted on his marital rights. He made a practice of muttering disparaging remarks about His Lordship both during and after their intimacy. It was clear that Michael no longer wanted her; he only wanted to punish Laughton. If he hated her enough to use her in this way, she could not rely on Michael's protection when Laughton discarded her.

Michael was not a contented man but he knew better than to challenge His Lordship directly. He was aware how much power His Lordship had and how far-reaching it was. But Michael had independent means thanks, in part at least, to her father. He might be persuaded to offer her parents a home at Mereside Lodge.

Ruth wished she had more time to accumulate the

means of escape. She had jewellery, carriages and horses but not money. A bank note from His Lordship here and there for notions from the draper would not pay her passage home from France. If only she didn't have the baby and could wait! One thoroughbred sold without his knowledge would get her to America and anonymity. She heaved a sigh. If only she didn't have the baby, she would not need to flee.

She unlocked her writing desk, took out her address book and flicked through the pages. Not many of her ladies' college friends had volunteered their details to a butler's daughter. But the girl whose mother was a baronet's mistress was there. Ruth hardly knew her and turned the page quickly. Finally she closed the book, took a sheet of writing paper embossed with *Mereside Lodge, Forest Chase, Yorkshire, NR*, and dipped her pen in the ink.

Dear Mother, I hope this letter finds you and Father in good health.

You will know by now that His Lordship is leaving England. I shall be going with him. I imagine this will please you as I am aware that my living arrangements give you much pain. However, I fear that you and Father will be required to quit your positions and your home. Michael may have a place for you here, although I have not had time to discuss this with him. I suggest that Father writes to him.

I have to tell you that His Lordship treats me well and I have no complaints. However, the worst has happened.

In spite of my vigilance I find that I am with child and I do not know who the father is.

Ruth stopped and reread the last sentence. It was a shockingly immoral sin to confess to her religious mother and she guessed it would cause her acute distress. But what had her mother expected? She needed her mother to realise how desperate she was. Ruth screwed up the page and began again, changing the sentence to:

I do not know whether the father is my husband or His Lordship.

She continued.

A child will be an encumbrance to His Lordship and so shall I. He will not want me or the child even if he believes that my baby is his. Michael hates me as much as he hates His Lordship and, now he can afford it, he drinks brandy for most of his time.

I shall not humiliate you with my presence at Waterley. However, I know that you have helped housemaids in my situation in the past and I am asking you to do the same for me. I shall be at The Admiral Hotel in London from next week. If you can furnish me with a name and address of one or two ladies who might assist me in any way, I can prepare myself.

Prepare myself? She thought. For what? For any solution that presented itself. She wasn't the only girl without means to land herself in trouble and it was never the men who paid the price. Some of these girls received help. Ruth simply wanted to be helped in the same way by people she could trust.

She sat back and reread her words. She was still their daughter and not yet twenty-one. Father had handed responsibility for her to His Lordship. Did that responsibility include an obligation to love her and care for her? She guessed not and reflected that neither Mother nor Father had demonstrated much love towards her, anyway; or indeed to each other. Their lives were driven by ambition for her father and religion for her mother. But they were her parents and Ruth felt she had no one else, no one at all, to turn to.

She signed the letter,

Your loving daughter, Ruth.

It was the only letter she wrote. She folded it and slid it inside one of the embossed envelopes, then hesitated. If a scandal was about to break, correspondence from Mereside Lodge would be suspect. She lit the tiny oil burner, picked up a stick of red sealing wax and watched it drip in blobs onto the closed envelope flap. She pressed the brass seal into the wax. No one would dare break a seal to examine the contents.

She placed it on a brass tray in the reception hall for a servant to carry to the post office then went for a long walk around the lake. Even in late winter, when the surrounding trees were bare twigs against the sky, it was beautiful and she would be sorry to leave. A few geese landed, disturbing the glassy water and she watched an ever-extending circle of ripples until they faded. Her existence as the scandalous mistress of Lord Laughton might fade in the same way if she lived abroad. No one would know her in France and she could start her life afresh.

But she had to decide about her baby first.

No matter how hard she prayed, Ivy could not find it within herself to forgive her husband or her daughter for their easy acceptance of their immoral ambitions. In her view, the thunderclouds of scandal that gathered over Waterley Hall were God's vengeance on the sinners.

Seth realised quickly that his days as house steward were numbered when he heard of Lord Laughton's plans to leave the country. He expected a cottage and a pension but neither was forthcoming. Lady Laughton dismissed him without notice and with some pleasure. Seth's resentment festered. On the day he received an official notice to quit his cottage he suffered a seizure that left him without the power of speech and the use of an arm and leg.

Ivy was unmoved. This was the wrath of God and Seth deserved it. She persuaded the doctor to place him in an almshouse for his last few months. Then she drove the trap and her belongings to Waterley Hall where she installed herself in an attic servant's room while she waited for Lady Laughton's decision on her position as housekeeper.

In this frame of mind, when Ivy received her daughter's letter, forwarded to the Hall, she regarded her with-child predicament as 'just deserts'. She marched into the kitchen, threw the letter on the cooking-range fire and watched it flare up with some satisfaction.

Of course no one wanted this child! The mother did not want it. His Lordship would never own it and Michael was too drunk to care. These wicked people deserved everything they got. Ivy stared at the flames until they died back to embers. Then she collected her prayer book from her sitting room and went outside to harness her trap. Waterley Hall was nearer to the Methodist chapel than the cottage. God was on her side.

PART TWO

Chapter 5

Waterley Edge, South Riding, Yorkshire, 1905

'Lettie, come here a minute.'

'What is it, Gran?' Lettie was sitting at the kitchen table cleaning the knives. She put down her buffing cloth and jumped to her feet. At nineteen, she had plenty of spare energy to use up and her grandmother relied on her for much of the rough work in the manse.

Gran closed the kitchen door behind her. 'The Reverend has a special meeting of the elders this afternoon. They'll be in the dining room from three o'clock.'

'I'll make sure it's ready.' Lettie cleared away the knives and stored her cleaning materials in the scullery cupboard. She folded the sheets of newspaper that had protected her carefully scrubbed table top and placed them on the pile for fire lighting.

Reverend Ennis did not have a wife. He was married

to his vocation as Methodist minister for Waterley Edge chapel and he depended on Gran to organise his life for the benefit of his calling. Gran was an intelligent old lady. As a young woman she had been a housekeeper to a lord in a large country house. She ran the manse with the same discipline. Lettie wore a serviceable cotton dress and housemaid's apron. Her long light brown hair was pulled back, plaited and left down her back or pinned up under a plain cap.

Lettie wondered what the meeting was about. 'Has someone passed away?' she asked.

'The Reverend buried him last month. He left a legacy for electric light in the mission hall. I hope they put it in here as well.' The manse had gas lights in the main rooms at the front, but still used oil lamps in the kitchen and bedrooms at the back of the house.

'So do I,' Lettie agreed. 'It will help your eyes.'

'There's nothing wrong with my eyes.'

Lettie disagreed but did not argue. 'Shall I sit in with you and take notes?'

'Not today, it's Friday. You'll have to stay in here for the egg man.'

'I could write up the minute book for you afterwards,' she offered.

'Thank you. You are such a help to me these days.'

Lettie would have done anything for her grandmother. Gran had looked after Lettie since she was a baby and brought her up to 'do everything properly' in the manse. But since she had left school, Lettie had been concerned about Gran's advancing years and anxious to shoulder much of the work herself. Consequently, Lettie hardly ever met people of her own age and, although she could never admit it to Gran, she was growing restless with her life at Waterley Edge.

She was secretly pleased that she didn't have to sit through the elders' meeting and tried not to let her excitement show. Thomas called with the delivery on Fridays. Normally Gran was present to pay him for the week, but mission duties always came first. Lettie liked Thomas. He was fun. She remembered him as one of the bigger boys at school. He lived in town and every time she walked the two miles to market she looked out for him cavorting around out on his delivery bicycle. He freewheeled down the hills with his legs stuck out in front of him and he made her laugh.

He was not what she would call handsome, but he was tall and strong, with thick dark hair. He worked for Mr Adley, a local smallholder, and when he wasn't delivering, he was on Adley's market stall selling eggs and vegetables. Last week, when Lettie walked to town for some sewing thread from the draper's, he had stopped to talk and asked her to go to the Midsummer Fair with him. He would be expecting a reply today.

Lettie collected a feather duster, broom and dustpan from the scullery. The dining room was already clean because it was summer and she hadn't lit a fire. 'Gran,' she asked, 'can I go to the fair on Saturday? Thomas has asked if he can take me.'

'Thomas?' Gran queried. 'Is that Thomas from chapel?'

'Thomas, who brings the eggs,' Lettie explained.

61

'You mean Thomas the delivery boy? What was he doing speaking to you? Who on earth does he think he is?'

He's not a delivery 'boy', Lettie thought. He's a young man, just as she was now a young woman, even if Gran wasn't aware of it. Why shouldn't Thomas want to walk out with her?

'I know him from school.' Lettie waited patiently for Gran to reply and, when she didn't, prompted, 'Well, can I go with him?'

'No, you most certainly cannot. His father's a coal miner and he's a roughneck. I'm surprised you even considered it. And you a Sunday school teacher, too.'

Lettie frowned at Gran's reaction and commented, 'Some of my Sunday school children have fathers who are coal miners.'

'Yes, well, their families are chapel folk. I haven't brought you up to mix with roughnecks.'

It had not occurred to Lettie that Gran would think Thomas wasn't good enough for her. But that's what she had implied.

'You stay away from that sort,' Gran warned. 'They're trouble, all of them.'

Lettie pressed her lips together to conceal her irritation. Thomas wasn't a coal miner anyway! And even if he was, it wouldn't have mattered to Lettie. She suppressed a sigh, wondering what she could say to Gran to change her mind. 'Mr Adley must trust him because he collects the money,' she muttered.

Gran scowled as she counted out some coins and piled them neatly on the kitchen table.

'Please, Gran.'

'I've said no and don't you go encouraging him. Now, remember to put the remains of the joint in the meat safe when you take the eggs down the cellar.'

'Yes, Gran.' Lettie was already a capable housekeeper and didn't have to be reminded what to do, but Gran still thought she did. Gran was full of wisdom and common sense but she could not shake off her habit of giving orders to servants and tradesmen – and to Lettie. It was her way and Lettie shrugged off her disappointment about the fair.

As she removed and folded the chenille table covering in the dining room, Lettie told herself she didn't mind missing the fair. But she did feel cross with Gran for her reaction to Thomas. The Reverend rarely interfered with Lettie's upbringing but if he did he sided with Gran. They were both too strict with her and she was becoming restless about her future. She stood back to admire her work. The mahogany table top shone. She arranged eight chairs neatly around it and checked that the sideboard had clear space for the tea tray.

Gran came in with ashtrays. The Reverend did not smoke tobacco but the elders were prosperous and one or two brought cigars. 'What time do you want tea for the gentlemen?' Lettie asked.

'The Reverend said three o'clock. Put out your jam sponge on the glass cake stand. It's going to be a long meeting.'

Lettie could see that Gran's eyes were already tired. 'He's lucky to have you to take the minutes,' she commented. 'Why can't he get a lay preacher to do it?'

'Because I do it for him and don't you be cheeky.'

'Well, I don't think your eyes are up to it.' Lettie had mentioned this before and Gran usually disagreed with her.

This time her grandmother didn't reply, so Lettie thought she might be right. She'd noticed that Gran didn't see colours as well as she used to and it was she who had suggested electric light in the manse as well as the mission hall. Lettie had noticed, too, that Gran had to stop for breath at the top of the stairs and she often asked Lettie to 'run and fetch me' items from upstairs.

The Reverend was a busy man. He was closely involved in miners' welfare, the almshouse and the orphanage. He worked tirelessly to raise funds for the mission, looked after his own pony and trap, and even kept a pig at the bottom of the garden. He relied on Gran for everything a housekeeper and clerk might do, including making sure that his chapel accounts were in order. Gran was more than happy to oblige as she was dedicated to chapel herself and she had always had Lettie to help her.

Lettie was not as devoted to chapel as her Gran was, but she had inherited her grandmother's quick wits and common sense. The manse at Waterley Edge was well run and comfortable – some said too comfortable for a manse – and most visitors appreciated their efforts. The ham and bacon from Reverend Ennis's pig was particularly desirable as Gran cured it herself in a zinc bath in one of the outhouses.

Gran took off her apron and said, 'I'm off to tidy myself up now. The cake is in the pantry.'

Where else would it be? Lettie thought uncharitably. She was used to Gran's ways but the old woman's reaction to Thomas had rattled her. She put away her broom and took her mending into the drawing room at the front, from where she could keep an eye out for Thomas. She had first noticed him from that window, pedalling down the road on his big black bicycle with its large basket in front of the handlebars.

She had simply wanted to go to the fair to have a little fun and maybe find out more about Thomas. She thought Gran was being unreasonable because she wouldn't even give Thomas a chance to show her he wasn't a roughneck. Maybe if she asked him to attend chapel Gran would approve?

Lettie had a big earthenware mixing bowl ready on the kitchen table for the eggs and, when she saw Thomas climb off his bicycle and wheel it down the path at the side of the house, she went to open the back kitchen door.

'Hello, Lettie!' He was carrying a large basket and looked past her into the gloom. 'Where's your gran? She's not ill, is she?'

'No, Thomas, she's at an elders' meeting. Your money's ready.'

'Thanks. Have you got a bowl for the eggs?'

'On the kitchen table. Why don't you come in and have a cup of tea?'

'Are you sure your gran won't mind?'

No, thought Lettie, I'm not sure, but she had to tell him she couldn't go to the fair and replied, 'It won't be for long.'

Thomas had a twinkle in his dark eyes as he grinned at her. 'While the cat's away, the mice will play.'

Lettie laughed. He was a friendly and cheery young man and made a welcome change to the sober and serious business of life in the manse. Not for the first time, she wondered what it would feel like to be kissed by him. Well, actually, she had been curious for a while about being kissed by a man, properly, on the lips. 'Kettle's on,' she said. 'Do you like sponge cake?'

'Yes please,' he replied. He counted out eggs from his basket and placed them in the bowl, then he deposited a newspaper-wrapped parcel on the table and pulled out a chair. 'You've some early runners, young carrots and lettuce hearts in there for the Reverend this week. He deserves the best on a Sunday after all his preaching.'

'Are you a chapel-goer?' she asked.

'Not me.' Thomas grinned. 'But a lot of Mr Adley's customers are and they like to know we look after the Reverend.'

Adley's market garden was one of the biggest in the area and his stall in town was popular because his prices were affordable to miners' and steelworkers' wives. His first-rate produce never went to market, though. He reserved it for his best customers who had regular deliveries and could pay full price.

'Did you ask your gran about the fair?'

'She said no.'

'Oh.' He looked disappointed and stared at her sadly for a moment.

'I'll just put these away, then,' Lettie muttered and

picked up the cooling mutton joint next to the bowl of eggs. It was on a big meat plate and heavier than she'd expected so it tipped slightly. 'Oops,' she commented.

Thomas darted forward. 'Shall I carry it for you?'

'I can manage, thank you. You mash the tea. The kettle's just boiled and the tea is in the pot.'

Lettie carried the meat carefully down a flight of stone steps that led to the cellar. There were two cellars under the manse: one for storing coal with an iron-grid covered opening in the ceiling for deliveries, and the other with a stone slab counter for keeping food. It was always cool in the cellar, even in a summer heatwave. A small amount of light penetrated down the steps through the open door at the top. She deposited the meat plate in the gauze meat safe and checked that the door catch was securely fastened. Then she turned and bumped straight into the bowl of eggs in Thomas's hands.

'Oh, you made me jump! What do you want down here?'

'I brought these down for you. Where shall I put them?'

'Over there next to the cheese dome.'

Thomas deposited the bowl carefully. 'I don't want to break any,' he said.

Lettie stepped to one side and watched him. He had to keep his head bowed in the low-ceilinged cellar. His wide shoulders seemed to fill the space. Normally there was plenty of room for her and Gran but Gran was tiny and Thomas was big so she was very aware that he was standing close to her. He seemed reluctant to return to the kitchen.

'Thomas?' she said.

'What is it, Lettie?'

'Will you kiss me?'

'Oh, I don't know, Lettie. I'd like to, but—'

'Please. There's nobody here.'

Lettie hadn't kissed anyone before, let alone a young man. Gran sometimes gave her a hug on her birthday and told her how much she loved her and she had only ever seen the Reverend shake hands with his congregation, even the women.

'All right, then, if you're sure.' Thomas stood in front of her and put his hands gently on her upper arms.

Lettie closed her eyes, puckered her lips and waited. When his mouth touched hers his lips were parted and as though by instinct her mouth opened too. She heard a growling noise in Thomas's throat and his grip on her arms strengthened. His tongue pushed between her lips and into her mouth and she felt her body tingle with excitement. Then he pulled her body against his and, startled, she pushed him away. 'Phew, Thomas, I didn't expect that.'

His face was flushed. 'Haven't you been kissed before?' he said. He sounded as surprised as she was but they were both brought back sharply to their right senses by a shadow in the doorway at the top of the cellar steps.

'What's going on down there?'

Lettie's hand flew to her mouth. 'Oh Lord, that's my gran!'

'I thought she was in the meeting!' Thomas whispered.

'She was.'

'Leave her to me,' Thomas whispered and dashed towards the steps. 'It's only me, Mrs Hargreaves. The egg bowl was too heavy for Lettie to carry down the cellar and she was showing me where to put them.'

Lettie grimaced. It was the truth but it felt like a lie to Lettie and she hoped Gran would believe him.

'Lettie! Are you down the cellar as well?'

'Yes, Gran.' Lettie stood beside Thomas and gazed up at the silhouette of Gran. 'Is something wrong?'

'Get yourself up here now.'

'Yes, Gran.' Lettie pushed passed Thomas and ran up the steps.

'What were you doing down there?'

'Nothing!' Lettie felt her cheeks grow hot.

'Then why have you gone red?'

Lettie put the cooling back of her hand on her cheek. She couldn't say she was hot from standing near the range. 'I must be sickening for something.'

Gran made an impatient sound in her throat. She wasn't stupid, nor did she have any time to waste. 'Don't make excuses. That Thomas is taking liberties with you.' Gran raised her voice and called over Lettie's shoulder, 'Up here this minute, young man!'

Thomas arrived in the kitchen with a serious expression on his face. 'I heard what you said, Mrs Hargreaves, and it's not true. I was only doing Lettie a favour.'

Lettie watched Gran's face set into her sternest expression as she replied, 'I don't believe you. You're all the same, your sort.'

'Gran!' Lettie was shocked. Thomas might have told

69

half a fib for her sake but there was no need for Gran to be so rude. 'It was my fault, Gran!' she cried.

'No, Lettie, it wasn't,' Thomas argued. He spoke directly to Gran. 'Mrs Hargreaves, I'd like to walk out with your Lettie. I want to take her to the Summer Fair and she wants to come with me. She says you won't let her.'

Lettie's eyes widened with delight. Thomas had said he wanted to walk out with her! No one had ever spoken up for like that before. He was very serious and polite and Lettie held her breath waiting for Gran to reply.

But Lettie's hopes were crushed as Gran replied, 'She's right. I won't. She's not going anywhere with you and don't you come near her again. D'you hear me?'

Thomas's mouth turned down at the corners.

'Well, do you?' Gran repeated.

'Yes, Mrs Hargreaves.'

'Get yourself off on your rounds, then.'

Thomas turned to Lettie and whispered, 'I'm sorry.' She smiled nervously but he wasn't smiling. He was cross and she hadn't seen him angry before. He took the coins on the table and left.

When he had gone, Gran turned on Lettie. 'I told you not to ask him in! Did you encourage him? Well, did you?'

'No, I didn't! Not like you think, anyway! But so what if I had? Most girls my age have sweethearts. Why shouldn't I?'

'You did encourage him! I knew it!'

'I like him, Gran,' Lettie protested.

Gran looked harassed and went on, 'You and I need

to sit down for a proper talk. I have to get back to my meeting now. Dear Lord! I only came out to say there are seven of us at the meeting. You'll need an extra cup and saucer on the tray.'

'But you've already told me. Look, I've put out seven like you said!'

Gran looked at the tray on the table and muttered, 'So I see.' Then she added firmly, 'Well, I saw Thomas out of the window and I wanted to make sure you were safe.'

'Thomas isn't dangerous!'

'You don't know anything about him.'

'Well, how can I if you won't let me walk out with him?'

'He's not suitable for you, Lettie.'

'You mean he's not good enough for me!'

'That's exactly what I mean. His father works down the pit.'

'But he's not a miner like his dad!'

'He's not chapel either.' The mantelpiece clock chimed. 'I'll talk to you about this after supper. The Reverend will be writing his sermon in his study so we can use the front room. We'll have it to ourselves.'

Gran picked up the tray. 'I'll take this in. You make the tea and bring it through with the cake.' She left in a hurry, leaving Lettie without further explanation.

Chapter 6

It's not fair, Lettie fumed. Thomas had done nothing wrong! She had asked him for a kiss and, although her first kiss had been brief, it had been exciting and she'd like to repeat it. She wanted to walk out with a man who would kiss her goodnight on the doorstep. Now, she wished she had not pushed him away. It had felt thrilling being close to a man. She remembered the smell of him and it had pleased her. Gran could not keep her cooped up in the manse like a child all her life!

Lettie brooded on what she had missed – the travelling bioscope show, a dance band in the town hall and now the fair. At first she had accepted that she couldn't go to dances in town because they had barrels of ale and cider for sale and chapel didn't approve of drink. Lettie understood that, but her gran took it further. Lettie wasn't allowed to go to any of the things that other young girls enjoyed, for example Sunday-afternoon walks in the Municipal Park or even village barn dances if they weren't chapel ones. She thought that it was time to make a stand. This was the twentieth century, after all!

The elders' meeting was long and Gran was tired by evening. Once the gentlemen had left, Lettie cooked the Reverend's six o'clock tea while Gran put the dining room back to rights. As soon as the Reverend disappeared into his study Gran insisted on her 'talk' with Lettie in the front room.

'I've done my best to protect you, Lettie, but you have to understand that a lady's reputation must be safeguarded. Young men do not always behave as you would want them to and you have to know them very well before you can trust them,' she explained. 'When I was in service, young ladies were not allowed to meet young gentlemen anywhere without a chaperone present.'

'It was different then. Gentry had to marry who their parents chose for them. And I heard that even the maids and footmen had to ask the butler's permission to walk out with each other in the old days.'

Gran's expression was stony. 'Who told you that?'

Lettie shrugged. 'I don't know. Somebody from the mission, I expect.'

'What else did they say?'

Lettie was puzzled. 'About what?' she queried.

Gran seemed to shake herself and pull herself together. 'Oh nothing,' she said. Her mouth smiled but her brow was frowning. 'You mentioned sweethearts this morning. Is that what you want: a sweetheart?'

'Not particularly,' Lettie muttered. Sweethearts usually married each other and Lettie couldn't imagine herself married to anybody yet. She didn't yearn for a husband and babies as some village girls did. Nonetheless she added, 'But why shouldn't I wish to marry one day?'

'I haven't said you shouldn't but I do expect you to choose someone suitable.'

'By suitable you mean chapel?'

'Eric from chapel is a schoolmaster.'

'And I suppose that makes him better than Thomas from Adley's?'

'Yes it does. He will be a faithful husband to his wife.'

Lettie wanted to say 'he's too dull to be anything else' and searched for words that didn't sound rude. 'He's . . . he's . . . he's a bit, well, serious about everything.'

'He has sober habits and that is in his favour. I should welcome him at our table.'

Lettie didn't know what to say. Eric was a few years older than she and had been to grammar school and Training College. He was a bony, wiry sort of fellow who taught at Waterley Board School and gave bible classes at the mission in his spare time. Lettie's face must have shown dismay at the thought of him because Gran shook her head and clicked her tongue, adding, 'Lettie, what is happening to you? You were always such a good little girl.'

'I've not been a little girl for a long time, Gran.' But when Gran spoke to her like this she felt like a little girl and sometimes she thought that Gran wanted to keep her looking like one. Her best blouses and skirts were plain, her hats unadorned, and she really ought to stop wearing her hair down her back like a schoolgirl. 'I want to go out and see a bit more of life,' she added.

'I thought you were happy here helping me to look after the Reverend?'

'I am and I love you both, but . . . but . . . oh, I don't know . . .' Lettie lapsed into silence. She didn't want to say she was bored with the manse, bored with the mission hall and bored with Eric and his ilk.

'You'd like some excitement in your life?' Gran suggested.

Lettie looked up quickly with a smile. 'Oh yes, Gran. Yes please.'

'I'll tell Eric to ask you to the next barn dance we have in the village. He'll take good care of you.'

Lettie's heart sank. Why would she want to go anywhere with a man who had to be prompted to invite her?

'I'd rather go to the fair, Gran.'

'No, dear, not the fair, there are too many . . .'

'Roughnecks?' Lettie finished the sentence for her.

Gran smiled. 'I knew you would see sense in the end.'

Then why don't you trust me? Lettie thought with a sigh. She tried to understand Gran's concern. Gran was her only living relative. She was also her guardian, a duty that Gran shouldered responsibly and diligently, which Lettie appreciated. But she wondered if her parents would have been so strict with her.

'I had a word with the Reverend while you were

washing up,' Gran said. 'He doesn't mind if I go elsewhere for his eggs and vegetables.'

'You can't give up Adley's! They're the best in town.'

'Actually, Boundary Farm is better. They supply . . . well, they supply Waterley Hall.'

'But that's Lord Laughton's estate and you hate him.'

'Who told you that?'

Lettie couldn't answer because nobody had. It was simply a feeling that she had developed over the years. Gran always shut down conversations about the Laughtons or their large house and grounds, not that there was ever much to say because Lord Laughton was never home and his wife was a recluse. Fortunately, Gran did not wait for her reply. She went on, 'The Reverend knows the grower there and he often has a surplus. Boundary Farm doesn't deliver, though.'

'Then don't cancel Adley's,' Lettie pleaded. 'Mr Adley will want to know why.'

'And I shall tell him.'

'You mustn't do that! Thomas will get into trouble.'

'He is already in trouble, my girl, and deservedly so.'

'Please don't do it, Gran. It was my fault. Honest.'

'I won't have you taking the blame. He took advantage of you while my back was turned.'

Lettie knew that it wasn't true and chewed on her lip as Gran went on, 'You are too young to know how deceitful men can be.'

'Thomas wasn't deceitful! He was honest with you!'

'I shall be the judge of that. I have spoken to the Reverend and he understands why I cannot have that boy calling at the manse.'

'Well, I'll shop at Mr Adley's market stall instead. I can walk to town every other day and carry the shopping home.' Lettie thought this was a splendid idea as she had plenty of surplus energy to use up.

'Yes, I do believe more walking will be of benefit to you, which is why I agree with the Reverend. He will change his supplier to Boundary Farm and you will walk over two or three times a week to fetch the order.'

This wasn't at all what Lettie wanted and she protested, 'Gran, please don't cancel Adley's order.'

'My mind is made up. You will not see or speak to that miner's son again.'

Lettie blew out her cheeks. She knew that Gran and the Reverend meant well, but she liked Thomas and she was determined not to give up his friendship. She didn't want to meet him in secret, but if she had to, she would; at least until she could persuade Gran to change her mind about him. 'You're not being fair, Gran,' she muttered.

'You'll thank me one day.' Gran rose to her feet and added, 'The matter is closed. Off you go to bed and ask for guidance in your prayers tonight.' She frowned at Lettie. 'Be patient, Lettie, and the Lord will show you the way.'

The following Monday, Reverend Ennis asked her to 'step into his study' after his midday dinner of cold mutton with bubble and squeak. He wasn't sitting at his desk, but in a comfortable chair by the fireplace. It was too warm for a fire and a polished brass fire-screen stood in the hearth. He indicated the chair opposite him. 'Sit down,

Lettie. Your grandmother has asked me to have a word with you.'

She was pleased to sink into a comfortable chair. Monday was washday and she had been turning the mangle in the wash house for most of the morning. Then she hung out all the sheets while Gran started the Reverend's dinner before running upstairs to change into a dress fit for Reverend's study.

Normally, Lettie had little formal contact with the Reverend because she ate in the kitchen with Gran and he took his meals in the dining room. Sometimes in the week, when he had finished his chapel work and put on his corduroys, he would join her and Gran at the kitchen table for a cup of tea and a slice of cake. But the conversation was usually about the weather or the Reverend's pig, which was fattening in a sty at the bottom of the garden. He never discussed chapel business or the fortunes of the nearby pit, and gossip about local people was frowned upon.

He opened their conversation. 'You are looking delightful in that summer frock, my dear. Your grandmother and I have noticed what a pretty young woman you have become.'

Lettie blinked. She hadn't expected him to compliment her on her appearance. 'Thank you, Reverend,' she said.

'It is natural for you to catch the eye of young men, but you must be careful of your reputation, my dear. Young men are not yet accustomed to the freedoms that ladies insist upon nowadays.'

Oh Lord, Lettie thought, that's what this is about. 'Gran had a talk with me about young men after . . . after I asked Thomas to step into the kitchen,' she said. 'I am nineteen, sir, and I can stand up for myself.'

'You still have much to learn about the ways of the world. Your grandmother has told me that you have thought about marriage. I think that is very sensible of you. Her mind will rest easy when you are safely married. Do you have a young gentleman in mind?'

'No, sir. I only mentioned to Gran that some girls of my age already have sweethearts. I wasn't thinking particularly of myself.'

'You are not against the institution of marriage, surely?'

'No, sir.' It was not generally a topic for conversation in the manse. Lettie had formed the opinion that Gran's husband, who had passed away years ago, was best forgotten and the Reverend maintained he was married to his vocation.

'Very well,' he went on. 'Your grandmother and I shall help you find someone. We have discussed it and I am prepared for you to have a young man call on you at the manse on Sundays for tea.'

Her eyes widened. She could ask Thomas and Gran would see him in his Sunday best. A smile spread across her features. It would be fun to sit in the kitchen and talk, eating scones that she'd baked for him. She wanted to know much more about Thomas.

The Reverend was satisfied with her reaction. 'I can see that my decision pleases you. However, there is a condition. Your grandmother must approve of the young man. Then you may entertain him in the drawing room if I am not using it for chapel business.'

Lettie tried not to let her disappointment show because she was grateful to the Reverend. It was his home, not hers, and it was very generous of him to allow her to use his front room as her own. But if she couldn't ask Thomas for tea, there was no one else. She said, 'Thank you, sir. But I don't have a follower to invite yet.'

'You will have, my dear. Be assured of that.' He gave her one of his rare smiles.

On the Wednesday afternoon, Lettie accompanied Gran to the chapel ladies' committee meeting at the mission hall. The ladies were wives of successful or important men in Waterley Edge who, of course, attended chapel. Officially, Gran was clerk to the group but it was Lettie who took the minutes and made the tea. Mrs Jones, who always took charge, brought a cake that her housemaid had baked. Before they set out, Gran glanced over Lettie's dress and hat. They were her Sunday best, as was befitting for her to wait on these ladies, especially Mrs Jones whose husband was a book-keeper for the Corporation in the nearby town.

'I think you ought to have a new outfit for best,' Gran said. 'I'll give you enough money to choose the stuff from the market tomorrow. You'll be able to make it up for chapel next week. Eric Jones will be there with his mother and father.'

Any other time Lettie would have been excited at the prospect of a new frock and ribbons for her best hat. But the implication that it was for Eric Jones's benefit took all the joy out of it. However, as she walked to town the following day, she realised that if she asked Thomas to come to chapel on Sunday, he would see her in her new outfit as well.

But Thomas wasn't on Adley's market stall. Mr Adley's son was serving and he had a queue. She joined it at first to ask when Thomas would be back, then realised his temper was frayed as he dealt with his customers. She didn't need eggs or vegetables and she didn't want to risk his sharp tongue so she moved away. Thomas was probably out on a delivery anyway.

But she chose her material with Thomas in mind and was pleased with some good white cotton for a blouse and a length of fine blue wool for a skirt. She had enough money left over for lace ribbon to decorate the front of her blouse. As she carried home her parcels, she had in mind a picture she had seen in a ladies' journal with a nipped-in waist and full sleeves. Gran would help her, although she'd have to do all the tiny stitching herself.

But Gran was no help with her hair. It was always plaited down her back. Lettie had tried winding the plaits round her head, but it made her look plain, like a governess. She wanted her hair piled high and framing her face, as in the picture. It can't be that difficult, she thought, and, on impulse, bought a packet of hair pins.

The skirt was straightforward but her blouse was tricky because it had a wide collar and fine pleats on the sleeve heads and down the front. Gran was disappointed it wasn't ready for Sunday but Lettie didn't mind. She hadn't seen Thomas to invite him to chapel yet. During the following week, Gran was happy for her to spend the hours sewing in her bedroom and Lettie used some of the time undoing her plait and piling up her hair.

When the next Sunday arrived her new outfit was finished and Gran insisted that she wore it to chapel. Lettie still hadn't set eyes on Thomas and wondered if he'd taken Gran's words to heart and given up on her. She'd be cross with him if he had! It was a fine day so maybe he'd be out for a walk after his Sunday dinner?

She pinned her summer hat with its new ribbon on top of her piled-up hair. It wasn't quite the look she wanted but she was satisfied with her appearance in the mirror. She was a proper young woman now.

Gran was waiting in the hall as she came downstairs. 'Goodness me!' she said. She seemed shocked and Lettie wondered if she'd cut her skirt too short. But ladies could show their ankles these days and she was wearing boots.

'Don't you like it?' she asked.

Gran seemed lost for words. Eventually she said, 'You've made yourself look very nice, dear.' As she opened the front door, Lettie heard her mutter, 'I suppose Eric is a trustworthy fellow.'

Lettie had forgotten about Eric because he had taken no notice of her last Sunday. Anyway, Gran had this notion about men in general. You couldn't trust them unless they were proven to be reliable, like the Reverend; and Eric, of course, because he was a schoolmaster.

She did turn a few heads when she walked into chapel and took her place in one of the front pews. During the service she even caught Eric staring at her. He didn't looked away either but sucked in his cheeks as his eyes darted over her. She didn't smile at him. Finally, the organ music faded, leaving the echo of its vibrations ringing in Lettie's ears, and gradually the congregation filed out into the bright morning sun.

One or two of the young women chatted to Lettie in the yard while Gran talked to Mrs Jones in the gloomy porch. When they emerged into the sunlight, instead of saying goodbye to each other and going their separate ways they both walked towards her.

Mrs Jones was a brisk buxom lady and Lettie frequently wondered whether she knew that her husband had a liking for patting the bottom of any young woman within his reach. One of them had said he'd gone further and put his hand up her skirt as well but Lettie didn't believe her. Mr Jones was respectable. He had a responsible position at the Town Hall and took care of the collection after each service. His was very proud of his clever son Eric. But Eric was a serious young man who was no fun and hardly ever smiled, and to Lettie's dismay he was now walking over to join his mother.

'Ah, there you are, Eric,' Mrs Jones began. 'I was looking for you. Your father will be a bit longer with the Reverend. You remember Lettie from Sunday school, don't you? Why don't you two go for a walk round while I talk to Mrs Hargreaves?'

'Very well, Mother.' Eric tugged at the cuffs of his jacket and crooked an elbow for Lettie to take his arm.

Lettie noticed that he didn't look at her. His eyes were scanning the chapel yard as the worshippers began to disperse to their homes. Perhaps he'd prefer to walk with someone else? She glanced at Gran who looked pleased and nodded at her, so she felt obliged to stand by his side. However, she didn't take his arm.

'Where do you want to walk?' he asked.

Nowhere with you, she thought but said, 'I don't mind.'

'We'll follow the path around the chapel.'

Lettie didn't think this was a good idea as it was always mossy and damp underfoot at the back of the building. She had a good look at him. He was taller than she and quite thin so that his collar looked too big for his neck. He had straight brown hair, darkened by pomade, small brown eyes and thin lips. Until today, Lettie had only ever spoken to him in Sunday school bible classes at the mission hall next door and she didn't think they had much in common at all.

She said, 'You don't have to take me for a walk if you don't want to.'

'Don't you want to come with me?' He sounded put out.

She didn't answer but she was conscious of the fact that Gran and Mrs Jones were watching them so, when he jutted his elbow towards her, reluctantly she took it. He headed along the cinder path that went alongside the chapel building.

They walked in silence for what seemed like an age to Lettie. She felt irritated by Eric. He was so stiff and starchy, and he didn't make any effort at conversation. They turned a corner of the building and were out of sight of the worshippers.

'Shall we go the other way? It might be slippy under-foot round here.'

'I shan't let you fall,' he said and placed his elbow against his body, trapping her arm.

She wanted to take her hand away but knew it would seem ungrateful and rude. It won't be for long, she thought, and said, 'I enjoyed the sermon today.'

'Did you? I could have done better myself.'

Lettie blinked with surprise. She had never heard anyone criticise the Reverend's sermons before and added, 'He didn't go on for too long.'

'I suppose you just wanted to get outside and talk to your friends.' He sounded critical.

'No I didn't. But why shouldn't I?'

She felt his arm stiffen. 'Do you answer back like that in the manse?'

Lettie's eyes widened. Well, yes she did, sometimes, she realised, but only to Gran and never, ever to the Reverend or one of his visitors. They turned a second corner and were now behind the chapel in the shade of several large trees. 'Shall we walk back now?' she suggested.

He clamped his elbow even closer to his side and he was strong.

'That hurts. Let me go, please,' she asked reasonably. When she tried to pull her hand out he took hold of it in his large bony fingers and held it in place.

'Mother said earlier to look out for you today,' he said.

'She spoke to you beforehand about me?'

'Your grandmother asked her, presumably because you told her to.'

'No, I didn't,' she denied.

'Well, what about all this . . . this dolling-up? You've

85

not done your hair like that before.' He indicated her appearance with a casual wave of his arm.

He thought it was all for his benefit. He must think that it was her idea and she wanted to walk out with him! Lettie frowned at him but he didn't appear to notice. He pushed her to one side and into a corner formed by the chapel wall and one of its flying buttresses. The sun never reached this side of the chapel. Ferns had taken over from grass and the stone wall felt damp against her back. Annoyed, she tried to push by him but he stepped to one side to stop her. Then he stood in front of her with his legs apart making it quite clear to her that he wasn't going to let her go.

With hindsight, Lettie realised that she ought to have made her views about Eric clearer to Gran. But it was too late for that now. She stared past him, over his shoulder at the tangled leafy branches of the trees and said, 'Well, I didn't do it for you. I think there's been a misunder-standing, Eric.'

'Not on my part, there hasn't,' he answered. His face loomed in front of hers so quickly that she squealed. Her squeal was immediately silenced by his mouth clamping over hers as he tried to kiss her. His teeth clashed with hers and his lips pressed so hard on her face that her head connected with the rough stone behind it, pushing her hat forward. Her instinctive objections were muffled in her throat. He put his hands on the swell of her breasts and then forced the lower half of his body hard on hers. She was pinned to the wall as he squeezed her flesh with his fingers and pushed his hips backwards and forwards against her.

Surely he must have been aware that the noises in her throat were a protest and that her eyes were wide open with fear? His eyes seemed glazed and looked straight through her as he kept pushing at her. Then he made a gravelly, groaning noise, slowed and stopped. He lifted his head and leaned, no *sagged* against her, breathing heavily.

She tried to push him off and waited for him to apologise. Instead, he muttered in her ear, 'That is your fault.'

Indignation caused her to blow out her cheeks. They were hot with embarrassment. 'How is it my fault?' she demanded.

'You flaunted yourself at me,' he replied.

Lettie had only done the same as other young women her age and if he thought that making herself look pretty was 'flaunting' then something was wrong with him! But Gran and the Reverend were as proud of Eric as his parents were. He could do no wrong in their eyes and he believed it of himself too.

'I didn't ask you to do that! You forced yourself on me,' she protested. All she wanted to do was get away from him so she went on, 'Now would you please step aside so I can go back to my gran?' She felt hot and bothered and knew she must look it as well. What on earth would Gran think if she emerged into the sunlight dishevelled and flushed? She placed her palms on her cheeks to cool them and said, 'Don't you ever do that to me again.'

He stared at her with raised eyebrows as though she had gone mad and said, 'Oh, be quiet and put your hat straight.'

She thought him rude but nonetheless tidied her hair as best she could, using one of the dingy rear windows of the chapel as a mirror. He waited until she had smoothed down her dress then held out his arm for her. She ignored it and tried to walk past him but he poked his elbow at her.

'You'd better take my arm,' he said. 'If we don't walk back together, they'll think I've been up to something.'

'Well, you have,' she replied irritably, but did as he suggested, feeling frustrated and cornered into a fib by his behaviour. She didn't care whether he was a schoolmaster or not, he took liberties and she didn't like him. She'd rather walk out with a miner's son who at least treated her with some respect.

Chapter 7

Lettie emerged into the sunshine hoping her cheeks did not appear as red as they felt. The last of the congregation had left. Gran and Mr and Mrs Jones were talking to the Reverend. Gran appeared pleased with herself. 'Here they are!' she called. 'My, they make a fine couple, don't they?'

Lettie realised that everyone heard this and protested, 'Gran!'

'Now don't be modest, dear.'

Lettie glanced around the small group. Everyone was smiling. Gran went on, 'You will come to the manse for tea today, won't you, Eric?'

'Thank you, Mrs Hargreaves, I should like that,' he replied.

Lettie resigned herself to this done deed, which seemed

to be what everyone wanted except her. 'Will you and Mr Jones come too?' she asked.

'Another time, dear.' Mrs Jones smiled. 'The Reverend has a double baptism this afternoon and we are expecting a large gathering. They have asked the mission ladies for tea in the hall.'

'It'll give you and Eric a chance to get to know each other,' Gran commented.

Lettie thought that she already knew more than she wanted to about Eric Jones. It shocked her that someone as outwardly pious as Eric could behave as he had. What was even more surprising was that Gran had been taken in by him. Hadn't Gran warned her, not so long ago, that men could be deceitful? Not chapel men, it seemed, only miners' sons. Lettie was cross. She wondered what words she could use to describe Eric's conduct towards her.

'Come along, dear,' Gran said, 'we have to get the Reverend's dinner on and the joint will need basting.'

As they hurried on ahead of the Reverend, Gran commented, 'Nice family, the Joneses. Mrs Jones works very hard for the mission and Mr Jones audits the manse accounts, which you do for me, of course. Nothing is ever too much trouble for either of them. What did Eric have to say for himself?'

'Nothing much.'

'Well, he has always been a quiet lad who keeps himself to himself. I suppose you can expect that with him being the studious sort. He's going to be a headmaster of the village school, you know.'

'No, I didn't.' Lettie preferred not to talk about Eric

because she could still feel the imprint of his fingers poking at the flesh of her breast, and the rough stone of the church wall on her back as his weight pressed against her.

But Gran went on about him. 'He'll be starting there after the summer and live in the school house. Have you ever been inside the school house? It's got front and back parlours and three good bedrooms as well as a box room. Make sure you give him a nice tea. You can make a sponge cake and some scones for him while the oven's on.'

'But I don't like him, Gran,' Lettie said.

'You haven't spent enough time in his company. He comes from a good hardworking family. You'll have a nice house and clever children, what more does a girl want?'

A man she respects and loves, Lettie thought, but didn't say it. Instead she replied, 'I don't think he likes me either.'

'Oh, I believe he does. In fact, I'd go so far as to say he's quite taken by you now you're a bit older. His mother told me he wouldn't need any persuading to come to tea.'

'You'll be there, won't you?'

'Well, I would be as a rule, but I've just been invited to attend this baptism. There'll be folk coming that I haven't seen in a while and they'll have travelled a long way. Besides, the mission ladies will need a hand giving them tea.' Gran beamed at her. 'It'll give you a chance to show Eric what a good little housekeeper you are.'

Lettie felt trapped. If she disagreed, Gran would be upset and annoyed and if she agreed, everyone, including

Eric, would get the wrong idea. She pressed her lips together in frustration. At least she had enough time to prepare what she would say to him. She had already made her feelings known to him so she only had to repeat herself to put him off for good. 'What time will you be back?' she asked.

'Why do you want to know that?' Gran queried. She sighed and went on, 'Sometimes, Lettie, I really worry about you. Eric has to see what a well-behaved young lady you are. I do hope I can trust you not to let me down in that respect. I don't want a repetition of that Thomas incident in the cellar, my girl.'

What about Eric? Lettie thought. He's the one who can't be trusted. Lettie considered telling Gran about his behaviour behind the chapel now, but with Gran in this frame of mind Lettie knew she wouldn't come out of it very well. Gran had already made up her mind that Eric could do no wrong. She felt irritated by Gran's injustice towards first Thomas and now her, so there was a touch of irony in her tone when she replied, 'But shouldn't I have a chaperone?'

Gran's serious expression became stern. 'Not all young men are like that Thomas. I blame myself for not speaking to you earlier about roughnecks. I assumed the fact that you lived in the manse would protect you from his sort.' She leaned over and patted her hand. 'Eric is chapel, my dear. The Reverend speaks very highly of him. He'll look after you.'

That made Lettie feel marginally better. If the Reverend thought well of Eric than she supposed he could be trusted to behave himself in the manse. And if Eric had agreed so readily to come to tea, perhaps he had been keen to walk out with her for a while. This possibility came as a shock to Lettie because she had not considered herself to be desirable in that way. Yet his actions behind the chapel had shown her he was . . . well . . . desperate to get his hands on her, quite literally.

Perhaps he was secretly in love with her and had had to wait for Gran's permission to court her? And perhaps that was a silly fantasy more likely to have occurred in one of the novels she read. Besides, it didn't alter the fact that she had never really liked him and his actions today had confirmed her opinion of him.

She liked Thomas. He was, she thought, clever in a different way from Eric. Thomas hadn't been to college but he was sharp and she reckoned that it wouldn't matter what kind of scrape he found himself in, Thomas would find a way out. On top of that he was fun. The thought of him made her smile.

'That's better, Lettie,' Gran responded. 'You are pretty when you smile.' Gran stared at her for a moment and repeated, 'Really very pretty indeed.' She looked down at the floor and muttered, 'Just like your mother, too pretty for her own good.'

Lettie wanted to pick up on that comment immediately and ask about her mother but Gran added briskly, 'Must get on, there is so much to do and you have to start your baking for this afternoon.'

This set Lettie thinking about all sorts of sabotage such as making the scones heavy or not leaving the sponge in the oven long enough. But it was not her way to waste good ingredients and Gran would be furious if she did.

I know what I'll do, Lettie decided as she creamed together butter and sugar for the cake. I'll make enough to take some to Thomas on the market stall in town.

She beat away at the mixture until her arms ached.

Eric arrived punctually and complimented Gran on the charm of the entrance hall at the manse. The Reverend had already left for the baptism and Gran was anxious not to be late. Lettie helped her with her hatpin in the hall and Eric held open the front door for her.

'Thank you, Eric. I know I can rely on you to take care of my granddaughter in my absence. Make yourself at home in the drawing room.'

'That is most kind of you, Mrs Hargreaves. Thank you,' he said.

'It's the Reverend's home, you must thank him.'

'I shall.'

Eric followed Lettie into the front room and walked over to the fireplace. It was too warm for a fire and the brass screen was in place.

'I'll go and put the kettle on.'

'Is there no one else here?'

'No. Do you think there ought to be?'

'Don't you have a maid for the scullery? Mother has a girl for the rough work.'

'Gran and I do everything in the manse.'

This seemed to impress him. 'Go on then,' he said, shrugging. 'But hurry up.'

'Tea will be in about half an hour,' she said when she

returned. She thought he might have offered to carry the tray in but he didn't. He sat proudly on the Reverend's couch with his legs splayed and a satisfied expression on his face. She wondered what he had to be so smug about and wandered over to look out of the window.

'Come away from the window and sit down over here,' he said firmly.

It was an order, she thought, and not a request, but the purpose of his visit was conversation so Lettie obeyed. She chose a fireside chair.

'No, over here with me on the settee,' he said.

'I'm comfortable here, thank you.'

'Well I'm not.' He got up, took her hand and yanked her to her feet. 'If you want to walk out with me you'd better learn to do as I say!'

'Who said I wanted to walk out with you?'

'Your grandmother did. She told my mother and she invited me here.'

'I thought you would have realised how I felt about you after this morning.'

'Oh that. You haven't been kissed before, have you? You'll soon learn. I'll show you if you come over here like I say.' He tugged on her arm so she fell against him, turned her round deftly and pushed her onto the settee. She scrambled to her feet. 'Aren't we supposed to have our tea and make conversation first?' she said.

'Your grandmother might be home by then,' he stated. 'Are you sure there's no one in the back?'

Lettie half laughed. He couldn't be serious about this. Surely he was not going to try to kiss her again, not after the last time? She was looking at his face, his shiny jumpy eyes and slack jaw. His regular features were not unattractive but at that precise moment they repulsed her. She kept her chin down so he couldn't kiss her in case he tried. That's when she saw his hands fumbling between them and they weren't on her because they weren't standing close enough. One hand was covering the bulge in his trousers and the other seemed to be wrestling with buttons in front of her and in full view! Lettie could barely believe her eyes and turned to exit the room as fast as she could. But he cut across her path and she tripped over his foot, only saving herself from falling by grasping the back of the settee.

He reached the door first and placed himself with his back against the door. 'Don't pretend to be stuffy with me. The word is out that your grandmother wants you married before you get yourself into trouble. We may as well find out as much as we can about each other while we have the chance.' She noticed his chest was rising and falling rapidly and she glimpsed a bulge of brown flesh pushing from his trouser opening. She spread the fingers of both hands in front to prevent him coming any nearer and said, 'You must stop this at once, Eric, and let me out.'

She heard him turn the key in the lock behind him and when he moved away there was no sign of it. He slid his hand in his jacket pocket presumably with the key and said, 'Come on, Lettie, I'm not courting a girl who won't do what I want.'

'Then that is just as well, Eric, because I have no desire for you to court me.'

'Don't play hard to get with me, Lettie. Your grandmother told my parents she wanted this and the Reverend agreed with her. You won't do any better than me in Waterley Edge. You might be the lass that all the fellows lust after but when it comes to marriage none of the toffs will consider you.'

'Marriage? Who said anything about marriage?'

'You'll have to marry soon. Who's going to look after you when your grandmother's gone?'

'I am quite capable of looking after myself, thank you.'

'No you're not. You won't last a week in the bottle factory and you've got no parents. You'll be a spinster of the parish, living in lodgings and asking for help from the mission.'

'I can find work.'

'Taking in washing and going out scrubbing for other folk? As my wife you'll have a lass to do that for you. And you'll be invited to sit on the mission hall ladies' committee.'

Her heart sank because some of what he said was true. She didn't have a proper occupation and Lettie could think of nothing more boring than arranging jumble sales and sewing circles for the mission welfare fund. It was noble work and she admired the ladies who did it, but she wanted to do something more challenging, something in the world outside the mission and the village. She didn't comment so he added, 'I thought your gran would have explained all that to you.'

'She warned me that some young men can't be trusted and you have shown me that she is right.'

He frowned and his face darkened. When he spoke he sounded exactly the same as her old headmaster in school. 'That's twice in one day I've been on the receiving end of your sharp tongue and it is quite enough. I can see you'll need taming if you're to be my wife.' He chewed the inside of his cheek. 'In school, the boys have the cane but I keep a leather slipper for the girls.'

Lettie was astounded. 'You would use a leather slipper on me?'

'As I say to the children, it depends entirely on whether or not you disobey me.'

He was quite serious. And to think that Gran approved of this potential match! She tried to appeal to Eric's reasoning. 'Why would you wish to marry a girl who has to be beaten into being the wife you want?'

The lines on his forehead deepened as though he was genuinely puzzled by this remark. 'I shall not need to because, as my wife, you will obey me.'

'Should I love and honour you as well?' she returned quickly, but her intended irony was wasted on him.

'I shall expect no less of you,' he replied.

'Then you ought not to marry me because I cannot meet your expectations.'

She saw anger flash in his eyes and suppressed a sigh. For an educated man he could be very obtuse. She spoke slowly and clearly. 'Eric, I do not love you.'

She ought to have saved her breath. He dismissed her argument with a wave of his hand, and sounded very confident when he responded. 'You will. I shall see to it.'

She wondered how he was going to do that, shuddered, and closed her mind to the possibilities. 'I shan't. I didn't ask for this, it was Gran's idea.'

'She's your guardian, isn't she? You have to do what she says. She knows what's best for you and you won't do better than me, not with you being an orphan and . . .' he hesitated before finishing, 'and all that.'

And all what? she thought. Her indignation must have shown on her face because he quickly added, 'Oh, don't worry, I shouldn't be ashamed of you standing by my side in chapel. I mean your grandmother is well respected and you are the prettiest girl at the mission. Besides, Mother and Father approve of you so everyone is satisfied.'

'Except me,' she said. 'I do not like the way you have behaved towards me. Shouldn't you at least wait until we are engaged?'

'We'll have an announcement in a few weeks, but a fellow likes to know a girl will' – he gave her a secretive little smile that sent a shiver down her back and lowered his voice – 'will suit his needs before he makes her any promises.'

And vice versa, Lettie thought. She regretted her irony about 'waiting until they were engaged' because now, heaven forbid, he presumed she had agreed to an engagement.

He stared at her thoughtfully for a few moments, and then said, 'You're not young but you've had a sheltered life here with your gran. You need to get used to being courted.' She was hugely relieved when he fumbled with his buttons again and closed up the gap in his trousers.

'Nonetheless,' he went on, 'I don't like to waste my time. You might be the prettiest girl in Waterley Edge but you have no background to speak of so you won't get a better offer than mine. I can wait.' He sat down heavily on the couch and tossed her the door key. 'I'll have my tea, now,' he said.

Lettie could think of nothing more to say to him and endured a gruelling hour of his conceit where conversation was limited to Eric's criticism of her scones and hints of shortcomings in her upbringing. She became quietly angered by this censure of her grandmother, which, she guessed, he must have realised eventually. After an extended silence he praised her cake. But, as he ate three pieces, this didn't help her mood because there would be none left for Thomas after she had put some by for Gran and the Reverend and she wished she hadn't eaten her slice. Her jam sponge was good, everybody said so.

She resisted blowing out her cheeks and heaving a sigh as he passed his cup across for a second refill. 'I'll refresh the pot,' she said, picking it up and moving swiftly to her feet.

She was in the kitchen before he could comment further and was standing at the range when she heard him follow her. He came up very close behind her and placed his hands on her waist. He stroked her hips, following the curve of her waist and bottom and she felt his breath on the back of her neck.

'You'll suit me very well, you know,' he whispered. 'It's a pity your grandmother will be home shortly. As soon as I'm installed in the school house, we can announce our engagement then you'll be able to come and take tea with me there, where no one will disturb us.'

Lettie splashed boiling water onto fresh tea in the pot and pushed away the uncharitable thoughts that flitted across her mind of where she'd like to splash it on him. She didn't want to waste her time any more than he did but decided that argument with him was futile. She needed to convince Gran and the Reverend that an engagement to Eric was a bad idea. She had to get them on her side.

Gran sensed an atmosphere between her and Eric when she came in from the baptism. Eric left shortly afterwards and Gran confronted her in the kitchen. 'Eric didn't look very pleased when he left. I hope you made an effort with him, my girl,' she scolded.

'I told you I didn't like him and I'd be hopeless as a headmaster's wife.'

'No you wouldn't and you'd have a good life.'

'Yes, but not the life I want.'

'Well, what do you want?' Gran was cross with her.

'I don't know yet; just something more than the mission ladies' committee!' Gran looked wounded and Lettie immediately regretted her words. 'I'm sorry, Gran; I didn't mean that, honestly.'

'I think you did,' Gran replied. 'You're headstrong, Lettie. Dear Lord, I've done my best with you but I hope you're not going turn out like your mother.' Gran shook her head sadly and went upstairs to take off her best hat and coat.

Gran rarely mentioned Lettie's mother, except to say that she 'had gone' or 'been taken from her'. But a comment recently about being pretty and now a second one concerning her behaviour had made Lettie question some of the things Eric had hinted about her background.

Chapter 8

Lettie used up the last of the eggs in her baking the following day. Gran hadn't checked them before she did last week's order so she didn't object to Lettie walking into town to buy some more from the provisions merchant in the high street.

She was nearly there when she heard a bicycle bell and turned quickly. Thomas was freewheeling down the hill towards the market square, but not with his feet stretched out in front of him as usual. He applied his brake and slid to a halt beside her. He was not on the Adley's delivery bicycle. This was some old bone-shaker she hadn't seen before. He climbed off, swinging one of his sturdy legs over the saddle. She was about to ask him where he'd been these past two weeks when he demanded, 'What have you said to your granny about me?'

'Nothing!' she answered. 'I am sorry about Gran but she was only trying to protect me.'

'You don't need protecting from me! What does she think I am?'

Thomas didn't expect an answer. He had a quick mind and he would easily have worked out why Gran didn't approve of him. He went on, 'She doesn't even know me!'

'I'm hoping to change that. She and the Reverend have agreed that I can have a . . . a foll—' She stopped. She mustn't presume too much and continued, 'A friend to call on me at the manse.' She gave him a hopeful smile. 'Providing Gran approves, of course.'

'Which rules me out, then.'

Her smile faded. 'I know. I'm sorry.'

'I'm the one who's sorry! Your granny wrote to Mr Adley and cancelled the Reverend's order. And she said why so old man Adley told me to leave.'

'Oh no,' Lettie groaned. 'I did ask her not to tell him. Will he change his mind?'

'Don't be daft!' Thomas was clearly upset and went on, 'My dad's furious with me.'

Lettie felt awful and repeated, 'I'm sorry.'

'Me too. He says I've got to go down the pit like my brothers, so my mam is mad with me an' all. She was really proud of me when I started at Adley's.'

'Gran gave me a telling-off as well. But I did make her see that I am old enough to walk out with someone if I want.'

'I should think so. I know girls your age who are married.'

'She's just over-protective. It's been hard for her bringing me up on her own.'

'And she's done a good job with you. You're a credit to her, but she ought to trust you more.'

Lettie agreed. She hesitated before adding, 'She would, I'm sure, if you were . . . that is . . . well, Gran said that you weren't suitable because you were not "chapel". If you came to chapel on Sunday, she might change her mind about you.'

'That's impossible! My mam and dad would never forgive me. We're Roman Catholic.'

'Oh. I didn't know.' Lettie was disappointed. She remembered an awful rumpus in the village when the eldest son of a well-to-do Roman Catholic family took up with a chapel girl. They married eventually but she had to take instruction and become a Roman Catholic too.

'I'll tell you what, though,' Thomas said, 'my dad wouldn't have judged you like your granny judged me! He'd have given you a proper chance to say your piece. Your granny just got rid of me as fast as she could.'

Lettie felt obliged to defend Gran and replied, 'She only has my interests at heart. She thinks any lad who's not chapel is not to be trusted. At least she knows I'm a grown-up now. I thought she was going to keep me a little girl for ever.'

'You ought to try and get way from that manse for a while.'

'And that's impossible for *me*!' she responded. Oh heavens, if their conversation carried on in this way they'd just end up squabbling and Lettie didn't want that. She pasted a bright smile on her face and asked, 'Which pit will you be working at?'

He tapped the side of his nose with his forefinger. 'Wait and see. I've got my own ideas. Are you off to the market?'

'The grocer's in the square, but I was going to come and look for you.'

'Were you?'

She nodded.

'That's nice of you to say so. I like you, Lettie.'

'Do you really mean that?'

'Yes.'

'Do you . . . do you lust after me, Thomas?'

'Lettie!' He glanced around. 'If you're going to say things like that, keep your voice down. Why are you asking me that?'

'Oh, it was just something that somebody said.'

'About you?'

'Never mind.'

'Who said it, Lettie?' Thomas insisted.

'It doesn't matter but he said that all the lads lusted after me. Is it true?'

'*He* said? Who said?'

'Is it true?'

'No, of course it's not. You don't flaunt yourself like some of the lasses. But you are very pretty and lads notice that in any girl.'

'Thank you for telling me,' she responded and he shrugged.

It was a shame that Gran had taken against Thomas

because Gran was so very wrong about him. He was decent and honest and she was determined to change Gran's mind.

'I'd best be on my way,' she added.

'Well, I'll look out for you. Ta-ra.'

'Ta-ra.'

Lettie felt better after seeing Thomas. She could talk to him about anything.

Later that week, Reverend Ennis asked to speak with Lettie again and this time she could guess what it was about.

'Your grandmother is concerned about you, Lettie,' he began. 'You were seen in town with that delivery boy.'

'If you mean Thomas, we were only talking.'

'Did he try to kiss you again?'

'He wouldn't,' she protested, 'not unless I asked him.'

'So did you ask him to kiss you in the cellar?' the Reverend queried.

Lettie blushed.

'And did he really kiss you?'

'Sort of, I pushed him away.'

'But he persisted?'

'No.'

'No? Didn't he want to kiss you?'

'Not at first, and then he did.'

'And your grandmother interrupted him.'

'No! I told you, I pushed him away.'

'Yet you had asked him to kiss you,' the Reverend pointed out. He suddenly looked grave and said, 'Your grandmother is disappointed that you don't want Eric Jones to call on you again.'

I'm not, Lettie thought and chewed on her lip, wondering whether to tell the Reverend the truth about Eric. She decided not to as it might not do her own reputation any good at the moment.

'Eric is a fine young man,' the Reverend went on.

When she didn't comment, he sighed. 'Lettie, you must begin to think about your future. Your grandmother will not live for ever and it would please her immensely to see you safely married quite soon.'

'I don't want to marry Eric Jones,' she stated.

'So I gather. But you must understand that you are an orphan with no means of support. A husband is your best option for the future.'

'I can work. I can be a housekeeper, like Gran.'

'It's far better for a young woman to keep her own house for her own husband.'

Lettie pressed her lips together. She hoped he wasn't going to browbeat her into changing her mind about Eric. He could be quite dominating in his sermons. He continued, 'I have suggested a solution to which your grandmother readily agreed. I have a sister in Wales, with a growing family who would welcome you to live with them for a while.'

'Gran agreed to that?'

'It was her idea. She is worried about you.'

'I don't mean to worry her, but sometimes, I feel . . .' She didn't want to say bored because it seemed rude. Anyway she had plenty to do, but somehow it wasn't enough for her. 'I feel restless.' She sounded inadequate and looked down.

'Yes, we thought as much. Your grandmother asked if I could find you a position where you might be more fully occupied; in another mission, perhaps.'

'I should have to leave Gran if I did that!' Lettie was shocked. She wouldn't dream of leaving Gran now she was getting old.

'Don't you want to meet new people?'

'Well, yes, but—'

'It was your grandmother's suggestion.'

'Gran wants to send me away?'

'She herself argued that it would be a positive experience for you to live in a proper family for a while, with other young ladies of your own age, and young men, too.'

'You mean she wants me to leave the manse and go and live with your sister in Wales? I couldn't do that. I can't leave. Gran can't manage without me.'

'She says she can, with a girl from the village for the rough work.'

It wasn't domestic help that Gran needed most but the Reverend wasn't aware of that. She said, 'Gran hasn't told you, has she?'

'What are you talking about, Lettie?'

'Her eyes are going. She'll deny it if you ask her but I know I'm right.'

The Reverend looked away from her and gazed at the fire-screen for what seemed to be a long time. When he turned back to her his expression was serious. 'Yes,' he said, 'that would explain one or two things that have happened recently.'

'And she always has to stop at the top of the stairs to catch her breath.'

'Indeed?' He frowned. 'I had not noticed that.'

'Please don't say I told you. She'll be cross with me.'

'But she ought to have told me herself.'

'Why? I can do everything in the manse that Gran does,' Lettie volunteered eagerly. 'She has trained me properly, just as she did her maids when she was young. Please don't send me away, Reverend. Gran needs me more than ever now.'

He gave a slight nod as though he agreed, but grimaced as he said, 'I know you think she does but the manse is not your responsibility. I agree with your grandmother. Your interests will be best served if you move away from Waterley Edge. I have several nieces and nephews doing excellent work with missions in the Welsh valleys.'

Her heart sank. She admired the Reverend and his good works, but she really did not want a future in a Methodist mission. And she most certainly was not going to desert Gran.

'What would happen to my grandmother if I left her?' she asked.

'You do not have to concern yourself with your grandmother. She has many friends at the mission here to help her and you are too young to be tied to looking after an old lady.'

Lettie had never considered Gran to be a burden and protested, 'But I want to look after her!'

The Reverend remained resolute. 'Her eyesight is failing, and from what you tell me, perhaps her heart as

110

well. I shall apply to the chapel welfare fund for her to see a physician. You do not have to worry about your grandmother, Lettie.'

But Lettie could be stubborn when she wanted and responded, 'Of course I do. She's my gran!'

'The mission ladies will look after her and my family will look after you.' The firmness in his tone made Lettie hesitate. Apart from Gran, the Reverend was the only person in the world for her to turn to and she respected his views. She did not doubt that he had her welfare at heart, nor did she doubt that this was all about keeping her away from Thomas.

'But I want to stay here where I have friends,' she argued.

'Do you mean Thomas?'

She refused to deny it and replied, 'He's a friend, yes.' He's the only one who seems to talk sense, she thought.

'You'll make new friends in Wales and forget about that delivery boy. He is not the sort of fellow that your grandmother wishes you to mix with, especially as he is not one of my congregation.'

Lettie knew that well enough. An awkward silence followed until the Reverend asked, 'What would you like to do with your life, Lettie?'

She hadn't given her future any serious thought because helping Gran had been her life so far. She didn't care to think about a time when Gran wouldn't be with her. She imagined that, one day, she would marry and have children. Meanwhile, Lettie took pride in everything she did and keeping to the high standard that Gran demanded. She wanted to manage the household perfectly just as Gran did. Gran had been appointed as a housekeeper at Waterley Hall when she was relatively young because she had been first-rate at it.

'You are a very good Sunday school teacher,' Reverend Ennis prompted.

Her headmaster at school had suggested, with his help, she could train to be a schoolteacher. But the women she had known as teachers either had married after a couple of years or were fusty old spinsters, and Lettie didn't want to turn out like them. There must be something more exciting that she could do?

'I don't want to be a teacher,' she replied.

The Reverend stood up. 'Well, you should think seriously about it. I shall write to my sister in South Wales and we shall see what can be done for you.'

A letter; is that all it took to change the course of her life? What was so wrong with Thomas anyway? She liked him and he liked her and she'd have much more fun with him than stuck in the school house with someone like Eric.

After tea that evening, Gran wanted to know how she had got on with the Reverend. They were tidying the pantry and Lettie was on the steps checking labels on bottles of preserves.

'Do you really want me to go away, Gran?' she said.

'Only if you won't reconsider Eric Jones,' she answered. 'He might give you another chance. His mother said he was quite taken by you, but thought you were a bit young.

I take responsibility for that and I don't regret it. You have plenty of time to become an adult.'

'*I don't like him.*'

Gran became impatient. 'He's a fine man, established in a good profession and a regular chapel-goer. You caused me and the Reverend a good deal of embarrassment when you refused to even consider him. *I'm* not getting any younger and *you* haven't got many options.' Gran put a hand to her breast. 'Oh goodness me, you've set off my palpitations. I'll have to sit down.' She staggered into the kitchen and sank onto a chair.

'Gran?' Lettie clambered down from the steps, thinking, What palpitations? 'What are you talking about, Gran? How long have you been having turns like this?'

Gran was catching her breath in gasps. 'It's nothing. Make me a cup of tea and I'll be fine.'

Gran couldn't blame this on the stairs but Lettie recognised when Gran was refusing to discuss something and obeyed silently. After Gran had drunk the tea and said she had recovered, Lettie queried it. Gran's face was ashen and Lettie suggested that she ask the Reverend to call the doctor.

'Nonsense, I'm as fit as a butcher's dog – always have been. Now, I do think it's a good idea of the Reverend's for you to go to his relations. It's a long way to South Wales but you'll be with people I can trust. You'll have to earn your keep, though. But you're a good little house-keeper so you won't be a burden to them.'

'You mean I'll be working for the Reverend's relations in South Wales?'

'For his sister; she has a big family and needs an extra pair of hands. Her eldest daughter is a schoolteacher. She'll be a good influence on you.'

Lettie considered she would be doing exactly the same work as she did at the manse but without her gran. It was the last thing Lettie wanted. Yet how could she say that when everyone had been so obliging? It was very kind of the Reverend to arrange this for her and she would be seen as extremely ungrateful if she refused. It seemed that he had decided on her future already and she wondered if Gran agreed wholeheartedly.

'The Reverend said it was your idea.'

'I asked him for advice and he recommended his family. He has an older brother too who is also a preacher and their chapel community is much bigger than ours. It is an extremely generous offer.' Gran's face was still pale but she took hold of Lettie's hand. 'The Reverend is as worried about you as I am.' She hesitated before adding, 'I had not intended to tell you but he . . . he will be your guardian if I should be taken by the Lord before you are twenty-one.'

Lettie was taken aback. Gran never spoke of her death and rarely mentioned her guardianship. It was something she avoided in conversation because Lettie always wanted to know about her parents and Gran wouldn't talk about them.

Gran went on hastily, her expression serious, 'I hope that it does not come to pass. But if I am called to God, I need someone I trust absolutely to care for you.'

Lettie stared at her. Gran would surely live for many

more years? She had been like a mother to her and the Reverend like a . . . a . . . Lettie realised with a start that the Reverend gave her the attention he would bestow on his own daughter. Her heart began to thump. 'The Reverend has agreed to be my guardian?' she commented. 'Why is he so kind and generous to me, Gran?'

'Why should he not be?' Gran's tone was sharp but her tired eyes were wary. Whenever Lettie asked questions that Gran didn't want to answer, Gran's conversation became guarded.

Lettie considered her words carefully. She was a young woman now and her life was changing. She wanted to know who she was. 'He's . . . he's not my father, is he?' she asked quietly.

Chapter 9

Her grandmother's jaw dropped open and her eyes widened. 'Good gracious me, no!' She was horrified. 'How dare you suggest such a slur on the Reverend?'

Lettie was frantic for a minute in case Gran had another attack. But Gran calmed down quickly and said, 'Whatever has given you that idea?'

Lettie hunched her shoulders. 'Why else would he care so much about me?'

'Because he is a good man, and believe me, Lettie, there are some who are not in this world!'

Lettie did believe her. Eric was one of those who were not, she thought, and from the information she had gleaned from Gran about her grandfather, he was another. She wondered what her own mother and father had thought of him and wished Gran would tell her. Over the years, when Lettie had asked after her parents, Gran had been evasive about them and the most she ever got in reply was: 'They've gone, both of them. It upsets me to talk of the past.' So Lettie had learned not to pursue her queries.

But some of the things Eric had said raised questions in Lettie's mind. Who was she, really? He had implied that Lettie's lineage was less than wholesome and she had wanted to challenge him on his comments. She couldn't do that, of course, unless she was in possession of the truth herself. What was the truth about her past? Perhaps now was not the best time to ask? But Lettie felt she had a right to know and Gran was getting on in years.

She was a Hargreaves so her father had been Gran's son or, or . . . her mother had not married. Lettie spoke quietly and clearly, 'Who was my father, Gran? You've never said. Was he a good man, or didn't you approve of him?'

Gran closed her tired eyes and kept them shut as she replied. 'He . . . he lost your mother and he could not look after you. I . . . I took you away for your own safety.'

That made sense to Lettie. While Gran was in this mood, she responded with the question that had smouldered in her mind for years, and since Eric's comments it now burned to be answered. It was the taboo question, the one you never asked because you might not like the answer. She kept her voice low. 'But they were married, though, weren't they? I'm not a . . .' She wanted to say 'bastard' but did not wish to shock her grandmother further and her words trailed away.

Lettie felt embarrassed by the look of horror that Gran gave her. Gran placed both her palms on the table and pushed herself to her feet. 'No you are not. Your mother was married when you were born and that is all you need to know,' she stated. 'Now, my dear, that's enough questions for now. Finish tidying the pantry for me. I really must get on with next week's orders.'

Gran had made it clear that the matter was closed. Lettie took the hint and moved on to a more mundane conversation. 'We need more laundry blue for the sheets. We'll be having a washday before the grocer does his rounds. Shall I walk into town tomorrow and get some?'

'All right. Take him the list for next week's delivery. You won't need the trap, but don't go looking for that delivery boy because he's not at Adley's any more.'

'Yes, Gran.' Lettie had use of the Reverend's pony and trap whenever he wasn't using it, but she preferred to walk anyway.

She set off the next day for the two miles to the grocer's shop on the high street. Waterley Edge used to be a separate village from the town, but they were more or less linked now by streets of houses for coal miners and steelworkers and their families. A horse rider passed her at a canter and she stood back to let him by. The horse was beautifully groomed and its gentleman rider sat tall in the saddle. She didn't recognise him as he looked down at her. He took a hand off the reins to raise his bowler hat. She bowed her head in acknowledgement and watched him for a few minutes. He was new to the area; probably a visitor to one of the big

118

houses built in the surrounding countryside for furnace and factory owners. He glanced back at her over his shoulder and she smiled.

Half a mile further on she noticed the horse tethered outside the cemetery and saw the man wandering through the burial ground, bending down to read the gravestones. She wondered why he was so interested in the dead and shivered. She was so intent on watching this stranger that she didn't hear a bicycle approaching until he rang his bell and distracted her.

'Thomas!'

He was out of breath. 'I was at the bottom of the hill,' he panted.

He'd said he'd look out for her and she was pleased to see him, but worried at the same time in case anyone saw them together and told Gran. She didn't want to upset her again.

'I'm not supposed to talk to you,' she said.

'Well, I haven't got much time either. How are you getting on with your granny?'

'She wants to send me away to South Wales.'

'Phew, that's a long way. She must be really worried about you staying here.'

'I don't know why. I haven't done anything wrong.'

'She thinks you might. This is a bit drastic, though, you won't know anybody.'

'I'd be living with the Reverend's relations.'

'Oh, I see. Won't your granny miss you?'

'Yes and I'll miss her. Except that I won't because I'm not going. She can't make me.'

'Yes she can. You're not twenty-one yet. What did she say when you refused?'

'I haven't told her yet.'

Thomas frowned. 'It sounds as though you've a row brewing there.'

'I know. That's why I haven't said anything. I don't want give her palpitations.'

Thomas sympathised and said, 'If you really have to go, I'll come with you and get a job in a Welsh coal mine.'

Lettie didn't take him seriously but it wouldn't have surprised her if Thomas did do just that. She glanced sideways at the graveyard. The stranger was writing something in a small notebook and it dawned on her what he was doing. He was looking at names and dates on the headstones. Was he an orphan like she, and searching for his father? Even if he wasn't, Lettie felt an immediate empathy for the man and it occurred to her that she could do the same.

'I shan't go,' she said to Thomas. 'I have things I want to do here.'

Thomas smiled. 'Is one of them to give me another kiss?'

'Stop it, Thomas,' she hissed. 'I'm in real trouble because of that kiss in the cellar.'

'You liked it, though, didn't you?'

'If I want to stay in Waterley Edge I'll have to find some way of persuading Gran to let me. So you've got to keep away from me – a least until this fuss dies down.'

'All right, Lettie,' he soothed. 'I was only joking. We're still friends, aren't we?'

She nodded and said, 'I'm sorry. Gran's not well and I'm a bit anxious about her.'

'Now I'm the one who's sorry. When I'm settled, I'll let you know where I'm working and you'll be able to get a message to me if I can do anything to help. Promise me you'll do that?'

'I will. Thanks, Thomas.'

He turned his bicycle round to face downhill. 'Ta-ra, then.'

'Ta-ra.'

She walked on but her mind wasn't on her errand. It was on where she might find her mother's grave, or her father's, or even her grandfather's. They wouldn't be in the cemetery she'd just passed because that was an over-flow from the parish church in town and Church of England. Gran was a Methodist. She'd start with the chapel burial ground.

But the more she thought about it the more she real-ised that they probably weren't around here because Gran never visited them. Lettie decided to choose her moment and ask Gran where they were. By the time she returned to the manse with the laundry blue she was quite anxious to talk to Gran before the Reverend wrote his letter to South Wales.

Gran was very tired by evening and Lettie was loath to say anything to upset her. So she tried to be calm when she asked, 'Gran, can you ask the Reverend not to write to his sister in Wales just yet?'

Gran was sitting in her rocking chair by the kitchen fire, her eyes closed. Lettie knew she wasn't asleep. Lettie ought to have been reading by the oil lamp on the kitchen table but she just couldn't concentrate until she'd had this out with Gran.

'Why should I do that?' Gran answered without opening her eyes.

'I really don't want to go to South Wales and I don't want to be a teacher either.'

Gran opened her eyes. 'Don't be awkward about this, Lettie. I know what's best for you.'

No you don't! Lettie wanted to say, but instead she said, 'Teachers turn into fusty old spinsters. I might want to marry and have babies instead.'

'Well, you can still do that. But you have refused Eric.'

'I don't mean with him!'

This seemed to startle Gran and she sat upright causing her chair to rock. 'You haven't done anything silly with that delivery boy, have you?'

'Silly? Oh, you think we have . . .' Lettie blushed in the lamplight. 'Oh no, I don't mean that. I mean . . .' What did she mean? It was so ungrateful of her to say that she simply wanted to do more with her life than work in a mission. She said, 'I was thinking about what you were doing at my age.'

Gran had told her she had been responsible for most of the housekeeping at Waterley Hall because she was head parlourmaid by eighteen and the housekeeper was too old to manage anything on her own.

Gran looked past her and out of the window. 'I was the youngest housekeeper in the Riding when I was appointed; probably the youngest in the county. Your

122

grandfather was butler at the time and then, years later, he became the new master's favourite.' Her expression soured. 'As thick as thieves, they were, but I didn't know that then.'

This wasn't the way Lettie had expected the conversation to go but she took an opportunity and asked lightly, 'Where is Grandfather buried?'

'Why do you want to know that?' Gran asked wearily.

'Well, I don't think he's in our chapel cemetery. You or the Reverend would have shown me.'

'No, he wasn't chapel so he stayed on the Waterley estate where he belonged,' Gran said. Her tone was sharp and Lettie bit back a barrage of questions. Gran was tired. She was an active lady, so much so that it was easy to forget how old she was in spite of her failing sight and her palpitations. She grew weary by nightfall. 'Shall I make some hot milk and honey to help you sleep?' Lettie suggested.

'Thank you, dear.' Gran rocked her chair and pushed herself out of it. 'Bring it upstairs and leave it outside my door.'

'Do you want me to brush out your hair?'

'Not tonight. I shall be too long at my prayers. Make sure you pray for guidance in yours, too.'

'Yes, Gran.'

Lettie mixed the warm nourishing drink in a stoneware mug and carried it carefully upstairs. She bent down to place it on the worn floorboards. A glow from an oil lamp was visible under the door and around the frame. Lettie could hear Gran at her prayers. The sound of her own name caused her to stop and listen.

*   *   *

123

Dear Lord, thank you for your leading me to Reverend Ennis and showing me the way forward to repentance. I beseech you to call my granddaughter Lettie to your service. Lead her towards an honourable life and give me the strength to bear our separation.

Please, Father, do not ask Lettie to suffer for her mother's sins. They were my sins too and I beg you to forgive me for them. Watch over my dearest Lettie and keep her pure and safe. Give her the wisdom to choose a more virtuous path than her mother . . .

Gran made a choking noise that muffled her words and then there was a silence followed by *Forgive me Lord.* Gran was weeping! Gran never cried and Lettie had to resist the temptation to dash into her bedroom and comfort her. But prayers were private and Lettie crept away, wondering if she had heard correctly. She could only guess at the sin her mother had committed that Gran blamed herself for. The answer seemed obvious and it would have brought shame on all the family. But Gran had been very firm when she said that Lettie was not born out of wedlock.

Yet she could not forget Gran's prayers. Lettie's mother had sinned in some unforgiveable manner and Gran was worried that Lettie was in danger of doing the same. Was she turning out to be like her sinful mother? Lettie thought not. Just because she had asked Thomas to kiss her didn't make her wicked! Of course she was aware what it might lead to – Eric had made that clear enough – but Lettie would not have allowed *that*; not before marriage. She heaved an impatient sigh. She didn't want to be a teacher or work in a mission either. No wonder Gran was worried about her.

Lettie did pray for guidance that night. Finding out a little about her father and mother had only whetted her appetite for more. She *had* to know what her mother had done and who her father was, who *she* was. Gran may be unyieldingly obstinate about revealing some parts of the past but the Lord might be more accommodating.

As Lettie lay awake in bed later that night, she realised that one of her prayers had been answered. Boundary Farm was on the borders of the Waterley estate. Waterley church and graveyard were about halfway between Boundary Farm and Waterley Hall. When she walked over to collect eggs and vegetables for the manse she could continue on to look for her grandfather's grave.

Boundary Farm had been standing for generations, some said longer than Waterley Hall itself. It was a well-worn stone building with a slate roof and a collection of wooden and brick outbuildings at the rear for horses and storage. But the main advantage for its occupant, Mr Osborne, was a large walled garden sheltered from the cold winter winds and enough acres for him to erect glass houses. He had a few small fields of staple vegetables but the larger areas from the old farmstead were leased to a nearby farmer as grazing pasture and growing crops for winter feed.

Mr Osborne was well known amongst the local gentry

for growing apricots and grapes as well as figs and berry fruits. The pick of his crop went to the kitchens of Waterley Hall but as the only resident was old Lady Laughton other larger residences in the Riding benefited from his produce. His wife greeted Lettie at the kitchen door when she arrived swinging her shopping baskets.

'Are you Lettie? I've been expecting you. Your mother housekeeps for the Reverend, is that right?'

'My grandmother,' Lettie corrected.

'I'm Mrs Osborne. Come with me to the barn and you can see what we have this week.'

'The Reverend said he knows you don't deliver but said to ask if Mr Osborne could take round a sack of potatoes when he's next in the village.'

'I'm sure he can.' Mrs Osborne was distracted by a young gentleman dressed for riding, leading a saddled horse from the stables. 'Good morning, sir.'

'Good morning, Mrs Osborne.' He stopped and took in Lettie's appearance, nodded briefly and added, 'Miss.'

He wasn't local, not even English, she thought, and replied, 'Good morning, sir.'

It was the same gentleman that she had seen wandering in the parish graveyard in town. He was well attired for riding, in jodhpurs and high leather boots, a brown woollen waistcoat and hacking jacket. Not very old, she thought, he had an even-featured face with an outdoor complexion and none of the whiskers that were so fashionable for the gentleman. She watched him with interest as he mounted the horse and clattered out of the cobbled farm yard.

'Handsome young fellow, isn't he?' Mrs Osborne remarked and walked on. 'This way, m'ducks.'

'Does Mr Osborne do livery as well?' Lettie queried.

'Dear me, no! He has his hands full with the gardening. The gentleman is lodging with us for the summer. That's his own horse and he looks after it himself.'

Lettie looked back at the young man over her shoulder and was embarrassed to see him doing the same to her as he cantered away. She filled her two shopping baskets, handed over payment and prepared to leave. 'Is it far to Waterley Hall church from here?'

'A good couple of miles in that direction, towards the house. Why do you ask?'

'Can I leave my baskets here while I walk over there?'

'Well, it's a fine day for the walk but I thought you were chapel, like, with you living in the manse.'

'I am but my grandfather wasn't and I think he's buried in the graveyard there. He was a butler to His Lordship before he died.'

'Well I never! Fancy that. Put your baskets in my scullery then and by the time you get back my scones'll be coming out of the oven.'

Lettie picked a posy of wild flowers on her way. She found the small church easily. The surrounding cemetery was tidy and dominated by ancient stone tombs, dark and mossy with age. They bore names and titles she did not recognise and none, apparently, for Lord Laughton's ancestors. She wandered around the smaller headstones and crosses, saddened by inscriptions such as *faithful servant* or *dearly loved sister* and eventually came across

Seth Hargreaves, House Steward, Husband of Ivy and Father of Ruth. This must be her grandfather! House steward? That was more important than butler. But it must be him because Gran's name was Ivy. Their daughter, presumably the daughter who had sinned and who was Lettie's mother – *her mother* – had been called Ruth. Lettie felt excitement bubble through her. Was her father buried here as well?

Lettie had never in her memory heard the name Ruth pass her grandmother's lips. She guessed that Ruth had died as a young woman and it hurt Gran to talk of her. She gave an involuntary cry and put her hand to her mouth as it occurred to her that her mother may have died in childbirth. The dates on her headstone would tell her, if only she could find her mother's grave. And it might give her father's name too so she would know who she really was. What would it say? *Ruth —, husband of —, mother of Lettie*, if Lettie was her full name. She hadn't questioned that before because everyone called her Lettie, even the Reverend.

She placed her posy at the base of the inscription on her grandfather's headstone and offered a short prayer. Then she searched the graveyard again for a Ruth and found one. This Ruth, however, had been a tenant farmer's dairymaid, and a much-loved sister of a coachman at the Hall, but there was no mention of her being a daughter, mother, wife or even widow. Disappointed, Lettie returned to her grandfather's headstone and frowned. Why did it not say *Beloved Husband* or *Loving Father* on his headstone? She looked at the dates. He had been much older than

Gran and died a long time ago. It was highly unlikely that anyone who remembered him apart from Gran was still alive.

Lettie walked back to Boundary Farm, confused and puzzled by her churchyard visit. Instead of answering her questions it had raised more in her mind and she was impatient for answers. Consequently she was in a restless mood when she collected her baskets from Mrs Osborne's scullery.

'Thank you, Mrs Osborne,' she called through the open door. 'I'll get off home now.'

Mrs Osborne cried immediately, 'You'll stay for a cuppa, won't you? It's not often I have company these days. My nippers are all grown and gone now and I do miss them. Did you find your grandfather?'

Lettie put down the baskets and went into the kitchen, which smelled appetisingly of baking scones. Mrs Osborne was a kindly lady and Lettie realised she was being rude by not acknowledging her hospitality. 'Thank you,' she said, 'I did find him. But I was surprised I couldn't find any Laughtons.'

'Lord Laughton's a newcomer. His father wasn't born a lord but he was as rich as one. When the old Waterley title died out the estate had to be sold and Queen Victoria, God rest her soul, had just made him a lord because of what he'd done.'

'Why, what had he done?'

'He'd made a pile of money out of steel and ships. His son and heir still does, an' all. An industrialist, they call him. They also say that he only bought the Waterley estate because he liked he sound of Lord Laughton of Waterley. He's never here, though.' Mrs Osborne glanced out of her kitchen window. 'Oh, there's Mr Boyer back. He'll be wanting some tea.' She rose stiffly to her feet. 'Scones'll be ready now.'

'Shall I take them out for you?' Lettie volunteered. It was one of the tasks she always did for Gran.

'Bless you, no, m'ducks. I can manage my baking.'

Lettie glanced out of the window and her attention was riveted by the sight of horse and rider as the stranger swung easily out of the saddle and led his horse to the stable. Behind her in the kitchen, Mrs Osborne groaned as she straightened up. Quickly, Lettie picked up a cloth, took the hot baking tray from the older woman and placed it on a wooden pot stand.

'Ta, m'ducks. I'm as stiff as a board these days.'

Lettie smiled. Her grandmother was more supple than Mrs Osborne and Gran must be ten or fifteen years older than her. Lettie realised that she was lucky to have her gran at all.

'He'll see to the beast first and then have a wash,' Mrs Osborne said. 'You couldn't carry the hot water up to his room for me, could you? My legs are not what they used to be.'

Lettie jumped to her feet. 'Of course I can. Is the jug in the scullery?'

'Use one of the brass hot-water cans on the floor. He has a washstand in his room so you'll see where to pour it.'

Lettie filled the can from the brass tap in the boiler

beside the fire that heated Mrs Osborne's cooking range. 'Which room?' she asked.

'It's straight in front of you at the top of the stairs.'

Lettie carried the heavy hot water upstairs and into Mr Boyer's room. It must be the best room in the house, she thought when she opened the door and light flooded from a large window onto the dim landing. A mahogany desk had been positioned under the window with one of those round-backed leather-studded chairs that she had seen in the municipal offices. The desktop held writing implements, books and leather folders of papers. Even with the desk, the room was large enough for a big mahogany bed, matching wardrobe and ottoman for blankets. There were heavy brocade drapes at the window and a counterpane on the bed in the same material. The effect was stately and comfortable. Lettie placed her can on the marble-topped washstand and then poured the hot water carefully into the decorated china ewer standing inside a similar gilt-edged wash basin. The hot steam rose to her face.

She was favourably impressed by the room and moved to the window to look at the view. As expected it was probably the best in the house, overlooking the front drive that led down through pasture towards the Waterley Hall road. Sheep grazed the lush grass. Their woolly coats were beginning to emerge again after early-summer shearing. She watched a couple of late-born lambs springing about, still trying to suckle their mother who kicked with her back legs and tossed them away with her head. So much for motherhood, she thought wryly.

The ewe's behaviour upset her and for a few minutes she was distracted, thinking about her own mother and wondering who she was. And who am I? she thought. Her dreaming was interrupted abruptly.

'My documents are private. Kindly leave.'

Chapter 10

The strong male voice left her in no doubt who was speaking and she turned away from the window quickly, clutching the warm metal jug.

'Beg pardon, sir.' Should she say she was looking at the lambs and not prying into his papers?

He had already removed his jacket, thrown it on the bed and was taking out his cufflinks. 'Kindly leave,' he repeated without looking at her.

His imperious tone reminded Lettie of Eric and she frowned, wanting to stay and defend herself. As well, she experienced a really strong urge to watch him roll up his sleeves. Discretion got the better of her and she obeyed silently, closing the door behind her. She walked slowly down the staircase wondering if his arms were sinewy like Eric's or brawny like Thomas's. The image of his capable fingers, manipulating the crisp cotton of his cuffs remained with her until she reached the kitchen. Mrs Osborne was laying his tea tray on the table.

'He's already washing,' Lettie said, wondering whether to tell her about his remarks.

'Yes, I heard the front door.'

'I . . . I was still in his room when he arrived.' Mrs Osborne didn't comment so she went on. 'I was watching the sheep out of the window and he thought I was looking at his desk.'

'Oh, I see. He likes to keep himself to himself. Was he angry?'

'He asked me to leave. I'm sorry, Mrs Osborne.'

'No harm done, I'm sure. I'll explain when I take in his tea.'

'I'd better get back. Gran will wonder where I've got to.'

This time Mrs Osborne didn't argue. 'All right, m'ducks. We'll have that cuppa another time.'

She's not happy with me, Lettie thought as she collected her baskets and left by the back door. She couldn't have read anything because all the books and binders were closed. But she had glanced at his desktop before she noticed the sheep so perhaps she was guilty of prying. She hurried along the path that led from the back of Boundary Farm to the wide track at the front, stopping briefly to admire the mellow stone of the handsome bay windows. A movement through the glass caught her attention.

Mr Boyer was standing in the bay and Mrs Osborne

appeared beside him to hand him a cup of tea and a plate of buttered scones. Lettie looked away quickly and lengthened her stride. As she walked away she felt two pairs of eyes burning into her back. The baskets grew heavy but she did not slacken her pace and was quite hot and bothered by the time the manse was in sight. Then she slowed. Why should she be so concerned about a stranger? He had hardly noticed her and a simple glance at the items on his desk was not, surely, such a terrible sin. She took a few deep breaths to calm herself and decided not to mention Mr Boyer to Gran.

'You were a long time over there,' Gran commented as Lettie placed her baskets on the quarry-tiled floor of the scullery.

'Mrs Osborne asked me to stay for cup of tea. She wanted a chat. I think she's lonely now her children have left home.'

'You might be right about that,' Gran considered. 'They say her husband spends all his time talking to his plants.'

'I didn't see him at all. I . . . I,' Lettie hesitated, wondering whether to mention her visit to the graveyard. But she had to if she wanted to know more about Grandfather and Ruth. 'I walked over to the Waterley church and looked for Grandfather's grave.'

Gran stopped lifting the vegetables into the stone sink. 'Did you find it?'

Lettie noticed that Gran didn't look up from examining the leeks. 'Yes,' she answered. 'It was very neat and tidy.'

'It's private to the estate and has gardeners tending all the graves.'

'I left a posy at his headstone and said a prayer.'

Gran turned on the big brass tap in the wall and water spluttered out into the shallow stone sink. 'These leeks are bigger than Mr Adley's.'

'Don't you want to talk about Grandfather, Gran?'

'No, I don't. I am sorry to have to tell you this but he was a wicked man and he is best forgotten. Now, can we get on with these vegetables?'

It was not a very charitable thing to say about her late husband but it would explain why he was not 'beloved'. What on earth had he done? Gran had said he'd been butler at Waterley Hall when they married. How does a wicked man reach the heights of house steward? There was so much more Lettie wanted to know but she recognised when Gran had closed down a conversation. Questions about Ruth would have to come later and she bit her tongue in frustration. Perhaps Gran might volunteer another snippet of information in a few minutes?

After a lengthy silence Lettie gave up waiting and said, 'These have got more muck on them than Adley's. I'll take them outside to give 'em a good scrub. You go and start on the Reverend's tea.' She took down her heavy sacking apron from the hook beside the sink.

The Reverend, like most ordinary folk in the Riding, had his dinner in the middle of the day and a substantial high tea in the dining room at six o'clock, often with a visitor connected to chapel. Lettie and Gran ate about half an hour later. Her chance came at the kitchen table when she and Gran had finished eating. The kettle was already boiling and Lettie stood up to make a fresh pot of tea.

'Why was Grandfather so wicked? What did he do?' she asked as she brought the pot to the table. Gran was cutting a piece of apple cake and she dropped the knife on the glass cake stand with a clatter. The pain on her face was so evident that Lettie regretted bringing up the topic again and she went on quickly, 'Oh, I'm sorry, Gran, but it's just that it's so long ago now, it really doesn't matter to me if he was sent to prison or something.'

'It was nothing like that. He was a favourite of Lord Laughton.'

'It says he was house steward on his headstone.'

'Ill-gotten gains,' Gran muttered.

Lettie could see she was becoming anxious by Lettie's questions. 'Don't upset yourself, Gran,' she said. 'You don't have to tell me.'

'You wouldn't understand if I did.'

'I might.'

Gran shook her head. 'Your innocence is your virtue.'

Lettie picked up the fallen knife to cut a piece of the cake and slide it across to Gran on a small plate. 'I may be innocent in comparison with some of my old school friends but I'm not a child. I read newspapers and I hear gossip in the mission hall.'

'What have you heard?'

'Nothing, nothing at all about Grandfather.' Although Eric had implied that there was gossip about her. She repeated, 'It was a long time ago, Gran, and nobody remembers him.'

'I do! I conspired in his wickedness and for that I shall shoulder the blame as much as he. I was a dutiful wife and a loyal servant. I obeyed my husband and my master against my conscience and I pray every day to the Lord for forgiveness.'

Lettie was astounded. It was the most Gran had ever said about the past and now Lettie understood why. Gran had been involved in the wickedness. 'What did you do?' she asked.

'Do not concern yourself with the past, my dear. When you move permanently to South Wales and live with the Reverend's family, you will mix with decent people and forget all about Waterley.'

'Move *permanently*? I thought it was just a visit!'

'There is no future for you in Waterley Edge. The Reverend has promised that, when I pass on, his family will take care of you.'

'But I don't want to go.'

'You have to; for my peace of mind. Lettie, you must understand your position. I am an old lady and I have only a small amount of money to leave you. We have a home here with the support of the Reverend and by the grace and favour of the church elders. When I am gone, the Reverend cannot have a young unmarried woman residing in the manse. You will have to live somewhere else.'

The Reverend was like a father to Lettie but she understood that for propriety's sake the elders would not permit her to stay, even as his housekeeper. Nonetheless, she protested, 'But that could be years in the future!'

'It is best to make the changes now.'

'Do you want to be rid of me for some reason?'

'Of course I do not and it will hurt me more than I can say to be separated from you. But I believe it is the Lord's will that you go.'

Lettie remembered her grandmother's prayer. She would feel the separation as much as Gran. 'Is my pain the Lord's will too?' she said. 'Does He wish me to abandon you when I know you need me more than ever, and then suffer that regret for the rest of my life?'

'I shall have the support of the mission. Truly, I am only doing what I think is best for you, as I have always done. Your head has been turned by the first young man to give you attention and—'

'This has nothing to do with Thomas! If it were I should go willingly because he has said he will follow me to South Wales anyway. I do understand my position as an orphan but I am sure I can find work here to support myself when I have to.'

'Doing what, may I ask?' Gran demanded.

'I don't see why I can't be a housekeeper as you were.'

'That is not a good idea for you and we have talked enough on this. Please can you pour my tea before it goes cold in the pot?'

Lettie did so and then picked up a tray to clear the Reverend's dining room. He had dined with a guest and they had already retreated to the drawing room. She stacked the tray with dirty dishes and left it on the hall table while she tapped on the drawing-room door. The conversation stopped when she entered and the

Reverend glanced up. 'Can I get you anything else, sir?' she asked.

'No thank you, Lettie.'

'Would you like another lamp?'

'I'll help myself from the scullery if I need one. I suggest you make sure your grandmother has an early night. She has been looking tired of late.'

'Very well. Goodnight then, sir.'

'Goodnight, Lettie.' He returned to his conversation.

She retreated gratefully, wondering if the Reverend had any information about her grandfather and decided not. He had much more pressing matters to deal with, many of which were confidential. Her duty was to look after Gran and not exhaust her with constant questions on a past she would prefer to forget. Lettie felt guilty about her selfishness and vowed in future to avoid anything that caused Gran anxiety. She would have to try very hard to be satisfied with what she knew for the time being.

A few days later Lettie was walking back from Boundary Farm with a basket full of vegetables when she saw Thomas leaning against the wall of the Miners' Arms with a tankard of beer in his hand. He wore heavy pit boots, a leather jerkin over his working clothes, and was black all over from coal dust. Goodness, if the day shift at the pit had finished already it was later than she'd thought. She quickened her pace, looking forward to exchanging a few words with him.

As soon as he saw her he pushed himself away from

the wall and stood up straight. 'Hello, Lettie,' he said. 'I thought I might see you. The landlord said you pass here on your way to and from Boundary Farm.'

'You can't do anything in this village without everybody knowing. The Reverend has his vegetables from there, now.'

'I heard. He was a bit hard on Mr Adley, I thought, because he'd already got rid of me.'

Close up, Lettie took in the whole of his blackened appearance and the word 'roughneck' crossed her mind. 'Have you started down the pit already?'

'I'm not down the pit. I'm working for Toogoods and I've found him two new customers from my Adley's round.'

Mr Toogood was a big name in coal haulage in the Riding and he was expanding, setting up coal yards near railway lines that brought in wagon loads of coal direct from the local pitheads. He had caused quite a stir when he bought a motorised vehicle for deliveries and had his name painted on the doors.

Lettie swung her head round to where the Toogoods wagon stood by the kerb, still carrying about twenty sacks of coal. 'Are you their new coalman?'

Thomas raised his glass in a toast. 'That's me. The landlord here always has a pint waiting for when I've filled his cellar.'

Lettie stared again at the wagon, which was huge compared with a bicycle. 'Do you mean you can drive that thing?'

''Course I can. Mr Adley had a motor car for when

141

he delivered to the inn and big houses in town. I used to back it up and turn it round for him reg'lar. One day I'll have my own.'

Lettie was impressed. 'I bet your mam is pleased.'

'And my dad.' He drained his tankard, adding, 'I needed that,' and placed it on a window ledge. Then he rapped on the window and said, 'I'd better get going. These sacks are for that row of farm cottages on the Sheffield road.'

Not Boundary Farm, she thought. They had coal delivered at a discount price direct from the pit, the same as Waterley Hall. The Reverend, too, had his delivered from the pithead on a cart pulled by two heavy horses. The pit owners were generous because they appreciated how well the mission looked after miners' families when they had troubles. The driver shovelled it off the back of the cart and a couple of lads from the Reverend's congregation shovelled it into the cellar for him.

Thomas walked by close to her as he returned to his truck and she shrank away from the coal dust that covered him. 'It washes off,' he commented. 'Have you got your gran to change her mind about me yet?'

'Give me a chance!' Lettie retaliated. But she knew it was a lost cause. Gran wanted her to be a schoolteacher or marry one. The fact that Thomas might have his own motor wagon one day would count for nothing in her eyes. Once a roughneck, always a roughneck was Gran's opinion. 'Was the fair any good?' she asked.

'It was better than last year. They had a new ride that sent you round and round as well as up and down. I went on it three times. Listen, I can see you this Sunday afternoon in the park if you like. Most of your village will be there because the colliery band is playing. I'll meet you by the bandstand and it'll look like a coincidence if anybody is watching.'

'I'll try,' she answered. She stayed to watch him crank the engine into life, climb up into the driver's seat and rumble away down the road.

A young woman came outside for his tankard and stood beside her to watch him drive away. 'Friendly sort, isn't he? Are you sweet on him?'

Lettie didn't answer. She was thinking about how she could get away from the manse on Sunday afternoon to go to the park. The woman prompted, 'Well, are you? I bet you are.'

Lettie thought about it. If being sweet on someone meant he was your sweetheart then she wasn't and she said so.

The woman didn't believe her. 'You're that stuck-up lass from the manse, aren't you?' she said. 'You'd better not be seen hanging about here. Chapel don't hold with us lot.' She snorted ungraciously. 'My dad's the landlord here and he says Reverend Ennis calls his ale "the demon drink".'

The woman went inside with the tankard and Lettie gazed down the empty road. She hadn't been called 'stuck-up' to her face since schooldays. But she guessed these names stayed with you for ever. She was more concerned with what Gran would think if she found out that Thomas drank beer in an ale house. It wouldn't do him any favours at all in her eyes. But it must be thirsty work heaving sacks of coal off the back of a wagon and up-ending them down cellar grates all day, so what was a working man to do?

Following morning service on Sunday, the talk outside chapel was about the colliery band in the Municipal Park and that it would be all right to go because they would be playing hymns. Both the Reverend and Gran approved so Lettie agreed to meet with others from chapel after dinner and walk to the park. She put on her new outfit with a ribbon bow at the front and another on her straw hat. After that unfortunate Sunday afternoon with Eric she had stopped being adventurous with coiling her hair but decided to pile it high for her day out. She was in a hurry and, annoyingly, her hair would not behave itself so in the end she brushed it out down her back. It was pretty enough but it made her appear younger than she was, which was even more noticeable when she joined the others from chapel for their walk.

The park was busy with men and women parading up and down in their summery finery making Lettie feel insignificant in comparison. Also, the other girls of her age had their hair coiled under flower-trimmed hats. Several wore skirts showing their ankles and matching short jackets that skimmed their waistlines. She eyed them with interest as she made her way to the bandstand. Rows of chairs were lined up all around, many already taken, and she scanned the gathering crowd for Thomas. He was standing up in the middle of a row and waved as soon as he saw her. Goodness, how clean and neat and tidy he was! She wished Gran could see him now.

'Oh, someone has saved me a seat,' she said to the others and detached herself from the group to weave her way through the crowd and shuffle down the row. 'Thomas, how did you get such good seats?'

'I came really early. Is your gran with you?'

'No, and she doesn't know I'm meeting you.'

'Will you tell her?'

'I'll say I saw you here but I don't think it will help. She's made up her mind about you and can be very stubborn when she wants.'

They sat down together and talked about the people they knew in the band and said which hymns they wanted to hear. Thomas was very easy to be with, she thought, and she felt safe with him after Eric. She stared at his profile for a while. He kept his eyes facing forwards but she noticed he smiled and that made her smile too.

'Who's that lady in the middle, a few rows down?' he said. 'She seems to know you.'

Lettie's eyes dodged between the large hats in front of her and realised it was Mrs Osborne, waving at her impatiently. She returned the wave and that seemed to satisfy her for she turned back and settled in her seat. Lettie noticed that even Mrs Osborne's grey hair was piled up elaborately underneath her hat, and her hat was trimmed with an ostrich feather. She fingered her long straight locks pensively as the band filed onto the circular stand with their shiny silver instruments. When they began to play, more folk gathered around the seating and stood to listen. After the finale, Thomas whispered, 'I enjoyed that, did you?' Lettie nodded and he added, 'Good, I'm glad. When do you have to be home?'

'I'm meeting the others by the gates at six.'

'Oh, we've plenty of time yet. Shall we go for a walk?'

The rows of chairs emptied gradually but when she and Thomas shuffled to the aisle she was waylaid by Mrs Osborne who materialised beside her, determined to talk.

'Wasn't that grand? We must ask the Corporation to make it a regular thing.' Mrs Osborne turned pointedly to Thomas. 'Good afternoon, young man.'

'This is Thomas,' Lettie said and went on quickly, 'We were at school together a few years ago and met each other just by chance.' Actually that was the truth, she thought, as it was chance that had brought them together, but it hadn't happened today.

Mrs Osborne nodded in Thomas's direction and he replied with a polite 'Good afternoon', then she turned back to Lettie. 'Will you be over tomorrow?'

'Not until Tuesday. It's washday tomorrow.'

'I'll look forward to Tuesday then.' Mrs Osborne gazed around. 'Now where is Mr Osborne? He'll be inspecting the flower beds, I expect. He didn't want to sit down. He can't keep still for two minutes at a time.' Mrs Osborne chatted on about the weather, her husband's glasshouses and her grown-up children. Lettie listened patiently until the older lady looked around and said, 'You haven't seen our Mr Boyer, have you?'

'Mr Boyer? Is he here, too?'

'He hired a trap, you know, to bring me here. Wasn't that kind of him? I find the walk into town too far these days and I can't ride in Mr Osborne's cart in my best frock, can I?'

'No, Mrs Osborne.' Lettie smiled. She glanced sideways at Thomas, who was waiting patiently. The crowd was thinning and through a gap she saw Mr Boyer, standing in the shade of a large oak tree, formally dressed in a dark suit and bowler hat with a black cane in his hand. 'Mr Boyer is over there,' she said. 'He's waiting for you at the other side.' She considered waving to attract his attention but didn't. He was a gentleman and it was hardly a ladylike gesture. And he would see her with Thomas if she did.

'We're going this way,' Thomas said and touched Lettie's arm with his hand.

Mrs Osborne noticed and her eyebrows moved up very slightly. 'I'll see you on Tuesday, then. Come after you've done your ironing and ask your gran if you can stay for a cuppa.'

'All right, Mrs Osborne. Bye, then.' Mrs Osborne turned round to search for her lodger and ride home.

Thomas tugged lightly on Lettie's hand. 'I thought we'd never get away from her.'

'She likes talking, that's all.'

The walkers continued to thin as many went straight home after the band finished playing.

'Shall we walk on the grass?' Lettie suggested. She liked the feel of the soft turf underfoot. 'We could cut across to the shrubbery.'

'Oh, I don't know.' Thomas slowed his pace. 'Let's stick to the path.'

147

Lettie was surprised. Several younger folk were walking that way and she watched them. Several *couples*, she noticed; not families with children and grandparents. There were lots of twists and turns and secluded corners in the shrubbery and Lettie guessed the reason for its popularity. She felt a blush rising and looked down. Thomas would be thinking she was very forward and she had to put that right.

'All right,' she said and shrugged, 'but I wasn't going to ask you to kiss me again.'

'You don't want me to kiss you anyway, do you?'

Chapter 11

No she didn't, not after Eric. She hadn't told Thomas about Eric so she asked, 'Why do you say that?'

'I don't think you wanted *me* to kiss you in the first place. You just wanted to be kissed.'

He was right and Lettie didn't know what to say so she kept quiet. Thomas went on, 'You still want to be kissed, though, don't you?'

'No! Well, yes, I do, but things are different now.'

Kissing led to other things. Thomas knew that, so did Gran and her warnings echoed in Lettie's ears. She liked being with Thomas and she had wanted to know what kissing was like and it . . . he . . . all of it . . . had surprised her. Proper kissing was . . . was . . . oh, she wasn't sure but it was something that she wanted to be special, with someone special, very special, with someone she . . . Lettie stared at the other couples walking across the grass. Were they all special to each other, or were they, as she was, simply finding out?

Thomas was nice, he was fun, but he wasn't, well, he wasn't special in the way she wanted him to be and if she asked him to kiss her again he would think he was.

He said, 'There's no wonder your gran is worried about you. She's protected you too much from ordinary life. In some ways you're still a child. You even look like my little sister today.'

'No, please don't say that! Gran doesn't let me come to the park as a rule.'

'That's what I mean! You need to grow up. I'm sorry, Lettie. I don't mean to be rude, but you should know what I think.'

They walked on in silence for a while until Lettie said, 'I want you to always tell me the truth, Thomas. Promise me you will.'

'That's easy. My dad brought me up never to tell lies.'

'Are we still friends, then?' she asked.

'Friends? I suppose so; for now.' He let out a sigh through the corner of his mouth. 'Shall we walk up to the fountain and make a wish?'

'All right,' she agreed.

She felt uncomfortable for a while. Thomas had under-lined what Gran had said about the value of going to Wales and living with other young folk in a proper family. Then Thomas began to talk about the Toogoods and she relaxed. In fact, she thought that Thomas was making an effort to be especially nice to her for the rest of the afternoon. He gave her a shiny new penny to throw in the fountain.

She tossed it high, watched it sparkle in the sun and fall with a plop into the clear water. As it sank she closed her eyes tightly and wished hard. She wished for something she had not prayed for. Guidance from God was all very well but she wanted to do something with her life that was more interesting than mission work and she wished for that; for something more exciting in her life.

When she opened her eyes Thomas was smiling at her and she smiled back.

'Come on,' he said. 'It's a long way back to the entrance.'

'We'd best separate before we get there.'

'I'll disappear at the bandstand. I can see the gates from under the trees.'

'Thank you for asking me here this afternoon. I've had a lovely time.'

'Me too. How often do you walk to Boundary Farm?'

'Two or three times a week, generally.'

'I'll look out for you by the inn when I'm delivering over that way.'

'All right,' she replied. 'Ta-ra, then.'

'Ta-ra, Lettie.'

The others questioned her about where she had been on her own and she gave them a half truth, saying she'd managed to get a seat at the bandstand and met up with Mrs Osborne from Boundary Farm. They all agreed that she had been lucky to get away from her before dark. They were in family groups and hurrying home to help their fathers clean and polish boots or help their mothers put laundry to soak for washday tomorrow. Lettie was no exception for this task and did it all herself because Gran was usually too tired by Sunday evening.

Gran and the Reverend had retired to their bedrooms when Lettie came in from the wash house. She ate the jam tarts that Gran had left out for her and poured warming milk from a pan on the edge of the hob into a cup. Then she rubbed lanolin cream into her hands to cure the wrinkling, blew out the lamp and took her milk upstairs by candlelight.

Eric had made her cautious about young men. She was sure she didn't want anything more to do with him, but she wanted to stay friends with Thomas. He had been kind to her this afternoon. But the more she thought about it the more she realised he had treated her like his little sister and she wasn't sure that's what she wanted. It was all very confusing and she couldn't talk to Gran about any of it. She wished she had a sister or even an aunty as the other young people in the mission did. She fell asleep eventually, wondering what advice her mother would have given her if she'd lived.

Gran insisted on using the wooden dolly to move around bed sheets in the wash tub even though she had to sit down every ten minutes to catch her breath. During one of her short rests Lettie asked, 'Gran, when I pick up the eggs and vegetables from Boundary Farm would you mind if I stayed to have a cup of tea with Mrs Osborne? She can't get out as much as she used to and I think she misses the company of her children.'

'I'm sure she does.' Gran stood up and nodded to herself. 'That's very thoughtful of you. It's just the kind of thing the Reverend expects of his mission ladies. You'll do very well in South Wales.'

Lettie tried not to frown. 'Has the Reverend written to his sister yet?'

'I haven't asked him. Can we get these sheets on the line before we have to stop and do the dinner?'

Lettie turned the mangle for most of the morning and it was hard work, but dinner was easy on Mondays. Cold meat and pickles with bubble and squeak and a rice pudding that was already in the oven. The Reverend came through the kitchen after his dinner to pick up the bucket of peelings for his pig. He never failed to say he had enjoyed his dinner, even when it was nothing special. Gran and Lettie were still finishing their pudding at the kitchen table. Lettie made a pot of tea for the Reverend to drink in his study when he came back, and a pot for her and Gran after they had done the washing-up. You could set your clock by the routine, Lettie thought. The following day at exactly the same time, she gulped back her scalding tea to set off with her baskets for Boundary Farm.

There was no sign of Thomas at the inn and no tell-tale coal debris around the grating in the yard. Lettie walked on slowly and looked back frequently until the inn was out of sight. Mrs Osborne was pleased to see her and her kitchen was full of the delicious smell of boiling jam. 'Aren't we lucky with the weather this year?' she said. 'Mr Osborne's fruit garden is bursting.'

'That reminds me,' Lettie responded, 'Gran says if you ever have any of your jam to spare, the Reverend will take it. Just put it on his bill.'

'I most certainly will. Did your gran say you could stay for tea?'

Lettie nodded enthusiastically.

'You can help me with the labelling when the jars have cooled. Let me have a little sit-down first.'

Lettie gazed out of the kitchen window for signs of a horse and rider but the yard was empty. 'Was Mr Boyer cross with me for being in his room last week?' she queried.

'Well, he asked who you were and where you were from. I persuaded him you weren't prying.'

'Where's he from, Mrs Osborne?'

'I don't rightly know, except that his family came from round these parts years ago and he was born in Canada. He's well-to-do, though.'

'How do you know that?'

'Oh, you can always tell by what folk expect and how they behave. I was at Redfern Abbey before I married Mr Osborne. Lord and Lady Redfern are proper gentry, you know, not like these newcomers in Waterley Hall.'

'I thought Lord and Lady Laughton had been there for years.'

'Bless you, m'ducks, not really. He was the first Laughton to live there. The Earl and Countess have been at Redfern Abbey for generations.'

'My gran doesn't like Lord Laughton.'

'Mrs Osborne rounded her eyes. 'It doesn't do to say

it around here, even though plenty would agree with her!' She squeezed Lettie's hand in a friendly way. 'He's lived abroad for years but his lady wife is still at Waterley Hall. Mind you, folk don't like her either. When the pig man came for his swill he said another of her maids had walked out after only a week and gone back to the mill. It's not like it was in the old days when young lasses had no choice. They can get factory work round here and even jobs at the pithead. They think they'll like being a maidservant and wearing a clean dress and pinny, but she's a right tartar is old Lady Laughton.'

'Do you know her, then?'

'Not me, m'ducks. Mr Osborne does. Why?'

'I was wondering whether, in the future, I might apply for a position at Waterley Hall.'

'After what I've just said? Years ago, Lady Laughton wanted me to be her lady's maid, like I was at Redfern Abbey, but Mr Osborne wouldn't hear of it. He knew what she was like.'

'You were a lady's maid? That sounds exciting.'

'Oh, it was. I've been to their shooting lodge in the Dales, and their London residence, and, of course, we came here to Waterley Hall once. That's when I met Mr Osborne.'

'Did you? How romantic.'

'Yes, I suppose it was. He was head gardener and Earl Redfern came looking for him to ask him how he grew his grapes. Now, it's not done to poach good servants from other estates and Earl Redfern wouldn't have dreamed of asking, but if Mr Osborne had wanted, he was sure he

155

could have gone to Redfern Abbey. We'd talked about it, you see, me and Mr Osborne, because we'd hit it off straightaway. When His Lordship here got wind of us, he offered Mr Osborne Boundary Farm tenancy if he stayed. Well, it meant we could wed and have children straightaway, and have a proper house to bring 'em up.' Mrs Osborne looked pensive for a moment. 'Mr Osborne said he was like that, Lord Laughton. He reckoned his money could buy him anything he wanted, even folk.'

Lettie didn't know what to say, but Mrs Osborne voiced her thoughts for her and added, 'Well, I suppose he could and he did. But me and Mr Osborne got what we wanted as well.'

'He must have been there when my grandfather was house steward.'

'Aye, but Mr Osborne answered to the land steward.'

'Would he mind if I asked him about grandfather?'

'He's never says much, m'ducks, and he won't talk about the old days. Best forgotten, he reckons.'

'Oh.' Lettie was disappointed and after a pause said brightly, 'This is a lovely home, Mrs Osborne.'

'Do you like it? I'm glad your granny has let you stay for tea. It can get lonely here because Mr Osborne won't have me go anywhere near Waterley Hall — he never has, nor my girls — and we're a long walk from the village. It's nice having a young lass around the house again.'

'You've got Mr Boyer.'

'He's different. He's a lodger, well, a paying guest, Mr Osborne calls him. Will you want to stay for tea every time you come over?'

'If I have the time. I'd really like to hear about Redfern Abbey.'

'I could tell you a tale or two, that's for sure.' Mrs Osborne rocked her chair to stand up. She groaned. 'My knees are playing me up again. Come along, Lettie, let's see what we have for the Reverend's basket today.' She walked awkwardly to the door then called over her shoulder, 'Fill the kettle and put it on the range for me, would you, m'ducks.'

Mrs Osborne allowed Lettie to choose which vegetables and fruit to take, including some luscious ripe gooseberries that were the Reverend's favourite.

'He's a lucky man, is the Reverend Ennis, to have you look after him as well as your grandmother.'

'He's a good man,' Lettie commented, echoing her granny's words. She remembered Gran's request for jam and added, 'He really likes your jam, Mrs Osborne.'

'He's not the only one, m'ducks. I'll tell you what; if you write me out the labels you can take some of my latest batch with you. Will you be able to carry all this?'

'Oh yes, it's not far and I stop by the inn for a rest.'

'Not for a glass of ale, I hope,' Mrs Osborne said. 'The Reverend wouldn't care for that at all.'

Nor Gran, Lettie thought; nonetheless, it was another thing, like kissing, that she wanted to try.

'I'll call you when the tea's mashed,' the older lady added.

Lettie sat at Mrs Osborne's writing table in her wide entrance hall and painstakingly wrote on tiny pieces of paper in her best handwriting: *gooseberry, strawberry, blackcurrant,* all followed by 1905. She had good hand-writing — her teachers had told her so — and she did not hurry. She heard the door through to the back kitchen open and close but did not look up as she finished the label. She was concentrating on adding a wavy line underneath.

Then she sat back and let out a sigh. 'There,' she said, 'all done. Shall I stick them on the jars for you, Mrs Os— Oh!' As she turned to speak she realised it was not Mrs Osborne standing behind her. It was Mr Boyer. 'Oh, I beg your pardon, sir, I thought you were someone else.'

'Clearly.' He placed his hat and riding crop on a side table by the front door and took a leather binder tied with tape from under his arm. 'I am looking for Mrs Osborne; do you know where she is?'

'Is she not in her kitchen?'

'I have just come from there,' he explained with, she thought, exaggerated patience.

She stood up, gazed at him with serious eyes and replied, 'I was not aware of that, sir. As you see, I have been occupied with my own tasks.'

He glanced past her at the desktop. 'Well, now you've finished, can you occupy yourself in looking for her and when you find her ask her to bring tea to my room today.'

'Very well, sir,' she replied. She bobbed a curtsey, something she had never done to the Reverend or any of his guests, turned her back on him and went through the kitchen door with a wry grin on her face. She wondered if he realised that she was mocking him. She was not a

158

servant at Boundary Farm and even if she were, he did not warrant a curtsey. This was not Waterley Hall and he was not a lord! He could be, though, she thought, because he dressed as one of the gentry and had a confidence and a presence that made people notice him.

The kitchen was empty but Mrs Osborne came in from the scullery with a bowl of eggs in her hand. 'I nearly forgot these. Did I hear Mr Boyer's horse in the yard?'

'You did and he wants his tea upstairs.'

'Oh drat! He'll be working on his papers again.'

'Shall I carry the tray upstairs for you?'

'Would you, m'ducks? I'll have to take it into his room after the last time but, yes, it would be a great help.'

'He spoke to me as though I were your maidservant. Is he always so abrupt with folk?'

'It's just his way. He's come over here looking up his family roots and I don't think he likes what he's finding out.'

'Oh.' Lettie felt again the empathy that she'd experienced when she saw him in the cemetery. Maybe his family had been in the workhouse or prison. Perhaps Gran was right and it's best not to know about your forebears. But Lettie knew what it felt like to be desperate to find out, to give you a proper sense of who you were and maybe to give you a family, like Mrs Osborne's – far flung, but people that you loved nonetheless.

She carried his jug of hot water to wash and then a laden tea tray up to the landing for Mrs Osborne to take into his room. 'I'll open the door for you,' she said as she

159

deposited the heavy tray in Mrs Osborne's hands. She held open the door and called, 'Your tea, sir,' then immediately closed it. She wasn't the least bit interested in his papers; she had her own antecedents to explore. And, she realised, she had to stay in the South Riding to make a start.

Later, when Mrs Osborne returned to the kitchen, they drank tea together at her scrubbed wooden table, and ate a piece of the seed cake, made for Mr Boyer's tea. 'This is delicious,' Lettie commented.

'It's a favourite of Mr Osborne.' She placed a gauze cover over the remainder to keep the flies away.

'Your hair looked lovely when I saw you in the park, all coils and swathes,' Lettie commented. 'How do you get it like that?'

'Ways and means, m'ducks.' Mrs Osborne smiled. 'I could show you how to do yours the same if you want.'

'Oh, would you?'

'I used to do Lady Redfern's hair all the time.'

'She must have been sorry to lose you.'

'Well, I trained up a nice young woman to take over. She was a lot like you, actually; lively and bright.'

'Will you show me how to do it today?'

'I'll have you looking every inch a lady, m'ducks. I use plenty of rolls and pads as my hair is thinning, but yours is beautiful and thick so I won't need so many. I can't do it in the kitchen, though. How do you want it to look?'

They went upstairs to a small dressing room at the end of the landing. It had a washstand and a small table with a mahogany-framed three-sided mirror standing on it and an upholstered chair. There was a fireplace, a tin bath hanging on the wall and a mahogany towel rail. 'My girls used this room all the time,' Mrs Osborne said wistfully. 'Sit yourself down.' She opened the drawers in the table and took out combs, hairpieces and wool pads, and a china bowl of hair pins. 'From what you've said, you've seen a picture of a Gibson Girl.'

Lettie watched, captivated by Mrs Osborne's deft fingers and, indeed, her own image in the mirror, as her hair took shape. Mrs Osborne kept making appreciative noises in her throat.

'You've got lovely hair, m'ducks, and a very pretty neck,' she said. 'In fact, I'd say this style is a great improvement. It's made you look like the young lady that you are.'

'It's . . . it's beautiful,' Lettie breathed. 'Thank you so much.' Lettie stared at her reflection. 'Do you think I could get a position as a lady's maid somewhere?'

'You might, for a family with a few daughters growing up. You'd certainly be above stairs, a parlourmaid, say. It's usually the head parlourmaid who looks after the daughters.'

Lettie fingered her hair. 'I wonder what Gran will think.'

'Well, leave it up and see. You can keep the padding and the extra hairpiece. You'll need it to do it up yourself. You'll be wanting extra-long hatpins as well. I'll see if I've got any to spare.'

Lettie wished Thomas could have been there to see her. This might change his mind about her being not-grown-up! She decided to walk home without her hat and placed it on top of the vegetables in her basket. As she hurried away from the farmhouse she stood for a moment and looked back fondly at the worn stone frontage. Mr Boyer was visible in the bay window of his bedroom. He was standing in front of his desk, she thought. He must have noticed her but he didn't move; neither did she. She felt pleased that he'd seen her with her hair done up. She didn't look like a servant girl now!

She wondered who his family were and whether they had lots of servants where he came from. To her knowledge there was no one in this part of the Riding called Boyer. It sounded foreign to her, but then he was from overseas according to Mrs Osborne. Canada, she mentioned. Didn't they speak French in Canada? Whoever Mr Boyer was, he was a fine horseman; that much she had noticed in her short association with him.

Lettie was so engrossed in her thoughts about Mr Boyer that she didn't realise she had hurried passed the inn until it was too late. She stopped in her tracks for a second. She had forgotten about Thomas and the coal wagon. He wasn't there, was he? She would have noticed. She would, wouldn't she? Unless he had taken the wagon round the back where it was nearer to the cellar grating? She glanced behind her and there was no sign of either. She put her hand up to touch her hair and wondered what Thomas would have thought of it. But she dare not linger as it was getting late. She shrugged and walked on. There'd be other days to see him.

Chapter 12

Gran was busy laying the table in the dining room when Lettie dumped her baskets on the scullery floor. 'I'm home,' she called.

She heard Gran's footsteps in the hall. 'Where on earth have you been until this hour? I was worried about you.'

'I stayed for tea with Mrs Osborne. You said I should.'

'Yes, but for all this time? I know she likes a chat but— Oh my goodness me! What have you done to yourself?'

Gran was in the kitchen as Lettie straightened up from emptying her baskets. Lettie patted her hair. 'Do you like it? Mrs Osborne did it for me.'

'She did that to you? And you let her?'

Lettie's pleasure in her new appearance drained away. 'I asked her to. I thought it would make me look more . . . more grown up.'

'Grown up? You like some music-hall actress. For goodness' sake, don't let the Reverend see you.'

'But Gran, all the ladies in Sheffield wear their hair this way. It's the fashion.'

'Don't be ridiculous! This is a manse, not some hippodrome.'

She had not expected Gran to be cross with her and Gran's agitation alarmed her. Mrs Osborne had spent ages on her hair and Lettie didn't want to undo all her handiwork but it seemed wise to offer. She said, 'Oh, all right then. I'll go upstairs and brush it out.'

'You haven't time now. The Reverend's been given a brown trout for his tea and I want you to gut it for me.' Normally, Gran did that herself. But the last time she cleaned a trout the Reverend's plate came back littered with a large number of tiny bones that Gran had missed. She simply had not seen them because she couldn't. Lettie had tactfully suggested turning up the lamp on the scullery wall. 'That's a waste of oil,' Gran had said. 'You'll have to clean them in future.'

'It's in the sink,' Gran added. She gazed at Lettie and clicked her tongue. 'Ridiculous,' she repeated.

Lettie blew out her cheeks and lifted an apron carefully over her head. She had been thinking of suggesting to Gran that she apply for a position at Waterley Hall instead of going to Wales. Clearly, now was not a suitable time to mention it. Perhaps Gran would be calmer after she had had her tea? 'What are we having?' she called as she slit the trout's belly.

'I've only time to do cheese and pickles for us,' Gran called back. 'Is the fish ready yet?'

Lettie placed the head and trimmings on an old tin plate for the mission hall cat and took the filleted trout into the kitchen for Gran to fry.

'I took a letter from the Reverend for Wales to the post today,' Gran said.

Lettie realised she had to say something now and it seemed easier if she didn't have to face her grandmother. She took down pots from the dresser to lay one end of the kitchen table for their tea. 'I'm not going to Wales, Gran.'

'I beg your pardon?'

'I don't want to leave you. I don't want to go.'

'And I'll not allow you to throw the Reverend's kindness back in his face.'

'But he isn't being kind if I don't want to go.'

'Sometimes you have to be cruel to be kind. It's for your own good. You have no idea what an opportunity this is for you.'

'There are opportunities here!'

'What opportunities? The bottle factory?'

The spat between them was over quickly. Gran served up the trout in silence and took it through to the Reverend. When she came back she said, 'He has everything he needs now. You can clear away after he goes into his study. I'm not having the Reverend see you all dolled-up. You'll be wearing lip rouge next.'

No I won't, Lettie thought rebelliously. She began to cut the bread, aware that Gran was watching her. 'I could find a position somewhere in the Riding,' she said.

'A teaching position? How?'

'Not teaching, Gran. I'll go into service.'

'You will do no such thing!'

Having mentioned it, Lettie was anxious to explain her reasoning and rushed on, 'But you were very good at it and you've taught me well, so why shouldn't I? I've been thinking about it since I heard there was a vacancy at Waterley Hall—' She stopped suddenly, bewildered by the look of horror that was spreading across Gran's features. 'There's nothing wrong with working in service. I could be a lady's maid and travel,' she finished lamely.

'You will not go to Waterley Hall.' Gran almost choked on her words and put one of her hands on a chair back to support herself.

Lettie immediately picked up the teapot to pour her a cup. 'Sit down, Gran, and tell me why not? Both you and grandfather were in service there and I know that Lady Laughton—'

'Lady Laughton?' Gran glared at Lettie. 'What do know about her?'

Gran's anger silenced Lettie for a moment and she decided to drop the subject. Now was not the time. She finished pouring and moved the milk jug nearer to where Gran was still standing. Gran repeated her question and after a further silence added, 'Well?'

Lettie gave a defensive shrug. 'Only that she is looking for a new maid.'

'Who told you?'

'Mrs Osborne.'

Gran looked sideways out of the window. The nights were drawing in and it would soon be dusk. 'I should

166

have known it was a mistake to let you go anywhere near the Waterley estate. What else has she said about Her Ladyship?'

'Nothing, except that she's a grumpy old lady. Mrs Osborne doesn't know her but Mr Osborne told her. She doesn't seem to be very well liked.'

'Then why do you want to work for her?'

Lettie found this a difficult question to answer without being totally honest and risk upsetting Gran further. The truth was that she wanted to find out more about grandfather – to find anyone who might have known him. She felt a huge sense of urgency to do this before – she shook her head slightly and gazed at her grandmother – before all of these people grew old like Gran. 'I don't,' she answered, 'but neither do I want to go to Wales and I have to do something with my future.' Her answer sounded petulant and feeble. Lettie wished she could explain it more.

'And you would rather fetch and carry for a bad-tempered mistress than be part of a respectable family who will give you a chance to be a pupil teacher in a mission school?'

Lettie looked down at her hands. The answer was yes and put like that it sounded pathetic. 'She might remember you . . . and . . . and grandfather; maybe even my mother and father.'

Gran closed her eyes for a second and sat down with a bump. She put a hand to her breast and began to breathe heavily. When her eyes opened they were wide and wild and her breathing was laboured.

'Gran! What's wrong? What's happening to you?'

Gran's eyes rolled as she struggled to get her breath. 'Fetch the Reverend,' she gasped.

Lettie dashed out of the door yelling, 'Reverend Ennis, come quick! It's Gran!'

He wasn't in the dining room or his study. She guessed he had finished his tea and gone out for his evening constitutional. He often walked after tea when the weather was fine. She rushed back through the kitchen, where Gran was slumped in her chair. 'I'll get you some water,' she said and hurried into the scullery with an earthenware mug.

After a few sips of water, Gran recovered a little. 'I'll help you upstairs to bed,' Lettie said.

'No, it was only my palpitations. I've had them before.'

Lettie frowned. 'But never as bad as this.'

'It's nothing and I'm better now.'

'Well, you don't look it. I think you should go and have a lie-down. I'll bring you some tea on a tray.'

'Well, don't tell the Reverend. I don't want to worry him.'

'You ought to have the doctor, Gran.'

'I'm not ill. Now stop fussing and give me hand up.'

Lettie helped Gran to the bottom of the stairs where Gran said, 'Bring me a chair. I'll sit down a minute before I go up.'

'I really think the Reverend should know you're not well.'

'Nonsense! When he comes in, just tell him I'm overtired. I'll be as right as rain in the morning.'

Lettie waited several minutes for her grandmother to

gather her strength until Gran sent her away to clear the dining room before the Reverend returned. It took Gran a long time to climb the stairs, even with Lettie's help. Eventually Lettie tucked her into bed, propped her up with pillows and said, 'I'll fetch you something to eat. What do you fancy?"

Gran shook her head. 'I can't eat anything. A glass of my tonic will do. Bring me one, will you, dear?'

'Of course I will.'

The next day, Gran's complexion was as grey as her hair and when Lettie took in her early-morning tea she was still in bed. Normally Gran would be up and dressed and lacing her boots.

Gran turned her head on the pillow. 'I think I might have caught a chill or something. Can you help me out of bed, love?'

Lettie placed the cup and saucer carefully on her bedside table. 'Gran, you're really poorly. I've got to tell the Reverend.'

Gran clutched at Lettie's arm. 'Give me your hand, Lettie. I need the po.'

'Can you hang on another minute? I'll fetch the commode from the closet.'

'Good girl.' Gran sank into her pillow.

As soon as Gran was settled back in bed, sitting up and drinking her tea, Lettie said, 'You will let me ask the Reverend to send for the doctor now, won't you?'

Gran nodded and Lettie hurried away to start cooking his breakfast.

For the whole of the following week, Lettie was so busy that she barely had time to think about Waterley Hall, or Mr Boyer, or even Thomas. It was clear to the doctor, the Reverend and now Gran herself what Lettie had known for a while: Gran could not continue in her present role. She was ordered by the doctor to stay in bed and rest.

Lettie stepped into Gran's housekeeping shoes, which fitted her well, and the mission ladies rallied round. By the second Monday, with a washerwoman in for the laundry, her fresh vegetable supplies getting low, and a desperate need to get out of the manse for a change of scenery, Lettie picked up her baskets and set off for Boundary Farm.

Mrs Osborne came out of her kitchen to meet her on the path. 'Ee, m'ducks, how are you? I heard about your granny. How is she now?'

'She's not her normal self yet and the doctor says she's not to do anything strenuous. The Reverend's looking for another housekeeper.'

'Doesn't he want you to take over from her? I'm sure you'd do a grand job.'

'He wants me to go to Wales and train to be a teacher when there's an opening for me. Gran does too.'

Mrs Osborne looked impressed. 'I see. I didn't know you were clever, although I should have guessed. You're like my eldest lad. He has quick wits, too.'

'Is he a teacher?'

'He has green fingers like his father. He's already in charge of the glasshouses at Redfern. He knows all about how they work and how the plants grow and he gives talks at the local institute.'

'You must be very proud of him.'

'I'm proud of all my children, m'ducks. I'm a fortunate old lady.'

Lettie thought that her children were the fortunate ones to have Mrs Osborne for a mother. She smiled and said, 'You're not old,' and they both laughed.

Lettie said she couldn't stop for tea as she had to get back for the Reverend, which was partly true. But with the washing taken care of and cold ham for tea, there was no real rush. If she reached the inn early she might catch Thomas, if he was in the area and if he was looking out for her. Too many ifs and buts, she thought, and pressed her lips together. She hadn't seen or had word of him since before Gran had had her turn and she wanted someone of her own age to talk to.

She hovered outside the inn for over ten minutes straining her ears for a sound of his lorry until the land-lord's buxom daughter came out with frown on her face.

'If you're waiting for that coalman again you're too early. Go away and come back in half an hour.'

'I'd rather wait,' Lettie replied.

'Well, my dad would rather you didn't. We're not some four-ale bar, y'know, with women hanging about outside.'

Lettie blushed to the roots of her hair. 'But I'm not—'

'I know you're not, but our customers don't. Now shift yourself.' The young woman stood her ground until Lettie moved away reluctantly. She went back the way she had

171

come and found a low stone wall to sit on that she hoped was out of sight but within earshot of the inn.

She heard the coal lorry rumble down the road, felt a flutter of pleasure and moved to where she could watch Thomas grasp the iron chain and lift off the heavy cellar grating in the inn yard. He must be quite strong, she thought, although he didn't look stocky like a miner. He took each sack of coal on his back to the open grate and up-ended it into the inn cellar. When he had finished and was enjoying his pint of ale, she stepped forward.

He didn't seem very pleased to see her. 'You're a stranger these days.'

'My gran was taken poorly. I thought you would have heard.'

He shook his head. 'No, I haven't. Is she better now?'

'She had to have the doctor.'

'It's not serious, is it?'

Lettie nodded. 'I've been doing everything at the manse. This is the first time I've been out for a fortnight.'

He stepped closer and she could see the coal dust clinging to his skin. She noticed the sympathy in his eyes and immediately felt better. 'I had no idea. Is she in bed, then?'

'She's got to stay there and rest. It's her heart, you see.'

'Oh, Lettie, I am sorry. No wonder I haven't seen you out and about.'

'I didn't want to leave her at all at first but it's going to take her a long time to get better.'

'You're not doing everything on your own, are you?'

172

'Oh no, some of the mission ladies help out occasionally.' But not often, she thought. Mainly, they visited and chatted to Gran and then left to look after their own families.

'Well, you need a bit of fresh air every now and then. Can you get to the park on Sunday afternoon?'

'Not really. I've got to look after the Reverend as well and Sunday is his busiest day.'

'I'll come round and take you out for a walk.'

Lettie thought that was really kind of Thomas but worried about being seen out with him and word of it getting back to Gran. 'The Reverend might see you,' she muttered.

'I'll wait until he goes to evensong. Take your granny her tea and I'll meet you in the lane behind the pigsty.'

It would be something cheering to look forward to and life wasn't very cheerful for her at present. 'All right, but I don't want anyone to see us.'

'They won't, I promise.'

He smiled and his teeth flashed white against the ingrained coal dust on his skin. 'You look as though you could do with a hug.' She could and she loved him for realising it. He went on, 'Don't worry, I've got four sisters and I know better than to risk dirtying your frock.'

Lettie smiled.

'That's better,' he said.

'How do you do it?' she said.

'Do what?'

'Always raise my spirits.'

'I take after my dad. His glass is never half empty, it's

always half full. So is mine.' He continued to smile at her. 'You might think yours is empty now, but it's not. Things will get better for you.'

'I hope so.' She heard a horse approaching and so did he.

'Best get on with my round,' he said. 'See you on Sunday.'

Four sisters, Lettie marvelled! He had brothers as well. They were a big family and they seemed to be happy. Lettie wished she had brothers and sisters; and a mother and father like Thomas. Goodness! That sounded so disloyal to Gran.

Gran knew the value of brothers and sisters, too. The Reverend's family in Wales would fill a gap in Lettie's upbringing and she ought to go and live with them. But she had to stay here now for Gran. And she had to find out as much as she could about her own family before it was too late. Nobody understood the desperate urgency she felt to do this. People got old and . . . She gulped back the thought. And they died and then it was too late . . .

Thomas cranked the lorry's engine into life and swung himself into the cab. The horse rider approached and Lettie realised she and Thomas had been in full view of the road. She hoped he'd realised they were just friends, passing the time of day. But it was Mr Boyer and she hadn't made a favourable impression on him so far. The words of the innkeeper's daughter ran through her head. *I know you're not, but our customers don't.* She blushed at the thought and put her hands on her cheeks defensively. She felt a piece of gritty coal dust clinging to her skin and looked down at her dress to see a small dusting on the front. It had blown up from an eddy in the yard. She tried to brush it away and only made it more noticeable by smudging.

Mr Boyer reined in his horse as he reached her and stared down. 'Good day, Lettie,' he said. His expression turned from curiosity to distaste. Did he really think she was a woman of easy virtue who hung about outside inns looking to pick up men to pay for her services? She felt she had to explain herself and stuttered, 'T–Thomas is a friend. He delivers coal to the inn.'

'So I see.'

She couldn't think of anything else to say. What was wrong with her? She was not usually tongued-tied. She glanced around for her baskets, located where she had dumped them and hastily took a step in that direction. Her sudden movement caused the horse to shy.

But Mr Boyer had control of the reins and turned the horse's head away from Lettie. She was left standing in the empty inn yard, feeling dusty and dishevelled, watching the well-groomed rump of the horse as it walked away. Mr Boyer sat high in the saddle, haughty and erect. His horse gave a swish of her tail as though swatting Lettie away like a fly.

Lettie slumped against the wall. Why did she feel the need to explain herself to this man? She guessed it would make no difference to him anyway. He'd probably made up his mind about the kind of girl she was – and what he had seen today had simply supported his views. Her anger simmered. He was wrong about her and just as bad as Gran in his prejudice!

175

Nonetheless, she hoped he wouldn't say anything about the incident to Mrs Osborne because she valued that lady's good opinion of her as much as she did her gran's. She wished she didn't have to arrange to see Thomas on Sunday against her Gran's wishes. But he was such a breath of fresh air in her life. She wished also that Gran were more like Mrs Osborne and then she could talk about him. Oh, why was everything so difficult!

Lettie stood in the middle of the empty inn yard and scowled until a farmer rolled out of the back bar towards the privy and leered at her. Hurriedly, she picked up her baskets and scuttled away, feeling inexplicably ashamed of her behaviour. When she arrived home, she was glad that Gran was upstairs in bed and did not see her smudgy face and dress before she cleaned it up.

Chapter 13

As Sunday evening approached, Lettie became more and more apprehensive. She looked forward to getting away from the manse for an hour or so, but where could she and Thomas walk without someone seeing them together? The lane was busy at certain times of the day because miners used it as a short cut from the pithead to the village. But the pit closed on Sunday so perhaps it would be quiet.

It was, but it wasn't deserted. When Lettie let herself out of the back garden gate, she saw a man and woman strolling along. He had his arm around her and her head rested on his shoulder. As soon as they saw her, he loosened his hold and they moved apart so Lettie looked down and pretended to be fixing the gate latch until they had passed her. The shrubs and trees lining the lane were hawthorn, holly and elderberry – too scratchy, she thought, for anyone to hide in them. But Thomas appeared from between them, glanced in each direction then called, 'Over here, Lettie.' He was clean and spruce and smiling.

She inhaled unsteadily and hurried towards him. He held back the thorns, making a pathway through the scrub. 'This way,' he added, 'there's a gap in the fencing ahead of you. Go through and I'll follow you.'

'But that field belongs to the old Farmer Watson. He doesn't like people on his land.'

'He'll be in church so he won't know, will he?'

Lettie hesitated. 'He has a big dog, Thomas.'

'It's chained up in the farmyard. I checked.'

She stopped. 'Even so, I don't want to trespass.'

'I'll go first, then. There is a footpath round the edge. We'll be all right as long as we stick to it. Mind the thorns on your frock as I squeeze by.'

There was plenty of room as it was obvious that others had used this way and broken away branches to form a makeshift track. Thomas helped her through the broken fence into the field. A few cows were grazing idly and over the other side a family group was gathering early blackberries from the hedgerow.

'Who are they, do you reckon?' Thomas said.

'I don't know but they're bound to be villagers. It's too early for town folk to be out blackberrying. I'd better go back.'

'Do you have to? It's a fine evening and you look as though you could do with the fresh air.'

'What do you mean?'

'Only that nursing your granny and housekeeping for the Reverend seem to be wearing you out. You've got dark circles under your eyes.'

'Have I?' Lettie had hardly looked in the mirror recently. She had gone back to plaiting her hair and as soon as she woke in the morning she was too concerned about Gran to worry about her appearance.

He took her hand in his and gave it a gentle tug. 'Come on, Lettie, we'll walk as far as the barn. They might be gone by then.'

She followed Thomas along the path around the edge of the field, enjoying the scent of wild honeysuckle. One or two of Farmer Watson's dairy herd looked up from their chewing. The group picking berries increased in numbers, effectively putting a stop to Thomas's plan.

'Shall we sit by the barn until they've gone?' he suggested.

'I'd rather not. Let's go the other way to the canal bridge.'

'There'll be a lot of couples on the towpath.'

Lettie groaned. 'It's no good. It doesn't matter where we go, somebody will see us.' She heard him sigh. 'I'm sorry,' she muttered.

'I'm the one who's sorry. All we're doing is going for a walk and this secrecy is daft.'

She remembered Mr Boyer's reaction to seeing her outside the inn. 'People can get the wrong idea.'

'Well, your granny can,' he responded tetchily.

'She's ever so poorly, Thomas. I daren't upset her now.'

179

He sighed again, more sympathetically this time. 'I know. Do you want to go back?'

'Yes, please.' But she didn't really. She wanted to ask Thomas about his family and where she might discover more about hers. He seemed to know so much more than she did about, well, about everything that she hadn't learned from books. All Lettie seemed to have learned apart from how to housekeep were stories from the Bible; but only the ones suitable for Sunday school. She wasn't interested enough to root around for the forbidden tales. Thomas had tried his best to raise her spirits and she was upset that he seemed displeased.

They said goodbye in the lane behind the pigsty. 'Will you look out for me at the inn?' she said hopefully.

'If that's what you want.'

He didn't sound very enthusiastic and she wondered if they were still friends. It was the first time he hadn't cheered her up and Lettie went indoors feeling disappointed and frustrated. She made a cup of tea for Gran and took it upstairs. Gran was dozing but she woke as soon as Lettie walked into her bedroom.

'Did you have a nice walk?'

'Yes thank you, Gran.'

'Where did you go?'

'Not far. There were people out blackberrying already.'

'They're early this year.'

'Yes.' Lettie helped Gran to sit up and plumped her pillows.

'Did you see anyone you know?'

'Just a friend.'

'You will be careful who you talk to, won't you? You ought to think again about Eric.'

'We've already discussed him, Gran.'

'Yes, but that was before I was taken poorly and I'm worried about what you'll do when I'm gone.'

'Don't say things like that.'

'I have to. Somebody told the Reverend he saw you speaking to a coalman in the inn yard the other day. What were you doing in the inn yard, Lettie?'

'I was on my way back from Boundary Farm and the coalman was doing his delivery as I went by.'

'Was it the same one that brings out coal from the pithead? I didn't know you knew him.'

'I don't. It wasn't him anyway.' Perhaps now was the time to own up to Gran. 'It was Thomas, Gran. When Mr Adley got rid of him he went to work for Toogoods. He can drive a wagon, you know.'

'Oh, Lettie,' Gran groaned, 'and you stopped to talk to him. What were you thinking of?'

'I was only telling him how pleased I was that he'd got another job. I wish you'd give him a chance, Gran. He's not a roughneck, honest, he isn't.'

Gran looked weary; worn out and grey. 'You haven't listened to a word I've said to you, have you?'

'I have. But you're wrong about Thomas.'

'Well, you don't want to be settling down with the first lad who turns your head.'

'I never said I wanted to settle down with him.'

'Well, you shouldn't be leading him on, then, because he'll think you do.'

'No, he won't!' Lettie felt quite irritated that Gran had made this leap in her imagination. 'We're friends, that's all.' But she wasn't even sure about that any more.

'Young fellows want more than friendship with a girl.'

Eric Jones certainly did. She wondered what Gran would say if she told her about Eric's behaviour. 'Maybe,' Lettie shrugged.

Gran handed the cup and saucer to Lettie. Then she closed her eyes for a minute and kept them closed as she spoke. 'Men do, you know. They want everything and they'll want it before they wed you if you'll let them.'

Lettie didn't need to be told that after her experience with Eric. 'I do know about these things, Gran. You don't have to worry about me.'

'Oh, but I do. You don't know how persuasive men can be, and how dishonest.'

'The Reverend isn't like that.'

'He's different, and you . . . well, you always see the best in folk.'

Until they prove otherwise, Lettie thought. She said, 'Is that such a bad thing?'

'No, but you can't let them have their way with you. You mustn't ever, not with anyone, not before he marries you.'

Lettie's eyes widened. What on earth had brought this on? Even in her most rebellious mood Lettie wouldn't dream of doing anything like that!

'Gran, you know I wouldn't.'

'You say that but men can be persuasive. They're crafty. They say they love you when they don't and then it's too late.' Gran reached out her hand and placed it over

182

Lettie's on the bed sheet. 'I want you to make me a solemn promise. I mean it, Lettie, I want you to swear on the Bible. Fetch it from the bookcase.'

Lettie carried the heavy book over to the bed. She often read from it to Gran when she asked. She placed it on the bedcover.

'Put your hand on it and promise.'

'Promise what, Gran?'

'Swear by almighty God with your hand on His holy book, that you will never, ever, have relations with a man before you wed him. I shan't rest easy unless I know you mean it. Promise me, Lettie,' Gran repeated.

Lettie didn't think it was necessary and felt cross that Gran didn't have enough faith in her without this little show. But Gran was a poorly old lady and Lettie loved her, so she placed her hand on the Bible and made her pledge. Gran seemed hugely relieved afterwards. Her head lolled to one side on the pillow, she closed her eyes and dozed.

Lettie sat with her, staring out of the window. Something in the past had happened to make Gran behave in this way and Gran had stated quite firmly that Lettie wasn't born out of wedlock. She supposed she might well have been conceived before marriage because that was a common occurrence. Or, Lettie realised, perhaps it was her mother Ruth who had been on the way when Gran made her vows at the altar? Was that why she thought grandfather was wicked? Surely that wasn't such a wicked thing to do? But it seemed a much more likely explanation to Lettie.

*　*　*

Gran's health improved slowly and Lettie continued to nurse her and run the manse, leaving her little time to think about herself. One or two of the mission ladies came in occasionally but they had their own homes to run as well as their welfare visits. Mrs Jones, however, had a housekeeper and a girl for the rough work so she had more free time and was only too pleased to help out for the Reverend. Mrs Jones was a good cook, her baking especially, and her pies and cakes were a welcome addition to the Reverend's pantry. She eased Lettie's workload significantly but she came with a special purpose of her own. Lettie soon realised that Mrs Jones had not given up the notion of a match between her Eric and Lettie.

Lettie's move to Wales was postponed until Gran was on her feet again. Secretly, Lettie didn't believe Gran would ever be back to her full strength but she went along with the possibility for Gran's sake. Apparently, the Reverend and Mrs Jones were of the same mind because at one of her visits, the older lady mentioned quite casually, 'The Reverend will have to find himself a new housekeeper one day.'

Lettie was drying her hands in the scullery. 'Please don't say that to Gran, will you?' she said anxiously. Mrs Jones's visits gave Lettie an opportunity to walk over to Boundary Farm and she had been looking forward to it until that remark.

'Of course not, my dear. We all want her to get better. It's you I am thinking of. You've shown everybody what a good little housekeeper you can be. You're a credit to your grandmother.'

'Thank you, Mrs Jones.'

'You know, my Eric was very taken by you.'

Lettie was pinning her hat on in the hall. Mrs Jones, with her fashionably elaborate grey hair and intricate blouse, came up behind her so that Lettie could see her image in the mirror. 'We rushed you a bit,' Mrs Jones went on, 'but you will suit him very well. We all understand that you've lived a sheltered life here at the manse and my Eric will look after you.' Mrs Jones smiled and raised her eyebrows.

Lettie had two hatpins in her mouth, which prevented her from replying.

Mrs Jones continued as she strolled away towards the kitchen, 'When your grandmother is better, you must bring her to tea with me and Mr Jones because Mr Jones would very much like to meet you properly.'

Lettie fixed her hat, and bit back her response, scowling at herself in the mirror. From what she knew about Eric and his father, they were two of a kind and the Joneses were the last family she wanted to associate with, let alone marry into. But she couldn't refuse to take Gran for tea with them when she was well enough. She replied, 'Thank you, Mrs Jones, I'll ask Gran.'

Mrs Jones stopped with her hand on the kitchen door-knob. 'Oh, I've already done that. She's looking forward to it.'

Lettie felt cornered and her anger bubbled as she walked briskly to Boundary Farm. She wanted to unburden her irritation in some way, to talk to someone, and Mrs Osborne was a willing listener. Lettie asked her if she would show her how to do her hair again, but not quite

185

so elaborate this time so she could pin her hat on to go home.

Mrs Osborne was delighted. 'Are you meeting that coalman at the inn again?'

'How did you now about him?'

'Mr Boyer saw you. You shouldn't be loitering outside an inn, m'ducks. I had to explain to him that he was mistaken about you as you lived in a manse and went to chapel.'

'Thomas is a friend,' Lettie said defensively.

'Well, he's a nice enough lad but you're a right lovely lass, well brought up and with your wits about you. You'd be a good catch for him and you could do better, m'ducks.'

Not Mrs Osborne as well! Lettie thought she would have been less critical of Thomas than Gran. 'I said he's just a friend,' she repeated. 'But I've been told that I have got a . . . a suitor.'

'Not this Thomas, then?'

'No. It's someone I don't really like. He seems to be keen on me, though. I've said no to him once already.'

'Oh, that's a fellow for you. They're all the same. If he's set his cap at you, he won't give up easily. You see it's all about you being *his* woman for all the world to see.'

Lettie frowned. 'He was very persistent and, well, he, you know . . . wanted to kiss me . . . and more.'

'Did he now? Your grandmother has told you that if you let him have his way with you, he's landed you at the altar as far as he's concerned?'

'Oh, I wouldn't do anything foolish. Honest I wouldn't.

Gran has made me promise not to, not before I'm married anyway.'

'So you do know what I'm talking about?'

'Y-y-yes.'

'And that even a gentleman can be very persuasive.' *Persuasive* – Gran had used that word, too, Lettie thought. Mrs Osborne continued, 'He'll tell you he loves you and all that.'

Lettie was decisive. 'Well, if he did and he was lying I wouldn't marry him.'

'Ah, but if you were in the family way, m'ducks, you'd have to get wed, wouldn't you?'

Goodness! Mrs Osborne didn't mince her words. 'I suppose you would,' she answered.

'There's no suppose about it, m'ducks.' Mrs Osborne smiled. 'That's what he'd be hoping for; hooked and in his keep net.'

Lettie wasn't happy to be likened to a salmon or a trout but she understood Mrs Osborne's meaning. It went some way to explaining Eric's behaviour towards her.

'Or worse, m'ducks,' Mrs Osborne went on, 'if he decided he didn't love you after all and threw you back into the stream.'

'Well, how do I know if he really loves me?' she demanded.

'How do you know if you really love him? It cuts both ways, m'ducks. But you'll know when it happens, believe me. Shall we do your hair before tea?'

Lettie spent a pleasant hour padding and pinning up her hair herself under Mrs Osborne's helpful guidance.

'You have a good eye for making the best of yourself,' the older lady said. 'And you're always clean and tidy. Have you thought any more about Waterley Hall? Lady Laughton is definitely looking for a new maid. I asked Mr Osborne to make sure. But,' Mrs Osborne lowered her voice as she continued, 'she's a crotchety old biddy and it's more of a nursemaid than a lady's maid she needs these days.'

'I'd like to apply but I can't leave Gran yet.'

'I thought the Reverend was getting his mission ladies to rally round?'

'Mrs Jones is helping out. She makes pies for the Reverend for me to warm up in the oven so I can see to Gran.'

'Is your granny not up and about yet?' Mrs Osborne frowned and pulled down the corners of her mouth.

Lettie chewed on her lip and shook her head. 'The doctor says she has to take her time. Before she took poorly she was planning to send me to Wales to stay with the Reverend's sister but I'm not going now. I didn't want to go anyway. I wanted to stay here and find out about my mother.'

'Don't you know anything about her?'

'Not really. Gran won't talk about the past. It upsets her.'

'Perhaps it's best if you don't find out then, m'ducks.'

'But if Gran is hiding something then it only makes me more curious. I know my mother was called Ruth yet I can't find out where she's buried. She's not with grandfather in Waterley Hall churchyard.'

'She must have moved away when she was wed. All my girls did. There might be nothing for you to find out around here.'

Lettie didn't argue. But she thought there might be a servant still at Waterley Hall from the old days when Grandfather was butler. If there was he would remember him, and Gran too. Long-serving maids and footmen who hadn't married were sometimes allowed to stay on when they grew old if the alternative was the work-house, especially if they could still see to sew or clean boots. A position at Waterley Hall would enable Lettie to ask questions.

Chapter 14

Gran's pallid colour remained despite all the bed rest, doctoring and nurturing care from Lettie. It was even tiring for her to sit out of bed to eat her dinner; not that she ever ate very much. Summer was turning into autumn and one day, at the Reverend's suggestion, Lettie lit a fire in the Reverend's front room. She and Mrs Jones helped Gran down the stairs for a change of scenery. But it was far too exhausting for Gran and her palpitations returned. She took her medicine, which calmed her down, but she couldn't summon up the strength to climb back upstairs so Lettie had to make up a bed on the couch for her. The Reverend was so concerned he called the doctor in again. The doctor recommended a proper convalescent home for Gran, at the seaside.

'We have a Methodist one in the East Riding,' the Reverend said. 'It's near Filey, I believe. I'll make enquiries.' He went into his study and Mrs Jones accompanied the doctor to the front door.

'Well, I guess I'll have to go,' Gran confided to Lettie, 'if it's the only way I'll get my strength back. I'm not ready to meet my maker just yet.'

'It won't be for ever, Gran.'

'I hope not but you won't be able to stay here without me. The Reverend will have to find a new housekeeper.'

Lettie was fighting back her tears, none of which were for her own dilemma. If Gran thought that about herself she was aware that she had, if anything, become weaker during the last few weeks. 'I'll ask if I can come with you,' she said.

Gran gave a rare, though weak, smile. 'I'd like that. I'm sure the Reverend will know a family you can lodge with. Then I can see you every day.'

Lettie managed to return her smile. 'I'll talk to him tomorrow.'

'Whatever he says, dear, you must promise me you'll do as the Reverend asks. He will be your guardian when I'm gone.'

'That won't be for a long time yet, but I promise.'

Gran lay back and closed her eyes. 'You're a good girl, Lettie. I'm proud of you.'

At Mrs Jones's suggestion, the Reverend sent a neighbour for Eric to carry Gran upstairs to bed. He was very polite to her in front of his mother but kept smiling at Lettie in a manner she could only describe

191

as a smirk. Lettie was thankful he was busy with his new school. He could not stay long and Lettie soon forgot about him.

She sat through the night with Gran, dozing from time to time in a fireside chair. Instead of being the resilient old lady that Lettie loved so dearly, Gran seemed to shrink before her eyes into a fragile birdlike creature. Her body had worn itself out, but her mind was still active and Gran was a fighter. 'I'll be fine as long as you're with me, Lettie,' she murmured frequently.

Reverend Ennis was sympathetic but he was hard working and his duties never diminished. When Lettie spoke with him in his study the following day, he was thankful for a solution and agreed to contact the mission in the East Riding to find lodgings for Lettie. 'Think of it as a holiday,' he said to her.

'I shall be able to read to her every morning as well as evening,' Lettie responded. 'She enjoys that. Have you finished with your newspaper?'

He hesitated. 'Er, no, not yet.' He glanced down at the wastepaper basket where it rested.

Lettie frowned. It wasn't yesterday's paper — she had read that one to Gran last night. She bent down to retrieve it. 'It must have fallen off your desk.'

The Reverend took it quickly from her grasp. 'Thank you, Lettie. I'll finish it after supper.' He paused. 'The doctor said your grandmother tires easily so I hope you don't keep her awake too long.'

'She insists that I read all of the paper to her. She does like to keep up with the news, sir.'

'Even so, she is very ill. Give the readings a miss tonight.' He nodded at her, expecting her agreement.

'Very well. She will be happy to hear that I can go with her to Filey.'

Gran was put out when Lettie said she wouldn't be reading. 'The Reverend asked me not to,' she explained. 'The doctor advised him. You have to rest.'

Gran grunted. 'What about a bible reading, then?'

'Not tonight, Gran. I'll ask the Reverend about that tomorrow.'

'Don't bother. I'll ask him myself when he comes in to say goodnight.'

In the past she had read to Gran by lamplight in her bedroom and learned what was happening in the Riding at the same time. No matter how tired Lettie was, it was still a part of the day that she looked forward to and she was as disappointed as Gran. She tidied the bedroom, picked up Gran's supper tray and stood in the open doorway.

'Goodnight, Gran,' she said. The doctor's sleeping draught was taking effect and she would be fast asleep by the time the Reverend tapped on her door later.

Lettie always waited in the kitchen until the Reverend retired. He was an early riser so he didn't sit up late. As soon as she heard the landing floorboards creak she raked out the fire ashes, and placed the kindling for tomorrow in the hearth. Then she crept into his study to retrieve the discarded newspaper intending to read it by lamplight in her own bedroom. It wasn't anywhere to be seen.

Her disappointment drove her to search the scullery

where clean old newspapers were kept to be torn into squares and threaded on a string for the privy. She carried her lamp through but it wasn't there either. She found it eventually outside the back door under the pig bucket to be added to the straw bedding in the sty. Well, the pig can sleep on it after I've read it, she thought.

As soon as she saw the front page her attention was riveted by the picture and headline.

LADY LAUGHTON DIES

The grainy photograph was of a much younger Lady Laughton, severe and formal, looking like a smaller version of old Queen Victoria before she died. Lettie sat down at the kitchen table and read, surprised to find out that she had been much older than Lord Laughton and previously married to his cousin; second cousin, it said. That meant their fathers had been first cousins. Between them the cousins owned the Laughton South Riding steelworks and east coast shipyards where Lord Laughton's fabled wealth came from. As a young woman, the newspaper reported, Lady Laughton had led a charmed life that was, sadly, beset by tragedy and she had withdrawn from public life many years ago.

No wonder she was a crabby old lady, thought Lettie, as she pieced together the scraps of information. She had had three daughters with her first husband, none of whom had survived infancy. 'Poor woman,' Lettie said out loud.

Her marriage to Lord Laughton, as everyone knew, was childless. It didn't say but Lettie guessed she had been past her childbearing years when she married him. Good heavens, she thought. It was known for older men to marry young women and although one or two gossips raised their eyebrows nobody questioned the sense of it, especially if the man had an income and his own home. But for an older woman to marry a younger man was almost unheard of! Well, they hadn't lived together for years so Lettie reckoned the marriage hadn't worked.

'I don't expect they loved each other,' she said to the kitchen shadows.

There was more about Lady Laughton's father who had been in shipping in the days of sail. He had transported raw pig iron from Russia and Sweden across the North Sea for the South Riding steel industry, where the abundant coal had contributed to making Sheffield the steel capital of the world. And at the end of the paragraph, Lettie read a telling sentence that made her think the Reverend knew what he was talking about when he preached that riches don't bring happiness. *She was his only surviving child and heiress to his fortune.* Lady Laughton's life had been an unhappy one, she thought. Even the rich have their tragedies.

She read the article again. Gran had never liked the Laughtons but she had worked for them as a younger woman. She would want to hear about Lady Laughton's death yet the Reverend had seen fit to keep it from her, from them both actually. He hadn't wanted Lettie to see it either, or he would have left the newspaper in the scullery for the privy.

Lettie blew out her cheeks. It would bring back memories for Gran, perhaps very distressing memories, so she respected the Reverend's wisdom. She put the newspaper back under the pig bucket and decided not to mention it.

But of course Lady Laughton's death was big news in Waterley Edge and gossip was rife in the town as well. The Reverend could not stop his mission ladies from talking so eventually Gran heard about it from one of them who came to visit. It was Monday, the day that Lettie helped the washerwoman. She was turning the mangle when the Reverend came into the wash house.

In the steamy heat, Lettie's face was red with effort and she was in her oldest gown covered by a sacking apron. The Reverend seemed quite taken aback by her appearance as she wiped her wet hands down the apron and pushed her damp hair under an equally damp cap.

'Is something amiss, sir?' She stepped outside, glad of the cooling breeze.

'One of my helpers said your grandmother had a bit of a turn when Lady Laughton's name came up in their conversation. I have sent her to fetch the doctor. You must come in and sit with her until he arrives.'

The washerwoman nodded in agreement and Lettie went indoors with the Reverend. He went on: 'She has taken one of her powders and is resting but it really is best not to speak to her of Waterley Hall or its former occupants at all.'

'Of course,' Lettie agreed. 'Do you know what happened, Reverend?'

'What do you mean?'

'What happened in the old days to make Gran hate the Laughtons so much?'

'You ought not to listen to gossip, Lettie. Your grand-mother has assured me she has told you all you need to know. If she chooses not to say more it is for your benefit. Look forward to your future, Lettie, not backwards to the past.'

But Lettie found that difficult when she was unsure of who her father was and therefore who she was. Why shouldn't she want to find out about her own parents? Surely she had a right to know where they were buried. However, she managed a smile and said, 'Very well, sir.'

The doctor said Gran wasn't any worse, but she wasn't any better either and exposing her to more anxiety might make her condition deteriorate. He lectured Lettie on keeping her calm at all times. Lettie agreed with every-thing the gentleman said. However, Gran was Gran and she couldn't change her nature. Her mind was still active and it needed occupying.

The Reverend decided that from now on Lettie should devote most of her day to Gran. Mrs Jones would take over his housekeeping and employ help. Lettie was relieved of some of her chores, notably the cleaning, ironing and scrubbing out, and this gave her plenty of time to spend with Gran. She was able to make sure the sick room was always fresh, keep Gran's hair looking dressed and tidy and prepare all the little delicacies that were Gran's favour-ites. And have time to sit and talk to her.

'Did you know about Lady Laughton?' Gran demanded one evening.

Lettie felt uncomfortable. 'I saw it in the newspaper. It was the one the Reverend asked me not to read to you.'

Gran sounded critical when she said, 'I wonder what Her Ladyship will have to say for herself when she meets her maker.'

'Surely she wasn't all bad?' Lettie ventured.

'No and I'll not speak ill of the dead. She didn't have a happy life and now she's gone.'

That echoed Lettie's own sentiments. 'Money isn't everything,' she said.

'Huh. Tell that to your grandfather. When's the funeral?'

'Soon, I think.' Lettie hadn't taken note of the date, although she did remember that present and former servants were invited to attend the service. 'Shall I ask the Reverend?'

Gran shook her head. 'I couldn't go anyway. It'll be in their private church.'

'I expect there will be enough mourners to fill it.'

'I mean I'm not strong enough to travel there and stand for any length of time yet.'

Lettie, aware that she ought to move their conversation away from Waterley Hall, said, 'The doctor's advised fresh air if you're well wrapped up. He suggested I take you out in a Bath chair when the weather is fine. The Reverend is trying to get hold of one for you. I can take you to chapel or to the mission hall.'

Her grandmother stared at the window. 'I'd like to see the old witch lowered into the ground.'

'Gran!' Lettie was shocked. 'That isn't very charitable of you.'

'No and neither was she. It wasn't my fault her husband left her but she dismissed me all the same. Nevertheless, I ought to pay my last respects.'

'Shall I go on your behalf? I'm sure folk will understand.'

'No, they won't!' Gran tried to sit up in bed. 'I don't want you there! It's bad enough you sneaking up there to find your grandfather's grave without you publicly mourning any of them.'

'But – but – I thought – please calm down, Gran. Remember what the doctor said.'

Oh dear, somehow Lettie had said the wrong thing. Gran had brought up the subject so what should she have done? Made some excuse to go out of the room? Yes, she should have done that; that's what she would do next time. Meanwhile Gran had started to breathe heavily and this increased her anxiety, which made her breathing more laboured. Lettie became alarmed. 'I'll mix you a powder,' she said. She poured some water into a glass from the carafe on her bedside table.

Gran shook her head wordlessly and waved her hand to say no, but Lettie ignored her. She hurried round the bed to Gran's marble-topped washstand, opened one of the packets, tipped it into the water and stirred it vigor-ously with a spoon.

'Come on, Gran, doctor's order.' She supported her head while, thankfully, Gran drank the draught. She gasped and choked as she swallowed. Lettie fretted as she held her hand and stroked her brow until, eventually, Gran's breathing calmed. It seemed like an age to Lettie and when it was over Gran looked even older and greyer, more tired and worn out. Lettie made her comfortable and when her powder took effect and Gran was dozing, she went downstairs, tapped on the study door and went straight in.

The Reverend looked up from his desk and peered at her over the reading spectacles perched on his nose. 'What is it, Lettie? I'm very busy.'

'I know and I shouldn't disturb you if it wasn't important but Gran's had another turn.'

The Reverend rose to his feet.

'She's sleeping now,' Lettie added quickly. 'But she looks much worse. Please can I fetch the doctor?'

'Of course. Call in the mission as you pass and send round one of the ladies. I'll sit with her until you get back.'

'Thank you, Reverend.'

Later that evening, Lettie took a tray of tea into the front room where the doctor was speaking to the Reverend and Mrs Jones.

'Come and sit down, Lettie,' Mrs Jones said. 'I'll pour.'

'Thank you.' Lettie was grateful to sit down for a few minutes. 'How is she, Doctor?'

'Sleeping, but she needs someone with her all the time now.'

'I'll stay with her,' Lettie said. 'I can sleep in the chair.'

'She is lucky to have you,' the doctor said. 'She's too ill for convalescence and anyway she is now too weak to travel. Rest and light nourishment is all she needs at present.' He drank his tea.

Mrs Jones took his empty cup. 'I'll ask if there's a room at our House of Help in town.'

The doctor shook his head. 'A move like that will put

too much of a strain on her heart, and they couldn't give her the nursing that she has here. She's more comfortable with those who love her.'

'Will she get any of her strength back, sir?' Lettie asked quietly.

The doctor leaned forward. 'With you to care for her, my dear, she is in the very best hands. It is important for you to keep up her spirits,' he glanced at the Reverend, 'and pray for her.'

A cold hand clutched at Lettie's heart. Gran wasn't going to get better. The Reverend had said prayers for Gran every Sunday since her first attack and it hadn't helped. She said, 'She'd like to go to chapel on Sundays. She misses it.'

'You could try but it might be too much for her. Did you manage to locate a Bath chair?'

Reverend Ennis answered, 'Yes, one of our elders has one in his outhouse. He will deliver it tomorrow.'

The doctor smiled. 'I'm sure that will do her as much good as anything I can prescribe. Give her what she wants.'

Lettie could hardly speak. This was much worse than she had realised. Gran might be, might be . . . might be . . . she stifled a sob rising in throat and croaked, 'How much time does she have left, Doctor?'

'It is very difficult for me to say in your grandmother's case, Miss Hargreaves. Her mind is strong but another attack like this one will further weaken her heart and it can only take so much.'

'Is there anything else I can do to help her?'

'You must keep her quiet. Any anxiety at all could precipitate another attack. I'll leave you some of the powders that help to calm her and a script for more.'

'Thank you.'

They stared silently at each other until Mrs Jones said, 'Would you care for another cup of tea, Doctor?'

He stood up. 'Thank you, no. I have two more patients to visit this evening.'

The Reverend accompanied him to the front door and Mrs Jones began to re-stack the tray. 'Don't worry, my dear,' she said, 'we're all here to help you.'

Lettie stared at the gas light, hissing on the wall. Installing the electric had been postponed while Gran was ill. She was all the family Lettie had. She had always been here for her, looking after her, teaching her, guiding her, chastising her and occasionally, yes occasionally, praising her.

'Why don't you?' Mrs Jones was speaking to her from the doorway, holding the loaded tray in her hands.

Lettie roused herself. 'Beg pardon, what was it you said?'

'I said why don't you go to bed and get some proper sleep while I see to these. I'll sit with her tonight and someone will be in to give you a hand in the morning.'

'You're all so kind.'

'It's what the mission does. You should think about joining us when . . . well, think about it anyway.'

Lettie nodded, sighed and stood up. She felt drained of all her energy and had to drag her feet up the stairs. But when she was in bed she found it difficult to sleep.

Gran wasn't going to get better. The doctor had all but said those words and that, with Lettie's care, she could still enjoy her last few weeks.

Lettie doubted it. Gran had needed to be kept busy and involved in chapel affairs. How satisfied would she be with little to look forward to except sitting in a Bath chair at her bedroom window and watching the world pass by? Of course, no one need tell her how poorly she was and Lettie could continue to make plans for her future. But Gran still had her wits and she knew her granddaughter well. Lettie would find it difficult to keep the truth from her. She fell asleep worrying.

Fortunately she did not have to carry the nursing burden totally alone as Mrs Jones arranged a supply of older ladies to sit with Gran and read to her. All understood the strict instruction to avoid any reference to the Laughtons or Waterley Hall. But the effect on Lettie of this ban only served to inflame her curiosity about the past and there was absolutely no possibility of questioning Gran now. She considered asking the Reverend what he knew but on reflection realised that her interest was likely to worry him and he had enough to deal with. Chapel work had not reduced because Gran was ill. If anything he had more to do and during quiet times, when others relieved her of her sick-room duties, Lettie sorted out meetings for the Reverend, kept the chapel accounts in order and informed Gran on her work. Chapel business was a safe topic of conversation.

Occasionally Lettie opened letters for the Reverend and placed them in neat stacks according to the type of response needed. At the end of each day she tidied his desk and emptied his wastepaper basket, retrieving the newspaper to take to her bedroom for later reading before it was put out for the privy or the pig.

Each week brought speculation from a reporter on the future of Waterley Hall and its former occupants. Would Lady Laughton's estranged husband attend her funeral? Would he return to Yorkshire or sell up in favour of his self-indulgent life in London and abroad? Who would buy Waterley Hall if he sold it? Lettie wished that she had time to visit Boundary Farm where, she was sure, Mrs Osborne would have some answers.

One Tuesday afternoon, when Gran was sleeping after her dinner, Mrs Jones came into the sick room and said, 'Mrs Osborne is downstairs.'

'She's here! Does she want to see Gran?'

'She's asking after you. She brought vegetables and fruit with her. I've shown her into the drawing room. Go down and thank her. You can make her a cup of tea while I sit with your grandmother.'

'Thank you. Gran's had a powder. She'll sleep for at least an hour.'

Mrs Osborne gave Lettie a hug and was so sympathetic that she wanted to cry.

Lettie sniffed. 'Gran's asleep at the moment. Did you want to see her?'

'I did, but I can wait until she wakes. I've missed your company, m'ducks.'

'Would you like some tea?'

'Oh, don't bother with all that yet. Come and sit here

beside me. Who is looking after you?' Mrs Osborne emphasised the 'you'.

'Oh, I'm all right.' Lettie yawned. 'Beg pardon, Mrs Osborne. I do most of the nights with Gran so the other ladies can be home with their families.'

'You sit up all night with her?'

'She likes to see I'm there if she wakes, and I don't want her falling out of bed. I usually read the Bible to her until she falls asleep and then I read to myself until I doze. The clock chimes in the hall always rouse me, though. When she wakes I help her to sit on the commode while I make the bed. Then I give her a drink or a powder if she wants one.'

'Can you go back to your own bed then?'

Lettie shook her head. 'It's hard for her to breathe so she has to stay sitting up. She might choke if she lolls over.'

'I see. She's really very poorly, then. Folk said she was. It must be tiring for you.'

'I don't mind. She's my gran and I love her. The Reverend lets me keep the lamp burning and I catch up on my reading.'

'You must know your bible backwards by now.'

'I read the newspaper mainly. I can just about stay awake for that!'

'How long do you think you'll be able to keep it up, m'ducks?'

Lettie didn't answer. She hadn't given the future a second thought. Mrs Osborne raised her eyebrows expecting an answer and Lettie shrugged. 'As long as it takes,' she said.

'You'll have read what's been going on at Waterley Hall, then?'

'We don't discuss it in the manse. It upsets Gran.'

'Well, it's the talk of Waterley Edge, and in the town, too.'

'Has Mr Osborne heard anything?'

'Oh aye, m'ducks. He doesn't say much, as you know, but he reckons His Lordship will come home now she's gone. It's whether he'll bring his floozy with him that folk really want to know. He can marry her now, of course. Oh dear me, look at your face. I've shocked you, haven't I?'

Chapter 15

Lettie was astounded. 'I hadn't heard anything about a floozy,' she murmured. No wonder Gran didn't approve of him, she thought.

'Well, Mr Osborne says that's why he left Her Ladyship in the first place. He and Lady Laughton never got on. They didn't even like each other, apparently.'

'Then why did they marry?'

'Isn't that obvious, m'ducks? She owned half of the fortune. His Lordship couldn't risk her being wed to somebody else and that somebody else muscling in on his empire. Mr Osborne says she never forgave her first husband for dying on her or her second one for going off with his floozy.'

'My gran thinks they were both as bad as each other.'

'Your granny's a wise old lady.'

'Yes, but when you go up to see her, you mustn't mention any of this. Promise me you won't. It was hearing about Lady Laughton that brought on her attack. She'll ask you as well so you have to be prepared to make an excuse and change the subject. We really don't talk about the Laughtons in the manse.'

'Well, if you say so, m'ducks.'

'I'll go up with you. I try to get her to sit in the Bath chair in the afternoons and wheel her to the window.'

'I can give you a hand with that.' Mrs Osborne put her head on one side. 'How are you getting on with that young fellow of yours?'

'Thomas? I've barely seen him since Gran took bad.' They hadn't parted on very good terms so she guessed he'd lost interest in her.

'Not the coalman. Didn't you say you had a follower?'

'A follower? Oh, you mean Eric, Mrs Jones's son?'

'Is that the young man? Isn't he the new head teacher at the village school?'

'I've really not had time to think about him, Mrs Osborne,' Lettie replied decisively. 'I've had other things on my mind.'

'I see. Out of sight, out of mind.'

Lettie supposed that was true because she hadn't thought about Eric since he'd called to carry Gran upstairs and the only time she'd remembered Thomas was when the coal was delivered last week. She had wondered how he was getting on at Toogoods and had experienced a pang of disloyalty towards him because she had spoiled their last afternoon together. On the whole she preferred not to talk about either of them and said the first thing that came into her head. 'Has Mr Boyer gone home to Canada?'

'Mr Boyer?'

As soon as Mrs Osborne repeated his name with her querulous tone, Lettie wished she hadn't asked. The truth was, thoughts of Mr Boyer had frequently crossed her mind, especially in those long wakeful night-time hours. She was intrigued by his presence and attracted to him despite his cold and distant manner.

She gave what she hoped was a nonchalant shrug. 'I just wondered if he was still staying with you at Boundary Farm.'

'Well, he is and he isn't, so to speak. He still has the front bedroom but he's been away more than he's been in there lately and Mr Osborne said he saw him at Waterley Hall when the lawyers were in talking to the servants.'

'I wonder what that was about.'

'It's whether they've still got positions there, m'ducks. Mr Osborne is a tenant so he's seeing a lawyer himself about his lease. You never know what'll happen when there's been a death. Shall we have that cup of tea, after all?'

Lettie rose to her feet. 'The kettle's already on the hob. Mrs Jones will come down and tell me when Gran wakes up.'

'I'll come through with you and tell you all about my girls.'

Two shopping baskets overflowing with early-autumn vegetables and fruit sat on the kitchen table.

'Goodness, Mrs Osborne, it's like the Harvest Festival already! The Reverend will be pleased.'

'I'll unpack them for you. Where shall I put them?'

'Just pile them in the scullery sink. Not the fruit, though. Did I see some grapes?'

'They're for your grandmother. They were Lady Laughton's favourite.'

'I'd better not tell that to Gran. How did you get here with all this?'

'Mr Boyer bought that trap he hired and he allows Mr Osborne to use it when he's away.'

'That's very kind of him.'

'Yes it is, isn't it? He's a bit stiff and starchy sometimes but underneath he's a thoroughly decent fellow.'

'Have you any idea what his business is in the South Riding?'

'I wish I did, but I know better than to poke my nose in where it's not wanted.'

Lettie took this as a mild rebuke and changed the subject. 'Is Mr Osborne with you, then? Will he join us for tea?'

'He's gone on into town. He'll call for me on his way back.'

Mrs Jones left as soon as Gran woke and Lettie spent a pleasant afternoon with Mrs Osborne and Gran, who was cheered by her chatter and enjoyed the grapes. Lettie left them to each other's company while she went downstairs to deal with the vegetables and clean out Mrs Osborne's baskets. Before Mrs Osborne left Lettie promised her she would find a couple of hours soon to visit her on the farm. 'It'll do you good to get out,' she said and Lettie agreed.

As she tidied the scullery at the end of the day she noticed the latest newspaper at the top of the pile. The Reverend must have taken it straight out there instead of placing it in the wastepaper basket and when she turned it over she saw why. The headline shouted at her.

LORD LAUGHTON RETURNS TO WATERLEY HALL
Speculation that absent landlord will return to his native Yorkshire

Lettie gazed at the grainy print of a photograph and guessed it had been taken a few years ago when Lord Laughton was much younger. He looked very handsome in his country tweeds, a shotgun in his hand and a couple of black gun dogs at his feet. A line of servants filled the background. He certainly appeared to be a wealthy and aristocratic country gentleman. Lettie took a minute to scan part of the lengthy article on his achievements then tucked the newspaper underneath the bib of her apron, planning to read it in bed before she went to sleep.

But the lady who was due to sit with Gran that night sent word to say her husband had been taken poorly and she couldn't leave him until the doctor had been. Lettie could have asked the mission to send someone else but it seemed an imposition as they were all busy ladies. She was already here and volunteered to sit up again. She had her paper to read for when Gran fell asleep and, sensibly,

211

left it in her own bedroom until Gran's powder took effect.

She crept along the landing to retrieve it as soon her grandmother's breathing slowed into the slumbering rhythm she recognised. When she returned, Gran looked peaceful. Lettie stroked her brow very gently, pushed back a straying lock of grey hair and bent to give her a light kiss on her forehead. Gran didn't stir. The new powders were stronger. The doctor had said that quiet rest was Gran's best treatment now. Lettie spread the newspaper on the counterpane and drew the lamp closer.

As she read she realised that Lord Laughton certainly lived life high off the hog. He and his late cousin, Lady Laughton's first husband, had built on their fathers' earlier fortunes in steel-making and shipbuilding. The report mentioned another cousin, too, who had married and left the country.

And then, right at the very end of the piece, the article told of the 'questions on everyone's lips': whether Lord Laughton would return to Waterley Hall and whether he would be alone or with his 'constant companion', an unnamed woman who had been seen with him at several race meetings in France and Germany.

Goodness, Lettie thought, surely this was not the floozy that Mrs Osborne mentioned? If it was then there was little wonder the Reverend did not wish her to see this article. He preached a very moral code in chapel and Gran echoed it. Was that why Gran would not have Lord Laughton's name mentioned? She smoothed the newspaper, stared at his photograph and wondered when it was taken.

In the background a line of footmen stood by the steps

leading to the front door of, she assumed, Waterley Hall. She took a closer look at the caption. *Lord Laughton with some of his loyal servants.* Were Gran and her grandfather among them? Her heart began to thump. Perhaps her mother or father was in the group as well? She fingered the picture lightly. It was hard to make out their features but she supposed a servant would recognise themselves or a close relative. She desperately wished she knew someone other than Gran who had been employed there and considered, again, approaching Mr Osborne. She sat back in her chair and yawned. Her eyelids drooped. The lamplight flickered and she focused her attention on moving shadows jumping across the wall. She yawned again. Then she closed her eyes for a minute intending to finish reading the newspaper . . . in a moment . . .

The next thing she knew was the sound of Gran making peculiar gurgling noises in her throat. Startled, she half rose to her feet. 'What is it, Gran? What do you need?' she cried.

The lamp still burned brightly. Gran's eyes were rolling, apparently helplessly. Her pillows were slipping away to right and left and she was trying to sit up but couldn't. Her breathing was difficult. Lettie stood up and attempted to get her upright again. Gran's bony fingers were clutching at the newspaper as though she were clinging onto it for her life. It was crumpled, scrunched up, even torn in places.

'Reverend!' Lettie called. 'Come quick!'

Gran lolled over towards her and the newspaper slipped to one side. Lettie managed to retrieve the pillows and

213

pushed them behind Gran as best she could. But Gran could not help herself to sit up. Her body was limp and her eyes had closed. For a second, Lettie thought that she had died until the gurgling in her throat resumed. She eased her back onto the pillows and the gurgling stopped.

'Say something, Gran,' Lettie pleaded.

Nothing was audible. No movement of her lips was visible. Where is the Reverend? she thought frantically. Lettie watched for what seemed like an age, trying to detect any movement that suggested breathing. Then she knew that the Reverend, or indeed the doctor, could not do any more for Gran now.

'Oh Gran,' Lettie breathed. 'Dearest Gran.' She leaned forward and took Gran's fragile form in her arms, cradling her gently against her soft bosom. 'Dearest Gran,' she repeated. 'I love you so much.'

Lettie inhaled suddenly and realised it was a sob so she pressed her lips together and sniffed. Gran's hair was awry and she wouldn't want anyone to see her looking so dishevelled. Lettie combed it for her, neatened the ribbon ties at the top of her nightgown, straightened the tumbled pillows behind her and tidied the bedcover. She looked more peaceful now and in her mind she could hear Gran say, *That's better, Lettie, much better.* The newspaper slid to the floor and Lettie bent to push it out of sight, under the bed with a stray pillow, before she went out onto the landing to tap on the Reverend's door.

He didn't take long to rouse and within a minute or so he had put on a heavy dressing gown and carpet slippers and was standing by the side of Gran's bed.

214

'I think she's gone, sir,' Lettie murmured.

'Yes, my dear. I'm very sorry.'

'Shall I fetch the doctor?'

'It's still dark. I'll get dressed and go. Will you be all right on your own?'

Lettie didn't reply. *On her own.* Without Gran she had nobody; no family, except the Reverend who was good and kind to her because that was his vocation. But he didn't love her like her gran had loved her. Gran had been the mother that Lettie had never known.

'I could fetch Mrs Jones or one of the others . . .' The Reverend prompted.

'No, there's no need,' she answered. 'I'd like to be alone with her for a while.'

He nodded and left quietly.

Lettie spoke softly as she continued to smooth the bedclothes. 'I know I haven't turned out exactly as you wished but I know you will be watching me from heaven and I shall do my best to make sure you are proud of me. I promise.' Then her tears began to flow and she tried to pull herself together but it was difficult. It was a long time before the Reverend returned with the doctor. She heard the side gate and went to the window to look. They were walking round to the back of the house. The sky was already streaked with grey and she heard the clock chime.

The doctor was very kindly when he confirmed what she and the Reverend knew already. Lettie simply stared at the wall as she tried to stem her tears.

'Why don't you go downstairs and get the fire going

for some tea,' the Reverend suggested so she nodded silently and went down to the kitchen, glad of a routine to be getting on with.

Both gentlemen joined her before the kettle had boiled. The fire was drawing well and the teapot was ready.

'I'll bring it into your study when it's ready, sir,' she said.

'It's cosier in here,' the Reverend replied and pulled out a couple of chairs for himself and the doctor.

The doctor put his black bag on the kitchen table and took out some folded paper packets. 'These will help you sleep, my dear,' he said. 'I want you to take one now and go straight to bed. Keep the others for night-time when you can't get off. They'll help.'

'What will happen now?' she asked.

'You will go to bed and sleep.' The doctor smiled.

'I mean, what will happen to Gran?'

The Reverend answered, 'I'll arrange for your grand-mother to be taken to the Chapel of Rest until the funeral. She left a will with her last wishes about burial, my dear. I have it in my study.'

'Oh. Can I see it?'

'Of course. When you are feeling stronger we shall have a long talk.'

The kettle began to bubble on the hob and the Reverend stood up to make the tea. 'Shall we have some of those fancy biscuits that your grandmother kept for the elders' meetings?' he suggested.

Lettie got up. 'I'll fetch them.'

When she returned with the biscuit barrel from the

dining room the Reverend had prepared a small tray for her and the doctor was stirring a powder in a small glass tumbler of water.

The doctor handed her the tray. 'I want you to take this upstairs to your bedroom, put on your nightgown, have your tea and biscuit and take the powder. Then climb into bed and I promise you'll feel better when you wake up.'

'Do as the doctor advises, Lettie,' the Reverend added. 'I'll take care of everything else.'

She inhaled a shuddering sob and then stifled a yawn and obeyed. She hadn't realised how exhausted she was. Her legs felt like the lead weights in window sashes and she had to summon all her strength to climb the stairs. In spite of the hot tea she felt cold and the sheets chilled her further as she fell into bed. Her last thought was of how cold her feet were and then she sank into slumber.

Daylight forced its way through the crack in the curtains when she woke, disorientated and with a dry mouth. After a second she remembered and lay there quite still, trying to quell the rising tears. When she got out of bed she found warm water in her ewer. Someone had been in to bring it and presumably to check on her. She wondered what time it was and waited for the clock to chime. But it only chimed the quarter hour so she turned back the covers and went to look out of the window. The sky was overcast although it was bright enough to be the middle of the day.

Her hands shook as she washed and dressed. She stood outside Gran's room for several minutes before she turned the knob and opened the door. The bed was empty, stripped of bedding, and the curtains at the window remained closed; and would until after the funeral. It was the custom. The room needed a good fettle now, Lettie thought.

She walked over to the commode and closed the lid. The pot had been taken away along with the miscellany of medicine, spectacles and pot-pourri on the bedside table and washstand. Gran's bible was still there and Lettie picked it up. She wasn't as devoted to God as her grandmother and had sometimes questioned the Reverend's sermons but had never said as much. Nonetheless this bible was so much part of Gran's life that if felt as though it were part of her. Lettie hugged it to her body and her tears flowed again.

'Is that you, Lettie?' she heard the Reverend call up the stairs. Putting down the bible, she went on to the landing.

'Come down and get something to eat. Mrs Jones has cooked a dinner and saved you some in the oven.'

It was so difficult to stop the tears and her legs now felt like jelly. She grasped the handrail as she went downstairs. The Reverend was waiting for her.

'I heard you get up. How are you, my dear?'

The Reverend didn't usually address her as 'my dear' but the doctor had called her that as well, she recalled. 'A bit shaky,' she answered. 'I slept quite heavily.'

'That would be the powder. The doctor said you would feel fine once you've come round. Mrs Jones has just gone and she left a tea tray laid up. She'll be in tomorrow as well, so you don't have to worry about a thing.'

'I . . . I'll turn out Gran's room. You'll need it for your new housekeeper.'

'There's no hurry, my dear.'

'I'll sort out Gran's belongings as well. She would want them to go to the mission – her best tweed coat and—' She couldn't go on.

He smiled sympathetically. 'Yes, my dear. We'll talk about that after the funeral.'

'When will it be?'

'Next week. There'll be a large attendance. Mrs Jones is arranging a tea afterwards at the mission hall.' He kept the gentle smile on his face. 'Why don't you go and eat your dinner now? I've finished my reports and I'll be seeing to the pig if you need me.'

He went upstairs to change into his old clothes.

Lettie did feel better after a lovely meal of meat and potato hash followed by stewed apples. The kettle simmered on the hob and the teapot stood ready. Lettie made some tea and walked down the garden with a steaming mug for the Reverend. He was leaning on the wall of the sty and scratching the pig's back with a stick. The pig seemed to really enjoy that and he snuffled and rolled on his side in the mud. Lettie smiled.

The Reverend had always kept a pig and he never gave it a name. You couldn't eat a pig that you'd given a name. She hoped the new housekeeper would be able to salt it down in just the way the Reverend wanted for his Christmas table. She left his mug of tea on the wall and he acknowledged her with a wave of his stick. Then she went back indoors to finish her tea and gather together some cleaning materials.

The bed was stripped and the mattress smelled of rosemary and lavender. Lettie rolled up the rugs to take outdoors and beat, and as she knelt on the floor she caught sight of the stray pillow under the bed; and then the crumpled newspaper. She stretched to retrieve them. The distorted headline brought those last few moments of her grandmother's life flooding back. Lettie relived the image of Gran, her wild rolling eyes, her fingers gripping the flimsy paper. And then she realised that Gran must have seen it. She had not been clutching it as the straw clutched by a drowning man. She had been tearing at it to destroy it.

Lettie remembered the report she had been reading when she dozed off. Gran had read it – or at least the headline and picture caption – and had . . . had what? Lettie would never know except that Gran had found the strength in her fingers to scrunch up the page. She stifled a cry in her throat. She had allowed Gran to read the very thing that the Reverend had advised against.

Lettie realised with a shock that Gran's final, fatal attack had been brought on by what she had seen in the paper and it was her fault! She had taken the paper into Gran's room despite the Reverend's warning. She had been the one to disobey. She had caused her grandmother's death.

Chapter 16

She screwed up the newspaper, rocked on her knees until her sobbing subsided and then attempted to smooth it out again on the waxed floorboards. She tried to think rationally. Gran had been seriously ill and could have gone at any time. But Lettie could not excuse herself from the blame. Seeing this picture and this headline had shortened her grandmother's life. It had been her actions that had brought on Gran's attack. Why had she hated Lord Laughton so much? Why? Lettie had to know.

She folded the newspaper carefully and placed it on the bed with the other things-to-keep. As she swept and dusted and polished, Lettie considered the questions she might ask the Reverend during their talk after the funeral. What had happened in the past to cause such hatred and anger in a steadfast God-fearing woman?

Gran's funeral was a large though not ostentatious affair. The chapel was filled to overflowing and mourners stood six deep at the burial. Tributes were small, floral arrangements or cards with purple ribbon and personal messages saying lovely things about her gran.

Lettie wanted to stay and read them all and asked the Reverend if he minded.

'You must be at the mission hall to receive the mourners, my dear. Allow them to express their condolences to you.'

Lettie nodded in agreement. This was the first funeral she had attended and she had never felt so lonely. Gran used to say that women never went to funerals when she was a girl but it was different now. Lettie had a black skirt and a dark grey blouse and wore a long black coat of Gran's that was fashionably short on her. Mrs Jones lent her a black hat and said that Eric would walk with her in the procession. In spite of the way she felt about him she was grateful for that gesture on the day. He was familiar with the service and order of events and she only had to keep her hand on his arm to be sure of doing things correctly. He behaved so well it crossed her mind that it was a pity she didn't like him.

Lettie found the occasion exhausting and would have preferred to grieve alone. She lost count of the numerous kindly folk who offered her their condolences. She couldn't remember the names of many, although she knew most of them by sight. Mrs Jones seemed to be in charge and she directed mourners to the tea and cake. The hall was crowded and stuffy and Lettie needed air. However, after about an hour, one or two of the elders left and others took this as their cue to say goodbye. Very soon, the stragglers who were left finishing the cake were more interested in talking to each other than to Lettie or the Reverend.

The Reverend whispered in her ear, 'Why don't you go and spend a few minutes by the grave on your own?'

'Thank you, sir.'

She slipped away and spent a tearful hour reading the many grateful messages on the tributes. She knew the strength of Gran's commitment to chapel but had no idea that Gran was so much appreciated in the village and even further afield in the town. Alone, Lettie reflected on the past and on Gran's more recent revelations about her late husband.

'I don't know what Grandfather did but you never forgave him, did you?' she murmured, adding, 'And the Reverend preaches forgiveness.' Lettie inhaled shakily, her sobbing over for now. She bent down to retrieve the small posy of wild flowers that she had picked and arranged for her gran. There were many similar tributes and one less would not take away from the display of affection and respect. She said, 'I am doing this for you, Gran, because you were too poorly to do it yourself. I hope you understand.' However, she wasn't entirely sure that Gran would approve of her actions as she set off for the private churchyard on the Waterley estate.

She took the short cut through woods and pasture, avoiding the road past the inn to Boundary Farm. The path was muddy in parts and the grass was wet so that when she arrived her boots had lost their shine and the hem of her skirt was soggy and soiled. She had walked briskly and felt her cheeks must be glowing in the cool air.

Grandfather's grave was much easier to find the second time and she stood at the foot of the simple grassy plot, alone with her thoughts for a long time. She heard the whine of a hinge and looked back at the gate. No one was there so she thought she must have imagined it. Lettie wasn't given to fanciful notions of spirits and visitations so this did not worry her. She bent to place her posy at the base of the headstone. Now she was here she didn't know what to say. The prayers she knew by heart were the ones she recited to the children at Sunday school and none seemed suitable. And then she considered it was God that Gran should ask to forgive her, and not her late husband.

The headstone ought to say more, she thought, and wondered if she could instruct a mason to add more words. The Reverend had already asked her about Gran's headstone and Seth Hargreaves was her grandfather, after all. 'What can I say about you?' she murmured and finally heaved a sigh. 'I just wish I had known you.'

'*Do you?*'

The voice was very close and it surprised her. She jumped and inhaled so sharply it sounded like a shriek.

'Oh! Where did you spring from?' she cried.

'The church,' he stated.

It was Mr Boyer. He must have returned to Boundary Farm. He had stepped from behind her and into her field of vision. He looked at her face briefly and added, 'It's you, I see.'

Lettie regained her composure quickly. 'Good afternoon, sir.'

He nodded an acknowledgement but did not walk on.

Was he waiting for her to speak? She wondered what he was doing here and assumed it was for the same reason as she. She said, 'I saw you searching the town cemetery last month. Are you looking for someone?'

'Is that what you were trying to find out when you were reading my papers?'

'I was not reading your papers,' she protested mildly. Goodness me, he still remembers, and he isn't being very friendly at all. She turned away from him and back to her grandfather's headstone, expecting him to leave.

'You wouldn't have wanted to know him, believe me,' Mr Boyer said.

Why would he say that? She whirled around. 'Did you know him? He . . . he was my grandfather.'

He looked astounded for a moment then recovered. 'That man was your grandfather?'

His tone was disparaging and Lettie felt herself blushing but she ignored the sneer. What business was it of his, anyway?

'Did you know my grandfather?'

'Of course not! How old do you think I am?'

Lettie was put off by his abrupt manner. Mrs Osborne had said he was a gentleman but he certainly wasn't behaving very much like one now. However, if he had some knowledge of her grandfather she was prepared to overlook his brusqueness on this occasion. 'But you know something about him? Please tell me. Please. You see, his headstone seems so . . . so bleak and I want to add a few words about him – something truthful – about the man he was.' She sounded emotional but did not care. It was how she felt at the moment. She lowered her voice and hunched her shoulders. 'There are no endearments and there ought to be.'

'Well, the truth is never wrong,' he said. Then he added, as if it were an afterthought, 'It is the telling of the truth that is right or wrong.'

He seemed to be mocking her in some way and she wasn't sure what to make of him. Was he saying that it was right not to add anything if it had to be the truth? This implied that Gran had been right not to tell her anything. She felt she should walk away from him but was not ready to leave Grandfather's grave yet. He had imposed himself on her and she wanted him to go. But not before he had explained himself. 'What do you know about him, sir?' she asked.

'Why don't you ask your grandmother?'

His question felt like a knife in her stomach. Her voice cracked and the tears threatened. 'I can't. I buried her today.'

His demeanour changed in a second and his sour expression turned to one of compassion. Was this the same face that had scorned her a moment before? 'Forgive me,' he said. 'I had no idea.' He looked past her to the posy of flowers resting at the base of the stone. 'I have intruded on your grief and for that I apologise most sincerely. Good afternoon, miss.' He turned and walked away, out of the graveyard without looking back.

Lettie was ready to collapse. Her legs seemed unable to support her and she placed a hand on the headstone to steady herself. Whatever Grandfather had done it was a long time ago and, surely, forgotten by all concerned. Perhaps *Rest in Peace* was the most fitting inscription for him.

She retraced her steps slowly across the pasture and through the woods to the manse. The Reverend had begun to worry about her absence and was relieved to see her. He urged an early night with one of her sleeping powders. Tomorrow, he planned to discuss the future with her. She supposed he meant Wales. It had not been possible when Gran was taken ill. Now, of course, it was an obvious choice and thoughts of the Welsh coalmining valleys jumbled with curiosity about Mr Boyer and her grandfather filled her mind until she fell asleep.

'Come in and sit down, Lettie my dear. Have you eaten breakfast?'

'Yes, thank you,' she replied, surprised at his interest in such detail about her welfare.

'Good. Mrs Jones has already found someone to take over from her for the next month. She will move in later today.'

'But I said I could manage until you found a permanent replacement.'

'No, my dear. You must allow her to do that. You have to leave chapel and manse affairs to others and think seriously about your future. As you know, your grandmother was keen for you to seek new pastures.'

'Did you write to your sister in Wales?'

'I did. And then I wrote again when your grandmother took poorly so no firm decisions were made. We — that is, you — must decide now.'

'Are you giving me a choice, sir?'

The Reverend was valued in Waterley Edge for a practical approach to his pastoral duty. His guidance was welcomed when his worshippers suffered crises in their lives. He was used to such interviews as this but Lettie thought he was considering his words extra carefully. She was prepared to listen but had mentally prepared herself for a disagreement. She added, 'I understood that you agreed with Gran so I suppose you still want me to go.'

'It would, in my view, be the best course of action for you. However, it has to be your decision and I shall not rest easy if you choose before, well, before I have discharged my duty towards you.'

My goodness, he does sound formal. He was an educated man with a good command of language as anyone might expect of a preacher. But now he was beginning to sound more like a lawyer than a pastor! Did he want to dispense with his responsibility towards her altogether? Gran had talked to her about her wishes so she said, 'Gran told me you would be my guardian when she . . . she . . .' Her voiced trailed away.

'None of us expected her to leave us so quickly, my dear. But, yes, she did confide in me with regard to your guardianship.'

'I could not wish for anyone else, sir. When I asked

Gran why you cared so much about me she told me it was because you are a good man.'

He smiled in a kindly fashion. 'It is my vocation, Lettie.'

And, she realised, he has a whole parish of worshippers to care for. He ought not to have his time taken up by one unfortunate orphan. 'I shall not be a burden to you. I told Gran I would find a position. I am convinced that I can.'

'So am I, my dear, which is why your grandmother wanted you to train for a proper vocation. You have a little money that she had saved for you, precisely for that purpose. What have you in mind?'

Not a teacher! She had to say it and wondered if he would argue with her. He was a clever man and credible in his arguments. He waited for her to respond and she said, 'I . . . I was thinking of applying to Waterley Hall before Her Ladyship died. But no one is quite sure what will happen there now. The newspaper said—'

'You really must put that idea right out of your mind. Your grandmother would not have approved.'

But that was because it holds secrets, Lettie thought defiantly, secrets about her past. Nonetheless, she had loved Gran and the Reverend was her guardian so she would have to abide by his wishes. Yet, he had said that she must decide for herself. She took a deep breath and said, 'I really do not want to be a teacher, Reverend. I am sorry to disappoint you but I don't want to go to Wales, either. Truly, I don't.'

'Why not? What do you have against the Welsh valleys?'

'Nothing at all, sir. It's just that I want to know who

I am. I have to. It's an urge in me that I cannot quell. Gran gave me a little information and warned me against further enquiry. But that has only made me want to find out more and I believe the answers must start here in Waterley, with my grandfather.'

The Reverend rested his forehead in the palm of his hand for a second. 'In some ways you have just made this interview much easier for me. Your grandmother said that you might be told when you reached twenty-one. I disagreed with her. You are an intelligent young woman and I think that you are mature enough to cope with it now.'

Now Lettie wanted to put her head in her hands. 'Cope with what, sir?'

'The truth, my dear.'

She felt an unusual shivering sensation spread through her body and swallowed. He knew something. She said the words that burned into her brain since she heard them yesterday: 'The truth is never wrong. It is whether you tell it or not that is right or wrong.'

'That is a very philosophical statement. Did you think of it yourself?'

'I wish I had.'

'Eric, then? He is a very well-read young man.'

'No, not Eric.' Eric wasn't interested in meaningful discussion with her, Far from it!

'Thomas, then? His father can be quite philosophical, I hear. He writes poetry.'

She shook her head. 'A gentleman I met at Mrs Osborne's.'

Reverend Ennis frowned. 'Another gentleman? I believe

230

your grandmother did speak fully with you about the dangers of being taken in by the flatteries of young men.'

'She did,' Lettie stated and considered, actually, that Mrs Osborne was much more help in explaining the actions of young men; as indeed the Reverend's sister in Wales might be. 'Do not concern yourself, sir. He did not flatter me.' Quite the opposite, she thought.

'Well, whoever said it was wise. It is precisely that dilemma that prompts me to go against your grandmother's wishes regarding your guardianship.'

This was a blow to Lettie and she floundered, lost for words for a moment. 'You . . . you will not be my guardian?'

He shook his head and a surge of disappointment washed over her. 'I am deferring my decision until I have gathered more information. When we talked of your guardianship your grandmother told me . . . certain facts of your background. She wanted me to promise to keep them from you.'

He knew something! Lettie's frustration deepened. The Reverend would not break his promise to Gran.

The Reverend had not finished and he went on, 'I replied that as your guardian I should have to consider what was in your best interests at the time.'

I wonder how Gran reacted to that, Lettie thought. She would not have been pleased.

'I am aware that your upbringing in the manse has been sheltered. You are not as . . . as worldly as some of the young women in the parish whose behaviour causes their parents endless worry.'

Well, those young women had been out in service or at the bottle factory for several years at her age, Lettie thought. If Gran had not felt the need to stop her from doing things that other nineteen-year-olds did, she may well have known what to expect from Eric Jones! She refocused her attention on the Reverend's speech.

'However,' he went on, 'your sense of right and wrong is well developed and I believe you can be trusted to behave in a proper manner, given a little more freedom.'

Lettie's eyebrows shot up in surprise. 'Did you say that to Gran?'

'I did not. I conveyed to her that I am prepared to act as your guardian and she passed away with that knowledge.'

'Thank you, sir.'

'However, I find my conscience is not at ease when I am aware that there is someone else with a better claim than I for the role.'

She wasn't sure she had heard him correctly. 'Beg pardon, sir, but could you say that again?'

'I understand this will come as a shock to you. It was, indeed, a surprise to me. In my role as your preacher as well as your guardian, I must do what I believe to be in your best interests.' He stopped to focus his attention on her face. 'Who am I to say that I will make a better guardian than your own father?'

Chapter 17

'My own father? But my father is dead.' What on earth is he talking about? she wondered.

'No, my dear, he may not be. He was estranged from your mother before you were born.'

Lettie's jaw slackened. 'Are you saying my father may still be alive?' she muttered. 'Surely not?'

'He has never owned you – that is, taken responsibility for you – as his child.'

'Then . . . he did not . . . want me?' This realisation devastated Lettie. 'Did he know about me?' she asked.

'I can only repeat what your grandmother told me a few months ago, when we discussed your guardianship. You see, I pressed her for information – any information on possible living relations, however distant. Blood is always best in matters of guardianship. She told me that your father had not passed away as she had led you to believe.'

'He may be alive?' Lettie sagged into her chair. 'My father may be alive and neither of you thought I should know?'

'Your grandmother has had no contact with him for nigh on twenty years.'

'But he's my father! Why didn't she tell me about him?'

'She spoke of him in a dismissive way. He was a man influenced by money and position, and, it seems, by your grandfather, too.'

Lettie sighed in frustration. 'Grandfather again! Well, Gran hated him so it's not surprising that she disliked my father as well. Even so, to have no contact with him whatsoever, it's . . . it's . . . it's just not fair.' Dear Lord, she had lost her mother and Gran had deprived her of her father too! Of course Gran must have had her reasons, but she thought it was a cruel thing to do. However, she could not say that to the Reverend. He was trying to make amends.

He said, 'Your grandmother was talking of when he was a young man. He may have changed with the years.' He paused before adding, 'If he is still alive, of course.'

Lettie stared past him and out of the window. 'If he is, he will remember my mother,' she murmured. Then she stood up smartly and said, 'I must find him, sir. You would not have told me about him if you did not believe that I have to search for him.'

'Not necessarily, my dear. I said I had to do as my conscience dictated. You must exercise caution in this matter. If your father is alive, he may have another wife and family. He may not wish to be reminded of you after all this time.'

'But he's my father—'

'He is a father who has never set eyes on you, let alone held you in his arms. Believe me, Lettie, since your grandmother passed away, I have prayed every single day for guidance in this matter. Now I pray for the Lord to guide you.' The Reverend continued in this vein, advising caution, prayer and reflection before action.

But Lettie was not listening as well as she ought. Her mind was racing. Her father's estrangement was to do with Grandfather. It had to be. Had he been a wicked man in the same way as grandfather had been? After Mother died, did Gran take her away from both of them because of what they did? She spoke her thoughts aloud and demanded, 'Do you know where he might be, where I might begin to search?'

Lettie's anxiety mounted. What if she were too late? There was not a moment to waste! The Reverend was very good at keeping calm in situations that were highly charged with all kinds of emotion and he remained unmoved; or at least he appeared to.

'You must be patient. I understand that you have many questions and I shall endeavour to answer them. I have already written to Lady Laughton's lawyer—'

'Lady Laughton? What has she to do with my father?'

'If you will allow me to finish, I shall tell you. Your grandmother said your father was butler at Waterley Hall before . . . that is, when Lord Laughton was in residence.

He was young for such a position but I guess he served His Lordship well and, of course, your grandfather was in a powerful position as house steward.'

'I knew it! I knew it was something to do with Grandfather! Lady Laughton dismissed all His Lordship's servants when he left her. Where did my father go?'

'That is precisely the question I have asked of Waterley Hall trustees. The estate must have kept records of their employees and I have asked them for information on all the indoor male servants in their service.' He smiled at Lettie. 'I await their reply.'

Lettie knew from the mission hall minutes that lawyers took forever to answer letters, especially from people who had not retained their services in the first place. She tried to quell the growing trembling inside her. What if they wouldn't say? What if her father had gone overseas? What if, heaven forbid, he had died? She could not bear that thought; to have lost him after all this time, after all the years when she might have known him and . . . and loved him. Gran must have been aware that someone had knowledge of his whereabouts. Why didn't she say?

'Did . . . did my grandmother ever try to find him?'

'I'm afraid not. He was part of a past that she steadfastly refused to acknowledge. It was only your future that concerned her, which is why she involved me.' He sat back in his chair. 'However, *if* your father is still alive, *if* I find him and *if* he is a suitable person to be your guardian, and *if* you and he desire it, I shall be happy to support both of you. My dear,' he looked directly into her eyes, 'you do understand that you must prepare yourself for the possibility of unwelcome news?'

'You mean he may have died?' That would be so dreadful to bear, especially now that Gran had gone.

'Do not forget that at some time in his life he had given up his right to be your father and he must have had a reason.'

Lettie closed her eyes. She had so much to think about, so much to plan, and all of it dependent on 'if's. If, if, if! How would she ever sleep until she had the answers?

The Reverend let the silence go on. He took a key from his waistcoat pocket, leaned down, and unlocked a drawer in the pedestal of his desk. Then he placed a battered metal cashbox on the surface in front of him and smiled.

'We shall decide on your long-term future when we have more substantial information about your father. At present I do not even know his name.'

'It will be Hargreaves, of course,' Lettie exclaimed. 'Gran told me. It's what they do in big houses. The family become accustomed to calling their butler by one name and they do not change it when he is replaced. Grandfather was Hargreaves to Lord Laughton before he became house steward, so father would have been addressed as Hargreaves too.'

'How confusing.' The Reverend frowned.

Lettie shrugged. 'Not to the family.'

'Well, I expect the records give his own name as well. In the meantime, I have more cheering news. Your grand-mother had a savings account that now belongs to you.

I am your trustee and I have decided to give you a quarterly allowance to spend as you wish so that you may become used to more independence.'

Lettie's eyes widened with gratitude. 'Thank you, sir. Gran allowed me a little money of my own, but I usually had to ask her for it.' And justify why I needed it, she thought and added hastily, 'Not that I minded.'

'Your grandmother felt her responsibility for you keenly. Your well-being was always her only motive.'

Lettie nodded briefly to show that she agreed. But she had already overheard a couple of the mission ladies talking about Gran being 'over-protective'. She remembered that one had said about Lettie, *She's not The Princess Royal*, whilst the other had responded, *No, but she is a lovely-looking lass,* and this had amused Lettie because how could someone with a tendency to freckle in the sun be called 'lovely'?

She assured the Reverend that she would account for her spending and told him about the small tin box kept in her bedroom containing her pencil and pocket book and where she noted her purchases. The Reverend seemed satisfied with his decision, counted out banknotes and coins and placed them in a small leather pouch. Banknotes! Goodness, she would have to take very great care of them. The coins jingled in a most satisfactory way as she felt the weight of the purse in her hand. She climbed the stairs to stow it away safely. Then she offered her services to the temporary housekeeper who responded briskly, 'I don't want you under my feet all day. Go away and help in the mission or something.'

Lettie was hurt by this rebuff and it must have shown in her face, because the woman changed her tone and went on, 'I'm sorry about your grandmother, lass, but your heart won't be in it with me in charge now. Besides, you've done enough for other folk lately. Why don't you go off and spend a bit of time on yourself for a change?'

Well, why don't I? Lettie echoed silently. Because she didn't know really where to start as the only young people she knew were chapel-goers. Although they were pleasant enough, their lives revolved around chapel life, which was not where Lettie saw her future. She sat in her bedroom and stared at her reflection in the mirror, fiddled with her hair for a minute and said out loud, 'Mrs Osborne.' Yes, Mrs Osborne, she thought. She treats me as she would her own daughters. I shall ask her to show me her journals, the ones with pictures and drawings of Gibson Girls. She grew excited as she planned her afternoon.

After dinner, eaten alone in the kitchen, Lettie asked the new housekeeper if she needed vegetables or eggs. She replied that her husband's allotment would be able to keep the Reverend supplied, so Lettie set off without the encumbrance of her baskets. She hardly noticed the walk. Her mind was on whether or not to tell Mrs Osborne about her father. Mrs Osborne was such a gossip. The Reverend had made it clear that his searches might all come to nothing so she decided to keep it to herself for now.

She realised quite suddenly that she had gone past the inn and felt a pang of disappointment that she hadn't seen Thomas. She didn't have any such qualms about telling him about her father because he could keep a confidence. She missed Thomas. They weren't walking out together or anything but she did not want to lose his friendship altogether and determined to look out for him on the way back.

Mrs Osborne was delighted to see her. 'They were saying at your grandmother's funeral that you'd be off to Wales as soon as the Reverend fixed it up for you. He hasn't asked you to step into your granny's shoes, then?'

'He wants me to be a teacher. Gran did too.'

'Well, it's a fine occupation for a spinster, if that's what you want to be. Mind, I reckon you wouldn't stay that for long. A bright young woman such as you will soon be snapped up. You could do quite well, you know.'

Lettie grew excited. 'Do you think so? I am thinking of going into service. Apparently titled ladies are desperate for lady's maids.'

Mrs Osborne raised her eyebrows. 'Got your ideas set on a young master, have you?'

'No. Why do you say that?'

'Didn't I just tell you you'd soon be wed?' Mrs Osborne shook her head good-naturedly at Lettie's puzzled expression. 'Oh, I see,' she went on, 'you thought I was talking about being snapped up for a position, didn't you?'

'Yes. Isn't that what we are talking about?'

Mrs Osborne laughed. 'Aye it is, m'ducks. Take no notice of me and put the kettle on.'

Lettie noticed Mrs Osborne hadn't laid up the tray for Mr Boyer's tea. She felt an acute sense of disappointment she wouldn't see him leading his horse across the yard. 'Has Mr Boyer gone away again?' she asked.

'No, m'ducks. He's out all day today and doesn't know when he'll be back. I'll be cooking his tea at eight o'clock tonight.'

'That was bedtime for Gran.'

'Aye and it was dinner time for Lady Laughton. That's how they have their meals up there. They don't have dinner and tea like we do.' Mrs Osborne put on her artificial aristocrat's air and added, 'She had luncheon at one thirty, ah-ah–afternoon tea at five and dinner at eight o'clock at night, a proper dinner an' all. I ask you, what time is that to be eating your dinner?'

Lettie laughed at her affected accent and said, 'Didn't they do that when you were at Redfern Abbey?'

'Yes but the Earl and Countess were different there somehow. They only fussed about meal times when they had guests. They were a proper lord and lady; not like these jumped-up Laughtons.'

Lettie pressed her lips together to suppress a smile. Mrs Osborne looked embarrassed and went on quickly, 'I shouldn't have said that, should I? But Mr Osborne said Her Ladyship was always complaining about something.' She paused to reflect on this and added, 'His Lordship had been generous, though, but then he was, with them that were loyal.' Mrs Osborne lowered her voice as though she might be overheard. 'You couldn't say that of Her Ladyship. Nothing was ever good enough for her.'

'My grandmother didn't have a pleasant word to say about either of them.'

'She wasn't on her own, m'ducks. But the old lady has gone now and what's left of the servants are wondering what the future holds for them.'

'Have some of them left already?'

'I gather so from Mr Osborne. The newspaper report said Waterley Hall was empty apart from a few servants.'

'It also said Lord Laughton was coming home.'

Mrs Osborne shook her head. 'That won't be until the shooting has finished in the New Year.'

'But there are servants still living there?' Lettie's mind raced. Maybe she wouldn't have to wait for the lawyer's letter? One of the servants might remember her father, might even know where he went when he left? She experienced a frantic urgency to question them before they disappeared to other positions.

'There's a bailiff and a gamekeeper, and a few indoor servants. They are mostly them that have been there for years.'

'Do you know if anyone up there could tell me about becoming a lady's maid?'

'I don't know. The last one left a while ago and Her Ladyship never replaced her.'

'Well, who looked after her then?'

'I've no idea, m'ducks. Nannies were sometimes drafted in at Redfern but Lady Laughton never had call for one of them at Waterley Hall. A head parlourmaid would do it if she had the knack, otherwise the housekeeper could always be trusted. They still have jobs up there, keeping the place spick and span just in case His Lordship arrives unexpected. Why don't you go up there and ask? I'm sure they won't mind.'

'I think I will.'

'Well, have a cup of tea first. I've had a letter from my eldest at Redfern.'

Over tea, and scones leftover from the day before, Mrs Osborne talked about her children and their children. Lettie was interested but listened with only half an ear as she imagined what she would say to the housekeeper at Waterley Hall. Mrs Osborne didn't seem to notice. After she had done the washing-up, Lettie came though from the scullery drying her hands on a towel and glanced at the kitchen clock. 'I'll have to get off now,' she said, 'but thanks ever so much for cheering me up.'

'It's a pleasure, m'ducks. Come again soon.'

'I will.'

If she hurried, there was still time to reach Waterley Hall, find the housekeeper and get home to the manse before the lamplighter came round for the gas lamps. The path forked just before the church. She carried straight on past fields of grazing sheep towards a jumble of outbuildings comprising stables, barns and a few poorly built brick buildings that looked empty and neglected. The rear of the house rose above this, grandly in comparison but probably not as grand as the Georgian frontage. Lettie had not actually seen the front yet, only a picture of it in the newspaper.

Everywhere looked shut up and dingy. The air of damp neglect made Lettie feel sad. She watched for several minutes until one of the doors on the ground floor opened and a man and a woman came out, sat on a wooden bench and lit cigarettes. They were in dark clothes and she guessed they were servants. They chatted with their heads together for a while then went back indoors still smoking their cigarettes. After a few more minutes, Lettie gathered her courage, walked up to the door and rapped on it as loudly as she could. She repeated her knocking after what seemed like a long time and the silence continued. She tried the large tarnished brass knob and the door opened so she stepped inside into a passage that had several doors leading off. One of the doors was slightly open and light from the gap fell onto the stone-flagged floor in front of her. She pushed it open further.

She was in a large scullery with wooden sinks on one wall opposite a large dresser laden with heavy crested china. A young girl in a dark serge dress and plain white apron looked up startled. 'Who are you?'

'Lettie. I've come to see the housekeeper.'

'Are you from the village?'

'Yes,' she answered truthfully.

'Oh good. We can use another pair of hands for tonight. Some o' the toffs are here; well, they're not really toffs, more professional gentlemen. Been here all day, they have, and expecting us to do for them like we used to for Her Ladyship. But most of the servants have found themselves positions and there's only a few left. My auntie's roped me in for the kitchen but Mrs S hasn't got anybody now.'

'I see,' Lettie responded. 'Where do I find Mrs S?'

'Don't let her hear you calling her that! She's in her room.' The maid went back to checking and counting plates.

'I don't know where the housekeeper's room is,' Lettie said.

The girl gave an impatient grunt. 'I'll show you but you'll have to help me carry these. Tell me if you spot a crack, will you? They're only supposed to be used in the servants' hall but one of the toffs has taken the butler's keys now he's gone an' all, so we're using 'em for upstairs. Mrs S is not happy about that at all, I can tell you. Here, take these and follow me.'

Lettie staggered under the weight of the heavy crockery until she placed it in a dumb waiter at the end of the passage as she was directed. Then she retraced a few steps and knocked on the housekeeper's door.

The housekeeper was surprised to see her but didn't question her reason to be present or, indeed, ask her name. 'You're here at last! Have you got a uniform?'

Chapter 18

Lettie shook her head. 'I'd like to talk to you if I may.'

'Later.' The housekeeper pulled her towards the window and examined her outfit. 'Well, your skirt will do and I'll lend you a blouse. Can you wait at table?'

'Yes, but I think I should explain.'

'No time for that now. We'll talk about your references if you can do the work. The trustees are here and everything is taking longer than expected so they've asked to be fed. It's early for dinner, I know, but I can't give a servants' tea to upstairs, can I? As it is, I'm having to use the servants' china because they won't let me have the keys. All the years I've been housekeeper here and I can't be trusted with the keys, not until after the inventory, they said. Where have you worked before?'

Lettie had already decided it was in her interests to

play along with the misunderstanding and answered, 'In the Methodist manse at Waterley Edge.'

'That's good enough for me tonight. You'll know how to mind your manners. You'll take the dishes from the dumb waiter to the sideboard and I'll serve. But you'll have to help with handing round the soup and clearing away so be on your best behaviour.'

'Yes Mrs S . . .?'

'Sinjun. It's spelt as St John and pronounced "Sinjun". Yes, I know you haven't heard of it before but you'll get used to it.'

Actually I have, Lettie thought, because I've read *Jane Eyre* and there's a St John in there and my teacher told me how to say it. 'Where can I wash my hands, Mrs St John?' she asked.

There were four of them present to cook and serve dinner to three gentlemen, which seemed more than enough servants to Lettie. Mrs St John left her to change into a plain high-necked, long-sleeved blouse and then cover most of it with a pretty lace-trimmed apron while she went to talk to the cook. Lettie stood in the dim draughty passage and waited until the housekeeper came out of the kitchen. Then she followed her up plain wooden stairs to a small landing. The dumb waiter full of crockery was waiting. It didn't have a door, only a wooden box opened at the front that was hoisted up and down a shaft with ropes around pulleys.

'Take those dishes and put them on the sideboard through there,' Mrs St John ordered.

Lettie smiled to herself. She sounded like Gran and it

was strangely comforting in the unfamiliar surroundings. Lettie obeyed and began to enjoy herself. She opened the door and faced a high black folding screen. Waterley Hall dining room, on the other side, was long with tall sash windows along one wall. She paused with her arms full to gaze out over the parkland stretching into the distance. The nights are drawing in, she thought. It will be dark when I get home. She heard Mrs St John call down the dumb waiter shaft behind her.

A polished wooden table and enormous sideboard dominated the room. Lettie reckoned there were twenty chairs around the table and more pushed back against the wall. Three places were laid at one end for dinner. Her footsteps echoed on the floorboards as she walked across to deposit the china. She stood to attention at the sideboard while the housekeeper walked slowly around the dining table checking the settings of shining silver and sparkling glass. Without looking up, Mrs St John said, 'Go and get the next load from out there.'

Lettie went back to the dumb waiter. The screen that hid the servants' entrance was ornately decorated in the Chinese style on the dining room side. The curtains at the windows were of a heavy brocade. Lady Laughton may have been a recluse but she did not live like a hermit.

Lettie returned with a large silver tureen of steaming soup. It smelled delicious but it was so heavy and hot that she almost dropped it before reaching the sideboard. She checked that everything was to hand on the sideboard while the gentlemen came in and sat down. They were talking, in low voices, about the late Lady Laughton and how prudent she had been during her lifetime. Lettie had not heard anyone speak of her in those terms before. The gentlemen sounded as though they approved of her careful control of affairs.

Mrs St John whispered in her ear, 'Carry the tureen on the tray to each diner in turn and I shall serve it. No talking and don't look at them.'

Lettie concentrated on not slopping the soup around as she followed the housekeeper cautiously to the end of the long table. The conversation ceased as they approached.

'Will you take soup, sir?' Mrs St John enquired.

Lettie was gazing at the back of the head of the man at the top of the table and thinking that he had lovely thick hair, although it could do with a tidy from the barber. He turned and glanced at the tureen and then at Lettie. Her eyebrows shot up. It was Mr Boyer.

His serious expression turned to one of consternation but he recovered his composure quickly and spoke tersely to Mrs St John. 'What is this girl doing here, madam?'

'She's my new maid, sir.'

He took his napkin from his lap, placed it on his waiting soup cup and sat back in his chair. 'She is not. She cannot stay.'

Lettie stood mortified and embarrassed as Mrs St John stammered a little and then said, 'Very well, sir.'

Mr Boyer rose to his feet and apologised to the others. 'Please excuse me, gentlemen. This is unexpected and I must deal with it.'

'But must you do it now, Boyer?' one of the others complained. 'We are all of us hungry.'

'I assure you that Lady Letitia would not want this girl in Waterley Hall.'

He relieved Lettie of the tray without looking at her and took it back to the sideboard. Mrs St John appeared unsure of what to do next. She said, 'Mr Boyer, forgive me, sir, but I only have a cook and kitchen maid in the house.'

'You may place all the dishes on the sideboard and we shall serve ourselves. This girl must leave Waterley Hall immediately. Mr Osborne will still be at work in the orangery. Send the kitchen maid to find him and he will escort her to Boundary Farm.'

'Very well, sir.' Mrs St John took a firm grip on Lettie's elbow and steered her towards the screen and door to the back stairs. As soon as they were out of earshot, she hissed, 'What have you done?'

'Nothing, honestly.'

'Well, he knows you from somewhere so you must have done something.' Mrs St John took her to the kitchen, pushed her into a corner and sent the kitchen maid to find Mr Osborne. Then she had a conversation with the cook, which Lettie could not hear.

Lettie was cross. She had done nothing wrong. Mr Boyer knew her from Boundary Farm only and Mrs Osborne had explained who she was. Oh, and there was the misunderstanding outside the inn with Thomas, and their exchange at Grandfather's graveside. Was this because of who her grandfather was? Lettie thought incredulously.

It has to be, she reflected. Grandfather was one of His Lordship's favourites. If Mr Boyer was one of Lady Laughton's trustees then he was duty bound to champion her cause and discredit His Lordship's supporters.

Lettie experienced a profound sense of disappointment. When Mr Boyer had been at Grandfather's grave and she'd told him about Gran, he had been contrite and she'd seen a flash of kindness and sympathy that . . . that she had cherished. Now that was gone. She was, once again, someone he despised because of who she was. Dear Lord, she prayed, who am I? Help me to find my father – and myself.

Mrs St John returned. 'Come with me,' she directed.

Lettie followed the housekeeper to her sitting room. It was comfortably furnished with a good fire in the grate and she invited Lettie to sit in one of the upholstered fireside chairs.

Mrs St John took the other and said, 'I've nothing against you, but I'm ordered to stay with you until Mr Osborne takes you away. You'd best tell me everything.'

Lettie told her about crossing Mr Boyer's path at Boundary Farm.

'Is that all?' the housekeeper commented.

Lettie grimaced and went on. 'I ran into him in the Waterley church graveyard and he was . . . well, he was bothered when he found out who my grandfather was.' The housekeeper frowned so she added, 'He worked for Lord Laughton when His Lordship was a young man.'

'Who was your grandfather?'

'Seth Hargreaves. He was butler when Lord Laughton

251

arrived here, and later his house steward. It was years ago. My grandmother told me.'

'Oh, that explains it.' The housekeeper appeared to relax and raised her eyes towards the ceiling. 'Those gentlemen are Her Ladyship's representatives.'

Lettie was very conscious of why she had come here in the first place and took advantage of the moment. 'I never met my grandfather. Do you know anything about him?'

Mrs St John shook her head. 'If it was in Lord Laughton's day it was before my time here. Anyway, if your grandfather was one of His Lordship's staff, Her Ladyship would have got rid of him. She cleared out all his servants after His Lordship left her.'

'Is . . . was Her Ladyship Lady Letitia, then?'

'She liked us to call her that. She was Lady Laughton by rights but it was common knowledge that she hated His Lordship, especially after he went off with . . . well, after he went off. She wouldn't have folk use his name in her hearing. Now, I expect the last of us will be given notice when His Lordship comes home.'

Lettie blew out her cheeks. 'What a waste of a beautiful house and grounds. They had all the money they needed so why couldn't they be happy here, living with each other?'

The housekeeper shrugged. 'Because she was older than His Lordship, I suppose. They never had any children. It's children that make a marriage in my opinion.'

'And love,' Lettie murmured.

She hadn't said it for the housekeeper's ears but she

heard her. 'Oh, there was love all right,' Mrs St John responded caustically. 'If we believe what Lady Letitia told us, His Lordship loved *her* shipyards and *his* women.'

Women? Not just one floozy then, Lettie thought. Perhaps Grandfather had been the same? That would explain why Gran described him as wicked. And Grandfather had had an attractive young wife in Gran. Poor Gran.

Mrs St John went on, 'That's what rich folk do to get richer. They marry more money.'

'But husbands don't get to keep their wives' money these days.'

'That's right. Half of Waterley Hall belonged to Lady Letitia and His Lordship wants all of it back.'

Well, he'll have it, Lettie thought, now that his wife has died, unless, of course, she's left it to someone else. Lettie's curiosity got the better of her discretion.

'Who are those gentlemen upstairs?'

'You do have a lot of questions, don't you?'

'Well, Mr Boyer has been staying at Boundary Farm for a while now. He's come all the way from Canada.'

'I'm not sure where he fits in. The other two are from Her Ladyship's bank and one of them is a legal man.' There was the sound of heavy boots in the passage and Mrs St John stood up. 'That's Mr Osborne. You'll leave with him now.' She sighed. 'I'm sorry you can't take the position here. You have the right manner and I could do with a useful pair of hands.'

'I should like to talk to you about your early days here, Mrs St John. Can I visit you?'

'No you cannot! You heard Mr Boyer. Her Ladyship, God rest her soul, would turn in her grave.'

'Was her name really Letitia?'

Mrs St John ignored her question and addressed the gardener. 'Don't come into my sitting room in your boots.' She grasped Lettie's arm and pushed her out of the door. 'Just take this one home with you.'

Lettie went out into the evening air with the taciturn Mr Osborne, her mind in turmoil. She attempted conversation. 'They're a rum lot at Waterley Hall, that's for sure.'

He did not comment.

'Mr Boyer is one of Her Ladyship's trustees.'

Still he made no response.

'I hope I haven't made you late for your tea. I didn't do anything wrong, you know. It's Mr Boyer, he's taken against me.'

'Aye,' he said. That was all.

She did not linger at Boundary Farm, but apologised to Mrs Osborne for causing her any embarrassment. 'Mr Boyer was there,' she explained, 'and you know what he thinks of me.'

Mrs Osborne raised her eyebrows and turned to her husband. 'You never said he had business at the big house.'

'Nowt to do wi' me,' he replied and went outside again.

'I am sorry,' Lettie repeated.

'You'd best get off home, m'ducks, and keep your visits to Tuesday and Friday like before.'

Lettie was frustrated but agreed. Anyway she had a question for the Reverend, which she presented him with in his study after breakfast the following day.

'Do you have my birth certificate in Gran's papers?' she asked.

'I have searched for it and it's not there.'

'It must be somewhere.'

'What do you want to see it for?'

'It's my name, that's all. Is it really Lettie?'

'Why would it be anything else?'

'It might be short for something.'

'Such as?'

'Well, Letitia, for example.'

'It's possible. But I do baptisms for babies called Maggie and not Margaret or Beth instead of Elizabeth. You may have been baptised Lettie.'

'Baptised! Of course! Did you baptise me as a baby? It will be in chapel records.'

'I didn't. Your grandmother assured me you were already baptised when you arrived.'

'Well, it would have been a chapel baptism and not the parish church. Is there any way I can find out, sir?'

The Reverend widened his eyes and spread his hands. 'Short of searching every Methodist chapel baptism record in Yorkshire, no, and that assumes you were baptised in Yorkshire.'

'Then that's what I shall do.'

'Your birth will be registered, my dear. I can make enquiries on your behalf.'

'Oh, would you? Thank you, sir.'

'Letitia, you think? Where have you got that idea from?'

'Lady Laughton was called Letitia. I . . . I thought I might have been named after her.'

'Now why on earth would you think that?'

'It's what you said about my father. You don't suppose that . . . that he and Lady Laughton were – you know – that I could be her . . . her . . .' She dare not say what was on her mind but the Reverend was not stupid.

He finished the sentence for her. 'Do you seriously believe that your father had an illicit affair with Lady Laughton?' She had not seen him quite so shocked with her before. But it was a stupidly fanciful notion and now she felt foolish.

He stood up, clearly alarmed. 'Put that outrageous idea right out of your head. It has no credence whatsoever! Your grandmother assured me that you had a mother and father and they were married; to each other.'

'I'm sorry,' she said.

'Sit down, Lettie.' He resumed his position behind his desk. 'I was not planning to tell you this until I had more information but I can see that these questions are eating away at your rationale. You are normally such a well-balanced young woman.'

A nervous tremble clutched at Lettie's heart. 'What have you found out, Reverend? Please tell me.'

'I have received a reply from Lady Laughton's representatives with an address that might be of help.'

'You have an address for my father?'

'No, I'm afraid not. Records were not kept as well as they ought to have been after Lord Laughton left and there were several upheavals amongst the servants. Their records show only one Hargreaves and he was Seth Hargreaves, house steward. They did not have a butler. It seems that your grandfather continued in that role as well.'

Lettie was disappointed until the Reverend went on, 'However, they did have the names of footmen employed by your grandfather, all of whom resigned or were let go when Lord Laughton left.'

'They may have known my father!'

'It is possible. I shall make further enquires. Do not raise your hopes at this stage. They did locate a forwarding address for a footman, a fellow called Powell, but it is from many years ago. I expect that he has moved on from there. However, I shall write at once to find out before you get any more of your silly ideas.'

Lettie didn't think it was silly. These things happened in great houses. She thought it was perfectly feasible that the lady of house, if disliked and rejected by her husband, might have had an affair with a handsome young servant and subsequently given birth to a child who was brought up on the estate. Except . . . She realised the flaw in her thinking. Her Ladyship had been much older than her husband and probably too old to bear children. Yes, it had been a silly idea.

'Will you tell me what the letter says, sir, so that I may help?'

'Not until I have made further investigations about this gentleman. The church is a useful organisation for such enquiries.'

Lettie had to be content with waiting and she tried her best to be patient. But she could not sleep that night. If her father was still alive, she had to know where he was and this Mr Powell might have the answer. A sense of urgency overtook her. She must find him before it was too late. Dear heaven, it might already be too late! But he may have told stories to his family, tales of his time in service at Waterley Hall. Someone might remember!

She gazed at the ceiling in the darkness. There was a bright moon – a hunter's moon. It kept dimming behind clouds and while she counted seconds for it to reappear she decided to start her search that minute. The house was silent. She crept on to the landing in her slippers and robe, listened for the soft steady snoring of the Reverend, and then stole downstairs first to the scullery for a candle and, quiet as a mouse, into the Reverend's study.

She found the letter, which came from the Waterley Hall land agent who had access to estate papers. The request had been passed on to him from Lady Laughton's lawyers.

The footman's name was Powell and he had removed to Mereside Lodge, Forest Chase, Yorkshire, NR. Yorkshire! It was a big county and NR was North Riding. There was no indication of the position he took up at Mereside Lodge. But the Hall had kept his records, which, Lettie guessed, indicated that he had been a respected servant, deserving of a reference then or later.

Was he still at Mereside Lodge? Was he still alive? She could barely wait until morning to act on this information.

The following day she walked into town with her shopping basket for the market and took a detour to the railway station where she asked the ticket clerk if she could catch a train to Forest Chase.

Chapter 19

'Forest Chase, miss? Yes, it's Harrogate way. You go from here to Sheffield and then change onto the line for Leeds and York. It'll stop at Mereside Halt, Forest Chase and then Stainthwaite.'

'Mereside Halt? What's at Mereside Halt?'

The ticket collector took off his peaked cap and scratched his brow. 'Mereside Halt? I don't rightly know these days, miss. There used to be a hunting lodge before the railway line opened. Set by a lake for fishing, I believe; the Mere, they called it.' He shrugged. 'It must still be there but we don't get many folk from these parts asking for it. Is that where you want to go?'

'How much will it cost?'

'First or third class, miss?'

She had her allowance from the Reverend, more than

enough for several third-class tickets. She walked away pensively, wondering what to do next. It was a long way to Mereside Halt and if she did go by railway train she would have to travel alone. But they had guards on the train to look after you and it was the twentieth century.

If only Thomas still worked at the Adley's stall on the market. She could go and ask him about travelling on railway trains and if he'd heard of Mereside Lodge. She needed a friend to talk to but didn't want to mention her search to anyone from chapel. They wouldn't understand and, anyway, nothing might come of it. Besides, if the Reverend found out he would be cross. He had been so wise and kind to her, she didn't want to disappoint him again.

As she came out of the railway station she noticed the gritty frontage of the coal merchant's office with the coal yard behind where goods trains from the pithead unloaded. It belonged to Toogoods now. Mr Toogood was setting up all over the Riding, wherever he saw an opportunity. She peered through the wrought-iron gates but there was no sign of Thomas or his wagon. A small mountain of coal waited to be bagged and a couple of hefty men were shovelling it into sacks on a weighbridge.

'Is Thomas here?' she called through the railings.

They stopped, straightened and wandered over. 'Who are you, then?' one replied. He grinned at her cheekily and his teeth contrasted sharply with his grimy skin.

'I'm looking for Thomas. He drives the lorry.'

'Aye, we know who Thomas is. What do you want him for?'

'I want to talk to him.'

'What about?'

'I think that's my business, not yours.'

'Ooh, touchy, aren't we?'

The other man said, 'He's out on the wagon. Ask in yon office. Gaffer'll know when he's due back.' He inclined his head towards the small sooty brick building that housed the merchant's office in the corner of the yard.

'Thanks.'

The door to the office opened directly onto the roadway, with another door at the back that led to the coal yard.

The gaffer was a small man with hardly any hair on his head and a pair of spectacles perched on his nose. He was sitting at a worn writing table. 'Yes, miss. What can I do for you?'

'Can you tell me when Thomas will be back?'

He pushed his pencil behind his ear and took a long look at her. 'I can but I don't see why I should. Have you come on behalf of your mistress?'

'No, sir. I'm not a customer. I'm a friend of Thomas's and I want to talk to him about something.'

'Not in my time, you don't. He finishes at half past six.'

She couldn't wait that long. The station ticket office might be closed by then. 'It's very important,' she said. 'I could talk to him while he waits for the wagon to be loaded.'

The gaffer took hold of his pencil again and looked down at his papers. 'Half past six, miss. Good day to you.'

She stood and watched him add up his figures for a moment then turned for the door. As she lifted the latch she heard him say, 'Who shall I say wants him?'

She swivelled around. He had not looked up from his invoices. 'Lettie Hargreaves,' she answered. 'Thank you, sir.' He still didn't look up and she left without another word.

It was a big decision to make without speaking to anyone about it but she did. She went back to the railway station ticket office and enquired about journey times then purchased a third-class ticket to Mereside Halt. Her intention was to go there the next day. She would be very late getting home and racked her brain to think of what she would tell the Reverend to explain her absence. Her grandmother had always taught her to tell the truth. But Gran had not always practised what she preached, if only by omission. Lettie considered this option. It reminded her of Mr Boyer's words about telling the truth and she couldn't decide whether she would be right or wrong. Mr Boyer would know everything about travelling and she wished he was here so that she could ask him.

She was beginning to understand why he was so set against her. It was probably for the same reason that Gran was so set against her grandfather and Lord Laughton. Even so, where was her father in all this? The now-familiar sense of urgency to find him overtook her. If she found this Mr Powell, and he had, indeed, been a footman at Waterley Hall he might be able to tell her about her mother too! This was something she had never, ever, even in her wildest flight of fancy, imagined was possible.

Every time her thoughts turned to Mr Powell, she felt an excitement bubble inside her, a thrill that shivered through her body and buzzed in her head. She might find out something, anything, about who she really was, and perhaps why she couldn't settle at the mission in the same way that Gran did. She prayed feverishly that Mr Powell was still alive and living in the North Riding.

Lettie completed her market shopping making extra purchases she thought she might need on her journey, and hurried home anxious to prepare for her long day of travelling. The Reverend was out at a meeting where he would be given supper afterwards and would not return until late. The temporary housekeeper had prepared a tray for Lettie and left it on the kitchen table with some soup on the range. As she washed up afterwards, Lettie realised that she would not see either of them in the morning before she left to catch the early-morning train to Sheffield. She sat down, thought long and hard, and wrote a note for the Reverend to say where she had gone and what time she would be home and asked him to forgive her impatience. The dining table was already laid up for his breakfast and she placed her folded sheet of paper on top of his table napkin.

She was amazed that she slept at all because she was frightened of not waking up in time. But she was exhausted from excitement and she must have dozed as she didn't hear the Reverend come in. She woke very early before the hall clock chimed five and dared not turn over for another half-hour in case she overslept. So she dressed quietly and crept downstairs with her small carpet bag already half full of items for the day. She added food from the pantry and let herself out of the back kitchen door. At the railway station she sat and yawned in the waiting room until the train arrived.

Sheffield railway station was big and she had to go over a footbridge to another platform for the York train. It was crowded. Factory men and women crammed into the third-class carriages only to spill out a few stops down the line for the mills and factories where they worked. Lettie got a seat but it was none too clean and very hard on her bottom. She felt grubby and dishevelled when, much later, she alighted with her bag at Mereside Halt.

The guard walked along the platform calling, 'Mereside Halt.' Lettie climbed out quickly in case the carriage started to move again but she needn't have. The guard was heaving large wickerwork hampers out of his guard's van and arranging them on the platform. After he had waved his flag and climbed aboard, the platform was deserted. Steam from the engine cleared and she was totally alone, except for the hampers, secured by leather straps and neatly stacked.

Mereside Halt did not have a ticket office or a waiting room and lavatory. It was simply a painted wooden fence separating the platform from a track through the trees that she hoped connected with a road around the corner. For the first time Lettie thought that this journey might not be a very wise undertaking after all.

If Mereside Lodge was a hunting lodge as the ticket officer had said, they would, of course, send a carriage or a motor car to collect visitors from the railway train.

265

Even a servant might be met by one of the outdoor staff with a cart. She was neither visitor nor servant, and she was uninvited. She unlatched the gate in the fence, went through and closed it behind her.

It was, actually, a very pleasant morning. A warm sun was out, lighting up trees and shrubs that had never been dulled by smoke from factory chimneys. Birds were chirruping around her and the ground was dry under-foot. She threaded her way through woodland to find a well-hidden spot to relieve herself. She had a damp flannel in her bag wrapped in a piece of oilcloth and used it to wipe over her face and hands. Then she adjusted her corset, smoothed down her skirt, re-pinned a few stray locks of hair and emerged on the track feeling fresher.

There has to be a proper road at the end of the track, she thought as she set off with a determined stride. There was and she stood for several minutes looking in both directions for any sign of humanity. Then she heard the steam whistle of a train, another one, approaching the Halt. Perhaps it will stop and set down a passenger! She hurried back down the track and waited. It came from the York direction and a young woman let herself out of third class. She was smartly dressed in a maroon skirt and a dark grey fitted jacket with a jaunty little hat perched high on her fashionably piled-up hair.

'Excuse me, miss,' Lettie said as she went by, 'are you going to Mereside?'

'I am. Have you been sent to meet me?'

'No, I'm afraid not. I'm a stranger to these parts and

266

I was hoping you were familiar with the area and could show me the way.'

'Are you here for the wedding, then? I am.'

'No, I came from . . . from Sheffield for the day. It's my first visit to Mereside.'

'Oh, I was born here,' the young woman replied airily. 'I live in York now.'

'May I walk with you?' Lettie asked.

'If you want to; who do you know here?' The young woman didn't wait for an answer. 'I know most folk in Mereside, 'cos my mam does for the vicar's wife and my dad's the sexton.'

They were church people! Lettie felt comfortable in her presence. 'Is Mereside Lodge the vicarage then?'

'Mereside Lodge? I'm talking about Mereside Church in the village.'

Lettie was confused. 'Oh, Mereside is a village.'

The young woman frowned. 'Ye-e-es. What did you think it was?'

'The ticket clerk told me it was a hunting lodge by a lake.'

'Ooooh, you mean Mereside Lodge up the hill. The lake's the other side of it. It used to be a hunting lodge years ago before they built the railway line. At least, that's what my dad says.' The woman paused and took a closer look at Lettie. 'They'd have sent a carriage for you if they were expecting you. Who are you?'

'I'm looking for Mr . . . er . . . I'm looking for the butler or the housekeeper.'

The young woman blew out her cheeks. 'Are you going

for a position there? Well, I don't want to put you off but my ma wouldn't have me anywhere near the place. She's not a prude or anything because she lets me stay in lodgings and work in a draper's shop in York, but she wouldn't let me go to Mereside Lodge.'

Lettie wondered why and frowned, an expression that the young woman misunderstood totally. 'Don't get the wrong idea of me. I haven't been dismissed or anything. They've let me have a day off today to be maid of honour at my sister's wedding.' The young woman quickened her pace. 'I've got to rush. There's a lot to do. When we get to the road, you go the opposite way to me. Good job it's nice weather 'cos it's a long walk. Actually, I'd go back to the Halt if I were you and wait for the cart from the Lodge. It'll be along to collect the hampers soon.' She broke into a run. 'I've got to dash. Ta-ra.'

'Ta-ra,' Lettie called to her back, 'and thank you.' She retraced her steps for a second time, wondering what was so unseemly about taking a position in a hunting lodge; unless it wasn't a hunting lodge any more. If much of the forest had been swallowed up by the railway line it may simply have reverted to a gentleman's country residence.

When she reached the Halt she went back to the platform and looked more closely at the labels tied to the rope handles with string. They were addressed to *Mereside Lodge, Mereside Halt,* but they were printed with details of the senders – big stores in Leeds and Sheffield with names that Lettie had heard of. Goodness, she thought, you didn't shop at those places without deep pockets. She didn't have to wait much longer before a horse and cart arrived to pick up the hampers and she asked the driver to take her with him to the house.

He was a stocky, ruddy-faced countryman, wearing thick outdoor trousers and a long battered jacket that had deep poacher's pockets. 'They never told me I had a passenger,' he said.

'I'm not expected.'

'No and you're not a guest either. They'd have sent a carriage for you. Who are you and what do you want?'

'I have business with a Mr Powell, if he still resides there.'

'He doesn't like unexpected nosy parkers and neither do I. You could be one of them newspaper men.'

That means he exists and he is still here! Lettie made a supreme effort to contain the exciting thrill that spread through her.

'Well, quite clearly I am not,' she said reasonably. 'I was, until very recently a . . . a housekeeper in a manse.'

'Oh, well, if you're here for a position, you'll be welcome if only by us lot. Can you climb up yourself?'

'Of course.'

'Go and get on the cart, then,' he replied, and waved her away.

The horse had moved a little way down the track to graze and had taken the cart with him. Lettie scrambled aboard but the driver was such a long time that she climbed down again to go back and offer her help. He was bending over one of the hampers buckling the leather straps that secured it.

'Can I assist you in any way?' she called.

'You can mind your own business,' he answered, rather rudely she thought, and started to drag the hampers towards the gate in the fence. She held the bridle as he hoisted them onto the cart then climbed up beside the driver. He didn't voice his thanks or attempt conversation so Lettie decided to stay silent as well. The horse plodded down the track and along the road to Mereside Lodge.

It was a pretty country house, large but not palatial, built of stone with some half-timbered elevations and gabled windows in the roof. The roof itself was tile, not slate, a warm red that nestled comfortably in the surrounding trees. A high stone wall stretched in both directions to right and left of the house until it disappeared into the trees. Bee boles containing woven straw beehives punctuated the wall at regular intervals.

'Whoa.' The surly driver stopped his cart. 'This is where you get off.'

'Oh! Shouldn't I go in the servants' entrance?'

'All newcomers have to go in that door.' He jerked his thumb in the direction of a sturdy but small wooden door at one end of the building. It was not the main front door. That was in the middle and protected by a porch with more red tiles on its pitched roof.

She climbed down, reached for her bag and muttered, 'Thank you.' The driver flicked the reins and the horse moved on. Lettie watched the cart disappear down a track by the wall, which, she presumed, led to a gateway. A few birds flew around twittering in the still air and Lettie sensed an atmosphere of quiet tranquillity about the house.

She straightened her shoulders and walked purposefully towards the small door.

As she passed the porch she noticed it had a beautiful red, black and white tiled floor laid in decorative pattern, but it was sorely in need of a good scrub and polish. Perhaps the owner was elderly like Lady Laughton and the servants were taking advantage. Certainly if Mr Powell was still here he would be of advanced years. The windows at this end, the servants' entrance she assumed, needed a coat of paint and there was a patch of green moss high on the stone wall beneath a dip in the guttering. She pulled at the wrought-iron ring and waited, staring at the graining on the small oak door. A maidservant answered, which surprised Lettie for she had been expecting a footman. The maid was a young woman, not a girl, of her own age perhaps if not older.

'Good morning, miss,' Lettie said. She had already decided to be totally honest about who she was and what she wanted. 'My name is Miss Hargreaves and I am looking for a Mr Powell.'

The maid's eyes rounded. 'Is he expecting you?' As an afterthought she added, 'Madam.'

He's here, Lettie thought excitedly. He's still alive and he lives here! She took a deep breath to quell her nervousness. 'I am afraid not but I am prepared to wait if he will see me.'

The maid's mouth turned down at the corners. 'He won't see you today. We're expecting Lord— I mean we are expecting an important guest.' She took a closer look at Lettie, taking in her boots, skirt, coat and hat, and went on slowly, 'And only the one party is due. Are you one of his servants?'

Lettie shook her head. 'If Mr Powell is busy, may I speak with the housekeeper?'

The maid grimaced.

Lettie glanced at the high wall stretching in both directions and hiding access to the domestic offices and suggested, 'Shall I go round to the servants' entrance?'

'No!' The maid chewed on her lip. 'If you're not with His Lordship's party and you haven't got an appointment you'll have to leave.' She began to close the door.

Lettie took a step forward onto the threshold and the door stopped against her boot. 'I've come a long way on the railway train and it's vital that I speak to Mr Powell.'

The maid frowned at her belligerently. 'He won't see you,' she repeated.

Lettie returned her fighting look. 'I am not going away without speaking to *someone*.'

The maid seemed to struggle with her thoughts for a moment. 'If you wait here, I'll fetch Dr Bretton. What name shall I give?'

Lettie told her and once again faced the closed door, for what seemed like a long time. Her initial euphoria turned to worry that if a doctor was coming to speak to her, Mr Powell might be ill. She prayed he was not. Eventually, the maid returned, opened the door and said, 'Come with me, Miss Hargreaves.'

PART THREE

Chapter 20

Mereside Lodge, Forest Chase, Yorkshire, North Riding

Lettie stepped into a lobby with plain plastered walls and a black and white chequered tiled floor. There were coat hooks on the wall and a small table at the end next to a closed door. Another door was open on one side. It led to the main entrance hall for the house and she glimpsed a square, wood-panelled room with a high wooden counter along one side and a rack of pigeon-holes with hooks on the wall behind it. Keys hung from some of the hooks and there was correspondence waiting in the pigeon-holes. A smartly dressed young man appeared from a room behind the counter and stared at her through the open door.

Lettie had seen this arrangement only once before, in the Waterley Arms in Waterley Edge back home. The Waterley Arms was an old coaching inn and in the game season it was full of visitors on their way to one or other of the Yorkshire estates for the shooting.

This wasn't a private house at all, she realised. It was a country hotel. A very discrete and private hotel, she thought, as she had no inkling of its function when she approached.

The maid pushed her across the entrance hall and into a small sitting room. A brass plate on the door said 'Morning Room'. Lettie's boots were silent on the thick Turkish carpet. 'He'll be along in a minute,' the maid said and left her alone.

It was a long minute for Lettie. The room contained very comfortable, upholstered furniture, bookcases and polished inlaid writing tables. And it had a view of the lake from its bay windows. This was the mere, she realised. Surrounded by trees, Lettie was mesmerised by its tranquil beauty. She stood at the window and watched a skein of geese descend from a clear sky and land on the glassy water, skating along the surface and making ever-expanding ripples.

'Miss Hargreaves? I am Dr Bretton. How may I assist you?' His English was good but he had a foreign accent of some sort. French, possibly, she thought, certainly not a drawl like Mr Boyer.

'I was hoping to speak with Mr Powell,' she replied. 'Will that be possible? I do hope he isn't ill.'

'May I ask the nature of your business with him?'

'Oh, it is a personal matter, sir, and I don't even know if he can help me. You see, I am looking for my father and I believe Mr Powell knew him as a young man.'

Dr Bretton stared at her. 'As a young man, you say? Mr Powell has lived here for many years so how would Mr Powell have known your father?'

'It would be from his time at Waterley Hall. It's in the South Riding near Sheffield and my grand . . .' She hesitated, aware of her grandmother's reaction to digging up the past. 'My father may have been a servant to Lord Laughton at the same time as Mr Powell was a footman.' She swallowed anxiously. 'At least, I think Mr Powell was a footman. He may remember him . . . and . . . and know what happened to him.'

'You are speaking of a very long time ago.'

'Twenty years, I should guess, sir.'

'Well, I'm afraid that I cannot help you. I have no knowledge of Mr Powell's early life. Nor, I suspect, have any of the people here.'

'Is Mr Powell ill, sir? I really should like to speak to him.'

Dr Bretton shook his head. 'That is quite impossible, Miss Hargreaves. I'm afraid you have had a wasted journey.'

Lettie could have wept with disappointment. She was exhausted from her travelling and had been tense with expectation. In spite of the Reverend's warnings she had allowed her hopes to be raised and now they were dashed.

Her voice trembled. 'He isn't going to die, is he? He can't! Not before I've had a chance to ask him about my father! I've prayed for Mr Powell to be still alive and to remember him. He's my only hope.' She swallowed a threatening sob.

'He is your only hope for what, Miss Hargreaves?'

She must have sounded garbled. But the strain of losing Gran, finding out about her father and then this journey all alone had taken its toll on Lettie's nerves. 'My grandmother told me my parents were dead, you see, but after she passed away Reverend Ennis – he's my guardian – told me that my father might still be alive and . . . and this Mr Powell left Waterley Hall about the same time as my father. You see, when Lord Laughton went to live abroad, Lady Laughton got rid of all his servants.'

Lettie shuddered. Her nerves were in shreds. Anxiety and exhaustion on top of her grief now got the better of her. Her throat closed and tears threatened. She fumbled in her coat pocket for a handkerchief to wipe her nose. 'Please excuse me, sir,' she muttered.

She was aware that Dr Bretton was watching her as he waited for her to compose herself. Finally, he stood up and said, 'I'll ask my nurse to speak to you.'

A nurse! Lettie was startled back to her senses. Oh, goodness me! Did Mr Powell need a nurse? He must be very ill. 'I'm too late,' she wailed. 'He's going to die, isn't he?' The misery and distress must have shown on Lettie's face because the doctor stood up and came over to her chair and looked closely at her face.

'You cannot stay here, Miss Hargreaves. Nonetheless, I can see that you are fatigued from your journey. You may rest on the couch until Miss Fanshaw is available. However, you must promise not to stir from this room.'

'I promise, sir. Thank you, sir.'

'Miss Fanshaw is very busy but she is well acquainted with Mr Powell. She may be able to help you.'

Lettie was trembling with anticipation. She had come this far. Even if it took her all day she was determined to find out whether Mr Powell had known her father. She gazed out of the window for a long time then stood up to examine a glass-fronted bookcase. It contained leather-bound volumes in sets, grouped according to their author. Some were tales of adventures in parts of the world Lettie had barely heard of. But others were novels by Mr Scott, Mr Dickens and Mr Hardy.

She recognised some of the titles and was tempted to take one out and read as she waited. *Tess of the D'Urbervilles* was there! Gran had said it was 'not fit for decent folk' and she shouldn't read it, which only made Lettie want to read it more and she had to wait a long time for the lending library copy. Poor Tess. She thought she was someone she wasn't and was duped by a gentleman who took advantage of her innocence.

As a child, Lettie had not been concerned about who she was. But now the need to know was dominating her life. It had become an itch that she couldn't scratch and it was always there, controlling her actions. She stood by one of the writing tables, drumming her fingers on its surface. Finally, the door to the morning room opened and the young woman who had answered the front door came in with a tray. 'I've brought you some refreshment, miss. Dr Bretton said that you may have a long wait and to make sure you had everything you needed.'

'Thank you. I should like to read if I may.'

'Of course you may. The bookcase isn't locked. There's a bell-pull by the fireplace if you want anything else.'

This maid was about the same age as herself and Lettie thought she detected a little sympathy in her eyes. 'Is Mr Powell very ill?' she asked.

The maid did not have to stop and think about her reply. 'Miss Fanshaw will answer your questions.'

But Lettie wasn't put off. 'You can trust me. I'm not from the newspapers or anything.'

The maid hesitated before responding. 'I am not supposed to speak to you.'

She remembered what the young woman at the Halt had told her. She could be in a house of ill-repute! Lettie looked pointedly at the tray and then back to the maid's face. 'Well, I shall have to trust you if I drink that. It could be drugged and you could be part of the white slave trade for all I know!'

'We most definitely are not!' The maid was, quite clearly, appalled and her dark eyes flashed. 'How dare you make such a suggestion,' she hissed.

Lettie immediately regretted her outburst. 'I'm sorry, but, please, you have to understand that I'm looking for my father and I believe Mr Powell knew him as a young man.'

Lettie saw that the maid wavered before answering. But her response was firm. 'I'll lose my position if I say anything about anybody here. But I can tell you this: don't believe the village gossip because they're wrong. Mereside Lodge is a respectable establishment and I am proud to be employed here.' She opened the door to leave, paused on the threshold and pointed to the tray. 'And that is very good. It's Dr Bretton's own restorative and you don't want to know how much we charge for it.'

She was gone from the room before Lettie could press her further. Lettie sat down for her 'tea'. It was very welcome. When she poured it from the pot it was an unusual khaki colour and the debris in the tea strainer was definitely not tea leaves. It was similar to one of the herbal infusions that Gran used to make to calm her nerves. The tray had honey and not sugar as a sweetener. From the beehives, she guessed. She tried a little of it on a spoon and it was delicious – and scented, she noticed. There were two dark-coloured baked biscuits on a matching tea plate. Lettie picked one up and sniffed it. It had a crest baked into the surface so she reckoned it must be special and, curious, bit into it. It was bland and gritty on her palate. She expected it to be sweeter than it tasted but it wasn't unpleasant. She sampled the brew and had to add all the honey to disguise its bitterness.

She was deciding which book to read when the door opened again and a mature woman dressed in a plain grey gown entered. Lettie would have assumed she was the housekeeper if Dr Bretton had not described her as a nurse.

'Miss Hargreaves? I am Miss Fanshaw. Are you feeling better?'

'Yes thank you, ma'am,' she answered truthfully.

Miss Fanshaw took one of the comfortable armchairs by the window and gestured to an adjacent one. 'Please come and sit down. I understand that you arrived at the

Halt unexpected and alone. If I may say so, that is a foolhardy action for a young woman.'

Perhaps so, Lettie agreed but said, 'I do have a good reason to come here.'

'So I hear. Why don't you tell me?'

Miss Fanshaw had a brisk manner that reminded her a little of Gran. She had a pleasant face, not especially beautiful or pretty but her features were even and although she had the lines of ageing, her skin was exceptionally fine. So much so that it was at odds with her greying hair.

'I'm searching for my father,' she repeated. 'I had been led to believe that he had passed away and found out, only recently, that this may not be true.'

'But why have you come here, Miss Hargreaves?'

'To speak with Mr Powell.'

'How could he possibly be of assistance to you?'

'I believe that he was a servant at Waterley Hall at the same time as my father.'

Miss Fanshaw's face remained composed. 'Assuming that to be true, how did you know that Mr Powell was here?'

'The Waterley estate land agent wrote to my guardian and told him that a Mr Powell took a position here many years ago when he left the service of Lord Laughton.' Lettie noticed surprise register on Miss Fanshaw's face. But she did not interrupt. 'It was about the same time as my father left. Lord Laughton went abroad and his servants had to find other places.'

Miss Fanshaw looked at her with widened eyes for a

moment then she seemed to compose herself and her features relaxed. 'They told you that he took a position here?'

Lettie thought that she almost smiled and responded eagerly. 'He would have been a footman, I think.' She raised her eyes to the decor and spread her hands. 'He may even have been the butler here. Mereside Lodge is a beautiful residence but it is much smaller than Waterley Hall.'

Lettie waited for a response of any sort and received only another silence.

'Mr Powell might remember where my father went.' Lettie stopped speaking again and wished Miss Fanshaw would say something – anything to indicate how she was reacting to Lettie's story. She wondered whether to mention her grandfather or not and decided that perhaps the whole truth was needed here. 'Of course with Waterley Hall being so big Lord Laughton had a steward. He was my grandfather, Seth Hargreaves. Mr Powell will surely remember him.'

Miss Fanshaw held up both her hands in a desperate gesture. 'You need not go on, Miss Hargreaves. You are very convincing.'

'You believe me?'

'I did not say that. Mereside Lodge is a very exclusive establishment and we pride ourselves on protecting the privacy of our . . . our visitors. I cannot tell you anything about anyone here.'

Lettie sagged into the chair. 'But I only wish to ask Mr Powell if he knows where my father went. You could ask him for me.'

'How do I know you are not a newspaper correspondent?'

Lettie was taken aback that anyone would think she was capable of such a situation. 'Well, I am not a gentleman for a start!'

'No, I do not believe an editor has sent you. But who are you really? You have wheedled your way in here no doubt looking for some titbit of information to whip up into a scandal.'

'I have told you the truth!'

'Our visitors require privacy, Miss Hargreaves, and if you knew anything at all about Mereside Lodge you would realise that our discretion is everything. You will not move from this room until I have arranged for you to be taken back to the Halt in good time for the railway connection to Leeds.'

Lettie's thoughts were tumbling to make sense of this information. Mereside Lodge wasn't a country hotel. It was a clinic of some sort. No wonder she couldn't get past the front entrance! Mr Powell was a patient here. She had so many questions but for the moment she could only hope that he would get better. After a weighty silence she said, 'Very well, Miss Fanshaw. Thank you for seeing me. May I leave a letter for when Mr Powell is well enough to read it?'

'You ought to have written in the first place.'

Miss Fanshaw was right and Reverend Ennis had advised her to wait. But neither of them was her, and had just discovered she had been deceived all her life by someone she loved and trusted. 'May I?' she repeated.

284

Miss Fanshaw waved her arm at a writing desk underneath one of the casement windows. 'You may. I shall send a maid to sit with you and escort you back to the Halt.'

Lettie closed the flap on the envelope and leaned back in her chair, satisfied that she had made her request to Mr Powell clear. The writing desk was a beautiful piece of carved mahogany furniture, designed to hold writing implements and an old-fashioned blotting block that she had rocked gently over her letter before folding it. The notepaper and envelopes were fine quality paper, with *Mereside Lodge, Forest Chase, Yorkshire, NR* embossed in blue. She noticed wax and a spirit burner for seals, a practice that was totally unnecessary now people used envelopes fastened with glue. A king or royal duke might seal documents with an imprint of his ring. She picked up the brass seal and examined the end. It was, she thought, an engraving of stag antlers, perhaps from the coat of arms when the house was a hunting lodge.

On impulse, Lettie lit the candle and picked up the stick of red wax. She melted the end and let it drip over the envelope flap to form a blob. Then she pressed the end of the brass seal into it and blew out the candle. It showed that she had written it here and was, she thought, an indication of her serious intentions. When the maid arrived in her hat and coat, Lettie gave her the letter, which she in turn left with the young man in the entrance hall. She then followed the maid to the side door.

'What's your name?' Lettie asked as they walked to the Halt.

'Cutler.'

'I mean your Christian name. I'm Lettie.'

'Agnes Cutler.'

'What is going on here, Agnes? Is it some kind of clinic?'

'I'm not allowed to talk about it.'

'Well, it's a long walk to the Halt, so what shall we talk about?'

Agnes didn't reply. Lettie continued, 'I met a girl from the village at the Halt and she said her mother and father wouldn't let her work at Mereside Lodge.'

'She doesn't know what she's talking about. I don't take any notice of gossip.'

'What do your parents say, then?'

'I haven't got any parents.'

'Are you an orphan, too?' Lettie knew what that felt like. She went on, 'I thought I was until recently. Then I heard my father might still be alive. That's why I'm here.'

'You don't think he's here, do you?'

'No, but how would you feel if you found out your father wasn't dead after all and you had the name of someone who might have known him? Mr Powell was in service with my father. He could help me find him.'

Agnes turned to face her. 'Is that true?'

'Of course it's true. I don't tell lies. I was brought up in a Methodist manse.'

'Did you write that in your letter?'

'Yes. Mr Powell will get to read it, won't he?'

'I don't know. Miss Fanshaw'll probably reply for him.'

'Can he not think for himself?'

'He's fine when he's well, but sometimes when he is not . . . well, we're all anxious about . . . our imminent visitor.'

Lettie sighed. 'It's not the King, is it?' Lettie wasn't really serious but Agnes was. She stopped abruptly and answered firmly. 'No it's not. Can we talk about something else?'

They walked on in silence for a while until Lettie asked, 'Have you worked here since you left the orphanage?'

'I had a position in a well-to-do household first. It was a below-stairs position and I wasn't very happy but I couldn't see a way out until I'd been there long enough for a reference. Then two winters ago a visiting dowager fell ill and needed someone with her round the clock so I was sent upstairs to help.' Agnes seemed to relax as she told her story. 'She was . . . well . . . oh, she was really tiresome. Nothing was ever right and no one else wanted to sit with her so it was always me who had to cope with her.'

'Oh you poor thing, how did you do that?'

'I just tried to do everything she asked and when she complained I always apologised.'

Lettie laughed. 'Is that all?'

'Why is that funny?'

'It sounds so easy but it can't have been.'

'No it wasn't, I can tell you. It paid off, though. When she was feeling better and I was back below stairs, she sent for me and told me if I wanted a better position she could help me. She's a regular patient at Mereside

Lodge. She knows the—' Again Agnes stopped talking abruptly.

A patient? Lettie thought. Her presumption had been correct. It was a clinic. 'Does this lady know Mr Powell?' Lettie asked.

But Agnes reverted to her formal voice. 'I'll see that Miss Fanshaw gets your letter. It's the best you can hope for. Listen, when we reach the track to the Halt, I'll leave you. You'll have a long wait for the train but I have some errands in the village for the patients. The villagers might disapprove of Mereside Lodge but the shopkeepers and the blacksmith make a good living out of us.'

They said goodbye to each other and Lettie was left with the impression that Agnes was more than just a parlourmaid. She walked briskly to the Halt then paced up and down the platform, wrestling with her thoughts. Instead of feeling pleased that she had located Mr Powell and written to him, she was dissatisfied that she had been close to the answers to her questions and was now on her way home. What was she to do with herself while she waited for Miss Fanshaw to reply? And what if she didn't write?

A stack of empty hampers awaited collection and she sat down with her thoughts until she heard the steam whistle of the approaching train. The big black engine hissed to a halt and clouds of steam swirled around the platform. No one alighted apart from the guard. She stood up while he stacked the hampers in his van and then waited patiently for her to climb aboard.

She couldn't do it. She had come so far in such a short

time; she could not leave without answers to her questions.

'All aboard, miss,' the guard called.

Lettie turned smartly away from the train and with a straight back marched through the white gate and away from the platform. She heard the huge steam engine huff and puff, and then grind into motion. It was too late, now, to change her mind and she continued walking, pushing all practical considerations out of her head.

Chapter 21

The road between Mereside Lodge and the village was deserted. She turned towards the village and as she approached it, passed a row of farm workers' cottages with slate roofs and then a pair that were thatched with pretty curtains at the windows and well-kept front gardens. When the green came into view, Lettie realised that Mereside was a well-to-do village with a row of shops along one side of the triangular patch of grassland. A church and school stood on another side and an inn on the third with a blacksmith's forge next door. There was a carriage and pair outside the inn. She was walking past the church when she saw Agnes step out of the draper's shop and join a cluster of women who were intent on chatting. Lettie quickly dodged into the churchyard and behind a yew tree, away from view. She wasn't sure why she was hiding except that it didn't seem sensible for Mereside Lodge to know she had not left as they wished.

She heard organ music from inside the church and remembered the girl off the railway train earlier, home for her sister's wedding. Lettie's heart began to thump. She had no wish to be caught out as a vagrant. Wedding guests would be milling around the churchyard soon. She moved to behind a beech hedge and stayed out of sight until the bride and groom emerged as husband and wife. Eventually, the party moved off and straggled across the green to the inn. It was Church of England and not Methodist but Lettie slipped inside while she worked out what to do. Her immediate reaction was one of delight. The flowers were enchanting, making a plain interior attractive and inviting. She chose a pew in the darkest corner and knelt down to say a prayer.

What had she done? Only stranded herself in a place she did not know! She must be out of her mind and thanked the Lord for keeping her safe until now. It had been a foolish idea to take the train to Mereside Halt in the first place without any sort of invitation or introduction. A young woman travelling alone was asking for trouble and she was lucky that Mereside Lodge wasn't some country hideaway established for race-goers and gamblers. Heavens, it could house activities just as sinister as the white slave trade and she had willingly gone inside! Her thoughts ran riot, but prayers helped. They anchored her jumbled ideas and made sense of her actions. She was determined not to leave Mereside until she had met with Mr Powell. Anything less would mean that she had wasted her journey.

It was cool inside the church and she went out into the sunlight to warm up. Across the green, the wedding party took up everyone's attention and the sun was already in the western sky. The days were getting shorter as autumn approached and with a clear sky the night was likely to be chilly. She hadn't passed a farm or a barn and she didn't know how much a night in the inn would cost.

There might be someone in the village who took in lodgers but she would have to knock on doors and ask. It was that or a church pew for her bed tonight! A landlady would, quite reasonably, wish to know her business in Mereside and what could she say? Certainly not 'I have business with Mr Powell of Mereside Lodge' if she wanted to be seen as respectable! Why hadn't she listened to Reverend Ennis and waited?

Gran had often advised her that a Methodist chapel was the best place to shelter in a storm, whether real or inside her head, and it seemed to Lettie that a church was the next best thing to a chapel. She returned to her shadowy spot and sat on hassocks with her knees drawn up and her back against the cold stone wall, hiding quietly until the vicar returned and went into his vestry to change. He went out again through the main door.

She was in luck. He did not lock the vestry and a winter cloak hung on a hook on the wall next to an umbrella. She wrapped herself in the cloak and returned to her pew, then finished the last of her oatmeal biscuits and apples and tried to sleep. The church clock chimed every quarter of an hour, but she must have dozed for while.

When she woke she felt refreshed. Her leg had gone to sleep and she got up to stretch and walk round. It was eerie in the silent empty building and she was glad of the flowers at the ends of the pews to cheer her. She massaged her leg then returned the cloak to its peg in the vestry. Her eyes were used to the darkness by then and she went outside to look at the clock. It was almost half past one and another four hours at least before folk started moving about.

She sat on a low wall and shivered. She didn't want to go back inside the church and spend the rest of the night huddled on the church floor. She wouldn't freeze to death out of doors at this time of year. But, more importantly she decided to return to Mereside Lodge, to walk back under cover of darkness and, somehow, find her way to the domestic offices at the rear until the household woke up. If she couldn't get to see Mr Powell via the front door, she would find another way.

She jumped at every rustle and squeak at first. But when she became accustomed to the nocturnal comings and goings of small animals and birds she relaxed. Even the fox seemed more scared of her than she was of him, although he did stop and stare at her for a minute.

She became aware of a low rumbling noise a long time before she identified the sound. It was a motor vehicle on the road behind her making slow progress in the dark. She darted off the road into a clump of trees and crouched down as it rumbled passed her. A motor vehicle was an unusual sight out here in the middle of the countryside and this was a delivery wagon like – good heavens! She straightened up, startled by the name on the door. She ran forward for a closer look at the name inscribed on the coachwork. It *was* a Toogoods wagon, just like the one Thomas drove, but it was empty of coal.

As she stared after it, it stopped in the middle of the road and the noise of the engine died away. The door to the driving seat opened and she retreated to the shadows of the trees.

'Wait!' the driver called.

He sounded just like Thomas. Thomas? Surely not?

'Wait,' he repeated, 'I'm looking for someone.'

'Thomas?'

'Lettie? Is that you? Oh, thank God. Are you all right? You're not hurt or anything?'

'No, I'm well. What are you doing here?'

'I'm searching for you! What do you think I'm doing! The foreman back at the yard told me you'd been in the office asking for me and then Reverend Ennis came looking for you.'

'Oh no. I didn't mean to worry him.'

'Well, you did. You left him a letter and he thought I might know more about it. We were all worried about you. Even my foreman got the wind up when the Reverend turned up at the yard. He knew your gran because he used to work at the Waterley Edge pit so he let me take the wagon to find you. What's all this about, Lettie?'

'It was something the Reverend said about my father. He might still be alive, Thomas, and if he is I have to find out.'

'Oh I see. I thought your gran said your parents were dead?'

'Not exactly. She never actually said they were dead, just that they'd gone.' Lettie shuddered suddenly and felt weary.

Thomas took up her hands and rubbed them between his palms. There were rough and covered in calluses but they were large and warm. 'You're cold,' he said. 'Come over here and stand by the engine.'

'You haven't got anything to eat, have you?' she asked.

He reached under the driver's seat and brought out a battered tin box. 'Try one of my mum's pasties.'

'Oh, thank you.'

'I've got some cold tea in a bottle if you're thirsty.'

'Thank you,' she repeated. 'God must be listening to me. I prayed in church for help and here you are. How did you know where I'd be?'

'Reverend Ennis told me what you'd put in your note to him and then the lads in the yard had seen you at the railway station, so I asked about you in the ticket office. What are you doing wandering around in the middle of the night?'

'I've been up to Mereside Lodge. I think it's a private clinic and there's a patient there who might have been at Waterley Hall at the same time as my father.'

'Have you spoken to him?'

'They wouldn't let me see him.'

'Were you surprised? I'm not. You could be anybody.'

'They let me leave a letter for him.'

'Then come home with me until he replies.'

295

'I can't. I'm too close to give up now.'

'You won't be giving up. You'll be being sensible.'

'I don't want to be sensible! I want to find my father! Nobody understands how it feels to be so close to something you have always wanted. I'm not leaving until I've seen Mr Powell. I'm not.'

'Lettie, you have to. I can't stay with you. I've promised to have the wagon back for morning. If I'm not in the yard at six o'clock loading it with coal, I'll be on my bicycle again.'

'Then you must go home now! You can't lose another job because of me!'

'Well, come back with me, then! I'll ask if I can borrow the wagon on Sunday and bring you over for the day.'

She shook her head. 'You're so kind, Thomas, but I've made up my mind. I am going to see this Mr Powell before I leave.'

'Please, Lettie. Let me take you home.'

She shook her head.

An owl hooted and, in the distance, the church clock chimed. 'It's a long way back, Lettie. I've got to set off now.'

'Then you go. I've already spoken to one of the maids up there. She's an orphan like me and understands why I'm here.'

'You're determined to do this, aren't you?'

'Yes.'

'I'll drive you up to the house then.'

'No, you can't. That thing makes too much noise.'

'Then I'll walk you up there, but *come on*.'

Lettie smiled in the dark. She knew she could rely on Thomas. 'Thank you,' she said. 'Keep to the trees. I want to find my way round to the back.'

The wall around Mereside Lodge stretched as far as Lettie could see it. 'Give me a leg-up over there,' she said. 'There's a tree the other side.'

'Are you sure about this? They might have dogs.'

Lettie hesitated. 'I don't think so. I didn't hear any earlier on.'

'I don't want to leave you.'

'I know what I'm doing. Help me up.'

He cupped his hands and she placed her boot in them, reaching for the top of the wall and hoisting herself up. She sat astride and whispered, 'It's easy. I can climb down the tree.'

'What's on the other side?'

'Just gardens.' She sat there watching for movement or a light. 'It's quiet.' She looked down at Thomas's anxious face. 'Thank you,' she said. 'I'll be all right now. It's a clinic. They take care of people. You'd better be off. Please tell Reverend Ennis that I'm safe and well.'

'But you're not!'

'I am,' she argued. 'As soon as I've spoken to Mr Powell I'll catch the railway train home.'

'Well, I hope this Mr Powell is worth it. I'll call in at the manse to see you on Sunday and if you're not there I'm coming to find you.'

'You're a good friend, Thomas.'

She stayed astride the wall as he walked away. A few minutes later she heard the low rumble of the motor engine and listened as the sound grew fainter and fainter until the air was silent again. She shivered, wavered for a moment, and then dragged herself onto a sturdy branch and climbed carefully down the tree. She brushed the flakes of bark and leaves from her clothes and yawned, suddenly feeling very tired. From the top of the wall she had noticed a summerhouse and she headed towards it. It wasn't locked and contained several pieces of wickerwork furniture. She piled the cushions onto a couple of chairs and placed them facing each other to make a bed. It was more comfortable than the church pew and she slept for a few hours.

Daylight woke her and she sat up quickly, alert for any sounds. But all was quiet. She stretched and yawned, wondering what time it was. There wasn't a soul in sight from the summerhouse windows. Nonetheless, Lettie decided she would be less noticeable if she were round the back of Mereside Lodge where the domestic offices must be situated. She replaced the furniture as she had found it and headed for a section of straggly shrubbery. The garden, she noticed, was neglected and untidy, which was a shame because it was laid out with flower borders and beds and could be quite beautiful.

From the cover of the shrubbery, Lettie was able to see the collection of buildings at the back of the Lodge. The nearest were the stables and coach house and they were as much in need of attention as the garden. But her eyes were drawn to a long building that formed a rear wing of the main house. Lettie identified a boiler room at the end by its chimney stack already giving out smoke. Outside a young man was shovelling coal from a heap into buckets and lining them up by the building. A maid came outside and called him in, presumably for his breakfast.

Lettie was considering her next move when she almost jumped out of her skin as a heavy hand grabbed her shoulder.

'What are you doing nosing around here?' She whirled round to see the surly man who had collected the hampers from the station the day before.

'I . . . I—'

'You come with me.'

His hand stayed firmly on her shoulder and he steered her towards the stabling where a gnarled and stooping stable hand was leading out a pony. 'Who's she?' he asked.

'She's trouble. I got a ticking-off from Fanny for bringing this 'un from the Halt yesterday.'

'Did she see owt?'

'Dunno, but she were supposed to be on her way yesterday so tek her with you when you go down for the hampers. See her into the railway carriage afore, y'know, you check owt. She's got eyes in the back of her head, this one.'

The stable hand grimaced. 'What shall I do wi' her till then?'

'Put her in the tack room and lock the door.'

'You can't do that to me!' Lettie protested. 'I came back to see the housekeeper.'

They ignored her and the gnarled old man let go of his pony, gripped her arm and tugged her in the direction of the coach house.

She tried to shake free and protested, 'I'm not going and you can't make me.'

'Shut up.' The other man gave her a hefty shove in the back.

She stumbled and fell to her knees, causing the old man to jerk sideways, swear and spook the pony. It reared its front legs, snatching the reins from the man's grasp. For a moment both men let go of Lettie, fearful, as she was, of receiving a kick from the frightened beast. Lettie saw her opportunity. She scrambled to her feet and ran in the direction of the coal heap and a door that she knew was open. They didn't follow her and she guessed they were more concerned about the pony than her. But she was left with a distinct impression that both of these men were up to no good.

The boilerman who had been shovelling coal and the maid who had called out to him were just inside the open door lolling against the wall and drinking mugs of tea. They were so interested in each other than they didn't notice her until she was virtually in front of them, catching her breath.

'Good morning,' she said brightly. 'Is the housekeeper's room this way?'

'What housekeeper? We haven't got a housekeeper,' the maid answered. The young man handed his empty mug to her and returned to shovelling coal.

'The butler then or whoever is in charge of the servants. I . . . I'm looking for a position.'

'Are you?' The maid gave her an interested glance. 'Can you start today?'

Lettie did not hesitate. 'Yes.'

'You'll want to see Fanny, then. That's Miss Fanshaw to you.'

Not her, Lettie groaned silently, she'll send me away again. 'Is there no one else I can talk to?' A crashing sound came from inside the house. 'Good heavens! What was that?'

The maid looked miserable. 'It's the scullery maid. The new cook uses her as an assistant cook and the poor girl isn't up to it.'

'Shall I go and help her?'

'Can you cook?' the girl asked.

'Have you got a clean apron? I can make a start in the kitchen while I'm waiting for Miss Fanshaw.'

'Would you? I don't know what Fanny'll say but to be honest if she doesn't get more help in, I'll be off an' all. Follow me.' She started to walk down the passage.

'Are servants always leaving, then?' Lettie asked. But the girl went through a door that she left open and returned a few seconds later with a fresh white apron and a hat.

'I'll put the hat on for you.' It was shaped like a close-fitting bonnet without a brim and had to be pinned to her head, squashing down her piled-up hair. 'Cor, you look different! Go and see what Cook wants. If she asks where I am, tell her I'm helping Agnes.' The girl pointed towards a door opposite and pulled on her own cap as she carried on down the passage towards the green baize door that separated domestic offices from the main house.

The kitchen was a huge high-ceilinged room with walls covered in white tiles. It was filled with the aromatic odour of sausages sizzling on the cooking range. But the light was poor as, Lettie noticed, all the windows needed cleaning. They were opposite the door and looked out on to the coal yard and, beyond that, the stables. Hastily, Lettie closed the kitchen door behind her, wondering if her earlier captors had followed her.

'Good morning, Cook.'

Cook did not turned around from her sausages. 'Where've you been? The men'll be in for their breakfast soon. Pick up those oven trays and lay out the bacon then bring me the frying pans for the eggs.'

Lettie tied on her apron, which, fortunately, covered most of her dress. The long scrubbed table appeared to be divided into three with polished silver serving dishes at one end and older tarnished ones at the other. A bowl of soaked prunes, another full of eggs and a pile of ready-sliced bacon were in the middle directly behind the cook. Lettie arranged the bacon on an oven tray and carried it to the range.

Cook's face was ruddy from the heat. 'Oh, you're new. About time too, what's your name?'

'Lettie.'

Cook examined the bacon and nodded. 'Put that in the top oven. Where are my frying pans?'

Lettie responded swiftly.

'Well, put them on the hotplate then,' Cook said. 'They won't heat up with you waving them around in the air.'

302

Lettie obeyed. A kettle was bubbling away and she suggested making the tea.

'Yes and carry it into the servants' hall; they'll be gasping for it by now.'

Lettie's recent visit to Waterley Hall had given her an idea of how servants' quarters were organised in a large household and Mereside Lodge wasn't as big. She stood in the passage with the heavy teapot and milk jug on a tray. Someone had closed the outer door and it was dark. But she reckoned that the scullery and pot store was the same side as the kitchen; so the housekeeper's and butler's rooms were likely to be opposite alongside the servants' hall. She stood with aching arms until the green baize door swung open and a liveried footman came through. It was the same one she had seen in the entrance hall yesterday.

Luckily he didn't recognise her in her kitchen maid's cap. 'I'll take that,' he said and did, disappearing through a door opposite as quickly as he had arrived.

Lettie returned to the kitchen and Cook immediately ordered her to take in the prunes and porridge. 'And tell them the bacon's not ready yet.'

Well, this is it, she thought. Someone is bound to recognise me now. As she picked up the bowls of prunes, the maid came in, quite out of breath and said, 'Fanny says Mr Powell wants his breakfast now.'

'Miss Fanshaw to you,' Cook snapped. 'Show this new girl what's needed, then.'

The maid groaned. 'Agnes wants me to help her.'

Lettie glanced at the silverware and linen stacked on

the table. 'I don't need to be shown,' she said and began to lay up one of the silver trays.

'He must be feeling better this morning,' Cook muttered. 'Hand me those dishes for the sausages.' Cook fried a dozen eggs in two huge frying pans and transferred them to shallow earthenware dishes warming on her hotplate. Then she dealt with the bacon before turning round to check Lettie's silver trays. She had completed half a dozen of them.

'Very nice. Have you done this before?'

'My grandmother was a housekeeper in service and she taught me.'

'Very nice,' Cook repeated. 'You'd best keep your apron clean for taking them upstairs. I'll get on with the servants' breakfast.'

'What about Mr Powell's breakfast?'

'It's in that bowl on the dresser. Squeeze the lemons into the glass jug, put three of those biscuits under the dome and fill the silver jug with hot water.'

'Is that all?'

'Dr Bretton's orders.' Cook shook her head. 'I can't see how half-starving a body will help it get well.'

Me neither, Lettie thought. 'Shall I take it up to Mr Powell?'

'Give it to Agnes or Miss Fanshaw then come back for your own breakfast before it gets cold.'

'Which room is he in?' Lettie asked. Her heart was beginning to thump with excitement and fear. She'd be bundled out as soon as she was recognised but there was a chance that she might get to see Mr Powell before that happened and it was worth the risk.

'Facing the lake but his name's on the door.'

'Is that on the first floor?' she asked.

It was and Lettie went out into the passage with Mr Powell's breakfast tray.

Chapter 22

She pushed open the green baize door with her bottom and found herself, as anticipated, at the rear of the entrance hall. She probably should have used the back stairs but she wasn't sure where they were and the entrance hall was deserted. She walked quickly towards the staircase that rose and turned out of sight. It was carpeted. Mereside Lodge had beautiful Turkish carpets in the rooms she had seen. The tray was nowhere near as heavy as those she had carried into the dining room at the manse but she was careful not to spill anything.

At the top of the stairs she turned to her left, past one of the fluted wooden pillars, remembering where the windows were located from outside the Lodge. Guessing which might have the finest view she peered at the white name card sitting in its brass holder on the outside of the door.

Lord Laughton. The shock nearly caused her to drop the tray. Lord Laughton! Here! Her mind raced. Was he ill? Was that the reason he was returning from abroad?

She heard a doorknob turn and huddled with her back to the door hoping she was shielded from view by the pillar. Someone came out of a room on the other side of the stairs and went down to the hall. Lettie leaned forward to see Miss Fanshaw hurrying away. Forgetting Lord Laughton, she crossed the landing to find Mr Powell's room and knocked on the door.

'Come in.' His voice sounded weary.

Lettie's heart was thumping in her mouth as she leaned down to turn the doorknob. Her feet crossed the carpet silently. It was not a huge room but it had a fine bay window that looked out over the lake. The bedroom furniture was heavy mahogany and a fire burned in the grate. Mr Powell was sitting in an upholstered chair at a round table positioned in the bay window. He had his back to her but she noticed that his hair was white. The soft furnishings in the room gave it a hushed comfort that Lettie found calming.

'Your breakfast is here, Mr Powell,' she said quietly.

'Is that you, Agnes? Speak up, will you?' He leaned forward to push some documents to one side.

Against all her grandmother's training of never looking directly at the faces of those you were serving, she did. He was not as old as his white hair indicated although he had lined features and dark shadows around his eyes. He had been handsome, she thought, for he had a

307

straight brow and nose, good cheekbones and jawline, although his sallow skin now sagged. He did not appear to be in good health. His eyes were a dull blue and when he caught sight of her, they opened wide. 'Good God,' he exclaimed, 'you startled me.'

'I beg your pardon, sir.'

'Who the devil are you?'

Every muscle in Lettie's body seemed to seize. She could hardly breathe. She had to be honest. 'I'm a new maid, sir.'

'Oh, I see. Your eyes, the way you speak, it reminded me of—' He stopped and glanced over the tray as she placed it before him. 'No brandy?'

'Shall I fetch you some, sir?'

He gave a short dry laugh. 'You would risk Miss Fanshaw's wrath? You have more courage than I.'

Lettie stood motionless, gathering her courage and formulating the words in her head. As she did, he waved a hand and said, 'That will be all.'

'Very good, sir.' She didn't move. She couldn't. Her legs seemed frozen to the spot. Ask him! What can he do to you? This is your chance, ask him now!

'Mr Powell.' Her voice was light and breathless.

'What is it, girl?' He twisted his head in her direction. 'What do I call you?'

'Mr Powell, please forgive me for this intrusion but I must speak with you. You see, I'm searching for my father and you may have known him as a young man. I believe he was in service for Lord Laughton when you were a footman. Can you help me, sir?'

There, she'd said it, and she had rehearsed it in her head so many times that it came out word perfect and she was satisfied with her delivery. 'Please, sir,' she added. 'You are my only hope.'

Within seconds the room seemed to be in chaos. Mr Powell shot to his feet and turned on her with a terrifying expression of disbelief and horror. 'Who are you?' he cried.

At the same time the bedroom door flew open, Miss Fanshaw rushed in and demanded, 'What are you doing in this house? How dare you come back here? Sneaking in, unannounced, who do you think you are?'

Mr Powell echoed her last question. 'Answer her, girl. Who are you?'

'I'm Lettie Hargreaves,' she answered. 'My grandfather was Seth Hargreaves.'

Mr Powell's face drained of the little colour it had, leaving a pasty, yellowing complexion. He sank into his chair. 'Dear God, is this true? Who sent you here?' There was desperation in his eyes as he turned to Miss Fanshaw. 'Did he send her, Frances? He means to get what he wants, doesn't he? What shall I do?' He looked pleadingly at Miss Fanshaw, whose face Lettie could only describe as a mixture of fury and anguish.

Miss Fanshaw was beside him with one arm across his shoulders and the other covering his hand. 'She's nothing to do with him, Michael,' Miss Fanshaw soothed. 'She's a nobody and I'll get rid of her. Calm down and take your breakfast. Dr Bretton will call in as usual.'

But Mr Powell would not be calmed. His voice had a hard edge to it. 'If he's sent her she is not a nobody. What is the old goat up to now? Oh God, I need a drink, Frances. You have to let me have a brandy, just a small one, only the one, I promise.'

Miss Fanshaw knelt down beside him and cupped his hand between hers. 'You know I can't do that. What would Dr Bretton say?' Then she twisted her head to look at Lettie over her shoulder, her face flushed with anger. 'Get out of here,' she ordered.

'I need a brandy, Frances. Just one,' Mr Powell pleaded.

'Get out this minute,' Miss Fanshaw repeated harshly. Lettie obeyed.

Agnes was hovering outside the bedroom door. 'It is you! I knew it! I said it was you in the kitchen!' she exclaimed. 'Miss Fanshaw would have told me if she'd taken on a new maid. You should have gone home yesterday on the railway train.'

'Would you have, when you were so close to discovering someone who might know where your father was?'

'Miss Fanshaw was livid after she realised you'd wormed your way back here. She'll call the constable. She will, so you'd better leave now.'

'I can't.' Lettie shook her head decisively. 'Mr Powell recognised my grandfather's name. He is the man I am looking for.' Lettie grimaced. 'I am sorry if I've upset him. I . . . I think I did give him a shock. He . . . he said something about a brandy.'

'Some patients take it with their morning tea,' Agnes replied. 'If Dr Bretton recommends it.'

Lettie didn't comment at first but it was clear to her that Mr Powell had really wanted his brandy. There had been a desperation in his eyes that made Lettie frown. She recalled what the Reverend and Gran said about men who liked their drink too much. He was one of those folk for whom 'one drink was too many because ten were not enough'. She murmured more to herself than to Agnes, 'He's a drunkard.'

After a moment Agnes added, 'Miss Fanshaw has given everyone strict orders never to serve drink of any kind to Mr Powell. He . . . he has been very poorly with the drink habit in the past and we have got this important visitor due.'

'Would that be Lord Laughton?'

'How do you know?'

Lettie pointed along the landing. 'His name's on that door.'

'You shouldn't be up here prying. I'm instructed to keep an eye on you.' Agnes gave her a little push towards the staircase, adding, 'And I want my breakfast.'

The servants' hall was smaller than Lettie had expected, but then she had seen only the one at Waterley Hall. It had a wooden floor and a fireplace flanked by two armchairs with a clock sitting on the mantelpiece. There was also a worn, spotted cheval mirror, an upright piano plus stool and an old sideboard where the servants helped themselves to food. The room was dominated by a long dining table covered with a white tablecloth. Lettie counted eighteen chairs around the table and they were all in use as different servants came and went constantly. Lettie realised that some of them were nurses. Eventually, the chaos eased, leaving Cook seated at the end nearest the sideboard with Lettie and Agnes, and a few outdoor servants including the two men from the stables further down the table.

'That's her!' one said. 'A right little madam, she is, she broke into the summerhouse.'

'Is that true?' Agnes queried.

'It wasn't locked so I slept inside.'

'All night?'

'Not exactly,' Lettie replied. 'I spent the first half of the night in the village church.'

'You don't want to believe a word she says,' the other man said. 'She told me a pack of lies yesterday.'

'I did not!'

Cook intervened. 'Now then, I don't want arguments in here. If you've got any complaints, speak to Miss Fanshaw. She's in charge now.'

'Only because she says so!' the man continued. 'How do we know it's what Mr Powell wants? He's been poorly for weeks. How do we know she hasn't drugged him with one of her fancy cures?'

'They burned her sort as witches in the old days,' the stableman added.

'Oh shut up, you two!' Agnes responded angrily. 'We have enough dealing with village gossip without you adding to it! Miss Fanshaw is a proper nurse. She nursed injured soldiers in Africa, in the war out there.'

'We managed well enough afore without her interference,' the man muttered.

Agnes retaliated. 'Haven't you got a carriage and pair to spruce up for when His Lordship's train arrives?'

Cook stood up and raised her voice. 'That's enough from all of you. If you outdoor lot have finished you can get off now. Dinner's at twelve sharp for everybody today.'

The outdoor servants rose to their feet and one of them said, 'Grand breakfast, that. At least summat's improved around here.'

'Aye and the sooner that new butler gets here, the better,' Cook muttered.

Agnes waited until they had closed the door behind them before she went to the sideboard to help herself. Lettie followed her. She was very hungry and helped herself to porridge, bacon, sausage, egg and a hunk of bread. The kitchen maid she had met earlier came in and sat next to her.

'I hope I haven't caused you any trouble?' Lettie whispered.

The girl glanced at Cook and Agnes with their heads close together deep in conversation. 'Cook said she didn't care who you were because you showed some gumption in the kitchen.'

'When's His Lordship arriving?'

'It must be today because Cook's planning seven courses for dinner tonight.'

The girl ate quickly and went back to her duties leaving Lettie on her own with Agnes and Cook. They stood up to leave.

Cook said to her, 'Come with me and wait in the kitchen for Miss Fanshaw. She'll be down in a minute to check the patients' breakfasts.'

313

'What can I do to help while I wait?'

'Trying to be nice won't make any difference to Miss Fanshaw. But I'm not going to turn down a useful pair of hands. Can you make meringues?'

Lettie hadn't made them often although both the Reverend and Gran had praised hers. As with her sponge cakes, she didn't stint on the beating. Meringues were easy as long as you left them long enough to dry out. She walked over to the oven range, opened the lower door and put her hand inside. 'That's just right now, but if it gets any hotter, they'll colour.'

'Get them in as soon as you can. I'll be roasting venison by teatime.'

Lettie became engrossed in her task and was piping the meringues into nests, as Cook had directed, when Miss Fanshaw came into the kitchen. Her task called for concentration and a steady hand so, although she heard their lowered voices, she didn't allow herself to be distracted until she had finished. She straightened and passed the back of her hand over her forehead.

Cook said, 'Very nice. I'll see those into the oven. Off you go with Miss Fanshaw.'

Lettie wiped her hands on a tea-towel and followed the starchy Miss Fanshaw across the passage through a door with a brass label 'Housekeeper'. It was a comfortable little sitting room with a fire laid but not lit. There were no pictures, journals or needlework bags. In fact, the room appeared to be unused.

'Sit down.' Miss Fanshaw indicated a dining chair at the small chenille-covered table. 'You are a very determined

314

young lady,' she began, 'but so am I and my main concern at present is Mr Powell.'

'I am sorry that I upset him, ma'am. Please assure Mr Powell that no one has sent me, least of all my grandfather who has been dead for many years.'

'Mr Powell was not speaking of your grandfather. He had not expected to hear from anyone bearing the name Hargreaves. Your arrival has been a great shock to him. His journey back to health is a long and difficult one and . . .' Miss Fanshaw's composure faltered and, for a second, Lettie glimpsed the compassionate side to her nature. But it did not last and her firm tone returned quickly. 'You are jeopardising his recovery. I assume you are one of His Lordship's servants who he has sent ahead of his party in secret. Now you must tell me why.' Miss Fanshaw glared at her and added, 'I am waiting.'

'I have nothing to do with Lord Laughton or his party. I have explained it to you and to Mr Powell. I believe he remembers my father from his days at Waterley Hall. Please, Miss Fanshaw, I beg you to let me speak to him. You see, I didn't know my father was alive—' Lettie continued with her well rehearsed little speech until Miss Fanshaw interrupted.

'He will see you.'

Lettie stopped, open mouthed. 'Beg pardon, ma'am.'

'Mr Powell will see you. He is inclined to believe who you are.'

'I am speaking the truth.'

Miss Fanshaw passed her hand over her brow and frowned. 'Unfortunately, it is the truth that is difficult for him to face. He has spoken very little of his past and the brandy bottle is an easy friend.'

'I didn't know. I'm sorry.' Lettie looked down at her hands resting lightly on the plush table cover.

She heard Miss Fanshaw sigh and then say, 'Cook wants you to stay and help her with tonight's banquet.'

'May I?'

'Do you not have a home to go to?'

'Not any more. I have no family left and I must find an occupation or . . . or marry, I suppose.' Lettie gave an involuntary shudder as she considered the latter with Eric Jones.

'Your clothes indicate that you are not destitute. Surely someone will be wondering why you have not returned?'

Reverend Ennis, she thought. But she had explained everything to Thomas and she trusted him to tell the Reverend.

'Well, Miss Hargreaves? There is a telegraph office in the village.'

'I have already sent a message to my guardian.' Miss Fanshaw assumed she meant a telegraph message and Lettie did not enlighten her. 'When will Mr Powell see me?'

'He has treatments throughout the morning as do most of the patients here. He rests after lunch so you may speak with him at tea. He takes tea at five o'clock in his room.'

'Thank you, ma'am.'

Miss Fanshaw stood up. 'You will not set foot out of

316

the servants' quarters until then.' She clicked her tongue. 'This is most tiresome. We are very busy and cannot watch over you every minute of the day.'

'Will you let me help where I can? I was an assistant housekeeper until recently and I can cook.'

'Yes, I noticed your meringues.' Miss Fanshaw stared at her while she decided. 'Very well,' she said at last. 'I shall inform Cook and you will take your orders from her.'

'Thank you, ma'am.'

'Make sure I do not regret this decision.'

'May I ask a question, ma'am?'

'What is it now?'

'What sort of clinic is Mereside Lodge?'

'It is a private one and none of your business.'

Miss Fanshaw left Lettie in the kitchen with Cook who seemed to be enjoying preparing the forthcoming dinner. Lettie spent most of her day picking over, peeling and turning vegetables and fruit. Cook gave the responsibility for the servants' dinner to Lettie, which consisted of boiling a whole brisket of beef and making two huge baked rice puddings. There were no complaints and Lettie gained the impression that meals had improved since Cook had taken over.

'Where were you before here?' Lettie asked her.

'I worked in the kitchens of an Earl and Countess once,' Cook replied. 'The cooks never ate with the rest of the servants there. We had our own dining room.'

'Was that your last position?' Lettie asked.

'No, m'dear. My last master was a Bradford mill owner.

He entertained local gentry from miles around. I used to cook dinners of several courses every night and they drank a different wine with each dish.'

'Will they do that tonight?'

'His Lordship will expect it. He's starting the cure tomorrow.'

'The cure?'

'The cure. It's what they do here.'

Lettie's imagination ran riot. 'A cure for what?'

'Gout, rheumatism.' Cook shrugged. 'Hydropathy can help lots of illnesses.'

'Hydropathy? What's that? I've never heard of it before.'

'The gentry go for it in a big way. Turkish baths and not much to eat, as far as I can make out. It's very popular with gentlemen who've lost their vigour, if you get my meaning.'

'I'm sorry, I don't.'

'Well, the ancient Romans had steam baths; and cold ones, and rubs and pummelling—'

'It sounds painful to me.'

'Invigorating, I'm told. They don't have much to eat either. Folk used to "take the waters" and now they have hydropathy. My last master used to go to an establishment in Harrogate. Haven't you heard of the Matlock House Hydro in Derbyshire? The King goes there.'

'I shouldn't think the King would take kindly to lemon juice and biscuits for his breakfast.'

'You'd be surprised. Now, I think those meringues will have to come out before they colour. Take them into the pastry room until I need them.'

'How many guests are you expecting for dinner?'

'Not many. His Lordship and another well-to-do gentleman who apparently telegraphed to say he was arriving today. Dr Bretton and Miss Fanshaw will be attending and one or two patients who have finished their treatments, and Mr Powell, of course. He's the host.'

'Mr Powell is the host? I thought he was a patient.'

'Mr Powell is the master here. He owns Mereside Lodge.'

Chapter 23

Goodness, thought Lettie, Mr Powell must be a rich man. Perhaps he wasn't a footman and my father was employed by him at some time. She felt her excitement bubble. If he had been Father's employer, he would be sure to know where Father went.

Lettie passed the afternoon in the pastry room lining tiny tin baking moulds with shortcrust and cutting sponge cake into shapes for decorating desserts. The time dragged slowly until Cook called her out to put on a clean cap and apron.

'Agnes says Mr Powell wants to see you and you're to take his tea. I want you back here in time to do the servants' high tea. They have it at six o'clock. It's cold meat and pickles tonight, followed by fruitcake and cheese, but the valets and footmen will want it punctual so don't be late.'

'Of course not, Cook,' Lettie said automatically. Less than an hour with him! Her mind was full of questions for Mr Powell about her father.

The tray was laid up with afternoon tea for two people. Agnes had made a plate of delicate cucumber sandwiches, which were hidden under a silver dome. Lettie carried it carefully up the main stairs and tapped on Mr Powell's door. Miss Fanshaw opened it. 'I've brought your tea, ma'am.'

Miss Fanshaw checked over the tray and nodded as though satisfied. 'You may speak with Mr Powell for half an hour. I shall wait outside on the landing.'

'But what about your tea?'

'It's for you and him; half an hour only.'

'Yes, Miss Fanshaw.'

Lettie stood inside the bedroom door. The stunning view of the mere distracted her for a moment. 'It's Miss Hargreaves, Mr Powell. I've brought your tea.'

'Bring it over here by the window, where I can see you.'

Lettie unloaded the tray, aware that he was watching her closely. 'Shall I pour it for you, sir?'

'Please; and for yourself.'

'Thank you, sir.'

He offered her the plate of cucumber sandwiches and took one for himself. 'Now, sit down and tell me who you are really and why you are here. I want the truth.'

Lettie tried to relax but it was difficult. Her mouth dried but she had to answer his questions. 'I told you the truth this morning, sir. I was orphaned as a baby and

321

brought up by my grandmother. She was Ivy Hargreaves. She passed away recently and my guardian—'

'Stop.' He held up his hand to silence her. 'Ivy Hargreaves has died? When was this?'

'Last month. Did you know her? She was housekeeper at Waterley Hall for many years.' He stared at her as she sipped her tea.

'What has she told you about her life before you were born?'

'Very little, sir. I understood it was a period in her life that she put firmly behind her. I am sorry to say that she had no affection for my grandfather.'

'Yes, I shared her sentiment.'

'Oh. You were acquainted with both of them? Did you know my father, sir? Have you knowledge of his whereabouts after he left Waterley Hall?'

He continued to gaze at her, not in a curious way but more in a thoughtful, almost affectionate, way. She thought he must feel sorry for her and cold fingers seemed to encircle her heart. He was going to tell her that something awful had happened to her father! He seemed to be undecided what to say.

She pressed him to respond. 'Please tell me anything you know about him, sir. There is no one else for me to ask.'

A frown furrowed his brow. Why would he not answer her? Perhaps her father had done something truly wicked. But she had prepared herself for the worst. At least she had *tried* to brace herself for bad news. Lettie could feel her heart beating louder. Is that why Gran hadn't told her? It had hurt Lettie to discover that the grandmother she had loved so dearly had not been totally honest with her. She knew Gran as a religious, somewhat pious woman. But in Lettie's experience, she had been intolerant of those who strayed and could be a harsh judge of others. Lettie hoped she would not be so quick to condemn others.

She found it difficult to sit still and sprang to her feet to stand at the window. Directly below there were gardeners at work with wheelbarrows full of debris, tidying flower beds and shrubberies. A few patients strolled along the paths. One of them was tall and straight. He reminded her of Mr Boyer in the way he walked. The truth is never wrong, Mr Boyer had said, only the telling of it. *Or the not telling of it.*

She turned to face Mr Powell. 'Was he sent to prison, sir?'

Mr Powell blinked and appeared genuinely startled. 'My dear girl, is that what you believe happened to your father?'

'I should rather know the truth about him, sir, however unpalatable.'

Mr Powell covered his face with his hand, drawing his fingers slowly down his features. His chest began to rise and fall as his breathing quickened. Lettie realised that she was distressing him with her questions and became anxious about his well-being.

'Shall I fetch Miss Fanshaw, sir?'

He shook his head. 'She cannot help me with this. I must get through this alone and I shall.'

'But if you are not well, sir, you need medicine or a doctor.'

He sat back in his chair, closed his eyes for a moment and then asked, 'Would you hand me my cup of tea.'

Lettie obeyed. 'Shall I leave you, sir?'

'Stay. I am quite well. It is strange that you speak of prison in connection with your father. His life was a kind of prison but be assured that he was not a criminal. His chains were of a wholly different nature.'

He knew something! There was some secret about her father's life and he knew it! Lettie hardly dare breathe as she waited for him to continue.

After a couple of minutes he seemed more composed and went on. 'Sit down, Lettie. You gave me quite a shock when you told me your name this morning.' He examined her features. 'You have your mother's eyes. Did your grandmother not speak of her?'

'Rarely. She was steadfast in her refusal. I believe it caused her too much hurt.'

'Yes, Ruth caused everybody a lot of hurt.'

He knew her mother! 'How, sir? Will you tell me about her? How well did you know her?'

He clasped his hands together and squeezed them together so firmly that his knuckles went white. He gazed past her out of the window and his features turned grim. 'I loved her once and she became my wife.'

The bitterness in his voice was evident to Lettie. Her eyes widened and she swallowed, causing her to cough. She picked up her napkin to cover her mouth as the realisation dawned on her. A burning, feverish sensation spread over her arms, back and neck and enveloped her head. It blotted out the tea table in front of her and the stunning view from the window.

She took a gulp of tea. 'Are you my father, sir?'

He gave a harsh ironic laugh, more of a grunt really, and commented, 'How can I be called your father when I did not even hold you as an infant in my arms.'

'Please tell me the truth, sir. Are you my father or was I, as I have always suspected, born out of wedlock?'

This seemed to bring Mr Powell back to his senses. He took a couple of deep breaths and turned his head to face her. His features had softened and his tone was kinder. 'You must never think that of yourself. Your mother and I were married in the sight of God. We were husband and wife when you were born.'

'But I am Lettie Hargreaves, not Lettie Powell.'

'That was your grandmother's wish. She took you away from me and I allowed it. It was for your own good.'

'Don't say that! Gran used to say that to me, and sometimes she was wrong!' Lettie's emotions were rising, taking over, and tears threatened but she composed herself quickly and added, 'How could it be for my own good if you were my father and you were alive?'

'I was no father to you. I was chained to the brandy bottle. It was – it is – my weakness and I should be long dead if it weren't for Miss Fanshaw's ministrations.'

Lettie had seen the outcome of this weakness in men and women at Waterley Edge. It ruined the lives of whole families and she understood why everyone who attended chapel was encouraged to 'take the pledge' and promise never to indulge in the 'demon drink'.

She was silenced for a minute and regretted her uncharitable thoughts about Gran. Of course Gran had had her best interests at heart! A drunken father could not bring up any child without its mother.

'Was it the loss of my mother that turned you to the drink, sir?' she asked.

He closed his eyes and gave a weary sigh. 'She was never really mine. She . . . she belonged to another and . . . There is so much you do not know.'

'Then will you enlighten me, sir?'

'Another day,' he said. 'We shall continue our conversation another day. I am dining with Lord Laughton tonight and I must prepare myself. It will be an ordeal for me after so long.'

'Of course,' she realised. 'There will be wine.'

'Frances – that's Miss Fanshaw – will be at my side.'

Miss Fanshaw will look after him. Lettie considered that their relationship was more than that of patient and nurse. She didn't want to leave yet but she rose to her feet and began to stack the tray. 'This has been a shock for me too, sir – er, Father. May I call you Father?'

'Please don't; not yet. It has to be our secret – ours and Frances's, until – well, for a few weeks yet. Promise me that you will not speak to anyone of our relationship within the servants' hearing. Valets pass on servants' hall gossip to their masters and I should prefer Lord Laughton not to know that you are here.'

'What has our connection to do with him?' Her initial

euphoria from finding her father was waning and she remembered being escorted from the premises of Waterley Hall when Mr Boyer discovered her presence.

He said, 'Please be patient, Lettie. Patience is something that Frances has taught me. Will you promise?'

Lettie suppressed her disappointment. Patience had not been one of her merits lately but she would try to keep her word. Perhaps a busy night in the kitchen was what she needed? She would not have time to dwell on the emotions and questions mushrooming through her heart and her head and taking over her reason.

'Very well,' she said. 'But I do look forward to the time when I may address you openly as my father.'

'So do I, my dear. Would you ask Frances to come in?'

She bent down and kissed her father lightly on his forehead. He seemed surprised and put his fingers on the spot. Then she picked up the tray and went out onto the landing.

Frances appeared from the shadows in front of Lettie. She seemed very anxious. 'How is he?' she asked.

Lettie considered again that her father was more than simply a patient to her. For her to find out that an interloper who has disobeyed her so flagrantly was his daughter would be a shock to her, too. 'He has something to tell you,' Lettie answered. Lettie had no idea how Frances would take the news and added as an afterthought, 'I shall be in the kitchen tonight as planned, helping Cook.'

In the servants' hall later, the outdoor servants enjoyed the attention as they informed everyone about the visitors they had collected that day from Mereside Halt.

The coachman was a much pleasanter person than the carter who collected the hampers. He was a recent addition to Mereside Lodge, like Cook and the new butler, Mr Norwich, who had arrived on the same railway train. Mr Norwich had taken his place at the head of the table and carved the cold remains of an aitch bone of beef for the servants who were now his responsibility. Under Gran's tutelage, Lettie had carved many hot and cold joints of meat during her years at the manse and watched him with interest. He did it well.

The coachman said, 'Lord Laughton was not pleased about sharing the coach. The two gentlemen from first class were not travelling together. We ought to have taken a second coach.'

Lord Laughton's valet added, 'Yes, they had a quite an argument. He should have gone on the luggage cart.'

'Don't be ridiculous,' Mr Norwich interrupted. 'He was a gentleman.'

'Are you sure? He didn't have a man with him.'

'He's an American,' the valet commented, as though it explained everything.

'Well, he's in one of the best suites,' Mr Norwich said. 'And his name is Laughton. I'll talk to Mr Powell about a second coach in the morning.'

'It was a family quarrel, I expect,' the valet muttered. 'I didn't realise he had any family left.'

'All right, that's enough gossip,' Mr Norwich said. 'We have much to do tonight. My head footman will act as valet to Mr Laughton and Lord Laughton's footman will be with me in the dining room. Any mishaps outside the kitchen, report directly to me. Cook will prepare cocoa for when we've finished.'

The valets and footmen went off first and Lettie followed Cook into the kitchen. Cook was relieved the new butler had arrived and said, 'At least I'll have somebody who knows what they're doing serving my lovely dinner.'

'What will happen about the patients' dinner tonight?'

'If they're taking the cure, it's pretty frugal and served early – often in their rooms. Miss Fanshaw will see to them but she has to dress for dinner so you can help her. I'll only need you for sauces and carrying.'

While Lettie was taking round patients' dinners under silver domes she checked name plates on the doors and found Mr Laughton's next to Lord Laughton's. *Alexander B. Laughton*, it read. A relative but perhaps not a friend of Lord Laughton by the sound of it, she thought.

The evening was fascinating for Lettie and, thankfully for all, uneventful. It was a lengthy meal that began at eight and went on until eleven. The servants were kept busy until after midnight. Lettie strained sauces in serving boats, cleaned up any smudged edges of dishes and carried them carefully to the white-gloved hands of waiting footmen. It was exhausting but it took Lettie's mind away from her own concerns for a few hours. She didn't really notice how tired she was until the last of the Rockingham china, Waterford crystal and silver cutlery had been locked away in the butler's pantry.

Mr Norwich assembled everyone in the servants' hall to thank them. He had a bottle of brandy and some glasses and Cook brought in a pot of tea and a jug of cocoa. The valets were with their respective gentleman. The kitchen maid and boot-boy, who had spent most of their time scrubbing cooking pots and washing tableware in the scullery, lit lamps and went off to their beds. Agnes and the footmen followed shortly afterwards, leaving Lettie with Cook and Mr Norwich sitting around the table in the servants' hall.

'Ought I to go up with Agnes?' Lettie suggested.

Cook replied, 'Miss Fanshaw asked for you to wait for her.'

Lettie stifled a yawn.

'Lord Laughton appeared satisfied with dinner,' Mr Norwich said. 'I've served him before in London and he is difficult to please.'

'Did they talk of anything interesting?' Cook asked.

'A good butler does not gossip about his employer,' Mr Norwich replied. But Lettie noticed he grinned as he said it.

'I'm not asking you about Mr Powell,' Cook protested, 'but I know something is in the air. Miss Fanshaw was quite keyed up.'

'Well, the atmosphere was icy between Lord Laughton and Mr Laughton. Dr Bretton managed to keep the conversation civil. He was speaking of recommending Mereside Lodge to his medical colleagues for their patients.'

'That's good, isn't it?' Lettie commented. She wasn't really interested and was trying to summon up the energy to go to bed.

'Not if Lord Laughton gets his way,' Mr Norwich said. 'He wants to buy the Lodge and, apparently, Mr Powell needs the money. Keep that to yourself. I don't want to alarm the servants.'

Lettie heard footsteps in the passage and turned to see Frances in the doorway. She looked beautiful, in a grey chiffon frock with a lace bodice and matching chiffon and lace jacket that skimmed her waist. Her hair was piled high and decorated with grey velvet ribbon and she wore grey kid shoes with a heel. She was carrying a lighted lamp.

'Miss Fanshaw!' Mr Norwich scrambled to his feet.

'Oh, do sit down, Mr Norwich, I'm not the lady of the house,' she said.

She could be, though, Lettie realised. She was more than ready for her bed, stifled a yawn and queried, 'Where shall I be sleeping?'

Miss Fanshaw said, 'I am sorry I've been so long. It has been a . . . a difficult evening for Mr Powell.'

'Will the lass be staying?' Cook asked. 'She'll be an asset. Don't you agree, Mr Norwich?'

'I do but I shall need sight of a testimonial,' he answered.

'That won't be necessary,' Miss Fanshaw said. 'Mr Powell will vouch for her.'

Cook raised her eyebrows. In response, Miss Fanshaw gave her a rare smile. 'Come with me, Lettie, I'll show you to your room.'

They went through to the main house and climbed the wide, carpeted staircase until they reached the first landing. Miss Fanshaw said, 'Michael – your father

– told me about you. We have no secrets from each other.'

'You are lucky, Miss Fanshaw. It seems that my life has been one huge secret since I was born.'

'Well, it was a shock for me. Do call me Frances when other servants are not within earshot.' She led the way. 'You are on the second landing, next to me.' As they climbed she went on, 'We have to keep quiet about it for now. I hope you understand.'

'Well, no actually. Father said it was to do with Lord Laughton. Is he ashamed of me?'

'No, of course not! Michael will tell you all in good time. For now he has other issues to consider.'

Such as the future of Mereside Lodge, Lettie realised. They reached the second landing and stopped. Frances opened one of the bedroom doors and said, 'You are in here, Lettie. My room is next door if you need anything.' They went inside. Two lamps were already burning, one on a dressing table and the other on a bedside table.

'Thank you.' It was the biggest bedroom Lettie had ever slept in. 'It looks very comfortable,' she said. 'Mereside Lodge used to belong to the Waterley estate, didn't it?'

'It was the hunting lodge, yes.' Frances took a deep breath. 'You may as well know. His Lordship gave it to your father many years ago and now he wants it back.'

'He *gave* it to my father? Then why must he give it back?'

'His Lordship is prepared to buy it and . . . and he is aware that Michael has need of a large sum of money.'

Lettie noticed that Frances looked embarrassed as she said this.

'Is Mereside Lodge losing money?'

'It is not as straightforward as that, Lettie. Lord Laughton wants Mereside Lodge for his own reasons and he is ruthless. He is also influential and powerful. It is a mistake to cross him.'

'Will Father sell?' she asked.

'I don't know. All I know is that Mereside Lodge could be the best hydro in Yorkshire. But it won't be if Lord Laughton gets his hands on it.' Frances sat down on the edge of the bed and added, 'Mereside Lodge is Michael's life's work!' She sounded emotional but after a few seconds pulled herself together and stood up. 'There is hot water in the ewer,' she said. She picked up a clean towel from the washstand and handed it to Lettie. 'Sleep for as long as you wish. Agnes has laid out nightwear and clean clothes for you. She will bring your tea in the morning and fresh water.'

'I'm not used to servants waiting on me.'

Frances smiled and it lit up her face so that, in spite of being exhausted, she looked pretty. 'You will be thankful in the morning,' she said. 'Shall I pull the curtains?'

'I'll do it. You must be very tired yourself.'

'I am. Goodnight, Lettie.'

'Goodnight, Frances.'

Lettie washed and put on the long nightgown. It was made of the softest cotton and trimmed with lace. Lettie was past her tiredness now. She had too much to think about to sleep. She wrapped a shawl around her shoulders and went over to the window, staring into the blackness, waiting for her eyes to become accustomed to the night. Her room overlooked the garden where the summerhouse was located. She was high up but she noticed a tiny intermittent glow of a cigar as one of the gentlemen walked in the garden. She wondered who he was, outside in the night air.

It was unlikely to be a patient; Lord Laughton perhaps or Dr Bretton or the American gentleman. She understood why the doctor was interested in the future of Mereside but what was the American gentleman's part in all this? Although he was a Laughton it seemed that he and His Lordship were not on good terms. Were these 'important visitors' simply vultures circling her father and his financial embarrassment, waiting for rich pickings? It must have been an ordeal for Father and she wished she had been at his side, helping to fend off these foes. As she stared into the darkness she felt a strong protective urge to fight for whatever her father wanted.

He's my father. She repeated the words softly, enjoying the warm feeling it gave her. Would she ever get used to saying them? It had been hard, at first, for her to understand why her grandmother had kept him from her. But Gran had wanted to protect her, perhaps too much, and Lettie appreciated that she was driven by love. She had never doubted that Gran loved her and knowing she was loved had given Lettie strength as a child. She wondered if her father might love her in the same way.

She realised that it was the thing she craved above all. A family that cared for her, not because it was their duty as it was in the church, but because they loved her, she belonged to them and loved them in return. She thought fondly of Thomas, of his belief in himself and his friendliness. She admired him for those qualities. He came from a big family, not well-off but hardworking and happy. Lettie wanted that for herself one day, when she fell in love. She wanted to fall in love and hoped it would happen to her. But the face that came to mind when she imagined herself in love was not Thomas's. It was Mr Boyer's: handsome, foreign and intriguing. She shook her head and rebuked herself for her foolishness.

Frances was in love with her father, Lettie had decided. She was convinced about this and wondered why she was so certain. Was Father aware of it? How did anyone know if someone truly loved them? She gave a shivery sigh. Life used to be so much simpler at the manse. She yawned and stretched. The tiny glow in the garden beneath her had stopped moving around and she realised the lamp in her room was making her visible to whoever was smoking his cigar in the garden beneath her. She pulled the curtains quickly, turned down her lamps and climbed into a soft feather bed.

Chapter 24

She woke to the sound of her bedroom door clicking softly and sat up with bleary eyes. Her room was empty and dark but chinks of bright light squeezed in around the curtains. She had slept late and a welcome aroma of freshly made tea drifted in her nose. A tray waited for her on the bedside table. She examined the biscuit. It was a special one with the crest. She had never seen them in any of the shops she frequented. No doubt they arrived by railway train in one of the hampers. She sat on the edge of the bed to eat her biscuit and drink the tea, noticing steam rising from the ewer on her washstand. It was time to get up.

Agnes had laid out a dark grey skirt with a matching tie, and fresh white blouse. Her own clothes had disappeared and she had noticed the evening before that they were grubby and crumpled. Agnes's choices were plain but they fitted her and were clean. She washed and spent more time than she ought to have on piling up her hair. She couldn't find her boots until she opened her bedroom door and found them sitting outside, nicely polished. Nonetheless, she wasn't a patient or an honoured visitor so she went down to the kitchen by the back stairs.

'Oh, there you are,' Cook said. 'You've missed breakfast but there's porridge keeping warm on the hotplate. Miss Fanshaw wants to see you in the housekeeper's sitting room when she's finished in the bath house.' Cook examined her clothes and added, 'Well, you can't help in here in those. That's what the upstairs maids wear.'

'I can't sit about all morning, either.'

'Can you sew?'

'Of course.'

'The sewing room is across the passage.'

It was a small, well-lit room lined with cupboards that reached the ceiling and dominated by a large table in the middle piled with linen and assorted items of servants' uniforms. Lettie found a well-stocked workbox and tackled some of the aprons that needed stitches here and there until it was time to see Frances.

Her hair was fuzzy and her face reddened from the steam in the bath house but Frances was more cheerful than the previous evening. They exchanged a few pleasantries then Frances said, 'This telegraph message came for you,' and handed it over.

Lettie opened the seal and read it. 'It's from Reverend

Ennis.' *Go to mission at Forest Chase stop Will send help,* she read. 'How far is Forest Chase?'

'It's the next stop on the railway line. Why?'

'The Reverend wants me to go to the Methodist chapel there. He's my guardian.'

'He must be worried about you.'

'It was rather foolish of me to set out alone for Mereside Lodge, but I had to come. You saw how I was.'

'Yes, and I understand why. Will you go to Forest Chase?'

'I don't know. I want to do what is best for Father.'

Frances chewed on her lip. 'Your presence is an added strain for him.'

'Do you think I should leave?'

'I do not want you to leave but . . .' She shook her head slightly. 'I want him to get well and you don't understand how difficult it has been for him to get this far.'

'I do. At least, I am aware that he has to take the pledge if he wants to stay alive.'

'He told you about the drinking?'

'It was the reason he gave me up.'

'I am so fearful that he will slip back into his old ways.' A tear glistened in Frances's eye. 'I couldn't bear to see him suffer again.'

'I want to help him, Frances,' Lettie urged. 'I do understand. I was brought up a Methodist in a pit village. He is lucky to have you, you know.'

Frances shook her head and murmured, 'I am the lucky one.'

She is definitely in love with him, Lettie thought, and this cheered her. They were allies in making Father better.

Frances stood up briskly. 'I have to check the energising drinks for patients.'

'May I assist you?'

'I'm sorry. Not until Lord Laughton has departed.'

'What shall I do for the rest of the day?' Lettie didn't look forward to staying in the sewing room for the afternoon.

'You are not a servant,' she glanced over her gown, 'although you are dressed as one. Your own clothes will be ready tomorrow.'

'Well, I shall have to occupy myself with something.'

'Go for a long walk. It's a couple of miles or so around the mere. It will clear your head and you will see why your father loves this place.'

Lettie needed the time to make sense of her thoughts. It was a fine day and warm for the time of year but she took her coat and pinned on her hat. She wandered across the pasture and stared at the calm water, occasionally rippled by a bird landing quietly on its surface.

Reverend Ennis had offered her an escape route if she wanted but she wasn't at all certain that she wished to take it. Of course he wasn't aware of her father's situation and she could well have spent a second night in the draughty church or summerhouse. No doubt the Methodist minister at Forest Chase would be expecting her and she ought to do as her guardian advised. At the very least she must reply to his telegraph.

A pathway took her away from the mere, through a

small wrought-iron gate in the wall and back to the road that led to the Halt. Deep in thought, she walked slowly, remembering how Thomas had risked his job to find her and had promised to make the journey again on Sunday. He must care for her quite a lot to do that.

The road seemed shorter than before; the track to the Halt was soon behind her and the church spire in view above the trees. The green was peopled with village housewives carrying shopping baskets, some trailing children pulling at their skirts. They glanced at her curiously as she walked by and one or two wished her good morning. She returned their greetings but moved on purposefully to the post office.

The postmistress was helpful as each word in a telegraph had to be paid for. She gave Lettie a scrap of paper and pencil stub to plan her message. What should she say to ease the Reverend's mind? *Safe stop Father alive stop Staying here stop Letter follows stop Lettie.*

She exhaled audibly as she paid for it. Sending this message to the Reverend had somehow confirmed her decision that she wanted to be involved in her father's life and help in any way she could. Satisfied, she turned to walk into the sunshine and found herself face to face with the very last person she expected to see.

'Mr Boyer! What are *you* doing here?' Heavens, she thought, how rude I must sound! Why shouldn't a foreign gentleman be travelling the more attractive parts of Yorkshire?

He raised his hat and bowed his head. 'Good morning, Miss Hargreaves.'

This was remarkably civil of him considering the way they had parted at Waterley Hall. She acknowledged him with a bow of her head, murmured an inoffensive 'sir' and waited for him to step aside so that she could pass. He didn't move and neither did she. She could have walked around him but her feet wouldn't budge and she guessed they – no, *she* – didn't want them to.

She was, she realised, unduly pleased to see him and to hear his rich voice and unusual vowels. True, his manner had been offhand and aloof but not all the time and his apology on the day of Gran's funeral had been sincere. And, she considered, although his reaction to her serving soup in the dining room at Waterley Hall had been a shock, there was something about him that appealed to her, something *physical* that stirred her senses as a woman. She was, when in his presence, very conscious that she was a woman.

He did not take his eyes off her face and they were penetrating eyes that seemed to pierce hers, making her unusually tongue tied. She looked away, desperately searching her mind for something to say to him. 'Mrs Osborne will be sad that you have left Boundary Farm.'

'My horse remains in the stables there.'

Oh. He intended to return then. Lettie wondered briefly if she would do the same. Waterley Edge seemed a long way away at present. The post-office door opened and a customer came in with a shopping basket over her arm. They both stepped to one side to give her more room.

Lettie said, 'Are you lodging at the inn? This is a beautiful part of Yorkshire, don't you think?'

341

'I do.'

'Did you travel here by the railway train?'

'I did.'

After a further silence Lettie realised he had not forgotten their parting and did not wish to make further conversation with her. Disappointed, she said, 'Well, good day to you, Mr Boyer.' But still he did not stand aside, or move to open the door for her. She would have to walk around him.

'I should like to speak with you, Miss Hargreaves.'

'You were anxious for me to leave your presence at our last meeting, sir.'

'I had my reasons and I wish to account for my behaviour.'

'There is no need, sir. I was simply trying to find my father and I believed one of the older servants at Waterley Hall might remember him. But I have found him now.'

'So you have discovered who you are?'

'I have.' She said it with some satisfaction and relief. Although she still had many questions for her father, her desperate urgency for answers had eased. She added, 'After growing up believing I was an orphan and then losing my only living relation, I have been blessed with someone who is my family. Do you know what that feels like, sir?'

'I cannot say that I do. You seem to have taken it very well. But you are a Hargreaves and you are strong. Do I take it that you are comfortable with the knowledge?'

'I am.'

Mr Boyer's face took on a guarded expression. 'You have met your father, haven't you?'

'I really don't see how it is any of your concern, sir, but yes, I have.'

'You must be cautious, Miss Hargreaves. You do not know him well and his behaviour in the past—'

She interrupted him. 'He told me about his past.'

Mr Boyer seemed concerned by her reaction. 'I understand your loyalty,' he said. 'He is, after all, your father, but where has he been all your life?'

'Mr Boyer, I really do not care what you think. My father and I have much to discover about each other. He has had his difficulties but now he has reformed.'

'He has not! He is the same—' He stopped as a customer at the post-office counter turned round to see who was raising their voice. He spoke more quietly and added, 'I really must speak privately with you. He has told you only his version.'

There was an insistence in his tone that made Lettie hesitate. 'Do you have a different story, sir?'

He kept his voice low. 'Not here. Will you take some refreshment at the inn with me?'

The nearest Lettie had been to an inn was in the outside coal yard on her walk to Boundary Farm. Her first thought was that the Reverend would be horrified and Gran would turn in her grave. The alarm must have shown on her face because he added, 'I am not suggesting we drink ale in the public bar. Will a pot of coffee be suitable for you?'

'Very well,' she agreed.

'Shall we?' He opened the post-office door for her, followed her into the sunlight and they set off the short distance to the inn. He must have rooms there, she thought. Perhaps he came for the wedding. She repeated her earlier question. 'Are you staying at the inn?'

'I thought you were.'

'My father asked me to stay at Mereside Lodge,' she explained.

'He did? Then he was pleased to see you? Perhaps he has mellowed towards you with the years.'

His comment stung. 'He gave me up because his situation meant that he was not able to look after me himself! That does not mean he did not love me!'

'I do apologise, Miss Hargreaves. My remark was ill-judged. Forgive me.'

'Do not be so quick to criticise, Mr Boyer. You have been mistaken about me in the past.'

'But I have known who you really are for a while now.'

Why should he be interested in who she was? Who was she to him? She stopped on the steps of the inn and said, 'Did you follow me into the post office?'

He didn't answer her question but offered his arm to climb the steps and said, 'I think we ought to continue this conversation in a more private place.'

She didn't take his arm. 'I shall not accompany you to your private rooms, sir. If that is what you expect then we must part here.'

He seemed mildly amused, which annoyed her. 'Surely you do not believe my intentions are dishonourable? I am not Lord Laughton.'

She did not move until he added, 'There is a small

parlour overlooking the rear garden. We shall not be alone but we may converse in private.'

Satisfied, she went inside, down a central corridor, to a small comfortably furnished room with a very pretty window made up of many small panes. Mr Boyer selected a couple of comfortable armchairs next to a low table. He waited for Lettie to settle before he sat down and ordered coffee. He had an air of quiet confidence that impressed her.

'You have the advantage of me, Mr Boyer,' she said. 'You appear to know who I am but I have little knowledge about you.'

'I am sure Mrs Osborne told you of my connection with the late Lady Laughton.'

'Actually, she didn't. It was Mrs St John. She said you were a trustee of Lady Laughton's estate.'

'It is an inherited duty. I am a distant relation, very distant.'

Lettie wondered why he had added 'very'. A relation was a relation and even more precious when you didn't have a family of your own. She said, 'I should be very pleased to discover I had relations, however distant.'

Her response caused him to raise an eycbrow. 'Would you, even if one turned out to be Seth Hargreaves?'

'My grandfather could not have been all bad.'

'You have a forgiving nature.'

'Perhaps that is because I don't accept the judgement of others readily! I prefer to draw my own conclusions. Don't you?' she challenged. Lettie thought he might. In spite of their apparent differences in background, she felt he might share this sentiment. She went on, 'My grand-mother was quick to condemn. It was a weakness in her character.' Lettie felt herself blushing for thinking and speaking ill of Gran and looked away.

'Maybe she had good reason to censure her husband.'

Her head twisted back sharply. 'Why do you say that? What do you know?'

'Seth Hargreaves was a confidante of Lord Laughton and everyone is aware of how badly he treated his wife.'

'Is it true that Lady Laughton owned half of the Waterley estate and Lord Laughton's industries?'

He raised his eyebrows so she added, 'Mrs St John told me that as well.'

'It was a third, actually.'

The coffee arrived and Mr Boyer had to move his legs out of the way for the landlord to set it down on the table. He was supple, she thought, a good horseman, tall and straight in the saddle; not especially muscular but agile. She had thought of him in these terms before and dismissed them as girlish whims. But in closer proximity to him it was these aspects that made her aware that she was not a girl any more. She was a young woman with all the aspirations it entailed. She wished she was wearing her own clothes instead of Agnes's.

He poured the coffee and offered her cream and sugar. She stirred her cup thoughtfully. 'Lady Laughton had a reputation for being a difficult old lady.'

'How diplomatic of you! She was an angry, bitter woman. She hated her husband with a vengeance because he only married her so that no one else would get their hands on the companies. Sadly, her bitterness extended to any and all of Lord Laughton's kin.'

'Did that include you?'

'She never met me and I kept it that way. My father's life was ruined by her efforts to disinherit him. Lady Laughton's one-third share was only a lifetime interest for her. Now she has passed away, her share reverts to the two remaining cousins and that is what she hated. She wanted to leave her share to her kin rather than to any of the Laughtons and couldn't because it was entailed.'

Lettie listened with interest, but didn't see that it was her concern. She wondered why he thought it was. Perhaps he just needed to talk. She understood that and responded, 'Are you saying that Lord Laughton has to share Lady Laughton's one-third with your father?'

'With me,' he corrected. 'My father is dead. My grandfather was the third cousin who left England for Canada as a young man, with his share. My father spent the latter years of his life fighting legal battles with the Laughtons and since he passed away I have spent all my time researching this whole sorry affair. That is how I know about you.'

'You're not making sense to me.' Lettie frowned. She didn't see how she fitted in to this at all.

He misunderstood her query and said, 'It's quite simple really. Lord Laughton and I each owned a third and now each of us has half of the remaining third.'

Lettie was good at figures. 'You own half of Waterley estate?'

'Including all the shipyards and steelworks. I'm proud

of my father and grandfather for their pioneering spirit, but I am sorry to say that I am a Laughton.'

'You told everyone your name was Boyer.'

'It is. It's my mother's family name.' He smiled. 'Alexander Boyer Laughton. My friends call me Alec. May I call you Lettie?'

He's *Alexander B. Laughton*, she realised. 'You are the American gentleman at Mereside Lodge?'

'Canadian. It's a common error among Europeans.'

Lettie had a sinking feeling about this information. She'd have preferred him to remain as Mr Boyer, rather than heir to half of the Laughton fortune. The knowledge of who he was seemed to distance him from her and she found that depressing. And she still didn't see why his family affairs were her concern. The coffee was finished and she felt it was time for her to leave. She said, 'Will you return to Canada soon?'

'Not until His Lordship and I have resolved our dispute. Of course, Mereside Lodge is at the centre of our disagreement.'

The mention of Mereside Lodge grabbed Lettie's attention. This did concern her. She remembered the servants' report of an argument at the Halt when they arrived.

'Lord Laughton does not give up easily,' Mr Boyer went on. 'He has not changed, believe me. He wants total control and he has decided to buy me off by giving me Mereside Lodge as compensation.'

'But Mereside Lodge doesn't belong to him!'

'Why should that stop him? He is used to buying his own way and he knows that Mr Powell needs money.'

348

'That is what I don't understand! Frances has told me he needs money but if Mereside Lodge is sold, he hasn't got a hydro to invest in, so what does he want the money for?'

'His divorce, of course. Mr Powell has to pay for his divorce, in order to marry Miss Fanshaw. Divorce is an expensive affair.'

Lettie was taken aback by mention of divorce. It was almost unheard of in Waterley Edge. 'I . . . I didn't know that my father was seeking a divorce.'

Mr Boyer sat back in his chair and frowned. In fact, he appeared to be genuinely puzzled. 'You said you knew who you were,' he murmured. His eyes widened and, for a gentleman normally so confident, he seemed at a loss to go on.

She added, 'I had no idea he had married again.'

His puzzled expression turned to one of dismay 'Dear God,' he muttered, 'what have I done? I assumed that you knew.'

'Knew what, sir?'

He didn't answer and his dismay appeared to degenerate into despair.

Chapter 25

'Mr Boyer – Alec – if this concerns me, I should like to hear what you assume I know already.'

'I have said far too much already. I . . . I don't have a right to say more. You must ask your . . . your father to tell you.'

Her frustration made her cross. 'But you have to tell me! My father has been reluctant to speak of the past and I am equally reluctant to press him. You know that he is not strong.'

'Even so, he is the person you must ask.'

'But what if he won't say? My grandmother kept *him* a secret from me all her life.' Lettie realised she was shaking and dangerously close to tears.

His reply gave her a crumb of comfort. 'You have hardly given him time yet. Speak to him, Lettie.' He seemed to be pleading with her and there was desperation in his eyes. 'Your sudden appearance was a shock to him. He is embarrassed by his relationship with Frances when he already has a wife.'

'My grandmother would turn in her grave if she knew!'

'Perhaps she did know? And that is why she kept him a secret.'

That made sense to Lettie and she calmed a little.

Alec took in a breath to speak further then seemed to change his mind.

Lettie sat with her thoughts for a minute. Alec had been honest with her but was drawing a line under further involvement and she didn't want that. She wanted to be involved with him. But what was she to him, apart from someone caught in the crossfire of his family feud? She said, 'Very well. I shall not compromise you with my questions any longer. You have been most kind in your considerations.'

'I fear I have not. I feel the need to make reparation.'

'For what? You have given me an insight into a past that I craved about.'

'On the contrary, Lettie, I have stirred a hornets' nest. I judged you to be strong enough but now I am not so sure. Is there no one else, no other relation you can turn to?' His eyes were questioning but he seemed wary of her response.

'I have my father. It is enough.'

Alec didn't respond immediately. He continued to frown and his eyes darted over her. She was not very well acquainted with him but he seemed fearful of something.

Finally he said, 'I have made a mistake in speaking with you. Your grandmother was right. It is better not to know anything than only a half truth.'

An odd feeling was spreading over Lettie and she began to feel lightheaded, as though the floor was falling away from beneath her. What did Alec mean? Her father had only given her a half truth? She could not bear it if this had been a wild-goose chase. 'I wish I'd never come here and started this search,' she muttered.

His face twisted in anguish and he seemed to be wrestling with his thoughts. 'This is my fault. I am to blame and I shall make amends. But there is only one person I am aware of who has the right to answer your questions and it is not me. You must ignore everything I have just said to you.'

Exasperated, she burst out, 'But I cannot!' She shook her head repeatedly. A sense of frustration and despair settled over her.

'And I cannot continue this conversation with you. I am truly sorry. It was not my intention to distress you in this way.'

But Lettie was distressed. She was exhausted after a tiring evening and late night yesterday, and troubled by her father's difficulties. As well, the worries of recent weeks had taken their toll on her. She felt shivery and tearful and didn't wish to break down in front of Alec. He had gained her respect and she wanted him to think well of her.

He gazed at her and there was sympathy in his eyes. 'You have turned quite pale, Lettie.'

352

'I feel unwell. I should go . . .' She was going to say 'go home' but she wasn't sure where home was any more. It didn't matter anyway and Alec seemed to understand.

He said, 'I'll order something to revive you first.' He raised an arm and called for the landlord. 'Bring a brandy for the lady; quickly, my good man, and do you have a carriage and driver available for hire?'

The brandy arrived and he handed it to her.

'I can't drink that,' she protested weakly.

'Take it as you would a medicine,' he urged, 'in one gulp.'

It was just a small amount and she tipped it to the back of her throat. The fiery liquid made her catch her breath and gasp, but its warmth soon spread through her veins. She began to feel better and composed herself after a few minutes.

'Another brandy?' he asked.

'Thank you, no. I'm ready to leave now.'

He said, 'I've ordered the inn carriage to take you back to Mereside Lodge.' Then he added, 'I shall ride with you as far as the Halt, if you have no objections.'

The landlord came to say the carriage was ready at the front steps. Alec offered her his hand to stand up but she didn't need it. However, she appreciated his help to step up into the carriage. It was a lightweight open trap, high off the ground with a flimsy step. 'Hold her steady,' he called to the driver at the pony's head.

He climbed in after her and unfolded one of the woollen blankets to wrap around her knees. As he leaned over to tuck in the edges his face came close to hers. He didn't have any whiskers and she caught the scent from his skin. It was an earthy, masculine aroma that excited her. He lingered and she could have stretched her neck a fraction and kissed him. Embarrassed that she wanted to, she shifted her position.

'Keep yourself warm,' he said, 'and when you get to the lodge, ask Miss Fanshaw for one of her new reviving drinks from America. They really do work.'

'Where to, sir?' the driver called.

'Stop at the Halt to set me down and then take the lady to Mereside Lodge. Ask for Miss Fanshaw and stay with her until she arrives.'

'Very good, sir.'

'I am not ill,' Lettie protested.

'Your colour has not returned yet.'

As the carriage approached the track though the trees to the Halt, he called again to the driver, 'I'll walk from the road. The train is not due yet.'

'Are you leaving?' Lettie queried. He had no luggage with him.

'I said that I would put right the distress I have caused you. I shall be away for – oh, a couple of weeks, perhaps. But I promise I shall return.'

'What shall I say to Frances?'

'I'll telegraph. Take care of yourself, Lettie.'

He climbed down and waited for the carriage to set off again before walking down the track. Lettie watched him until he had disappeared. She didn't know what to make of him. He was a law unto himself. But she was very much aware that she would be counting the days until he came back.

Frances put her to bed with a cup of calming camomile tea. She slept for a short time and woke feeling refreshed. Lettie had a long letter to write to Reverend Ennis and she went down to the morning room to find paper and pen. She smiled at a footman on duty in the entrance hall as she went in. She was alone but a few minutes later Agnes came in.

'What are you doing in here?' Agnes said.

'I have to write to my guardian. Frances – I mean, Miss Fanshaw – said I could.'

'Oh, did she? I suppose it's all right then. She told me you were above stairs now. What are you going to do?'

'I'm not sure yet.'

Agnes glanced over her serviceable skirt and blouse. 'Well, you'll be asked by the patients to serve tea dressed in those clothes.'

'I won't be long. I want to take this to the post office today.'

'Shall I bring you some tea? It's a bit early but I can make some.'

'May I have some of that new American drink?'

'Have you tried it before? It is not to everyone's taste.'

'Why, what's in it?'

'It's a herbal tonic made from the coca plant mixed with an extract of kola leaves. It's guaranteed to revive you.'

'I'll try it, then.'

In her letter, she thanked the Reverend for sending Thomas, apologised for causing him distress but hoped he would understand her hastiness. She explained her father's situation and it clarified her thinking about him and Frances and Mereside Lodge. Agnes arrived with her drink as she was in the middle of her letter; she left it on the table and retreated quietly.

When Lettie had finished writing she knew what she wanted to do. She was determined to help her father and Frances in whatever way she could. Why should he give up his life's work because Lord Laughton did not wish to share Waterley Hall with his cousin? But she suspected her father's future happiness depended on marriage to Frances as well. She sat back, gazed out at the mere through the window and said aloud, 'Father must not sell. There has to be another way.' The drink restored her energy and she ran upstairs for her hat and coat then set off to post her letter.

On her way back she saw the cart from Mereside Lodge making slow progress up the road with hampers from the afternoon train. She remembered her arrival at the Halt and the length of time the carter had taken to load them. Curious, she turned off to walk down to the Halt but stepped off the road into the trees and approached the platform unseen.

A pony pulling an old governess cart was tethered outside the gate in the fence and she recognised the stable hand from Mereside Lodge. He was heaving two hampers into the cart. He covered them with sacking, unhitched the reins and climbed into the driver's seat. Lettie stayed out of sight as the pony ambled away but she followed it as it bounced its way along a rutted bridleway through the woodland. It was heading away from Mereside Lodge.

Halfway to the village and under cover of the trees she watched the stable hand transfer packages, including a whole ham wrapped in muslin, from the hampers to a couple of men with a handcart. She could not recall seeing a ham boiling or roasting in the Mereside Lodge kitchens so far and now she knew why. A banknote and coins exchanged hands.

Lettie was cross with what she saw but not especially surprised. She had suspected something underhand was going on when she arrived. However, fearful of discovery, she hurried in the opposite direction towards Mereside Lodge. She dawdled when she reached the road and waited for the returning governess cart to catch up with her, raising her hand to hail a lift.

'How fortunate you came along, my feet are quite worn out,' she commented cheerily as she climbed up the steps at the rear of the cart. The stable hand did not reply and she noted that the empty hampers had disappeared; presumably he had left them at the Halt for the railway train guard to load into his van. She wondered if Father was aware his servants were stealing from him. Probably not, but she decided not to increase his anxiety by discussing it with him when she was quite capable of doing something about it herself.

Back at the Lodge, she climbed the stairs to the second landing thoughtfully.

Agnes had sponged and pressed her clothes and returned

them with a note from her father. It was an invitation to join him for dinner in the small dining room at nine, after the patients had returned to their rooms for the night. This was a late hour for Lettie who was used to keeping manse hours. She dressed carefully and spent half an hour on her hair. When she looked in the mirror she imagined Mrs Osborne advising her and thought fondly of her afternoons at Boundary Farm. She had met Alec there and had been intrigued by who he was. She realised now that her interest in him had been more than curiosity. It had been, and remained, a deeper appeal. Lettie was lost in thought when Frances knocked on her door to ask if she was ready.

Frances was transformed into a graceful woman when she was not wearing the plain grey outfit of a hydropathic nurse. She was poised and charming in a delicate blue floating dress with an overskirt and long jacket, and feathers in her hair. Lettie thought that she was a perfect antidote for her father.

'Your father has told Dr Bretton and Agnes that you are his daughter,' Frances said. 'They will keep it to themselves for the present.'

They went along the landing together. Father and Dr Bretton were waiting in the hall below, looking unnervingly formal in evening dress with white ties. Lettie urged Frances to go on ahead of her while she lingered at the top of the stairs to compose herself. She took a deep breath, straightened her back and took hold of the banister rail. It was a grand staircase, wide with carved wooden balustrades, and Lettie felt grand – elegant and grand – as she walked down. She could hear her father speaking to Dr Bretton.

'Is everything satisfactory for Lord Laughton?' he asked.

'I believe so,' Dr Bretton replied. 'It is hard to tell because his manner is quite obnoxious.'

'I did warn you, Take care. His bad opinion can be damaging.'

'Well, he has been recommended to my regimen and he is following it closely. He says he will marry again soon and is determined to renew his vigour.'

'Really?'

'His wants an heir and his mistress is young enough.'

'He's going to marry his mistress?' Her father sounded surprised.

Dr Bretton nodded. 'He spoke of her during his consultation. She lives in France, I believe.'

'Dear God, no! Not her! He can't bring her back with him!'

Frances had joined them and intervened. 'Michael, dearest, hush now. Your daughter is here.'

Her father stopped talking and turned round. He looked much improved this evening but she noticed that he swallowed at the sight of her. She had tried very hard to impress him and now she wasn't sure that he liked what he saw. Nevertheless, she smiled and said, 'Good evening, Father.' She loved the sound of that and went down the last few steps quickly.

'You look very lovely, my dear.' He bent to kiss her gently on each cheek.

'Thank you, Father. Good evening, Dr Bretton,' Lettie responded.

They exchanged pleasantries and went into the dining room. She had not overheard much of their conversation but neither gentleman had referred to Lord Laughton in sympathetic tones. Rather the opposite, she thought. They didn't seem to have much respect for him at all.

The small dining room at Mereside Lodge was for patients taking the cure who did not wish to dine in their rooms. It was a square, wood-panelled room, well lit by oil lamps. Each table had a silver candelabrum to set off the white linen and crystal. The effect was of a restful grace, disturbed only by the sound of cutlery on china. The food, though, was very plain and had little in common with the banquet that had been served in the main dining room the evening before, or indeed the menu that evening for those not taking the cure. In the small dining room patients could order only vege-tables or salads with grilled fish or an omelette if their regimen allowed it. Some simply took the consommé and did not linger to be tempted further.

'We occasionally have dinner in here after the patients had finished,' her father explained as they sat down. Lettie recognised the footman who took their order.

The ensuing silence felt awkward to Lettie and she guessed that her presence was limiting their conversation. 'How long will Lord Laughton stay?' she began.

'I don't know,' her father answered.

'Until he gets what he wants, I imagine,' Frances added quietly.

'Well, will you sell to him, Father?' Lettie asked.

Three pairs of enquiring eyes turned in her direction. 'How do you know that I am considering it?' Father queried.

'I . . . I met Mr Laughton at the post office in the village and we took coffee together at the inn.'

Frances raised her eyebrows. 'You went to an inn with a gentleman you are not acquainted with?'

'Oh, but I am acquainted with him! He has been staying at Boundary Farm near Waterley Edge. We had an . . . an interesting conversation.'

'What has he said to you, Lettie?' her father asked.

'Not much, except that he's entitled to half of Waterley estate and Lord Laughton has offered him Mereside Lodge instead.'

'They argued about it – at least, Lord Laughton did – all through dinner yesterday,' Frances complained. 'It was quite exhausting.'

Dr Bretton added, 'If part of the estate had been willed to others he'd no business giving any of it away in the first place.'

'Well, he did. I have the title deeds. He had Lady Laughton's willing consent at the time. She wanted . . .' Her father hesitated. 'She wanted me out of Waterley Hall and agreed to sign.'

The memory appeared to trouble her father, causing Lettie to hesitate with more questions. Frances took up the conversation, 'Mr Laughton is not at all like his cousin. I thought he was very civil.'

'I sincerely hope he is not going to stir up more trouble with His Lordship,' her father commented.

361

Lettie grimaced. 'I think it's too late to hope for that, Father. He has little regard for either Lord or Lady Laughton. He told me that his father spent most of his life in legal battles with one Laughton or the other.'

'Considering you are a stranger to him, he seems to have told you a great deal.'

'He appeared to think I should know. Actually, I think he was explaining his involvement as a kind of apology for his earlier behaviour towards me. He took a dislike to me at first, especially when he found out who my grandfather was.'

Her father exchanged a questioning glance with Frances. She returned a faltering smile. Their soup arrived accompanied by the gritty biscuits that Dr Bretton called crackers and crumbled them into his consommé. Her father waited until the footman had disappeared before asking Lettie what else Alec had divulged.

'Not much that I haven't told you already.' She took a deep breath. 'Well, I . . . I do know why you want the money.'

She saw her father glance at Frances who tried to maintain her cheerfulness. 'Selling up is the only way for us to be together in the way we wish,' she said and added firmly, 'You have to tell her, Michael.'

Lettie noticed that her eyes were sad and she realised that her father had already made up his mind to sell. 'But what will you do if you leave here?' she demanded.

'We'll have enough left over for a guest house at the seaside,' Frances answered. She appeared to be happy with this solution.

362

Her father, too, managed a smile and Lettie realised that the only time he seemed happy was in Frances's company. He loved her and he needed her and it was clear to Lettie that Frances would do anything for him. That's love, she thought. They wanted to be together as husband and wife. Father was estranged from his wife but Frances, clearly, was not prepared to live with him as his mistress and play the part of the Lady of the House at Mereside Lodge. Lettie admired her for that stance.

'You have already decided to sell,' Lettie stated.

'We don't want any more battles.'

'Then Lord Laughton has won!' she exclaimed. 'You can't let him do that. He's a bully and it's not fair!'

Chapter 26

'I shall have Frances as my wife. That is worth any amount of money.'

Lettie was forced to agree with him. But her sense of injustice was strong. 'You can't give in without a fight!'

'Yes I can.' Her father put down his soup spoon. 'I am worn out with fighting,' he said.

This silenced Lettie for a moment as she realised he had been fighting his own personal battles for most of his life. Yet Mereside Lodge *was* his life! A guest house in Scarborough was hardly the same.

'But Frances isn't,' she exclaimed and swivelled to face her. 'Are you?'

Dr Bretton intervened, 'You would be a notable loss to hydropathy, Frances. And Michael is not ready for a major upheaval. He needs more time to complete his recovery and this is the best place for him.'

'Father will recover, won't he?' Lettie asked him anxiously. She was very aware that her sudden appearance had come as a shock to him and he had been tempted back to the brandy bottle.

'Your arrival has been my biggest test in recent months,' her father admitted.

'I know and I am sorry. I want to make amends.' She turned to Dr Bretton. 'Is there anything I can do to help with Father's recovery?'

'Very little, Lettie. He must do it for himself.'

Frances added, 'But you can do what I do and be there for him when the temptation is greatest.'

'That is enough about me!' her father interrupted. 'May we not enjoy our dinner? Our new cook has proved to be an excellent choice and Mereside Lodge will continue as a hydropathic establishment until the deed of sale is signed.'

'If Lord Laughton is going to give it to his cousin, Mr Laughton may wish for it to continue as such,' Dr Bretton commented. 'I know he was favourably impressed.'

'Did Mr Laughton take the cure?' Lettie queried.

'He planned to but that was before he was called away. However, I did have an interesting conversation with him on the merits of radioactive tonic water.' Dr Bretton warmed to this topic as a footman cleared the soup plates. 'Healing waters from natural springs have been scientific-ally proven to possess radium emanation. There is a company in San Francisco selling ceramic water dispensers lined with radium ore. The tonic eases pain from gout and rheumatism.'

Lettie had no idea what he was talking about, but Frances did. 'The water cures at Bath and Harrogate involve drinking the water as well as bathing in it. We ought to have our spring water tested for radioactivity.'

'I'll see to it,' Dr Bretton said. He poured water from a jug into their drinking glasses.

Lettie hesitated before she drank. It did taste slightly different from the water at the manse and didn't lather as well either.

Lettie had noticed that the table was not laid with wine glasses. Her eyes roamed round the room. All the tables were the same. Quite a contrast, she thought, with the selection offered by the butler the previous evening. He must have made the choices for her father.

Mr Norwich came in with their Dover sole on a large silver platter, which he offered to each of them in turn. The footmen followed with neatly turned and beautifully presented vegetables. After they had left, her father commented, 'Mr Norwich was worth waiting for. He was an under butler in the household of a duke. When I watch him at work I remember my days as a young man.'

Lettie wanted to know more about those times and asked, 'Did you enjoy your years in service, Father?'

'I did. It was my vocation. Whilst I am here, Mereside Lodge will be run as a gentleman's country residence ought to be.'

Lettie resisted a strong temptation to voice other questions running through her mind, judging it to be unwise.

Instead she said, 'I should like to learn about hydropathy, if I may. The patients take steam baths, I understand.'

'Perhaps the two of us might spend tomorrow afternoon together?' Frances responded. 'I'll show you the bath house and treatment rooms.'

'I should like that very much.'

Lettie went to sleep that night contented that, although she still had much to discover about her father and Mereside Lodge, she had made a friend of Frances. They had had a difficult start because of her rash impulsiveness and Lettie wanted to make it up to her. She now felt some easing of the impatient urgency she suffered at first. Father had, she thought, accepted Lettie although there was obviously some residual anxiety about her existence. It was an apprehensive time for her as well, but she was young and strong, whatever Alec Laughton had implied earlier.

Would he be the owner of Mereside Lodge in future? When he had told her about Lord Laughton's plans, he had not seemed predisposed to go along with them. Where had Alec gone, she wondered, and with what purpose? He said he would telegraph so perhaps Frances would tell her tomorrow; if she asked.

She met up with Frances at the end of morning treatments in the palm court, a conservatory adorned with large glossy green plants and colonial bamboo furniture. A straggle of patients wearing bathrobes were exchanging comments on their treatments and waiting for luncheon. They were mainly gentlemen smoking cigars and enjoying the view. Lettie followed Frances along a corridor of windows to the bath house. As they walked Lettie commented on how much she had enjoyed dinner last evening.

'Your father did, too,' Francs responded.

'Have you ever met Father's wife?' Lettie asked.

'No, never, they have lived apart for many years.'

'It must have been a short marriage. She cannot have loved him very much.'

'He believes that she did not love him at all.'

'Then why did she marry him?'

'I really do not know and he will not speak of it. I assumed at first that she was a maidservant and she married him for his position but he once said that she was a woman of independent means.'

'And you are sure she is still alive?'

'Oh yes. She lives abroad and that makes a divorce even more difficult. Lawyers are so expensive and it is, of course, not a gentlemanly thing to do. There has to be a . . . a third party. Michael has to have evidence of – you know – her . . . her adultery, and the newspapers these days are so aggressive in their reporting. It will not be easy for any of us.'

'Doesn't she want the divorce as well?'

'I imagine so but I don't know yet. We cannot instruct a lawyer without the means to pay him. I have offered to allow her to cite me as the guilty party but Michael won't hear of it. He gets angry because it would be a lie. He insists that she is the guilty one.'

Lettie noticed that talking of divorce was making

Frances anxious so she didn't pursue the conversation. They reached the bath house and this cheered Frances as she explained to Lettie what went on in a twentieth-century health hydro and how modern science was improving on the old methods.

The bath house was a long low building containing rooms of different sizes for various hydropathic treatments. The atmosphere was warm and oppressively humid in some areas. Frances had a team of assistants – female hydropathic nurses and male bath attendants who administered treatments to their patients and kept the bath house clean. An aroma of scented oil filled Lettie's nostrils.

The steam rooms were lined with white tiles and fitted with similarly tiled benches. They had adjacent cubicles for cold water treatments, which sounded quite brutal to Lettie. Some of the cubicles had long bathtubs, permanently situated with their own piped water supply and drain hole, for sulphur mud or peat treatments.

Mereside Lodge had taken delivery recently of some patented 'sitz' baths from Germany. Lettie thought they were attractive hip baths until she learned that, although the water in the sitz bath was warm, the treatment consisted of sitting in it with the feet in icy water. This sounded unpleasant enough, but the treatment also required that the patient then move to a cold sitz bath with the feet in warm water and alternate between the two. Excellent for gout and rheumatism, France advised.

The larger baths used for immersing the whole body in warm ocean salts or seaweed seemed a much better proposition. Lettie was undecided about the massage tables but totally enamoured of a delightfully warm and dry room at one end containing a row of comfortable couches with pillows and blankets for patient relaxation at the end of their treatments. Frances knocked on a door labelled 'Consultations' and a voice answered, 'Come in.'

Dr Bretton was sitting behind a desk reading a journal by the light of an oil lamp with a glass chimney. He had a pair of reading spectacles hooked round his ears.

'Are we disturbing you?' Frances said.

He stood up. 'Not at all. Come in and sit down. I have been reading about a new design of sitz bath that is divided into two halves and holds the hot and cold water in one utensil.' He took off his spectacles, massaged his eyes with his fingers and muttered, 'We must seriously consider putting in electric light.'

Lettie glanced around the room for a gas mantle on the wall and queried, 'Why don't you have gas lights at Mereside Lodge? We had them in the downstairs rooms at the manse.'

Frances replied, 'It costs far too much to lay the pipes. They don't have gas lamps in the village either.'

'The Reverend is having electric light in the mission hall at Waterley Edge.'

'But electric is dangerous,' Frances said. 'I mean, it can kill you, can't it?'

'Only if you touch it,' Dr Bretton replied.

'But you can't see it so how would you know?'

'It travels along wires inside rubber tubes. We ought to consider it, Frances. I have been reading about patient treatments using electric.'

'It does cost a lot, though,' Lettie explained. 'I used to write up minutes for the elders' meetings and I saw the figures. Our chapel had a legacy to pay for it.'

'I'll talk to Michael about it. More treatments mean more patients,' Dr Bretton said.

'And now we have better servants we can take more patients,' Frances added.

'Perhaps we can make savings, too?' Lettie suggested. Neither Frances nor Dr Bretton queried the fact that she was including herself in the future of Mereside Lodge. She went on, 'Those daily hampers from Leeds and Sheffield must cost a fortune. I know how much a whole ham costs.'

Frances shook her head emphatically. 'Michael will not compromise on his daily deliveries of provisions. He insists on the best suppliers. Patients expect the same high standards that they have in their own country residences.'

'Do you ever check that they are sending you the full order?'

Frances raised her eyebrows and looked helpless for a second. 'I cannot do everything, Lettie! I never have a minute to spare on some days and I am a hydropathic nurse not a housekeeper.'

'We do have a housekeeper, normally,' Dr Bretton explained. 'Unfortunately, the last one turned out to be most unsuitable. She came with testimonials but we think they were not genuine.'

'I can housekeep,' Lettie suggested. 'My grandmother used to be a housekeeper at Waterley Hall and she taught

371

me everything. I've never used half of what I learned but Gran said I should know anyway.'

Frances smiled. 'Lettie, managing a manse is hardly the same as here.'

'I had the mission hall and chapel accounts to look after as well. I checked all the ordering and invoices and kept the books balanced for the Reverend.' Lettie felt excited by the thought of being involved in her father's venture.

'Someone to help with housekeeping records would be useful, Frances,' Dr Bretton pointed out.

'You cannot do housekeeping and nursing,' Lettie added. 'Of course, I'll only do it if Father agrees.'

'You are far too young for such a position,' Frances said.

'I'm not suggesting I am the housekeeper, or even that you call me housekeeper. Cook and Mr Norwich would probably walk out if you did. But I could be your assistant, Frances, doing the housekeeping work for you until you have made a new appointment.'

Frances was undecided until Lettie added, 'I should be acting on your instructions all the time.' Lettie recalled the meticulous minute books recording mission business and suggested enthusiastically, 'I'll write a full report for you and Father every day.'

'Well, I can't say that I don't need your help,' Frances said slowly then added more briskly, 'Very well. You can start with the laundry lists.' She stood up and went on, 'We'll leave Dr Bretton to his reading and I'll show you where the keys are. The linen cupboards are next to the housekeeper's sitting room.'

'I know. I did some sewing in there.'

They went out of the bath house through the servants' entrance at the opposite end from the palm court and passed the laundry, which had completed most of its work for the day. As they skirted the coal yard to return to the servants' hall, Frances muttered, 'Coals are getting low again. Michael will have to send word to the coal merchant.'

Lettie reflected that Toogoods wouldn't need a reminder to deliver supplies. They knew how much coal their customers used and replenished their cellars on a regular basis. Life was different in the countryside. They didn't even have the gas light here.

'Who is your coalman?' she asked.

'I can't recall his name but I'll show you where I keep the invoices and record books.' Frances led the way into the housekeeper's sitting room and said, 'Wait here while I fetch some refreshment.'

Lettie sat by the unlit fire, her gaze wandering over the bookcases with interest until Frances returned with a pot of aromatic coffee on a tray.

'The house servants are eating their dinner. We'll have ours at second sitting with the hydro nurses and bath attendants so I've brought cake to keep you going,' Frances said. 'Do you like cherry cake? It's just out of the oven.' She placed the tray on a small table between the two fireside chairs.

'I like all cake,' Lettie replied. 'Shall I pour?'

Frances outlined how she managed the housekeeping and pointed out where the relevant books were kept. 'I'm afraid I haven't kept the linen records up to date, and the invoices haven't been sorted for over two months. But every one is there, so you can find out anything you need to know. The previous housekeeper ordered food supplies as well.'

'I gather she didn't stay long,' Lettie commented.

'Michael had to let her go. I agreed with him but I haven't been able to replace her yet.' Frances looked unhappy for a moment, then said more cheerily, 'Now Mr Norwich has joined us, he will order his own supplies and Cook can manage food provisions. They can be trusted. Both come with good references that Michael has checked himself.'

Lettie didn't comment but she guessed the old housekeeper had been in collusion with the outdoor staff to steal food. Frances's record-keeping was, indeed, in a sorry state and Lettie decided she would begin with stock-taking and inventories.

After tea, Frances took her into the butler's pantry. Mr Norwich was poring over his own inventories. He was very pleased to learn that he would be receiving regular housekeeping returns from Miss Fanshaw in future and Lettie itched to get started.

The following day, Lettie was unexpectedly called away from her task by Frances who said, 'Your father has had a visitor who insists on meeting you before he leaves. He's waiting in the morning room.'

Intrigued, Lettie took off her apron and tidied her hair. A mature gentleman, plainly dressed and wearing an ecclesiastical collar, was waiting for her. He stood up as soon as she entered the room and approached her with an air of briskness.

'Are you Miss Hargreaves?' He appeared to be examining her appearance in some detail.

'I am, sir.'

He nodded. 'Yes. You match the description I have. Excellent! My name is Reverend Pryce from Mereside Church. Your guardian has requested that I place myself at your service.'

'Reverend Ennis asked you to come here?'

'Actually, no. It was his colleague from the Methodist chapel in Forest Chase. We are acquainted. Your guardian sent word that you were here and requested that I confirm you are well and it is your wish to remain here. A gentleman who claims to be your father received me and gave me such confirmation, but I must hear it from you.'

'The gentleman is my father, sir, and please be assured that he speaks the truth. I have written to the Reverend to explain this.'

'Yes, yes, but he is concerned, and rightly so. Mereside Lodge is not an establishment for young girls.'

'That is nonsense!' Reverend Pryce raised his eyebrows and Lettie searched for words to redeem her rudeness. She remembered the words that Agnes had used about the Lodge's reputation and added, 'Forgive me, sir, but this is a respectable house, whatever you may have heard.'

His mouth turned down at the corners but he responded positively. 'Very well. I have done my duty and shall report my findings as requested. Good day to you.'

'I'll show you out, sir.' She opened the morning-room

door, followed him out and handed him his hat and cane from the hall closet. When she held the front door she said, 'Thank you for taking the trouble to find me. I am sure some of our . . . our guests will be pleased to attend your Sunday services if you advise us of the times.'

'Indeed?' he answered with a query in his voice.

'Guests at Mereside Lodge are here to improve their health, sir, and I am sure my father has a high regard for their spiritual well-being too. I shall arrange the carriage for evensong.' She wondered if she'd had been too forward, but smiled anyway. 'Good day to you, sir.'

He raised his hat to acknowledge her as he walked down the steps and she closed the front door softly. There was so much to be done at Mereside Lodge and she looked forward to returning to the servants' hall and catching up with Agnes. Agnes was in charge of the upstairs maids and an important ally of any housekeeper.

Engrossed in her new challenge, the days flew by. Alec had telegraphed to say he was going abroad and would return to Mereside Lodge within the month. Lettie counted the days on the calendar in the housekeeper's sitting room and her mind registered the date every day. Occasionally, when she was walking alone by the mere and heckled by the geese, she allowed herself to daydream about him. She imagined hearing the approaching thud of hooves behind her as he rode up to sweep her up onto his horse and carry her away to she knew not where.

It was a girlish fantasy and she reproached herself for it afterwards. But she believed his chivalrous nature to be real. He was a gentleman in every sense of the word and he would protect his chosen lady to the death. Sadly, she thought, that lady was not likely to be her. Alec's lady would be more akin to one of the elegant aristocratic creatures who came to Mereside Lodge to recover from a hectic and exhausting season of parties and balls.

Chapter 27

Michael gained in strength every day and cheered notice-
ably when several new patients arrived. Lettie assumed
they had been influenced by Lord Laughton's presence.
His Lordship took the cure for a week and, against Dr
Breton's advice, insisted on a further week. Lettie was
curious about him and she saw him once, in the palm
court.

She had been asked by Frances to make a needlework
repair on the ribbon of a satin bedroom slipper for one
of the lady patients. The lady was elderly, not titled but
connected to a baronet's family through her marriage,
and Lettie was instructed to take the slippers to her in
the palm court at teatime. They were very pretty embroi-
dered slippers and Lettie wrapped them in clean muslin
to return them.

Palm court was a popular venue for patients taking the cure. It had a restful ambience and a relaxed dress code. Those on strict regimens could remain in their hydropath bathrobes and take tea amongst the greenery, perhaps sharing conversation with new-found acquaintances. Afternoon tea did not vary. The traditional beverage with milk or lemon as patients wished, or a herbal alternative, a few very dainty cucumber sandwiches, even in winter when the cucumbers came from glasshouses, and a slice of Russian cake.

Lettie was intrigued by the Russian cake. It was the same every day and baked in loaf tins by Cook to a special recipe without butter, solely for patients taking the cure. The ingredients of eggs, flour and a mix of minced dried fruits were assured to keep sluggish digestions in working order. One slice at teatime was obligatory for the cure.

Lettie delivered the slippers and was admiring the plants when she was distracted by a commotion from one of the gentlemen. She overheard a patient comment, 'Lord Laughton again. When is he going home?'

Lord Laughton was a gentleman of middling years with greying hair and whiskers. He was running to fat, Lettie noticed, and it made him look like King Edward. He must have been handsome as a younger man but his face was deeply lined so that his expression was angry even when he was calm. He did not seem to care that he had disturbed other patients by his demands. A young footman, one of Mr Norwich's recent additions, was standing in front of him with a silver tea tray.

'You heard me! Dundee cake and a glass of whiskey to wash it down,' His Lordship demanded.

'Your order card has light diet on it, sir,' the footman replied.

'I've had enough of that. Fit as a fiddle now, everything in good working order.' He threw a coin on the tray and said, 'Whiskey, a large one.'

The footman placed the tray on a low table. 'I beg your pardon, sir. I cannot accept a tip. House rules, sir.'

Lord Laughton added another coin. 'You'll fetch me a whiskey if you want to keep your position.'

'I'll ask Mr Norwich. Excuse me, sir.'

As the footman walked by Lettie, he said, 'He's always complaining about something. And he knows about the tipping.' The young man added indignantly, 'I am not a waiter.'

Lettie agreed that Lord Laughton should have known better. Father was proud of his 'gentleman's country house' traditions at Mereside Lodge. Guests in country houses presented monetary gifts to servants discreetly in envelopes at the end of their stay. Of course His Lordship knew! She recalled a comment of Mrs Osborne that Lord Laughton thought he could buy anyone, and grimaced. Well, he's not buying my father's life, she thought crossly, not if I can help it. She spoke quietly to the footman. 'Mr Norwich won't change it without Dr Bretton's say-so. I'll fetch him.'

Lettie explained the situation to Dr Bretton and he went to speak to His Lordship immediately. She hovered in the background, half hidden by the large glossy leaves of a magnificent rubber plant. Dr Bretton suggested that Lord Laughton dispensed with the cure as he had advised earlier. One week was the normal prescription. Eventually, His Lordship agreed to continue the discussion in Dr Bretton's consulting room, to the relief of other patients.

It was a minor incident yet it made Lettie determined that her father would not give in to His Lordship's demands to sell. Mereside Lodge was her father's life, and now hers as well. But his divorce was equally as important to him and he ought to have both. At the manse she had had to account for every penny that was spent. It appeared that no one had applied the same principles here for a long time and Lettie resolved to change that.

Lettie spoke with her father on most days. She ate her breakfast and dinner in the servants' hall but took tea or dinner with her father, either in his room or in the small dining room for patients. She preferred tea when they were alone as Frances and Dr Bretton were present at dinner and the conversation different. Alone with father, she talked fondly of her grandmother and childhood at the manse, and saw that this gave him pleasure. But for Lettie, questions about her mother were constantly on her mind. However, although she remained intensely curious about her mother, she had to be satisfied, for the present, to have found her father.

As he gained in strength he talked of earlier years at Mereside Lodge, at least those he could remember. He had 'given up the drink' several times on the advice of his physician and more than ten years ago had visited a famous hydro in Derbyshire frequented by the then Prince of Wales. It was there that he met Frances, fell in love, and with her help began his slow and very rocky road to recovery. But, following that visit, his vision for the future of Mereside Lodge had remained steadfast. He sold his thriving woodland concern to pay for the bath house and other changes. Frances contacted Dr Bretton, a colleague from her years as a nurse in Africa, and persuaded him to join them.

On one occasion Lettie outlined her ideas for savings. Michael readily accepted her request to investigate coal supplies and it made her think of Thomas. He could advise her and she wondered if he would drive over in the coal wagon one Sunday as he had promised. She realised that she missed him.

'Father,' she asked one evening, 'why do you buy York hams from a London supplier when they come from Yorkshire?'

'I only have the very best quality, my dear. London stores supply the great houses of our lords and ladies.'

'But I could go direct to the pig curers for the very same hams.'

'And how would they get here? London stores deliver every day on the railway.'

'The provisions merchant in Mereside village has York ham. His wife cooks it and he slices it, weighs it out and sells it to his customers. In fact, he could probably supply you at a saving.'

'I have no intention of reducing my standards. I should rather close down.'

'I agree with you, Father, but will you let me look into it?'

'If you wish. Frances says you are proving to be a good housekeeper.'

'Gran taught me well.'

He gazed out of the window. 'Yes, she was a good woman. But your grandfather was powerful. He controlled his own home as he did the servants' hall at Waterley.'

'Tell me about my mother,' she said softly.

Pain washed over her father's face and he closed his eyes.

'I'm sorry, Father. I didn't mean to upset you.'

'It's not your fault. Your grandmother and I were as one in that respect. Why should a daughter suffer for her father's evils?'

Lettie didn't understand and said, 'I . . . I haven't suffered, Father.'

'I believe you have,' he replied, 'and it has been because of my actions. However, I was not speaking of you.'

'Then who?'

'Your mother. She suffered from your grandfather's ambition. It ruled him and infected her and I . . . I went along with his ways. I was weak, I see that with hindsight.'

'But you are strong now! You have conquered your weakness.'

She realised that he was distressed and immediately talked of other things: her arrangement for Sunday worshippers at the village church, and the governess cart. She said, 'I should like to buy some notions from the draper's in the village and I thought I might use the old governess cart in the stables.'

'Certainly. The stableman will take you.'

'I am able to drive myself, Father. Now I am Frances's assistant, I often want to make small purchases. May I not have the governess cart for my own use?'

'Why, that is a splendid idea! It will need some renovation. I'll speak to Norwich about it.'

'Thank you. I wasn't aware Mr Norwich was responsible for the outdoor staff as well.'

'He has to be for the present. I used to have a steward, a reliable fellow who managed all the servants for me.'

'Where is he now?'

'I couldn't pay him, you see. But he was loyal. He stayed as long as he could, but he had a family to support . . .'

'Well, that won't happen again. We have more new patients expected this week. Lord Laughton may be difficult but his presence here has helped.'

'No, my dear, His Lordship has not helped at all. We are constantly offering patients extra services to apologise for his behaviour. It was his cousin, Mr Laughton, who recommended us to his London acquaintances.'

Lettie's heart lifted. If that were the case then Alec did not want Mereside Lodge to close! When Father sold to Lord Laughton, it might remain as a hydro, with Father and Frances and Dr Bretton and . . . *and me*, she realised happily. Nothing would change and soon she would see Alec again.

'When is Mr Laughton returning?' she asked.

Her happiness was short lived. Father replied, 'He has written to say he has been delayed. The letter was posted overseas.'

She realised that travelling was a part of Alec's life and he would return home to Canada as soon as his business with Lord Laughton was finished. She found this a depressing thought and sighed unconsciously.

'Are you sad about our new patients?'

'No, of course not, it's . . . it's good news for the hydro.' She rallied her thoughts. 'I . . . I want to examine our coal costs. Is Mr Norwich in charge of the boilerman as well?'

'He is. I shall not make any further appointments now. Mereside Lodge will need an engineer in future even if the hydro closes. A house of these proportions must have electric light and a motor vehicle.'

'But it will still need coal for the boilers and fires.'

'Everybody needs coal,' her father said with a smile.

Lettie agreed and her thoughts turned to Thomas. She wanted his advice so it was with some delight that the following Sunday afternoon, when she said 'Come in' after a tap on her door, Thomas walked in to the house-keeper's room.

'Well, look at you, Lettie Hargreaves, the housekeeper already.'

'Thomas! How lovely to see you. Sit down.'

'I like the grey outfit.' He grinned, referring to her

dark, serviceable housekeeper's dress. 'It makes you look, er, um . . .'

'It makes me look what?' she prompted.

'Your age,' he said, 'but in a nice way; grown up and capable.'

She wasn't flattered and she frowned.

'It's what you are,' he added quickly. 'It's you, especially with your hair done up like that.'

When she didn't reply he went on, 'Reverend Ennis told me you were staying on here and I said I'd be back if you didn't come home so here am I.'

'So here you are,' she repeated and decided not to dwell on what he thought about her appearance. 'And I am very pleased to see you. Reverend Ennis sent a spy from the local church to check up on me.'

'I know. I've called into the manse several times and he told me. He was worried about you and he couldn't leave the mission. You found your father, then? I'm happy for you, Lettie. What kind of place is this?'

'Oh, I've so much to tell you.' She closed her account books carefully, pushed them aside and began.

After about half an hour he said, 'Do you know that you look different when you talk about here. Your eyes light up and you smile a lot.'

'I'm happy here, Thomas. Whatever happens to Mereside Lodge, Father will marry a lovely lady and he will be happy too. I'll have a family.' After she had said it, Lettie realised how satisfying that sounded to her. Thomas wouldn't understand. He had always been surrounded by a large and loving family. But she hadn't and she smiled to herself every time she thought about it. She couldn't help herself.

'I'm thirsty now,' she said. 'And you must be hungry after your long drive. Let me get you some refreshment. Tea? Or coffee? The coffee here is very good.'

'Then I'll have coffee please.'

'With cream?'

'No, ta. Have you got sugar?'

'Of course we have! Wait here.' Lettie went off to the still room next to the scullery.

Agnes was laying up tea trays for the patients and Lettie explained who Thomas was as she warmed a silver coffee pot.

'We were all wondering,' Agnes replied, 'because he came round the back in a motor wagon. You go back and talk to him. I'll bring your coffee. Large slices of cake?'

'And sandwiches, he'll be hungry.'

Agnes lingered to serve Thomas his coffee and hand round sandwiches and cake. 'Can I fetch you anything else?' she asked.

'No thank you,' Lettie answered, aware that the patients' teas were waiting.

'I'll come back for the tray,' Agnes volunteered.

'No need, you've a lot to do out there,' Lettie said.

'It's no trouble,' Agnes replied as she left.

After the door had closed, Thomas commented, 'Do the maids always wait on you as well?'

'No, they don't. I'm not even the housekeeper, just an

assistant, and I normally do everything for myself.' Agnes knows that, she thought.

Thomas pulled down the cuffs of his Sunday suit and straightened up in his chair. 'Perhaps she thinks I'm somebody important.'

'She saw you arrive in the coal wagon, that's all, so don't get above yourself,' Lettie commented, smiling. 'And speaking of coal, I may be able to give you an order for Mr Toogood. How much will he charge a ton for regular deliveries here?'

'To here? I don't know. It'd have to come from a pithead via a yard around these parts.'

'Well, has he got one?' Lettie got up to find a piece of paper, an invoice for the Lodge's latest load of coal. She waved it in front of his face. 'Can he beat this price?'

'Keep it still, then.' Thomas took hold of the document and read it. He blew out his cheeks. 'That's a bit dear, isn't it?'

'I thought so too. And the Lodge uses a lot.'

'It doesn't look that big a house to me.'

'It's not, but we have the bath house. You know, Turkish baths and so on, every morning.'

'I know about them. My dad says they're supposed to be good for you.'

'They are, especially when you've been ill like my father has.'

Thomas gave her a sympathetic look. 'He'll need you and Frances on his side for ever.'

'I know. He's got us, both of us.'

'He's a lucky man. Tell me more about this place. My dad'll be fascinated.'

Lettie spent another very pleasant hour with Thomas before Agnes came back for the tray. 'Your father was asking where you were today,' she said to Lettie.

'I sometimes have my tea with him, if he feels up to it,' Lettie explained to Thomas.

'And I've kept you from him,' he said. 'Go and see him for half an hour.'

'What about you?'

'Well, I'd like to see the size of the boilers here before I leave.'

'I'll find one of the men to show you after I've seen father.'

'I can do that for you, Lettie,' Agnes suggested.

'Thank you, I'd like that.' Thomas smiled and stood up. 'Have you worked here long, Agnes?'

As Agnes returned Thomas's smile, Lettie felt excluded from this hasty arrangement. Before Agnes could reply Lettie asked, 'Will you be able to stay for servants' tea? It's at five o'clock on Sundays.'

'Yes please! I've a long drive home.'

'I'll take him to the servants' hall,' Agnes volunteered. 'We'll wait for you in there.'

Lettie had little choice but to agree. 'Well, if you're sure, Thomas?' she muttered.

'Don't neglect your father for my sake,' Thomas said. 'I'll be in good hands with Agnes.'

Lettie knew that and watched them walk out of her room with a frown. Thomas was *her* friend. He'd come

389

to see *her* and she wanted to show him round. But Father was asking for her so she quelled her feelings and gave some attention to her appearance.

She was late arriving for tea in the servants' hall, which, on Sundays, was cold cuts with fresh and pickled vegetables followed by fruit cake and cheese. She wasn't hungry anyway and went straight over to Thomas and Agnes who were deep in conversation.

'Did you see the boilers?' she asked brightly.

'I did, and I had a talk with your boilerman. You know that invoice you showed me?'

'Ye-e-es,' Lettie answered.

'Is that every fortnight?'

'Every week.'

'You do get through a lot of coal,' he responded with raised eyebrows.

Agnes stood up. 'I've got sewing to organise this evening. It was nice to meet you, Thomas. You'll come again, won't you?'

'If I'm invited,' he answered. When Agnes had left the room he added, 'She's a lovely girl, isn't she?'

'I like her. She's a good friend as well as being reliable.'

Thomas lowered his voice. 'I wouldn't say that about some others employed here.'

'What do you mean?' She knew the answer, of course.

'Even if those boilers are going all day and night, you wouldn't get through that much coal every week. Where else do you use it?'

'Nowhere. It's the same with the food deliveries,' she whispered. 'Stuff goes missing before it even gets here. Come back to the housekeeper's room. I want your help.'

Lettie told him what she had seen with the food hampers.

'If you know who it is you'll have to get the constable in,' Thomas concluded.

'I can't do that because it'll get in the newspapers and cause a scandal and that won't do the Lodge's reputation any good at all. Father can't afford to lose any patients but he says I can look at all costings. I've got a better idea.'

'Watch your back, Lettie. These people have no scruples.'

Lettie put his mind at ease by outlining her plan to change suppliers and the way provisions were delivered and remove the opportunities for stealing.

'Yes, but you'll need someone to find you new suppliers – someone like me who knows the traders. And he'd need a motor vehicle out here.'

Lettie gave a short laugh. 'Do you mean you?'

Thomas was surprised, thought about it for a moment and said, 'I don't see why not. I'll ask Mr Toogood about the coal order. What with all these mill and factory owners building their big houses and living like the gentry, he has interests all over the Yorkshire coal fields.'

'You must have impressed him to let you borrow the coal wagon again.'

'Reverend Ennis asked my foreman if I could. That reminds me, he sent some of your things from the manse.' He stood up. 'I'll fetch them in, and then I'd best make a start for home. Can I say goodbye to Agnes before I leave?'

'I'll find her for you.'

But Agnes was already outside, cutting spikes of lavender for the linen cupboard. By the time Lettie caught up with her she was sitting on a garden seat with her trug of scented flower stalks, near to where the coal wagon was parked. Thomas was sitting next to her.

Lettie gazed at them and frowned, pressing her lips together in thought. She recognised her Gran's old travelling box on the ground by the wagon and walked over to it. Thomas and Agnes joined her a minute later.

'Where do you want your box?' Thomas asked, bending down to pick it up. He heaved it onto his shoulder.

'Leave it in the passage,' Lettie said. 'The footmen will carry it upstairs.'

'It'll take two of them,' Agnes commented as she watched Thomas walk away.

Left on their own, Lettie and Agnes stared at each other in silence until Agnes said, 'I have to check on the maids in the sewing room,' and followed Thomas indoors.

Lettie waited by the wagon until he came out again. She was trying to make sense of her feelings. Thomas was *her* friend but there was no doubt in her mind that he was attracted to Agnes, and that Agnes was welcoming his attentions. As Thomas cranked the engine into life, climbed into the driver's seat and waved goodbye, she noticed that Agnes was standing in the open doorway, watching them.

Chapter 28

Lettie walked over to the stables to see the coachman. He was supervising renovations on the governess cart. The last coat of varnish was dry and it looked very spruce. The coachman had selected a pony for it and he showed her where the tack was hung. Mr Norwich had made him ostler, in charge of all the horses, carriage and carts – and the men who worked them.

The carter and stableman were not happy but Mr Norwich had already made his presence felt, outdoors and indoors, as the most senior servant at Mereside Lodge. Cook and the head gardener, who were rulers in their own realms at Mereside Lodge, respected his word. And Cook was very popular with the outdoor men because she looked after their stomachs.

The carter appeared as they were admiring the trap.

'You'll need one of us to tek care of it fer you,' he said.

The coachman replied for her: 'I've a lad from the village starting next week. You and the stableman are needed with the heavy horses, clearing woodland and watercourses round the mere.'

'What about the hampers waiting fer fetching from the Halt?' the carter demanded.

'Oh, I'll collect those in future,' Lettie answered.

'You can't lift them on your own.'

'Then I'll take the new stable hand.' She paused before adding, 'Ordering is different now so I'll know what to expect.'

The carter grunted and wandered away. Lettie thanked the coachman and looked forward to speedier journeys into Mereside village. She went indoors to tidy the paperwork that she had been doing when Thomas arrived. The door to the laundry store and sewing room was open and the maids were packing away. Agnes had been supervising running repairs on uniforms, and repairing worn bed linen from patients' rooms for its second life in the servants' attics.

Lettie fingered the fabrics spread out on the table. 'Do they make their own dresses?' she asked.

Agnes looked up from her task. 'Not any more. They're sent over from a factory in Leeds.'

The room was warm because a fire had been lit to heat up the flat irons. They were cooling on the fender. 'If we have the electric light, I can buy flat irons that work off them,' she commented.

'Really?' Agnes continued checking the linen and sewing box contents. After a few more minutes she sent off the maids and locked the cupboards. Then she turned to Lettie and said, 'Can I ask you a question about Thomas?'

Lettie closed the door and sat down at the sewing table. 'You like him, don't you?'

Agnes didn't reply. Instead she asked, 'Do you have an understanding with him?'

Yes! No! Yes! Lettie didn't know what to say at first. But Agnes expected an answer and the directness of her question made Lettie think seriously about her relationship with Thomas. It wasn't what Agnes thought. It was a friendship, a close friendship, because Lettie didn't have the privilege of brothers and sisters. And her so-called friends from the mission were not the ones she would choose. She chose Thomas as her friend and she did not want to lose him; which, she realised, was the reason why she was jealous of Agnes's interference.

'Yes, we have,' she replied.

'He says not,' Agnes responded.

'Why ask me if you know!'

'Because we are friends and I do not want to spoil that!'

'Then stay away from him!'

Agnes drew out a chair and sat down opposite her. 'I don't want to.' She looked directly into Lettie's eyes. 'He will be here again, won't he?'

Lettie felt uncomfortable. If she was honest with herself, she didn't *love* Thomas. And he had spent as much time with Agnes as he had with her that afternoon. She didn't want to lose him as her friend. If she made an enemy of Agnes and . . . and Thomas preferred Agnes's company to hers . . . Oh, that didn't bear thinking about! Yet it had been clear to Lettie that Thomas was instantly attracted to Agnes; and she to him.

She took a deep breath and started again. 'Yes, we do have an understanding but it's not what you think. We are friends, close friends, and for my part I want to keep it that way.'

'He said the same about you when I asked him.'

'You didn't waste any time, did you?'

'I know my own mind, Lettie.'

'Yes you do,' she agreed, 'and I want us to stay friends as well.'

'So do I.'

'And so does Thomas.'

'He said that to you?'

Agnes nodded.

He didn't waste any time either, Lettie thought. She didn't own him and she wanted him to be happy. Nonetheless, although it was hard for her to say it, she did: 'Well, good luck with him, Agnes.'

Lettie managed a smile. She felt that she was letting something precious slip away from her. She wasn't devastated but she was sad because their friendship would never be quite the same in future.

'Thanks, Lettie. I didn't want to quarrel with you.'

Agnes seemed happier and Lettie left the sewing room.

* * *

397

The following day, after her dinner in the servants' hall, Lettie changed into her best outfit and went over to the stables in the sunshine. She harnessed the docile pony herself, backed him into the shafts and secured the reins. She hadn't driven a trap for a while and the seat seemed higher than the Reverend's, but the rudiments of driving returned and her pony was well behaved.

The draper's in Mereside village was run by two spinster sisters who fashioned gowns from the fabrics they sold and displayed them in their shop window for sale to ladies whose husbands could afford them. Lettie purchased her threads and enquired of one of the ladies if she had used one of the new treadle machines for sewing.

'Certainly not,' she replied. 'Our garments are hand-made, every one of them.'

'And they are very beautiful. But I am from Mereside Lodge and the sewing room has a pile of bed sheets waiting for sides-to-middle. Perhaps you know of a local girl who can help?'

The sisters exchanged a glance. 'We offer that service to larger households. If you would care to bring your linen here I am sure we can come to an arrangement.'

'Then I shall,' Lettie replied. 'Expect me tomorrow afternoon. Good day to you.'

One of the sisters came around the counter to open the shop door for her. 'Good day, Miss . . .?'

'Hargreaves; Miss Hargreaves.'

Feeling confident, Lettie went next door to the provisions merchant, stared in the plate-glass window for a minute then opened the door. The interior was large and much more impressive than anything she had seen in Waterley Edge, or indeed their nearby town. The floor was tiled in a black and white chequered design, strewn with sawdust. There was a ladder-back chair to sit on, and two glass-fronted counters displaying cheeses and a variety of cooked meats. A wall of mahogany shelving held bottles, jars and a few cans of preserved goods, some of them with labels in a foreign language. Lettie gazed around in awe.

A young man in shirtsleeves and a waistcoat covered by a long white apron stood behind a polished mahogany-topped counter with brass edgings and corners. 'Good morning, miss,' he said.

'Is the proprietor available?'

'That would be my father. He's not here today. Can I help you?'

'I am looking for a supplier of lemons.'

'Lemons?' He climbed a small ladder to reach down a preserve jar from one of the higher shelves, wiping it free of dust before placing it on the counter. 'Best there is, miss. They come in from Italy.'

'I am looking for fresh lemons, they must be fresh.'

The young man's eyes widened for a second. 'Not much call for them around here. We'll be having oranges in from Spain in a few weeks' time.'

'Lemons,' she repeated.

He took the pencil from behind his ear and picked up a notebook. 'My father will get them for you, miss. He prides himself on supplying every request. What name shall I give him?'

'Miss Hargreaves, Mereside Lodge.'

He stopped writing for a second and then continued, 'The Lodge, eh?' he said. 'I'd heard there were a few changes going on up there. Is there anything else I can help you with, Miss Hargreaves?'

Lettie glanced at the fresh provisions displayed under glass domes on the counter. 'I'll take some York ham and . . . Wensleydale, I think. Yes, some Wensleydale cheese.' She watched as the young man sliced and weighed out her purchases and then wrapped them neatly in clean crisp paper. 'There's no need to send them on for me. I have my trap outside.'

'I'll carry them outside for you, Miss Hargreaves.' The young man walked round his counter and opened the door for her. Then he stowed her packages safely in the trap and helped her into the driving seat. When he handed her the reins he said, 'It's a pleasure to serve you, Miss Hargreaves.'

'Thank you.' She smiled. 'I'll call again when your father is home. Good day.'

Lettie flicked the reins gently and set off for the Halt. She was on the platform before the railway train with the hampers was due. Shortly after she arrived another small carriage appeared on the track behind her, the driver wearing the livery jacket of the inn. He waited on the platform too and when the railway engine hissed to a steamy halt, both went directly to the guard's van. The guard handed out two hampers, a travelling trunk and a valise.

Lettie's hampers were light enough for her to handle as they didn't contain hams. Quails eggs, cucumbers and cinnamon sticks were not heavy, although dried fruits for the Russian cake were. The driver from the inn was kind enough to offer help and she did not refuse him. A lady and gentleman, who had alighted from first class, walked out in front of them to their waiting carriage.

Lettie had been so concerned about her hampers that she had not taken any notice of the passengers. But, as she looked up, she saw the gentleman help the lady into their carriage and recognised Alec. Her heart gave a peculiar little lurch. He was so tall and handsome, so smartly dressed, that she experienced an immediate pang of envy for the lady who accompanied him. He appeared to be very attentive towards her and Lettie wished she had seen more of her. She wore a large feathered hat that shaded her features from the sun. But even without seeing her face, Lettie's overriding impression was that she was a lady of elegance and fashion.

'Who is the lady?' she whispered.

'She's a guest at the inn, miss.'

'She isn't a local lady, then?' she queried. But he didn't answer her because he had moved away to collect his passengers' luggage.

Alec didn't even glance in her direction before he climbed into the carriage after the lady. It was hardly surprising, she shrugged. Lettie may be wearing her best outfit and feel confident that the village traders had taken her seriously, but she felt dowdy in comparison to Alec's companion. The thought depressed her. She wanted Alec to think well of her. Perhaps, intent on the comforts of his companion, he had not even noticed her. If he had, he hadn't acknowledged her and this depressed her further.

Who was the lady? The answer dropped into her mind like a stone in a well, plummeting to its depths. She was Alec's wife. He had a wife and why would he not have one? He was a gentleman of means, educated and well-travelled, and the most attractive man she had ever set eyes on. His wife had accompanied him from Canada and remained in London while he completed his business in the North of England. She stood at the rear of her trap waiting for the inn carriage to move off and felt her new-found poise drain away.

When she reached the road, the inn carriage was well on its way to the village and Lettie considered that Alec must be staying at the inn with his wife for . . . for how long? For the time being? Until her father had agreed the sale with Lord Laughton and His Lordship had left? Yes, of course, although Lord Laughton was a relation of Alec's, His Lordship was an unpleasant gentleman and Alec was protecting his wife from His Lordship's domineering behaviour.

Father will know! Lettie realised. Alec, surely, has telegraphed her father about his return. As far as she knew, Alec had not given up his suite at the Lodge. She flicked the reins eagerly and called, 'Gee-up!' The pony ignored her and she was obliged to quell her impatience.

Michael and Frances did not change for dinner every evening and instead took supper on a tray at their own convenience in Michael's room. Frances was in the still room preparing it when Lettie found her.

'Is that for you and Father?'

'And you, if you can join us. Michael has something to tell you.'

'What about? Do you know?'

'I do, but I shall not say. What have you got there?'

Lettie placed her packages on the wooden dresser.

'I've brought something from the village for him to sample; York ham and a tomato from the hamper. Is there any Dundee cake left? I have Wensleydale, too, and it goes particularly well with Cook's Dundee.'

Lettie thought that Frances was not as excited as Father about the news. He stood by the window gazing at the mere as the daylight faded and announced, 'I have decided that I shall not sell to Lord Laughton. My life is here.'

Lettie was overjoyed. She leapt to her feet and went over to hug him. It was an impulsive gesture and he was surprised. But he hugged her back and he looked pleased. 'Does Dr Bretton know?' she asked.

'I've been having discussions with him and Mr Norwich and we are in agreement. We can make Mereside Lodge profitable.'

'And Frances?' Lettie turned round to face her. She was smiling but her eyes were sad. 'How will you pay for the divorce?' she asked.

Michael stretched out his hand towards Frances. 'Frances has been involved in all our decisions. It will be hard for both of us, but we have agreed to wait.'

Frances came forward. 'We are quite used to waiting

now. Installing the electric light is important for a twentieth-century hydro.'

'I wish there was another way,' Lettie said.

'Michael and I are together,' Frances argued, 'not as we would wish to be, but we have hopes for our future.'

It was a bitter-sweet celebration, Lettie thought, although they were as happy as they could be in the circumstances. She was happy for them and pleased with plans for the changes at Mereside Lodge. Father approved the quality of her ham and cheese and questioned her about the village provisions merchant.

'I expect Lord Laughton will be angry,' Lettie commented later.

'He is. He was the first to know,' Michael nodded.

'He's leaving for Waterley Hall tomorrow,' Frances added. 'He and Mr Laughton can take their squabbles there.'

'Has Mr Laughton given up his suite as well?' Lettie queried.

'Actually, he hasn't,' Michael said. 'Why do you ask?'

'I saw him today,' Lettie explained. 'He arrived at the Halt this afternoon.'

'He isn't here,' Frances stated.

'No, he went to the inn. He was with a lady.'

'But he has a suite here! How strange. He'll call or write to inform us, I'm sure.'

'I hope so,' Michael added. 'There is the matter of his bill.'

Lettie's eyes widened. 'He wouldn't *not* pay you, Father!' she exclaimed.

Michael and Frances looked at her, surprised at her outburst. 'These things do happen,' Frances pointed out.

'Alec is an honest man,' Lettie stated indignantly. But she noticed Frances and Michael exchanged a questioning glance and this irritated her. She knew him better than they did.

They retired shortly afterwards and the following morning after breakfast in the servants' hall, Agnes came into the housekeeper's room with a message for Lettie to see her father immediately.

He was dressed and standing in the middle of his room. But he had a helpless look in his eyes and he was clutching an opened letter.

'Frances is packing,' he said. 'She says she cannot stay, it wouldn't be decent.'

Lettie couldn't believe her ears. Frances was having a crisis of conscience? After all this time? 'Of course it's decent!' Lettie cried. 'Your relationship is respectable. Heavens, your rooms are on separate floors!'

'You don't understand. She's here! She's in the village, staying at the inn!'

Baffled, Lettie stared at him.

'My wife,' he anguished. 'My wife has come back.'

Chapter 29

Lettie blew out her cheeks and sat down on the nearest chair. She collected her thoughts for a moment and said, 'But that is good, Father, because you can talk to her about your divorce.'

'Not without Frances by my side. I can't do anything without Frances. You must go and persuade her to stay!'

Lettie raced upstairs. Frances was adamant that she should not be in the same house as Michael while his wife was here. Lettie argued that his wife wasn't at Mereside Lodge yet and anyway Frances couldn't leave her team of hydropathy nurses. And if Mrs Powell moved into Mereside Lodge then Frances could live in the village until she left. Surely Michael's wife did not want to return permanently? Did she?

She was such a distant person in his life that, in Lettie's

mind, she hardly existed. Yet she did, and her father was in a close relationship with another woman while he had a living wife. Apart from the impropriety, which would have horrified Gran, it would cause a scandal if it got out, and that would not do the hydro's reputation any good at all.

Frances left a packed suitcase in her room, ready to quit at short notice, and went down to the bath house. Lettie reported back to her father. He was relieved and gestured to the letter lying half folded on table. 'You will have to meet her.' He seemed very depressed about this and added, 'I'll . . . I'll organise it. I'm sorry, Lettie. I am so sorry.'

It was a setback for her father and Frances, she agreed. She glanced at the letter. The beginning was innocent enough, enquiring about his health and so on . . . *I should like to arrange a meeting with you. We have much to discuss . . .* But the words that riveted her attention were in the engraved heading on the notepaper. Mrs Powell was residing at the inn in Mereside village. Mrs Powell was the lady that Alec had brought to Mereside!

This was Alec's doing. It was something to do with him, and Lettie wanted him to explain himself. She left her father writing his response to the letter and went to her room for her coat and hat. She didn't stop to change out of her dark grey housekeeper's dress but hurried to the stables for her trap.

At the inn she asked to see Mr Laughton. The landlord took her name and called his wife from the back. 'There's a Miss Hargreaves to see Mr Laughton. He's just ordered refreshment in the back parlour.'

'Thank you,' Lettie replied. 'I know the way.' And she set off down the carpeted passage.

'Just a minute, miss!' the landlord called after her.

She ignored him. The small parlour was empty apart from Alec and Mrs Powell. Alec was sitting in the same chair he had used when he had brought her here. Lettie slowed and stared. Mrs Powell was less flamboyantly dressed this morning with a smaller hat that showed her features. There was something vaguely familiar about her face but she was . . . she was much older than Alec, and much older than Lettie had imagined. Of course she was! She was her stepmother! This realisation made Lettie stop and take a breath. Alec was on his feet as soon as he saw her, and the landlord caught up with her as well.

'Sorry, sir,' the landlord apologised, 'this lady barged in before I could—'

'She is welcome, landlord,' Alec said. 'Bring another cup with our coffee, if you please.' He hesitated then added, 'And brandy, I think.'

He stood in front of Lettie, effectively blocking her view of Mrs Powell. His face was serious but not angry, she thought.

He went on, 'Sit down, Lettie. This meeting was supposed to happen later this week. But I should have known your father would tell you and you would not wait.' He stepped back to allow her to sit down and gestured towards his companion. 'This is—'

'My stepmother,' Lettie interrupted. 'I know.'

Alec frowned, a painful anguished frown. Lettie looked at her stepmother and was shocked to see that she was distressed. Her eyes were brimming and her mouth was trembling. She was shaking her head very slightly.

Alec kept his voice steady and addressed the older lady. 'The deception has gone on for too long. You must tell her the truth now.'

'The truth?' Lettie queried. Dear Lord, not more lies, more secrets, more revelations about her father. 'Are you not Mrs Powell?'

The lady composed herself. She was, Lettie realised, very beautiful and had a grace and poise that Lettie wished she possessed. And she *was* vaguely familiar. Perhaps she had seen her picture somewhere.

The lady inhaled and straightened her spine, something Lettie did when she needed to gather her courage. 'I am Mrs Powell,' she replied. 'I am your mother.'

'Stepmother,' Lettie corrected gently. 'My mother is dead.'

Mrs Powell continued to shake her head very slightly. 'I am your mother and I am alive. You are my daughter. You were born in France and I baptised you Collette.' She looked down and to one side. 'Your grandmother said the name was too fanciful and, when she took you away, she called you Lettie, Lettie Hargreaves.'

Yes, Gran would do something like that, Lettie thought irreverently, and swivelled her eyes onto Alec. 'Is this true?' He nodded. 'And you knew? All this time, you knew?'

He spread his hands in a gesture of helplessness. 'When we were speaking together, here in this room, I thought you knew too. I assumed you knew every-thing about your parents – your real parents – but I was wrong. When I realised I had made a mistake I believed there was only one person who could correct it and that was your mother.'

'Alec is right,' Mrs Powell said. 'You see, it was my secret and when you were born your grandmother insisted that it should remain so. She did not want you to suffer because of me.'

Lettie's father had spoken of her 'suffering' as well. 'Are you really my mother?' she asked.

'I am.'

'Then why did Gran deny your existence to me? All my life I believed you were dead! I don't understand. Didn't you want me?'

Lettie's heart was thumping and her eyes were filling up. She'd had a father and mother all along! She understood why Gran had taken her from her father. But to deprive her of her *mother* for all these years?

Her tears began to spill over. She swallowed and then sniffed. A handkerchief appeared and she clutched it. She shot a grateful glance at Alec and she wiped her nose. Her . . . her mother was doing the same with a delicate lace-edged hanky that fitted her fragile beauty so very well.

Alec moved away, behind her, and she heard him speak to the landlord. He reappeared with a tray and placed it on a nearby table and said, 'Tell her, Ruth. Tell her everything. I shall make sure you are not disturbed.'

'Don't go, Alec,' Lettie begged him. 'You know all this anyway and . . . and I . . . I want you to stay.' It was more than that, she thought. She needed him to be there. He

410

seemed to understand her and how much the truth meant to her.

'Ruth?' he queried.

'Yes, stay,' Ruth agreed.

He poured coffee and handed it round then sat down again as Ruth related her story.

'Before I tell you,' she began, 'I want to say how much I regret what happened. I was young – younger than you are now – and ambitious, like my father. I was, I thought, destined to marry a gentleman of means. I was unaware that more powerful influences were at work.'

Lettie's coffee went cold as she listened. She was shocked, she couldn't deny it, and she tried not to let it show. But hiding her feelings was not one of Lettie's strengths. She had little wonder that Gran had kept this scandalous, sorry affair from her. Knowing Gran as she had, it must have been very difficult for Gran to come to terms with her daughter's life. Lettie understood why chapel had become so important to her.

'When I fled to France,' Ruth continued, 'I believed I was the only person that wanted you. I asked your grandmother for help. She misunderstood my plea and thought I wished to be rid of you.' Ruth choked slightly on her words, but she went on, 'I felt that I was trapped and, whatever happened to me, I wanted to be sure you would be well cared for.'

'I was,' Lettie said. 'Gran did her best for me.'

'She didn't reply to my letter and I was desperate. I wrote to her again from London and pleaded with her to find me someone trustworthy and reliable. I can't

411

remember what I wrote, but she had a change of heart, arrived at The Admiral and travelled with me to France.' Ruth stopped talking for a moment and inhaled with a shudder.

'A brandy?' Alec queried.

'Yes please,' Ruth answered.

'Lettie?'

She nodded. 'Just a tot for me.' Lettie was thinking that it was not surprising her father turned to drink. Michael had all her sympathy. She said, 'Well, Lord Laughton is free to marry you now if you will divorce Father.'

'Laughton does not want to marry me! He was angry about . . . about you, and he lost interest in me a long time ago. His current mistress is some Italian countess, I believe.'

'But you stayed in France.'

'Yorkshire folk have long memories for scandals and my concern was always for you. Lady Laughton was as powerful and vindictive as her husband. I have, however, wanted to make contact with you for many years.'

'I wish you had.'

Ruth didn't reply. She looked as sad as Lettie felt. What a waste of those years, Lettie thought. She said, 'You will divorce Father, won't you? He has Frances now.'

'I'll do more than that. Alec has explained Michael's position and his own in relation to Laughton. I shall make it as easy as I can for Michael to divorce me. The lawyers will work something out and I shall pay them for both of us. Michael was deceived by all of us and I owe him that, at the very least.'

412

Lettie found this offer difficult to believe and wondered if it was an empty promise. 'Divorce is very expensive!' she exclaimed. 'How can you afford it?'

'When Laughton left me, he took his racehorses and left me the farm. It was purchased in my name anyway and I was wise to his ways by then. I had my own horses and some valuable jewellery and objets d'art as investments for my future. I learned to farm. I live a simple country life but I have wealth. Be assured that I can afford it.'

'Then you must go and tell him now,' Lettie urged. 'He and Frances will be so pleased. Frances means such a lot to Father and it is very awkward for her to be thought of . . . to be a . . .'

'To be what I was?' Ruth embarrassed Lettie by finishing the sentence for her.

'I – I'm sorry,' Lettie muttered. 'This is difficult for me, as well.' She was finding it impossible to call this woman her mother. Yet she had had no such qualms with her father.

'I am the one who is sorry,' Ruth replied. 'You did not choose your parents.'

'Nor you,' she said, and a spark of sympathy glimmered in her heart. Ruth's story concurred with Gran's opinion of her grandfather. Lettie was overcome, quite suddenly, by a surge of tearfulness. She sat in silence to compose herself. No one spoke. The only sounds came from the inn reception along the corridor.

Finally, Alec broke the stillness. He said, 'There is something else, isn't there, Ruth?'

'I don't think so,' Ruth answered.

'There is the matter of Lettie's father.'

'Alec, please! Michael is her father.'

Alec stood up. 'Wait here.'

'Where's he gone?' Lettie asked.

'I don't know but we ought to do as he asks.'

They stared at each for a couple of minutes then Ruth said, 'Your grandmother decided what was best for you and I had made too many mistakes to argue with her. You grew up untainted by the scandal that kept me in France. Very few people know the truth.'

'Alec does and he found it out for himself.'

'He has his own reasons for searching out the truth. He was very insistent that I came back to Mereside Lodge with him. He said he wouldn't leave the farm without me. Have you any idea why?'

Lettie didn't and she shrugged. 'He's a gentleman so I trust his reasons are honourable. He's an admirable man, which is more than I can say about some.'

Ruth raised her eyebrows. 'You have no idea at all why he came for me?'

'Have you?'

Ruth seemed mildly irritated by her response. 'But he did it for you, of course! He did it for you because the truth is important to you and . . . and because he loves you. Didn't you know?'

Lettie blinked. Well, yes, she knew the bit about the truth, but not . . . but not the . . . the rest. Was this true? Her heart began to stir with a peculiar fluttering. She opened her mouth to ask Ruth how she knew, but Ruth's attention was already diverted by Alec as he returned.

414

He carried a folder – one of the leather ones Lettie had seen on his desk at Boundary Farm. He undid the ties and took out some pictures, sepia photographs, all of the same lady, and handed them round. He said, 'Lettie has your eyes, Ruth, but don't you think there is a greater resemblance to this lady?'

Ruth agreed. So did Lettie and she asked, 'Who is she?'

'Lord Laughton's elder sister, late elder sister.' He turned to Ruth. 'You did know he was Lettie's father, didn't you?'

Ruth covered her face with her hands and groaned. 'We all knew, as soon as you were born. The likeness was obvious then. You have grown more like me, I am pleased to say.'

Lettie was aghast, 'But you have let Michael believe . . .'

'He knows. We have lived the lie to protect you from the . . . from my disgrace.'

From the truth, Lettie realised, from the stigma of illegitimacy.

Ruth added more harshly, 'Well, who would want Laughton as a father?' She sounded stronger now.

'But Michael has accepted me . . .'

'None of that dreadful scandal was your fault,' Ruth stressed. 'Why should you have to suffer the repercussions? Your grandmother provided a way out for you. She took you home and brought you up as her orphaned grandchild.'

Lettie gazed at her, at this woman who was her mother, and whispered, 'Have you any idea how much I have dreamed and wondered about you?'

Lettie saw the pain cross Ruth's features but she did not flinch from her reply. 'Of course I have. Not a day has passed when I have not thought of you, of how you had grown, and of how much I loved you. I gave you up because I loved you.'

Lettie could not make a response. She was exhausted, emotionally drained, and confused. She was confused about her feelings for this woman who was her mother.

Ruth went on, 'I have many regrets about my past, not least of which was agreeing with your grandmother that I should never be part of your life. I should have liked to have made up our differences and I am so very sorry that she has passed on.'

'Did Alec tell you?'

Ruth nodded and fell silent.

Lettie hadn't drunk her coffee or tot of brandy but her head was fuzzy. She needed to think, she needed air, and she needed a walk to clear her head. Ruth had made mistakes, but then who hadn't? She looked at Alec. There was much about him that she did not know, yet that didn't seem to matter to Lettie. She needed him. Was Ruth right in her observations about him? Love meant wanting to spend the rest of your life with someone. How on earth could Alec love her knowing that she was Lord Laughton's daughter?

She stood up and said, 'I need to think. May I meet again with you later, Ruth?'

'Of course you may. Why not join us for dinner tonight?'

'Us?'

Alec answered, 'This is a difficult situation for your

mother as well, Lettie. I shall stay at the inn for her until she has resolved matters with Michael.'

'Very well,' Lettie agreed. 'In the meantime, I should like to ask a favour.'

'Anything,' Ruth said.

'Please don't go up to the Lodge to see Michael. You will upset Frances. Michael is writing to you and I am sure he will come here.'

Alec offered to drive back to the Lodge. She thanked him and told him she had her own trap now. He accompanied her outside and helped her climb in then unhitched the pony for her.

'Thank you,' she said once again as he handed her the reins. She was glad that he was there, that he was staying at the inn for Ruth, and she was sincere when she added, 'Thank you for everything.'

An expression of relief crossed his features. 'It was a gamble for me to bring Ruth here. I did it for you and I wasn't sure that you would be pleased. But I was very sure that you deserved the truth.'

He held onto her hands as he passed across the reins and she felt his strength flood into her. *I love him*, she thought. She pressed her lips together to stop them trembling. *I want to spend the rest of my life with him*. They stared at each other until he stepped back to allow her to drive away.

She drove the trap back to Mereside Lodge, left it at the stables and took the path around the mere on foot. It had a calming influence on her muddled emotions. Her real father, a man that few people had any kind of

417

regard for, had not wanted her. It was clear in her mind that, lord or not, she did not want him either. She felt that she understood Michael and his battles and admired him for the man he was.

But her mother? How did she feel about her mother? I don't know, she thought. Then, she knew so little about her, aside from her part in a scandal that had happened years ago. She had criticised Gran for her quick judgements on people and vowed not to do the same herself. So what did she really know about this woman who was her mother? Heavens, she knew more about Alec and that was little enough!

A cackle of duck and geese, squabbling over territory, disturbed her thoughts. She plodded on through the trampled undergrowth following the curve of the bank, her mind returning constantly to the man who had precipitated this present situation. She wanted him here now, walking beside her. Alec's presence gave her strength and she didn't want him ever to go back to Canada. Yet Canada was his home and he would wish to return. But just the thought of him leaving left her feeling empty and alone.

She walked all the way round the mere and sat on one of the rustic wooden seats in sight of the bath house. It was near the end of morning treatments and servants' dinner would be almost ready. She was hungry but did not want to speak to anyone; not yet anyway. She heard someone approach and guessed she would have to make an effort. She glanced sideways to see Alec sitting down at the far end of the bench.

'I'll just sit here and wait for you,' he said. He stretched out his legs and stared at the geese on the mere.

After a few minutes she said, 'When are you going back to Canada?'

'I haven't decided. My half of Waterley Estates will keep me occupied for months. I'm gearing up for some battles with Lord Laughton.' He sounded as though he looked forward to the fight and that made her smile.

'What about your family?'

'My brothers? They are taking care of our agricultural concerns back home. They packed me off willingly to sort out the English part of our father's legacy.'

'You have brothers, how lucky.'

'And aunts on my mother's side, with cousins.'

He's very lucky, Lettie thought, except for his titled Yorkshire cousin. She said, 'I suppose I am related to you as well.'

'Oh, I think that's stretching it a bit; third cousins at one remove or something. Not what you would call family at all, really. Would you prefer it to be different?'

She liked the fact that he was different from Lord Laughton. He was foreign and with fresh ideas. She turned to face him and shook her head.

'I would,' he said, and shuffled along the smooth wooden seat towards her. 'I want us to be much closer. I want us to married. I love you, Lettie.'

She ought to have been elated because she loved him too. But all of his recent disclosures to Lettie had, invariably, come with a sting in the tail. She said, 'How can you love me when you know who my father is?'

'I'm following my heart, Lettie, and my heart is telling me all I need to know. What is your heart saying to you?'

'It's saying I love you too.'

He put his arms around her and kissed her, hesitantly at first and then, when she offered no resistance, deeply and longingly and satisfyingly. When they parted, out of breath, he stayed close to her with his arm around her shoulders, watching the ducks bobbing and foraging in the shallows of the mere.

Eventually he said, 'I am meeting with Michael for luncheon today. I want to buy a piece of land from him, well away from the Lodge on the edge of his estate. I'm going to build a house on it. What do you think?'

'For you to live in?'

'For us both to live in. That's if you'll marry me. Will you marry me, Lettie?'

Lettie sat up straight to look at him directly. He was smiling and so was she. 'Of course I'll marry you.'

'I have to ask Michael's permission first. Do you think he will object? I am Lord Laughton's cousin after all.' He was making light of it and there was a twinkle in his eye as he added, 'If he does object I shall bribe him with an offer to pay for the electric in the Lodge.'

'But he won't need a bribe if he sells you some land,' she pointed out.

'I know.'

She smiled again, feeling confident in her future, married to Alec, helping Frances and Father in his hydro and . . . and . . . where did Ruth fit into her life? 'You'd better go or you'll be late for your meeting,' she said. 'I'll see you tonight for dinner at the inn.'

He kissed her again and left reluctantly. She stayed watching the waterfowl until she was sure that servants' dinner was over. Then she helped herself to a piece of cold pie and ate it in the housekeeper's room. She did not want to be distracted from her thoughts about Ruth and what she would say to her that evening.

So, she spoke with confidence when she arrived at the inn for dinner. She wore her Sunday-best outfit and dressed her hair carefully. She had finished with her frantic searching. She had her answers and although she did not like some of them, she knew, at last, who she was and, more importantly, what she wanted. She wanted what she believed she had: Alec, her father and Frances and the challenge of Mereside Lodge; and one thing more.

Lettie and Alec and Ruth dined well at the inn. They celebrated Lettie's as yet unofficial engagement to Alec with French champagne. Ruth, Lettie realised, had a taste for it.

'We shall not make a proper announcement until you have settled your divorce arrangements with Michael,' Alec said to Ruth.

'Anyway, he has to court me first,' Lettie stated proudly. 'I look forward to that.'

'I'm very pleased for both of you,' Ruth smiled.

Lettie returned her smile and commented, 'Earlier today, you said that we cannot choose our parents. But I believe that I am an exception, and that I can.'

A wary look came into Ruth's eyes. 'What do you mean?'

'I mean that I can choose who my father is and I choose Michael, as you did.'

'With Frances as your mother?' Ruth queried.

Lettie noticed the wariness had returned to Ruth's eyes. She said, 'Frances is my friend. You are my mother. You.'

Lettie reached across the polished-oak table with her fingers. Ruth's hand closed over them, held them and squeezed them gently.

'Thank you,' Ruth said.

THE SECRET DAUGHTER

Catherine King

A gripping, gritty novel set during the run-up to the launch of the Titanic.

Loss

Phyllis Kimber's entire future is called into question after her father is killed in Earl Redfern's employ. But the earl knows something about Phyllis that means she will always be looked after.

Lies

As lady's maid to Martha, Phyllis is the American heiress's only confidant in England: she knows Martha doesn't love the recently widowed Lord Melton, the man Martha's socially ambitious father is determined she marries, but there's another secret – a secret that makes Phyllis give up everything to protect her friend.

Loyalty

Martha begins making preparations to return to America with Phyllis, her father and new husband on the *Titanic* but the burden of deception eclipses Phyllis's hope for a new future. As she struggles to protect Martha, Phyllis must decide where her loyalties lie, unaware of the undiscovered secrets in her own past and of the tragedy that is about to unfold on that fateful crossing.

Out now.

A SISTER'S COURAGE

Catherine King

Out of tragedy, came her strength and hope.

Sacrifice

When her mother passed away, Meg Parker was forced to
sacrifice her chance at love for the sake of her family. She
hopes she will be able to live a full life once again after
her father remarries – until tragedy strikes a second time.
Suddenly, Meg is facing a darker future altogether.

Struggles

Lady Alice Langton is travelling the Yorkshire Dales,
spreading the suffragette message. Florence Brookes, the
daughter of a prosperous grocer, accompanies her, impas-
sioned by the cause but seeking distraction from her own
troubles. Appalled by their lack of domestic skills, Meg
decides to flee her old life and joins the two women as
their maidservant as they make their way to London.

Strength

When Meg is reunited with her old flame, she is hesitant
about her feelings for him – not least because of the rift
this causes between her and Lady Alice. It's not until
Florence's actions land them in jeopardy that Meg realises
she must find the courage to make a heartbreaking choice.

Out now.

Find out more about **Catherine King**'s books at

www.catherineking.info

Or you can follow her on Twitter

@cathkingauthor

And keep up to date with

@LittleBrownUK
@LittleBookCafe

To buy any Catherine King books and to find out more about all other Little, Brown titles go to our website

www.littlebrown.co.uk

To order any Sphere titles p & p free in the UK, please contact our mail order supplier on:
+ 44 (0)1832 737525

Customers not based in the UK should contact the same number for appropriate postage and packing costs.